IN THE HEAT OF THE NIGHT

Ella wasn't sure what had suddenly possessed her. It could have been the haunting romantic air of the glade, or the fact that she was full of energy after such a long rest, but she felt alive, sensual, and daring. She wanted Harrigan to make love to her. Even more, she wanted to enflame him. Casting Harrigan a faintly taunting look, she began to undo her gown.

"You're going to have a swim?" he asked.

"Yes. It looks lovely and cool and very clear." She wiggled out of her gown and placed it carefully on the grass, then tugged off her shoes. Setting her foot up on one of the many rocks littering the banks, she slowly unrolled her stockings, knowing that Harrigan was watching her.

"If you want to take a swim, fine, do so, but I think you ought to be a little more careful," he said. "You're tempting fate with the way you're carrying on."

Ella kept her back to him as she undid her camisole. She slipped it off, held it out to the side, and let it drop onto the pile of her clothes. Her heart pounding, she tugged off her pantaloons, savoring the feel of the cool night air on her body.

"Tempting fate, am I? I had rather hoped that I was tempting you . . ."

Books by Hannah Howell

THE MURRAYS

Highland Destiny
Highland Honor
Highland Promise
Highland Vow
Highland Knight
Highland Bride
Highland Angel
Highland Groom
Highland Warrior
Highland Conqueror
Highland Champion
Highland Lover
Highland Barbarian
Highland Savage
Highland Wolf
Highland Sinner
Highland Protector
Highland Avenger
Highland Master

THE WHERLOCKES

If He's Wicked
If He's Sinful
If He's Wild
If He's Dangerous
If He's Tempted
If He's Daring

VAMPIRE ROMANCE

Highland Vampire
The Eternal Highlander
My Immortal Highlander
Highland Thirst
Nature of the Beast
Yours for Eternity
Highland Hunger
Born to Bite

STAND-ALONE NOVELS

Only for You
My Valiant Knight
Unconquered
Wild Roses
A Taste of Fire
A Stockingful of Joy
Highland Hearts
Reckless
Conqueror's Kiss
Beauty and the Beast
Highland Wedding

Silver Flame
Highland Fire
Highland Captive
My Lady Captor
Wild Conquest
Kentucky Bride
Compromised Hearts
Stolen Ecstasy
Highland Hero
His Bonnie Bride

Published by Kensington Publishing Corporation

WILD ROSES

HANNAH HOWELL

ZEBRA BOOKS
Kensington Publishing Corp.
www.kensingtonbooks.com

ZEBRA BOOKS are published by

Kensington Publishing Corp.
119 West 40th Street
New York, NY 10018

All Kensington titles, imprints, and distributed lines are available at special quantity discounts for bulk purchases for sales promotion, premiums, fund-raising, educational, or institutional use.

Special book excerpts or customized printings can also be created to fit specific needs. For details, write or phone the office of the Kensington Special Sales Manager: Attn.: Special Sales Department. Kensington Publishing Corp., 119 West 40th Street, New York, NY 10018. Phone: 1-800-221-2647.

Zebra and the Z logo Reg. U.S. Pat. & TM Off.

First Mass-Market Paperback Printing: June 1997
ISBN-13: 978-1-4201-3242-7
ISBN-10: 1-4201-3242-3

First Electronic Edition: August 2008
eISBN-13: 978-1-4201-3517-6
eISBN-10: 1-4201-3517-1

10 9 8

Printed in the United States of America

Chapter One

Wyoming, Spring 1874

"I hope you can forgive us, sir, but it was necessary to lock up your wife." Deputy Smith wiped a stained handkerchief across his sweaty forehead.

Harrigan Mahoney smiled politely at the nervous man, immensely satisfied with the deputy's gullibility. "She made a fuss, did she?"

When the rotund deputy hefted his short, soft body out of his chair, Harrigan stood up as well. It did not surprise him in the least that Ella Carson was stirring up trouble. He had been persistently warned about her volatile temperament by her Eastern relatives before he came to the wilds of Wyoming to get her. All he could do was pray that she would give up the fight once she knew she could not win. The thought that he might have to deal with a spoiled rich girl's tantrums and pouts for the entire long journey back to Philadelphia made him shudder inwardly.

"It took three of my men to drag her from that aunt's house," the deputy said as he tugged on his tobacco-stained shirt. "They're all nursing bruises now. That damned aunt of hers nearly shot my man Clement. That ain't no way for women to act. I'll be right pleased to see the last of her. Taking that aunt of hers too?''

"I hadn't intended to."

"A real shame, that is," muttered Smith as he lumbered toward the cells at the rear of the squat wooden building. "It'd be a damned sight quieter around here with Louise Carson gone."

Clasping his hands behind his back, Harrigan strolled after the deputy. The next few minutes would be tricky. He could only hope that the deputy felt so much animosity toward Ella Carson that he would not heed a word she said. If he had judged Smith right, the man would never take a woman's word over a man's and that could only serve him well.

It was difficult to maintain his air of calm when Smith stopped before Ella Carson's cell. Harrigan cursed inwardly. The picture her relatives had given him had shown her to be a passably attractive young woman. It had not prepared him for the thick waves of dark auburn hair tumbling down her slim back to her tiny waist. No photograph could have done justice to her alabaster skin, now touched with a becoming flush of anger. The dull tones of the picture had also stolen the beauty of her rich green eyes, a beauty only enhanced by the glint of rage sparkling in them as she glared at him. The soft dark green gown she wore, though wrinkled and dirty, complemented both her slim figure and her coloring. Ella Carson was tiny, delicate, enchantingly lovely, and as furious as any woman he had ever seen.

"Your husband is here," the deputy grumbled as he fumbled with the key to the lock on her cell door. "You shoulda told us you was wed, Mrs. Mahoney."

"I do not have a husband, you empty-skulled piece of refuse," Ella snapped.

She glared at the tall man standing next to Deputy Smith. She hastily shook aside the traitorous thought that she would not mind calling such a handsome man *husband*.

He had to be six feet tall or more, broad-shouldered, lean, and strong. That strength was clear to see in the way he stood and in every line of his elegant form, which was well displayed in a tailored black suit and crisp, white shirt. His glossy black hair was thick, wavy, and a little long, hanging just below his shirt collar. High cheekbones, a strong jaw, a perfectly angled nose, and a slightly full mouth formed a face that was very easy on the eye. When she finally met his gaze, she caught his brief cocking of one smoothly arched brow and the hint of mockery in his heather-grey eyes, and renewed fury pushed aside her attraction to him.

"Now, darlin', you can't keep playing that game," Harrigan drawled. "I've told the deputy the whole sordid tale."

If she had a gun, Harrigan mused, *she would shoot me dead.* It was abundantly clear that Ella Carson had the wit to know exactly why he was there and who had sent him. It was also abundantly clear that she did not want to return home. The trip to Philadelphia could prove to be a very long one.

"Oh, this is a very clever game, this is—Mahoney, is it?—but do not think that it will succeed."

Harrigan pulled a mournful face and slowly shook his head. "Why do you persist in this, sweet girl?" What little he could hear of her furious muttering made Harrigan glad that he could not understand it all. "Now, for once in your life, just come along quietly."

The deputy moved closer to Harrigan. "You sure you want her back, Mr. Mahoney?"

"She is the burden I must bear," Harrigan replied. "And it is well past time that I relieved you of it."

"Suits me."

The instant the deputy opened the cell door Ella made a dash for freedom. Harrigan was ready. He caught her up against his chest in a tight but not painful hold. She displayed no such concern for his well-being. He winced as her small booted feet belabored his shins. Only half listening to her soft but persistent tirade, he decided that she had spent too much time near the docks in Philadelphia. For the benefit of the deputy, he heaved a deep sigh of resignation as he draped her over his shoulder.

"Y'know," muttered the deputy as he followed Harrigan away from the cells, struggling to keep up with the younger man's long strides, "I ain't never held with a man beating his wife, but I'm beginning to think there might be cause now and again. Yes, indeedy, and a wife or two what'd be the better for it."

"Put me down," Ella snapped, "and I'll show you who'd be the better for a good thrashing, Smith, you bloated sack of pig swill." She lifted her head up a little and, through the curtain of her tangled hair, she saw the deputy flush a deep red. "You had better put a stop to this, Deputy Smith, or, as soon as I get free of this thick-necked ruffian, I will have you charged as an accessory to kidnapping."

"Now, darlin'," Harrigan said as he patted her slender, well-shaped backside and ignored her gasp of outrage, "the deputy knows the whole unpleasant truth."

"The deputy doesn't know squat, and if you call me *darlin'* again, I'll cut your lying tongue out."

"We shouldn't be airing our differences in public like this, sweet thing. I mean to prove to you that that woman didn't mean a thing to me." Harrigan saw the way the deputy nodded solemnly as he held the door open for him, and mentally patted himself on the back for concocting the tiff over an affair tale, one well embellished with hints of past marital turbulence.

"Sometimes a man just can't help himself," agreed Smith. "Women oughta understand that. A man has to taste his pleasures. It's the way of the world," he intoned heavily as he followed Harrigan out onto the creaking wooden sidewalk.

Ella gaped, unable to believe what she was hearing, and managed to raise herself up enough to look at the perspiring deputy with pure disgust. "Intelligence has not graced your family for many a generation, has it, Smith?" She frowned, certain she felt laughter ripple through the man holding her.

Deputy Smith opened his mouth to reply to her insult, then suddenly gaped, staring down the rutted street of town. "Oh, hell. That aunt of hers has gotten free."

Harrigan looked in the direction Smith was staring and nearly gaped as well. A tiny woman, nearly as delicate of build as the one he carried, was marching toward them. Her thick chestnut hair was half pinned up and half tumbling around her slim shoulders. What held his gaze was the fine new Henry rifle she carried. When she stopped and aimed it at him, handling the weapon with ease and skill, he found it hard to believe that such a tiny, pretty lady would shoot him. Blind instinct made him dodge to the left just as she fired.

The two men who were chasing the woman finally caught up with her and tackled her onto the dusty road. As they struggled with her, finally wrestling the rifle from her grasp, Harrigan glanced behind him at the wall of the jail. Judging from where the bullet had splintered the rough wooden clapboards, Harrigan knew that, if he had not moved, she would have shot a very large hole in his right leg. He felt sure that the swearing, struggling woman being dragged toward them had intended to maim him. The job he had been hired to do, one he had seen as a quick, easy way to earn money, was looking more difficult by the minute.

"Hell's bells, Louise," shouted Smith as the men holding Louise paused in front of him. "You coulda killed the man."

"That would have been my pleasure," hissed Louise, tossing her head to clear the tangled hair out of her face, "but even an idiot like you knows that I always hit what I aim for. If you'd just fix your squinty pig eyes on the hole I put in your jail, you bloated fool, you'd see clear that I wasn't aiming to kill the bastard."

Ella looked at her furious aunt. "Thank you kindly for trying, Auntie."

"I'm not done trying yet, Ella," Louise vowed. "This is not over. Not by a long shot."

"Oh, yes it is," snapped Smith. "I'm locking you up, you mad woman."

"You've got no right to do that," protested Ella. "There is no law against shooting a building."

"Don't you go telling me what the law is, girlie," Smith said, glaring at Ella.

"Someone has to. You are too stupid to know it yourself."

Before the flushed deputy could respond to yet another insult, Harrigan said, "It would help me some, Smith, if you could hold the woman until I am clear of this town."

"Glad to oblige," answered Smith. "Sure you don't wanna press charges? Then I could hold her a lot longer than that."

"No need. Holding her until I leave will be good enough."

"Well, I think you're making a big mistake there, but . . ." Smith shrugged. "Lock her up men. And Clement," he called to a gangly young man crossing the street to join them, "you escort Mr. Mahoney to the train. Don't want any of Louise's boys causing him trouble."

"Don't you fret, Ella," Louise called as the two men holding her dragged her into the jailhouse. "I'll get you free of this. This low, stinking hireling won't get you back to Philadelphia. I won't let those thieving, murdering leeches who call themselves our kin get their slimy hands on you."

The deputy slammed the door shut behind Louise the minute the men got her inside. "Damned troublesome female." He frowned at Harrigan. "Has kin back east, huh? More like that?"

"Good God, no." Harrigan shuddered with distaste. "A much more refined branch of the family tree. I am praying that their influence will calm my wife's fractious nature."

"They will calm me, alright," Ella snapped. "They'll calm me right into my grave. You take me back to Philadelphia and you'll be an accessory to murder."

Harrigan shook his head and sighed, then briefly shook the deputy's soft, plump hand. "Thank you for all your help, sir. Just let me get on the train and on my way. Then you may let Miss Louise Carson go.''

"You sure?'' The deputy frowned at the jailhouse door. "Maybe if I hold her until you get to Philadelphia—''

"No need, Deputy Smith.'' Harrigan started toward the train station at the far end of town. "What can she do once the train leaves?''

"You clearly do not know my auntie,'' Ella drawled, glancing up in time to see the deputy shaking his head as he reentered the jailhouse. She turned her attention on the young man following them, his downcast expression revealing how much he hated the chore. "Clement, you know this is wrong.''

"It ain't wrong for a husband to be taking his wife home.'' He shook his head then looked at her accusingly. "You shoulda told us you was wed.''

"I *am not* married! I do not even know who this slinking cur is!''

"Harrigan Mahoney, at your service, ma'am,'' Harrigan said quietly so that Clement could not overhear him. "No point in arguing with them. They all believe me.''

"That simply proves that you are a skilled liar and they are stupid, Clement,'' she said, giving the young man as beseeching a look as she could manage while hanging upside down. "Have I ever lied to you?''

"Well, no,'' Clement agreed reluctantly, "but I ain't known you for too long. This might be something you would lie about.''

"Fine,'' she ground out, her teeth clenched in fury and frustration, "but even if I am married to this hulking fool, it is not right to allow someone to take me away when I do not want to go.''

"I reckon a husband can do it. Uh-oh.'' Clement tensed, moved closer, and placed his hand on his gun. "It's a couple of your aunt's boys.''

Harrigan frowned as three tall young men moved to stand directly between him and the waiting train. The darkest of the three moved a little closer, peering around him at Ella. When the youth looked back at him, his black eyes were hard and narrowed, and Harrigan tensed. He doubted the youth was long into his twenties, but the lean face he now looked at said that those had been hard years.

"I think it would be wise if you'd put our Miss Ella down now, sir," the youth said, his voice deep and cold.

"Now, Joshua," said Clement, "this here is Ella's husband."

"Husband?" Joshua looked Harrigan up and down slowly. "I don't think so. Ella ain't wed."

"He says—"

"Don't give two damns what he says. What say you, Ella?"

"I am *not* married to anyone," Ella answered, feeling the tension in the man who held her and wishing she could see what was happening. "That scum in Philadelphia hired this fool to take me back to them."

"Well, I think we'll put an end to that plan here and now."

When the young man pulled his gun, Harrigan silently cursed. He could almost hear the deputy's young man trembling beside him. Joshua was steady and calm, as were his two companions, who slowly drew their pistols as well. The few people who were loitering in the area hastily moved away. He wished he could do the same, but he had signed an agreement that he would do all he could to bring Ella Carson back to Philadelphia. Harrigan was trying to decide if that meant he should allow himself to be shot down in the dusty road of a struggling, dirty little town when he saw his assistant George Morgan slip out of the train and begin to silently advance on them, a rifle in his hands. Things could still turn deadly, but Harrigan felt a little less helpless and cornered.

"This is between Miss Carson and her family," Harrigan said. "Why not leave them to sort it all out?"

"If they want to discuss things, they can come here. Put her down," Joshua ordered.

"I think it'd be a fine idea if you boys'd put those guns

away," said a deep voice followed by the ominous sound of a rifle being cocked.

Ella cursed, tried to lift herself up, then tried to peer around Mahoney. Although she could not see anyone's face clearly, she recognized Joshua's boots and ornate belt buckle. He was flanked by two more of the youths everyone referred to as Louise's boys. What made her tense was the pair of legs she could see directly behind them. Instinct told her that that man was the one who had cocked the rifle. What she could see clearly was that everyone except the man she was draped over was holding a gun and the tension between the men was so thick she could feel it pressing in on her. Although she was terrified about being put in the reach of her Philadelphia kin, she did not want anyone to die trying to save her.

"Give it up, Joshua," she said. "This isn't worth dying over."

"No? Didn't you say those folks back east are eager to see you dead?" Joshua asked, never taking his gaze from the unarmed Harrigan.

"They are, but I'm not in their hands yet."

"This bastard means to put you there."

"There are a lot of miles between here and there. You can't win this standoff. And that pig, Smith, has put Auntie in his jail. She could use some help and I could certainly use her free and fighting for me."

For one long minute the tense confrontation held, then Joshua and his friends put their guns away. Ella breathed a sigh of relief and felt it faintly echoed in Mahoney. She intended to fight hard and long every step of the way to Philadelphia, but she did not want the trail to be littered with the bodies of her friends.

"Don't you worry none, Ella," Joshua said as he and his friends began cautiously to move away. "We'll get Louise out of trouble and then we'll get you free of this. That flock of carrion back east won't be picking on your bones."

"How colorfully put," Ella murmured as she watched her three erstwhile rescuers walk away.

"Phew," Clement said as he reholstered his gun with a shaky hand. "I thought Joshua was going to shoot you dead, Mr. Mahoney."

"Oh, not with you here to protect me, Clement," drawled Harrigan as he nodded his thanks to George and started toward the train.

"Sir, I couldn't shoot a man. Hell, I can't hit anything I shoot at. Joshua knows that, too."

Harrigan glanced at a morose Clement and suddenly realized that none of the young men had aimed their guns at Clement. In fact, they had mostly ignored the timid youth. Since the deputy had made it clear that he was glad to see the Carson woman leave, and that he expected trouble from "Louise's boys," Harrigan could not understand why he had been given such an inept guard. Smith was either incompetent, or unaware of Clement's failings. One look at Clement's morose face was enough to make Harrigan decide not to file any complaint against the young man.

"I think it would be best if we got out of here as speedily as possible," said George, pausing at the door of the train to let Harrigan board first. "This job isn't looking as easy as you thought it would be."

After murmuring his thanks to Clement, who left them with a graceless haste, Harrigan nodded, briefly grimacing at his assistant. "Once we're on our way, the situation will grow calmer, George."

"I am beginning to think you have about as much wit as the deputy," said Ella, cringing a little as they strode through the passenger car, for she recognized several of the people there. "My aunt will be hot on our trail as soon as that idiot Smith releases her."

"Her aunt?" murmured George as he helped Harrigan settle Ella on a seat.

Harrigan briefly told George about the confrontation at the jail. "We will be on a train rolling steadily toward Philadelphia. I don't see her as much of a threat."

Ella was just about to reply when Harrigan clicked shut

a pair of wrist shackles, chaining her right arm to the arm of the seat. For a brief moment she was stunned, then mortified, certain that every other person in the train car was staring at her. Then fury pushed aside all other feeling. Harrigan sprawled in the seat next to her and she glared at him.

"This is not necessary," she said in a cold voice as she fruitlessly tried to free her wrist.

"I will release you once we are moving and have put a goodly distance between us and this dusty town," Harrigan said.

She looked at the other man, the one Harrigan had called George, who sat across from them. George was not much taller than she was and slender of build. His somewhat narrow face was softened by thick waves of dark brown hair and surprisingly large hazel eyes. Those eyes revealed his discomfort, and Ella wondered if she could use that to her advantage.

"Don't waste your time," drawled Harrigan, smiling faintly when she scowled at him. "George may not agree with all I do, but he will not go against my wishes."

"Ah, I see. The lackey has a lackey."

"This journey will go much more quickly and smoothly if you would cease to hone your tongue on my skin."

"I do not see why I should consider your comfort when you are taking me to my death."

Harrigan studied her closely and frowned. He was beginning to think that she really believed what she was saying. For one brief moment, he considered the possibility that she was telling the truth, then shrugged it aside. She did not want to go home and was simply trying to sway him to her side. The rich were good liars, he thought bitterly, and would say or do anything to get what they wanted.

"That is utter nonsense. You might as well give up that lie because I will not swallow it."

"I do not lie."

He uttered a short, scornful laugh. "The rich always lie."

"You are Irish, Mr. Mahoney, and I would have thought that you would know well the folly of such sweeping condemnations."

She was pleased to see the flicker of discomfort on his face, but still inwardly cursed. There had been a wealth of bitterness behind his insulting words. Some wealthy person had done him a wrong and now she would pay for that. It was unfair, but she would be foolish to ignore the fact. Nor did she have the time to change his mind. It surprised her to realize how badly she wished to do so.

"What you believe or do not believe," she continued, "does not matter to me in the slightest." She hoped he could not detect the lack of conviction behind her words, something that deeply troubled her. "I will not be in your company long enough for it to affect me."

"No? Already planning your escape?"

Ella ignored the derision in his deep voice. "Yes, and I am sure that Aunt Louise will soon be along to assist me."

"Your faith in your aunt is admirable, but misplaced. She is nearly as delicate as you are and we are secure within a moving train. There is nothing she can do." He frowned and felt a twinge of unease when she slowly smiled.

"You do not know my auntie."

Chapter Two

"Louise, are you sure we ought to do this?" Joshua Longtree asked quietly as he sprawled in a delicate chair. He warily watched Louise Carson march in and out of the front parlour of her small house throwing the things she thought she needed for a trip to Philadelphia onto a plush burgundy settee.

Louise stopped after tossing a large bowie knife onto a tangled pile of clothes, and slowly turned to face Joshua and his three equally concerned companions, Edward, Manuel, and Thomas. Joshua and Thomas were half Indian, Manuel and Edward half Mexican. All of them had known little more than abuse and hatred in their lives and it had made them hard. She had saved the life of each one of the young men, taken them in, nursed their wounds, and given them work on her small ranch. She had never asked any return for her kindnesses, but had gained their unfaltering loyalty. There was no doubt in her mind that they would follow her to the gates of hell if she asked them to. Following Ella to Philadelphia and trying to rescue her could be just as dangerous, and she could not willingly push them into the middle of that.

"*I* have to do this. *You* do not," she said as she started to stuff her clothes into a small carpetbag.

Joshua looked at his three friends, who subtly nodded, then looked back at Louise, smiling faintly over her unusual agitation. "If you go, we go." The other three youths nodded again.

"That is so good of you," she murmured, and sat down on the settee. "This could be very dangerous. Ella and I were not victims of female hysteria when we told you that her life was in danger."

"Never thought it."

"Those people in Philadelphia want only one thing—Ella's death. They will not see any of us as an impediment to that plan. They will sweep us all aside if they can. You know they will feel free to be rid of you, seeing you as no more than half-breeds and outcasts. They will see me in much the same light. I know I have always jested about it, but I truly did leave Philadelphia in disgrace. There are many people back there who still suspect that Robin Abernathy was my lover and that I killed him in a fit of jealous rage. What I am trying to say is that, although I am a Carson and the Carsons are highly placed in that society, I am not. I will be no protection for you."

Joshua moved to sit next to Louise, lightly patting her tightly clenched hands. "If you're fretting that we'll do something we don't really want to because we feel we owe you, stop it. I won't say that a sense of obligation ain't part of what's prodding us, but there ain't no shame in that. Ella treated us kindly and that little miss sure as hell doesn't deserve to die just so her kin can take what don't belong to them. We don't want you doing something dangerous without us and you don't want us in danger either. Ain't no choice though, so why don't we just all agree to watch out for each other and get down to the business of saving poor Ella." He flushed when Louise impulsively hugged him and then scowled when the others laughed.

It was almost noon before they had everything ready for their rescue attempt, and Louise cursed softly as they rode away from her small ranch. The train now had a two-hour head start. Although they could take a more direct route than a train, and the one Ella was on would make a lot of stops, catching up to it was not going to be easy. Getting Ella off of that train could well prove to be impossible. Even if they were able to snatch Ella from her captors, that would not put an end to the danger she was in. It would only postpone the inevitable confrontation. Louise had the sinking feeling that the time had finally come to face the threat that had hung over them all for three long years. All she could do was pray that they could successfully eradicate it and that they would all survive.

An ear-splitting scream erupted from Ella, and Harrigan pulled away from her so quickly he nearly fell out of his seat. He glanced at the other passengers in the train car and flushed slightly under their accusatory stares. When he looked back at Ella she was no longer asleep but sitting calmly and tidying her hair. His first thought had been that she had suffered from some terrible nightmare, but his initial stirrings of sympathy abruptly faded. He now suspected that it was just another one of her ploys intended to discomfort him.

"You seem to have recovered from your bad dream very quickly," he drawled as he relaxed in his seat.

"Bad dream?" Ella looked at him, feigning innocence, and could tell by his narrowed eyes that he did not believe her act. "Ah, that. Yes, it was rather horrible. For one brief, terrifying moment, as I woke, I feared that I been thrust into the pits of hell. I was quite certain I could feel the devil's hot breath upon my cheek. I could even smell its foulness."

Harrigan clasped his hands over his stomach, sternly resisting the urge to cup a hand over his mouth, breathe into it, and test the freshness of his breath. He knew she was referring to him, to the way he had been leaning so close to her as he had prepared to nudge her awake. For a moment he had lingered in that position, struck by the sweetness of her expression. He had been strongly drawn to the fullness of her mouth and the way her lips had been faintly parted in innocent invitation. He had even found the length and thickness of her dark lashes of intense interest. It was a little embarrassing to have been caught in his observation, but he would never give her the satisfaction of knowing that.

"I am pleased that you have calmed yourself, have realized that it was only a dream."

"Was it?"

"You are hardly in hell, Miss Carson. You greatly exaggerate your situation."

"You, sir, know nothing about my situation."

"I know all I need to know."

"You know only the lies my conniving relations have told you."

"And you are the sole voice of truth, are you?"

His sarcastic tone enraged her, but Ella fought to control that emotion. Screaming insults at the man would do little to aid her cause. It would probably just confirm every lie her relatives had told him. A calm, steady repetition of the truth was what was needed. There was the chance that, if she said the truth often enough, and firmly enough, the man might at least begin to question the tale he had been told.

"Yes, I am, at least concerning this matter," she said, pleased at how polite and at ease she sounded. "My relatives in Philadelphia no doubt told you that I am some wild, spoiled child who ran away from her loving family and all of her obligations, a foolish girl who makes up tales of dangers and threats."

Harrigan swallowed a brief surge of unease over how precisely she had guessed what he had been told. Her family had said that she often tried to flee so it was possible that she knew exactly what they said about her. They had probably even said it to her face. They had also told him that she was very clever.

"More or less," he murmured, watching her closely for some sign that she was lying or was one of those sad people prone to delusions. "I am sure you have heard it all before."

"Yes. They have made it their business to tell that story to all who will sit still long enough to hear it. I fear I lacked the wit and the guile to ingratiate myself with the people of power and high standing in Philadelphia, so I suspect that many were more than willing to believe such a tale." She idly twisted the manacle encircling her wrist. "Therefore, I suppose I cannot blame you for believing it. Everyone you must have spoken to before accepting this appalling job must have readily confirmed that story."

Harrigan subtly glanced at George, who avoided his gaze, concentrating instead on smoothing down some imaginary wrinkles in his black waistcoat. George had repeatedly suggested that they investigate the Carson's claims before taking the job on, but Harrigan had always shrugged that good advice aside. He knew his own prejudices against the rich made him susceptible to believing any tale of their stupidity or rash, unthinking actions. He did not want to think that the Carsons may well have used that prejudice against him. Nor did he want an encroaching sense of guilt to make him believe anything the dangerously alluring Ella Carson chose to tell him.

"Just because everyone believes something does not mean it is the truth," she continued, glancing at him and wondering why there was no expression on his face. It was as if he was making a real effort to conceal his thoughts from her.

"Just as it can mean that it *is* the truth," he replied. "I find their tale of an errant, imaginative child far easier to believe than your story of conspiracies and attempted murder."

Ella turned in her seat slightly, so that she was facing him more directly. "I begin to think, Mr. Mahoney, that you have some deep mistrust and dislike of rich people. I also suspect that those feelings are even stronger when the rich person happens to be of English descent. So why do you so quickly and firmly reject the idea that such people could conspire against each other, even to planning the death of one of their own?''

"If they wished to murder you, they would not involve strangers. They would have come after you themselves.''

"The Carsons do their own dirty work? Surely you jest. They would never sully their hands so. And, if they were convicted of my murder, they would lose all that they can gain from my untimely death. It might behoove you to watch your back a little more closely. The Carsons may well have a plan to implicate you in my death.'' She peeked at George, pleased to catch the dark frown on his face, for it meant that she had at least roused some suspicion and doubt in his mind. "In truth, I am surprised that my relatives would even know an Irishman.''

"They know me well enough. It was one of their closest friends who stole my father's business, and, as a result, my inheritance,'' Harrigan said coldly.

"Ah, and therein lies the dislike of *my kind.*'' Ella inwardly cursed. Reminding him of the many wrongs done to him was no way to sway him to her side. "I would wager that you refer to the Templetons. I doubt that it will do me any good to remind you that women are usually given little control over or knowledge of business dealings.'' When Harrigan just scowled at her, she shrugged with an air of disinterest, then abruptly tensed. "Mahoney? Wasn't Templeton's daughter Eleanor acquainted with a man named Mahoney?''

"You could say she was *acquainted* with one. She was engaged to me.''

Worse and worse, Ella thought. "Was?''

"She called off the wedding when my father lost the business to her father.''

Distracted from her own troubles for a moment, Ella closely studied Harrigan.

Eleanor Templeton was a voluptuous blond, beautiful and haughty. It had astounded Ella when she had heard that the woman had betrothed herself to some unknown Irishman. When the wedding had been abruptly canceled, no one had been surprised, least of all herself. Gossip about the ill-fated match had been thick and constant. It was at that time, however, that Ella had discovered the perfidy of her relatives, realized her life was in danger, and fled to Wyoming. In the nearly three years since then, she had had far more important things on her mind than the whims and follies of Philadelphia's elite. She supposed that was why the name Mahoney had roused no memory when she had first heard it.

Now, however, memories flooded her mind, including the memory of a few suspicions she had had about Eleanor, as well as about her own cousin Margaret. The small crimes she had begun to suspect them of had faded into insignificance when she had realized her life was threatened. Both Eleanor and Margaret were society beauties and both had shown a tendency to become engaged to men their society considered unsuitable. Those engagements were usually short-lived as the young men or their families had suddenly had an unexpected turn of bad luck. At the time, she had begun to wonder if the two young women had had something to do with that bad luck, especially since their families had almost always benefited from the downfall of their betrotheds. Breaking a betrothal was also scandalous, and it had seemed curious that Margaret and Eleanor had risked their much prized reputations so repeatedly.

"You are staring," Harrigan said quietly, a little discomforted by her intense gaze.

"Is Eleanor Templeton married now?"

"I believe she might be in a month or two, as she is currently engaged to a man of her own standing. She was betrothed three more times between me and her current fool."

"And my cousin Margaret Carson? Do you know if she has wed?"

"She is now engaged for the fifth time since you ran away. I do not believe you will be attending any wedding, however. The man is from a poor background, born of a poor Scotsman who began a business twenty years ago and has only recently turned the corner to prosperity."

Ella smiled faintly when she saw the curiosity he could not hide. "Does it not strike you as passing strange that Eleanor and Margaret make and break so many betrothals? That they risk their reputations and standing in the society they love with apparent callousness? Or that they keep promising marriage to young men who are taking their first steps into the society Eleanor and Margaret were born into, making matches that none of their family or friends could possibly approve of? Odd that they would be willing to brave ostracism and scorn for love yet flee when the man becomes poor again? I find it a little sad that, each time they choose a man who has struggled up from the bottom and finally has wealth in his grasp, he loses it all. One must wonder if those women carry some strange curse, or if they just choose unwisely."

"Or if they are working for their fathers."

Fury had whitened his features, and Ella wondered if she had stupidly given him yet another reason to distrust and dislike her. He had already revealed how easily he could condemn an entire group of people for the crimes of a few. It was possible that he could now think she was hand in fist with Eleanor and Margaret. She had hoped to enhance her standing in his opinion by revealing such deception, but may well have done just the opposite. After taking a deep breath to steady herself, she decided to persevere. Any other action might simply harden his suspicions.

"That is what I was suddenly wondering. In truth, just before I left Philadelphia, I began to wonder what game they played. Margaret and Eleanor are not women given to whims and fancies. They are also very proud and aware of their place in society. I then began to wonder how they were even meeting these men, men who would never be acceptable to their friends and family. Even the objections of their families seemed weak, and, well, almost practiced."

"But you did not pursue it."

The strong hint of accusation in his deep voice irritated her. "At that time, Mr. Mahoney, something of far greater importance came to my attention—the threat to my life. I am sorry if you think it selfish of me, but I fear I decided that staying alive took precedence over all else."

Before Harrigan could reply, a short, plump man stepped up to his seat and, after nervously clearing his throat, said, "Sir, I do not know what crime this young woman is guilty of—"

"The most foul," Ella said. "I ran away from home." She met Harrigan's angry glance with a sweet smile.

Harrigan met the man's gaze and inwardly flinched at the condemnation he could read there. There was no way to defend himself. No man would believe that the sweetly smiling Ella was such a threat she needed to be manacled, at least not until they had dealt with her. The concern and good manners of the people he traveled with could prove to be a real problem, especially since Ella was clever enough to take full advantage of it.

"Sir," he finally said in a firm, coolly polite voice, "her family hired me to return her to Philadelphia. She is a chronic runaway."

"A young woman should indeed be safe within the care of her family, but does she need to be taken there in chains?"

"Chains? Hardly that, sir. A simple wrist manacle to ensure that she does not slip away again."

"Surely she cannot do so on a moving train with two grown men watching her." The portly man glanced nervously toward two equally plump women at the front of the car. "The sight of a woman being treated in such a rough manner upsets the ladies, I fear."

Harrigan wanted to tell him that none of this was his concern and that he could keep his bulbous nose out of other people's business, but he forced himself to smile. "Perhaps, while the train is actually in motion, I can relieve their distress." He fought to ignore Ella's small, triumphant smile as he undid the manacle around her slender wrist. "However, sir, safely returning this young lady to her family is far more important than the delicate sensibilities of strangers. I may need to act forcefully again, so I would strongly suggest that you speak to your female companions and impress that need upon them."

The way the man grunted, warily eyed the women he was traveling with, and shuffled back to his seat told Harrigan the man would do little to change their minds. They had pushed the man to interfere in another's business once, they would probably do so again. He exchanged a look of irritation with George then turned his attention to Ella. Her expression was too smug to suit him.

"This is no victory," Harrigan said, "merely a reprieve."

"And now he accuses me of unbecoming gloating," she murmured. "Is there no end to the insults I must endure?"

"How dramatic. You *were* gloating."

"You misread me. My expression was not one of triumph, but one of amusement. I was but entertained by your display of mastery over your true inclinations. You were so polite when what you truly wished to do was tell the fellow to mind his own damned business and waddle back to his masters."

Harrigan dimmed George's grin with one dark frown, then returned his gaze to Ella. She had judged his feelings perfectly, and that was a little disturbing. If he was going to successfully return her to her family, he had to be one step ahead of her at all times. He was now convinced that that was not going to be easy. Since there was no sense in denying what she had just said, he decided to just ignore it.

"I believe we were discussing the perfidy of your relatives before the gentleman interrupted us," he said, pretending he did not see her wry expression or delicately raised brows.

"It is odd that you so readily believe that they would trick and deceive your family into ruin yet scoff at my claim that they wish me dead," Ella said.

"There is a vast difference between believing people are

thieves and believing they are murderers. Many people do not blink an eye at stealing, but would never think of taking a person's life. And your family probably believes they acted in the name of good business, not thievery. A lot of people in their position do not realize that it can all be one and the same."

"If it involves trickery and deceit of the sort we think they employed, then they knew it was pure thievery. They have found a way to get what belongs to others without the poor fools knowing it is gone or even how it was taken away. That is thievery. Giving it a pretty, respectable name does not change that."

"You speak very harshly of your own family."

"They are only family because of a complicated series of marriages. And, it is easy to speak harshly of people who want you dead."

Harrigan slouched in his seat and gave her an exasperated look. "Are you planning to whistle that tune all the way to Philadelphia?"

"Until you start whistling along."

"I might do so if what you claim made any sense. It does not."

"Considering the way you feel about the rich, I am quite surprised that you would doubt any accusation against them." She studied him for a moment, wondering why she did not just give up. "What would make you consider the possibility that I am telling the truth?"

"You want me to tell you how to convince me that your delusions are real?" When she just lifted one delicate brow and continued to stare at him, he muttered a mild oath. "I certainly need some reason of consequence, something more than the fact that you are an irritation to them."

"I am an irritation to them because I have a lot of something they dearly love—money."

Harrigan sat up a little straighter, a flicker of unease teasing at his mind. "You have your own money?" George's dark frown made it all the harder for Harrigan to fight the doubt creeping through him.

"Of course I do. If I was some poor, penniless relative living off their kindness, do you really think they would be so eager to get me back?" She smiled crookedly when he just scowled at her and did not answer. "My mother, father, and infant brother drowned in a boating accident seven years ago." Ella idly stroked the silver, rose-embossed locket hanging around her neck. "They were not as wealthy as Uncle Harold, but they were far from poor. It all came to me, but my uncle had discretionary control over it until I am one and twenty, or married."

"So, he already has control over your money."

"Only a little. There is a whole pack of lawyers watching everything he does. He can only bleed the fund a little from time to time. Uncle watches me and they watch him."

"Then write a will and leave everything to your aunt or someone else."

"I have," she said, failing to keep all the sharpness out of her voice. How stupid did the man think she was? "I do not believe it will hold firm. Uncle Harold has his hands on my inheritance. Because Aunt Louise left Philadelphia under a large cloud of scandal, and because Uncle Harold can afford to hire some very clever lawyers, the will I wrote could easily be cast aside. That is assuming that it is ever allowed to come to light, of course. No, Uncle Harold wants my money and he will stoop to anything to get it. Even to hiring someone to lead me to the slaughter."

Harrigan just muttered a curse. The situation was getting more complicated by the minute. He still was not sure he believed Ella's claim that her life was in danger, but he could no longer treat it with complete scorn. He was caught firmly in someone else's tangled web of deception, but was it hers, or Harold Carson's? The hard truth of the matter was that he had no way of telling which Carson he should believe. The answers were all in Philadelphia, and would take time to ferret out.

"You are trying very hard not to believe me, aren't you?" Ella said softly.

"No. I was just thinking that it might be wise not to

believe you or your uncle and just wait until we get to Philadelphia to find out what the hell the truth really is."

"My death waits in Philadelphia."

"So does the truth. And there really is no other choice but to wait."

She smiled faintly and turned to stare out the window. "There is always Aunt Louise."

Chapter Three

"The train has stopped."

George's quiet but tense announcement almost made Ella open her eyes and look around. She continued to feign sleep, however, not wanting to expose the sudden surge of hope that warmed her blood. There were a dozen reasons for the train to stop. Once during the long night they had stopped for water. This time it could be for coal or wood or whatever they were using to fuel the engine. It did not have to be her Aunt Louise. Ella was not sure how her Aunt Louise could stop a train anyway.

"Have we reached a town?" asked Harrigan as he stood up and stretched.

"Not that I can see. Couldn't see a water tower either. Looks like we've stopped in the middle of nowhere."

"There was supposed to be a stop soon. Let's see if there's anyone we can talk to."

Ella waited for a moment after listening to the two men walk away before she cautiously opened her eyes. A look out the window told her nothing except that it was early in the morning and that George might just be right. It certainly looked as if they were in the middle of nowhere.

The same open, empty land could be seen through the window on the other side of the train car. Even if she was not shackled to the seat again, escape would be nearly impossible and probably very foolhardy. There did not look to be a decent place to hide for miles.

Despite the apparent hopelessness of even attempting an escape, Ella slipped a hairpin from her hair. Her aunt had spent many long hours teaching her how to pick a lock. It had been great fun. It had also been intended to help her get out of a locked room, something her uncle was very fond of putting her in. Louise had never once considered the possibility of manacles. Ella briefly prayed that her uncle had not either.

After several fruitless attempts at the lock, she cursed, then looked around nervously. She might yet have some use for the sympathy of her fellow passengers and she could not afford to lose it because they had overheard her talking like some dock worker. Ella was relieved to see that no one was near enough to hear her. It annoyed her, however, to discover that they were all covertly watching her, but not one of them offered to help. Their sympathy apparently extended only so far. The small hope she had nurtured that one of them would be moved to help her slowly began to die.

"Aunt Louise, I pray that it is you who has stopped this train," she muttered as she renewed her efforts to unlock her shackles. "It looks as if you are my only hope."

"This has got to be the stupidest plan you have ever thought of," drawled Joshua, frowning at Louise.

Louise brushed a stray lock of hair from her flushed face and glared at Joshua, who stood beside the railroad tracks and a safe distance from the outer rail. She too was beginning to have doubts about her plan to stop the train. Standing in the middle of the tracks, the train would soon come rolling over had caused her to question not only the wisdom of her plan, but her own sanity. She had struggled long hours to think of a way to stop the train without endangering it or the passengers it carried. If the engineer was alerted to trouble on the track he would slow to a safe stop. The least endangering and most easily removed difficulty she was able to think of was herself. Unfortunately, Joshua's continuous complaints and insults were making her envision far too many things that could go wrong—horribly, fatally wrong.

"If you do your part correctly, everything will be fine," she said as she studied her small booted foot and wondered if it really looked wedged in the tracks. She could not afford raising the engineer's suspicions too quickly.

"He won't stop for me. He'll just roll right over you. Might even do it just because stupid women annoy the hell out of him."

"No man will run a train over a woman no matter how stupid he thinks she is."

"You have too much faith in your fellow man."

"Look, I am well aware that this plan has holes in it big enough to stampede a herd of horses through. However, it is the safest one I could think of."

"Safe for everyone but you."

"I will be safe enough. Now, go, and make sure the other boys know what to do." When he hesitated, still scowling at her, she repeated, "Go, or we will still be standing here arguing this as the train thunders over me."

After muttering a few soft curses, Joshua left, and Louise breathed a sigh of relief. She knew that if Joshua had stayed any longer, he could have succeeded in talking her out of her plan. The idea of facing a speeding train was not only mad, it was terrifying. Although she had carefully considered all possible contingencies, there was no certainty that she would succeed in either stopping the train or getting out of the way if it was not going to stop. She cursed Harold Carson, the railroad, and Harrigan Mahoney as she wriggled her foot around in an attempt to make it look truly wedged even from a distance.

Suddenly, a sharp pain ran up her foot and wrapped

around her ankle. A cold knot formed in her stomach as she looked down. Not only was her foot definitely wedged but she could feel it begin to swell and something sharp was pressing dangerously into the top of her foot. She bent down and unbuttoned her high-top boot. One gentle tug on her foot brought a sharp pain and the sure knowledge that she would rip her foot open even if she was able to pull it free without fainting from the pain.

"God help us, Joshua, you better be able to stop that train," she whispered as she fought the urge to succumb to the panic tightening its grip on her. "I am now reduced to two grim choices—lose my life or lose my foot."

By the time George and Harrigan reached the front of the train, the engineer and his two fellow workers were already standing outside looking at something on the tracks. George immediately hopped down and started toward the other men. The moment Harrigan's feet touched the ground he knew he had made a mistake. He cursed as he heard the distinct sound of a rifle being cocked. Very carefully, keeping his hands held out to the side, he turned his head just enough to glance behind him. The way Joshua grinned only added to his anger and frustration. The two other youths he had seen with Joshua back in Wyoming nimbly boarded the train.

"I think stopping a train is a crime," Harrigan drawled, obeying Joshua's silent signal to move toward the others gathered at the front of the train.

"Possibly, but I don't think anyone will bother with us. We ain't robbing it, just taking a friend off it."

"You needed rifles for that?"

"Thought you might complain." As they stopped, Joshua scowled at Louise, who was still standing in the middle of the tracks. "You can move now, Louise. We'll have Ella free in a minute. Thomas and Edward have probably found her already."

"I am glad to hear it." Louise grimaced and glanced

first at Joshua then at Manuel, who held a gun on the engineer and his men. "I think I might need a little help."

Joshua cursed softly. "Don't tell me there's been a small problem with your brilliant plan?"

"Sarcasm will not help get me free."

"Aren't you going to do anything to stop this?" Harrigan asked the engineer, who looked far too at ease for his liking. "These people have held up the train."

"They've just stopped it for a little while," the burly man replied, rubbing his bristly chin and eyeing Harrigan with dislike. "It seems someone kidnapped a friend of theirs."

"It was not kidnapping. I was hired by the family to bring the girl back to Philadelphia."

"That ain't none of my business." The engineer clapped his skinny brakeman on the arm and moved toward Louise. "C'mon, Billy boy, let's get the little lady free, so we can move along."

Harrigan shook his head and cursed. He had become the villain in this little play. When he heard Joshua laugh softly, he glared at the youth.

"Louise has a cozening way about her when she chooses to use it," Joshua said, then shook his head as he watched a now freed Louise hobble toward him. "She also has a brain when she chooses to use it. This wasn't one of those times."

"It worked," Louise said as she carefully stayed out of Harrigan's reach while she limped around him.

"Auntie," cried Ella as she stepped off the train and ran up to Louise, Edward and Thomas strolling after her. "What happened to your foot?"

"We can talk about that later," Louise replied as she returned Ella's hug. "Thomas, get the horses." She looked at Harrigan. "When you see that sore excuse for a man, Harold, you can tell him that Louise wishes him her worst, that I know exactly what game he plays, and that he will never win, not as long as I still breathe."

"When I see Harold Carson again I will tell him that

the cost of my services has soared," drawled Harrigan. "He
told me how much trouble his niece was." Harrigan just
cocked one eyebrow when Ella glared at him. "But he
neglected to tell me anything about her equally troublesome aunt. Bringing Miss Ella Carson back to Philadelphia
is worth far more than he has offered."

"Yes, you should be charging dearly to take part in a
murder," snapped Ella.

"We don't have time for this argument," said Joshua as
he nudged the two women toward the horses Thomas led
over to them.

For one brief moment Harrigan considered the possibility of disarming Joshua and turning the tables on Ella and
her friends. A close look at Joshua put a swift death to that
plan. The youth was still watching him closely. Despite his
appearance of a relaxed guard, Harrigan knew he would
not get two steps before Joshua offered him a choice of
being shot or backing down. He found himself wondering
how the diminutive Louise had won the loyalty of such a
hard young man.

An involuntary smile touched Harrigan's face when Ella
and Louise mounted their horses. Neither woman paid
any heed to how their skirts were hitched up as they sat
astride their horses, their slim stockinged legs displayed
past the knee. When he looked up he met Ella's glare with
a smile. He knew his look held some of the lechery he felt
and, at the moment, he found that more amusing than
alarming.

The moment Ella and her valiant rescuers rode away,
Harrigan looked at the engineer. That man was staring at
him as if he was something nasty the man could not scrape
off his boots. It took Harrigan a moment to quell his anger
and outrage enough so that they would not creep out into
his voice.

"How far ahead is the next town?" he asked the man.

"About an hour," replied the engineer, wiping his hands
on his oil-stained pants and turning back toward the train.

"Is the train going to stop there?" Harrigan followed

the man, biting back his resentment over the way the engineer had turned his back on him and was walking away.

"Yup."

"For how long?"

"Don't see that you need to know that."

Harrigan clenched his fists at his side as the engineer stopped in the doorway of the locomotive and stared down at him. "I need to know if I will have enough time to get Miss Carson back and still catch the train or if I will have to meet up with you at another stop." The engineer stepped back a little into the cab of the locomotive and Harrigan decided he was doing a very poor job of hiding his urge to strike the man.

"It don't matter how long we set at the next stop or where we go after that. Not to you. When we stop at that town up ahead you're getting off my train and staying off it."

"You can't do that. I've paid for three passages."

"I can do most anything I damn well feel like on my train. The passengers have been complaining about how you treated that little lady and now we've been held at gunpoint. You're trouble, mister, and I don't need trouble."

"I'm not the one who held you at gunpoint."

"Nope, but you made those folks do that so they could save their friend."

"The authorities won't see it that way." Harrigan had no intention of speaking to any lawman about Louise stopping the train, but the engineer did not have to know that.

"You can talk to the law all you want, mister. If they come and ask me about this, all I'm saying is that a little girl decided she didn't want to go back East, so I let her off the train. Now I suggest you get back on this train unless you're inclined to walk to the next town."

Harrigan swore and strode back to the passenger car. He and George had barely stepped up into the car when the train jerked to a start. When he reached his seat and saw the empty shackles dangling from of the arm of the seat, he cursed again. As he sprawled in his seat, he caught the look on George's face and sighed, massaging his temples in a vain attempt to rub away a growing headache. His partner would continue to work with him, but it was clear that George now hated the job they had been hired to do. Harrigan silently admitted that he was beginning to detest it himself.

"I should have listened more closely to Ella when she said I did not know her auntie," Harrigan drawled as he began to get his anger under control.

"*That* was her aunt?" George asked, a brief look of astonishment flickering over his usually expressionless face.

"Yes, that was Louise Carson, the bane of the Philadelphia Carsons, and, if one can believe anything Sheriff Smith says, the bane of Wyoming as well. Didn't you hear Ella call the woman auntie?" Harrigan frowned when a blush fleetingly put a hint of color in George's pale cheeks.

"I fear I paid little heed to what occurred once I set eyes on Miss Louise Carson," George confessed quietly.

"She does have a skill at drawing one's attention."

"Yes, although I realize you do not speak kindly. I had not realized Miss Ella's aunt was so young or so lovely." He suddenly smiled, an expression as short-lived as all the others he employed. "I do not believe she had intended to be truly stuck, only to appear as if she was."

"The fool is damned lucky Joshua could get the train to stop." Harrigan shook his head as he stuffed the now useless shackles into his carpetbag. "Joshua speaks plain to her, but he clearly has no power over her. I am sure that he did not like this plan at all. He certainly didn't sound as if he did."

"What do you think Joshua is to her?"

"Like a nephew or a son if I judge it right." Harrigan met George's look squarely. "I am not sure it's a good idea to cast your eye that way, old friend."

"You mean to go after the girl."

"I do. We were hired to bring her back to Philadelphia.

The right or wrong of it is not our concern. And I don't intend to be beaten by two tiny ladies and a ragtag group of boys.''

Ella gratefully accepted the canteen Joshua held out to her. She rinsed her mouth out, took a small drink, and then dampened her handkerchief so that she could wipe off her face and neck. They had ridden hard for about an hour and her body was reminding her that it had been a long time since she had indulged in such strenuous activity. Cooking, cleaning, and tending gardens could be hard work but it did not prepare one well for a long, hard gallop. Once they were back at Louise's ranch, Ella promised herself, she would make the time to do some riding and, perhaps, toughen up some of the tender parts that were already complaining. She did not even want to think about how much further they had to ride.

What troubled her more than her own discomfort and the promise of more to come was her own confused feelings. She knew she ought to be elated. She had escaped. Yet again she had eluded Harold's deadly grasp. Everyone had survived the rescue. There was more than enough reason for her to celebrate, yet she felt no joy at all.

The longer she considered the matter, the more certain she was that Harrigan Mahoney was the reason she did not feel joyous about her freedom. Ella was slightly horrified when she realized that she regretted leaving him. The man had snatched her from her home, shackled her, and was determined to take her to Harold. He was in the pay of her enemies. She should be delighted to see the back of him, but she was not. Ella decided that her poor confused mind wanted it all—freedom and Harrigan Mahoney. She was going to have to push such mad thoughts aside. Harrigan Mahoney wanted to take her back to Philadelphia and Harold. Reluctantly, she admitted that she was intrigued by the man and strongly attracted to him, but he was a real threat to her. Her interest in him only added to that danger. She was determined to kill that reckless attraction.

"I would have thought you'd look a bit happier," murmured Louise as she rode up next to Ella.

"I am happy, and deeply grateful to all of you." She included Joshua and the others in her glance. "I cannot believe you put yourself in front of a train." Ella shook her head, glanced down at her aunt's foot, and gasped when she saw how swollen Louise's bootless foot was. "My God, you were really trapped on those rails!"

Louise looked at her foot, tried to wriggle her swollen toes, and winced. "That was not part of my plan. I was standing there thinking that my foot didn't look trapped enough, wriggled it about and, lo and behold, got myself well and truly stuck. Never mind that. It will heal. Now, I know you're glad to be free, but you didn't look too happy. I want to know why. Did that bastard hurt you? Besides shackling you in that barbaric way, I mean."

"Ah, so you were told about the shackles. It was just a small manacle around my wrist. You can't really blame the man for fearing that I would run away. We all made it abundantly clear that the last place I wanted to go was Philadelphia."

"Alright, I will grant him that. He's no better than some bounty hunter, however, so that is all I will grant him." Louise studied Ella closely for a moment. "I know you, girl, better than you might like. That is because we are so much alike. Something is gnawing at you. If you would just spit it out, we could chew it over together, and then the problem might not seem so big."

Ella smiled faintly, saw that the men were too far ahead to overhear them, and said, "I'm not sure it's a problem. More of a puzzle, really. I am delighted to be free yet I find that I regret seeing the last of Harrigan Mahoney." She gaped slightly when her aunt began to laugh. "I don't see the humor in this conundrum."

"You will some day." Louise struggled to subdue her amusement. "Child, even as I was aiming my Henry at that tall fool, I could see that he was a fine figure of a man. A woman doesn't see many like that in her lifetime. You wouldn't be a woman if you didn't appreciate a man as beautiful as that.''

"Auntie, he was taking me to Harold, to my death. He thinks I am a spoiled, rich child given to lies and fancies. He shackled me to my seat. He carried me to the train like a sack of meal.''

"And I bet that, for one brief moment, you thought it was a fine broad shoulder.'' She laughed again when Ella blushed faintly. "It might seem mad to give him any thought at all, but, I swear to you, any other woman with eyes in her head would find herself in the same quandary. You're still running away from him, aren't you?''

"Of course I am. He was taking me to that pig, Harold, who desperately wants me dead before his guardianship of me ends.''

"Exactly. True madness would be if you walked back to him. Thinking about a handsome man yet still protecting yourself and your heart is just natural. What you're regretting right now is that you didn't meet him under different circumstances. Don't worry, Ella, there will be another one.''

A voice in Ella's head adamantly declared that she did not want another one, she wanted Harrigan, but she fought hard to silence it. She would put that man right out of her mind. She was not one to bemoan what she could not have and Harrigan Mahoney would not be allowed to change that. He was out of her life now and would not return. A chill ran down her spine and she decided that was a statement she would need to repeat a few times. Ella fixed her gaze upon the land stretching out ahead of them and sternly resisted the urge to look behind her.

Chapter Four

Harrigan sighed, tipped his hat back, and wiped the sweat from his brow with his handkerchief. Luck had been with them so far. The train had reached the next stop in under an hour, he had gotten some of his ticket money back, the horses and supplies had been easy to acquire, and Ella's trail was clear to follow. He prayed that good luck would continue. A quick look at George told him that his partner was not as pleased with their good fortune as he was and Harrigan sighed again.

"George, I wish you would shake free of that gloom that's settled over you," Harrigan said. "We *both* agreed to do this job for Harold Carson. We *both* need the money."

"I know," George replied, then shook his head. "I know I reveal no secrets when I confess that I have grown to like this job less and less. And, now that I have seen Miss Louise, I begin to feel like the basest of traitors."

"You only saw the woman once, when she stupidly got her foot stuck on the railroad tracks."

"One look is all it takes sometimes."

A part of Harrigan agreed and he brutally silenced it. "George, Louise Carson is unquestionably a lovely woman.

She is also the woman who tried to shoot a hole in my leg, who has been galloping over the countryside with four young men of dubious background, and who stuck herself in front of a moving train.''

"All of which reveals spirit and a deep sense of responsibility for her niece's safety."

Harrigan briefly lifted his hat and dragged his fingers through his hair. "You have picked a damned poor time to suffer a first love."

"And what makes you think it is my first?"

The bite in George's soft, melodious voice caused Harrigan to stare at his friend in surprise. "I meant no insult. Hell, George, I've known you for what, seven years or more, and you've never had much to do with the ladies. I just assumed you were, well, too quiet or shy. Considering you're only two and thirty, I just figured the way you've behaved for the last seven years is the way you've always acted."

Harrigan watched the tight anger slowly leave George's face and inwardly breathed a sigh of relief. He had never considered the possibility that George would have a sore spot somewhere, and he was not really pleased to have found it. At the moment, it seemed like George was the only one who was not angry with him, and he did not want to lose his only ally.

"Sorry," George murmured. "I was married once, you know."

"Married?" Harrigan was so shocked he nearly choked on the water he was drinking. "You're a widower?"

"No, I got divorced." George smiled faintly at Harrigan's open-mouthed astonishment. "I shocked myself nearly as much at the time, but it did not stop me. That is, however, why I moved from Boston to Philadelphia. No one blamed me for divorcing the woman. In truth, they all sympathized. That might be one reason that I could no longer abide living there."

"What happened?"

"I just grew weary of finding my side of the bed occupied

with another man. I think I might have been inclined to stay, to try and win her back, if it had been the same man. It was not. This was not a matter of her loving another. I began to wonder if she was just pulling them in off the street as they walked by the house.''

"Hell, George, I'm surprised you didn't just shoot her." Harrigan briefly thought of how it would feel to see Ella in bed with a man and was surprised at how angry the image made him. "I don't think I would've paused to wonder if she loved the man. I would've just reached for my rifle and wondered which one of them to shoot first."

"There was one time when I came very close to doing just that. That was when I decided the scandal of divorce would be acceptable. A scandal is a lot easier to bear than a noose around one's neck."

Harrigan decided that George's painful tale made his own problems with women look a bit small and insignificant. "I would think that, after that bitter experience, you'd have the sense not to decide on a woman with just one look."

George shrugged. "Louise is not like my wife, nor would she ever be like that."

"Damn it, how can you be so sure of that?"

"For one thing, my wife Ellen would never lift a finger to save or help anyone. I cannot explain why I think Miss Louise is completely different from Ellen. I just know it."

"Didn't you just *know* it about Ellen?"

"No." A short, faintly bitter laugh escaped George. "All I saw was Ellen's beauty. All I knew was that I ached for her. She could clear my mind of all questions, all thought, with one inviting smile. There were rumors, whispers of scandals, but my lust for the woman made me deaf to them. That and the arrogance of youth. I was sure that, if what people said about her was even partly true, I would be the one who would make her change her ways."

Harrigan echoed George's bitter laugh and shook his head. "I had some of the same stupid ideas about Eleanor."

As George began to speak, Harrigan tensed, and held up his hand to silence his friend. He lifted himself up a little in the saddle and listened intently, then slowly smiled. The soft spring breezes were carrying more than a refreshing coolness. They also held the faint sound of voices. Harrigan could see nothing amongst the scattered trees and tall grasses they rode through, but he was certain that they had finally located their quarry.

"Gird your loins, old friend," he said to George even as he nudged his horse in the direction of the voices. "You are about to get another look at your cantankerous, guntoting lady love."

"You intend to taunt me with that for a while, don't you," George murmured as he followed Harrigan.

"Quite probably. Now, let's go get little Miss Ella."

"We have to get back on our horses," Louise said, her voice weak and unsteady as she tried to stand up.

Ella gently but firmly pushed her aunt back down onto the blanket spread beneath a gnarled tree. "You are staying right there until we can get the swelling in your foot to go down."

"I can ride."

"Of course you can. That's why you fell out of your saddle. You're lucky you didn't break your damned neck. Do you think all of us are squatting here staring at you out of pure admiration?" Ella briefly exchanged a grin with a chuckling Joshua.

When Ella had watched her aunt turn white and tumble out of her saddle, she had felt choked with panic. Louise was the last of her family, certainly the last one who cared anything about her. The moment Louise's body had hit the ground, Ella had felt the impact deep in the pit of her stomach. As she had rapidly dismounted, Joshua and the others swiftly joining her as she knelt by Louise, the fear that she was now completely alone had almost overwhelmed her. She had nearly wept when she saw Louise breathe and realized that the woman had only fainted.

As the four young men had helped her settle Louise on a blanket in the shade of a tree, Ella had seen clearly how much Louise meant to her *boys*. Even Joshua had paled when she had tumbled to the ground. Louise was their family. For most of them she was probably the only one who had ever given a damn about them and they adored her for it. Although Louise was only seven and twenty, not much older than many of her boys, it was not a romantic love Ella had glimpsed in the four hard faces. Theirs was a love born of Louise's freely given friendship, trust, and respect.

"Your bedside manner could use some softening, Doctor Carson," Louise muttered as she raised herself up enough to take a good look at her injured foot. "What is that rag draped over my foot? And why is it set on top of Joshua's saddlebags?"

"The cloth is wet with cold water from the creek to bring down the swelling and your foot is set up on the saddlebags so that it is raised, which will also help. Margaret turned her well-bred little ankle once and this is what the doctor told her to do to reduce the swelling. It seemed to work."

"We can do this back at the ranch."

"We will do it here and now." Ella handed Manuel the rag. "Could you please go to the creek and soak this in the cold water again?" As soon as Manuel left, Ella sat back on her heels and gave her aunt a stern look. "You will rest here until the swelling eases and I can think of a way to let you ride while still pampering that foot."

"When did you become so autocratic?"

"When you fell off your horse in a swoon because you stuck your foot in front of a train. You scared us all to death, Auntie, and now you will placate us by trying to take care of yourself. At least for a little while."

Louise stared at Ella, Joshua, Edward, and Thomas, sighed, and laid back down. "Oh, as you wish. I suppose the horses could do with a little rest."

"Such a gracious concession. I wonder what happened to Manuel? It shouldn't be taking him this long," Ella mused aloud as she gently settled her aunt's swollen foot more comfortably on the saddlebags. "It already looks better."

"I'm glad of that," Joshua said in a tight voice as he, Thomas, and Edward slowly rose to their feet, "because everything else is looking pretty damned bad right about now."

Ella looked in the direction the men were staring in and echoed her aunt's curse. Manuel was returning from the creek, the wet rag held tightly in one of his raised hands. Close behind him was Harrigan Mahoney, holding a rifle on the youth. George trailed behind the pair, leading the two horses. Ella decided that Harrigan looked far too pleased with himself. She briefly wondered why George looked so downcast as she carefully stood up.

"I see that you decided not to ride the train back to Philadelphia and concede that this battle is lost," Ella said, ruthlessly silencing that reckless part of her that was dangerously pleased to see him.

"You've lost this battle, not me," Harrigan said, stopping just out of their reach. "Now, everyone toss their weapons over to George—very carefully."

"Better do it, boys," Louise said when Joshua hesitated. "We can't be sure how desperate this rogue is to collect his blood money."

"Taking a fee for returning a runaway child to her family is not taking blood money," Harrigan responded in a tone that revealed his sense of insult. "Tie them up, George."

"Louise is injured," protested Ella. "You can't tie an injured woman up and leave her out in the middle of nowhere. Even you can't be that callous, that brutal."

"I can, and she wouldn't be hurt if she hadn't stuck her little foot in front of a train." Harrigan nudged Manuel toward the others. "Now, arrange yourselves prettily around that tree. All except you, Ella." He grabbed Ella by the wrist and tugged her close to his side. "Don't worry.

George is a gentleman. He will tie them up in a way that will allow them to squirm free in a little while, but not soon enough to catch up with us." He caught Ella eyeing his rifle speculatively and smiled. "If you try to grab this gun, darlin', it could easily go off. You might want to take a minute to recall who it is aimed at."

Ella paled slightly and stood very still. She ached to put up a fight, but knew Harrigan was correct. That would not be the safest thing to do when there was a cocked rifle aimed at her family and friends. She did not really believe that Harrigan wanted to shoot anyone, but his gun was loaded and ready, and that made him dangerous. It pleased her to see that George allowed Manuel to cover Louise's swollen foot with the cold cloth before he tied them all to the tree, but that was the only thing she could find to be pleased about.

"When I get free of this, I'm going to hunt you two bastards down and gut you," snapped Louise as George finished tightening the last knot and stepped back.

"Now, I am sure you don't really mean that, Miss Louise," George said.

"You'll think differently, little man, when you're staring at your own innards."

"Oh, I like that one, Auntie," Ella said. "That has to be the best of all your threats."

"Thank you," Louise said. "The heartfelt ones are always the best," she added, meeting George's nervous glance with a too sweet smile.

"You are both quite mad," Harrigan said as he shook his head. "George, get one of their horses for Ella." He looked down at Ella, who was not able to hide the hope glinting in her eyes fast enough. "And you can stop plotting. You will have your own horse, but not the reins."

"Mine is the brown mare," she called to George, inwardly cursing over Harrigan's uncanny ability to read her thoughts. "At least this time I will have a change of clothes when I am kidnapped."

"You are not being kidnapped," Harrigan snapped as

he tossed her up onto the saddle of the little mare George led over.

"If you don't like the name, quit the job," she said. "You are taking someone where she does not want to go. Sounds like kidnapping to me."

"I have already discovered that you have your own unique way of seeing things."

"Yes, I suppose someone as pigheaded and ignorant as you would see the truth as unique. Or is it because I am a mere woman that you refuse to listen to a word I say? If I was a man you would listen, would you?" When Harrigan said nothing, just stared at her while George mounted his horse, she finally demanded, "What are you gawking at?"

"I was just wondering how you could make the word *man* sound like the vilest curse."

"Sometimes that's just what it is."

"Now, look here."

George moved his horse close enough to Harrigan's to bump it and draw Harrigan's attention. "If your plan is to get so far ahead of these people before they free themselves that they can never catch up, I suggest you have this argument later," George said, casting one last, sad look toward a glaring Louise before he spurred his horse to a trot and rode away.

Muttering a curse, Harrigan quickly followed his friend. Ella Carson certainly had a sharp tongue, but he did not understand why he allowed it to stir his anger. He had dealt with sharp-tongued women before and had been able to do so with calm. Their complaints and insults had simply bounced off him. Ella's went straight to his heart and that disturbed him, almost frightened him. After Eleanor's deceit had cost him so dearly, he had sworn that no woman would touch him. He spared one quick glare for Ella before concentrating on the route they rode over, and decided that he needed to toughen his hide. No tiny, green-eyed girl was going to make him forget the hard lessons he had learned.

Ella looked back, but only got one last glimpse of Louise

and the boys before they disappeared behind the scattered trees and high grasses. She prayed that Harrigan was telling the truth and that George had tied them in such a way that they would be able to free themselves. It could be deadly to be left so helpless in the wilderness. There were dangerous animals and dangerous men wandering the unsettled areas.

She scolded herself for such selfish thoughts, but she also worried that Louise and the boys would not be able to ride to her rescue this time. Even if they got free, Louise was in no condition to go galloping across the countryside. The boys might try it on their own once they got Louise settled safely and comfortably, but that could bring new problems. Because of their mixed heritage, they were not often welcomed by people, no one would listen to them so they would be unable to enlist any help, and they could even come face to face with the dangerous prejudices that had caused them so much trouble in the past. Louise's presence sometimes softened those threats. People might think some very unpleasant things about her and her companions, but Louise had the presence and the training to overcome those difficulties or at least cause people to hesitate long enough so that she and the boys could get out of harm's way.

Ella forced herself to accept that she might well be on her own this time. It was hard not to give in to the fear that welled up inside of her. Fear was a destructive emotion and stole her ability to think clearly. While she was still in Harrigan and George's hands, her life was not in danger. She did not believe either man wanted to hurt her in any way. That was certainly something she could use to her advantage.

There was only one thing she had to give some very careful thought to and that was what she should do if she did have the chance to escape. She did not know the country they rode over. She had grown up in Philadelphia and spent her time at her aunt's within the confines of the ranch and the town. There was also the fact that she

would be traveling around alone, at least in the beginning.
It was a daunting thought. Only the certainty that Harold
wanted her dead kept her from casting aside all thoughts
of escape. She was in a fight for her life, whether Harrigan
Mahoney deigned to believe her or not, and she could not
let timidity stop her from grasping any chance to escape.

As carefully as she could, not wanting Harrigan to catch
her at it, Ella studied George Morgan. He was suffering
from a change of heart. Whether he was beginning to
believe her or was simply infatuated with Louise did not
matter. Ella was sure that George was heartily regretting
signing on for this job. It was another thing she could use
to her advantage if she could get some time alone with
the man. Harrigan could have been overestimating his
friend's loyalty when he had said that George would never
work against him no matter how much the man hated
the job he was doing. Harrigan had never considered the
possibility that his friend would cast a covetous eye at their
prisoner's aunt, something Ella was now sure George was
doing. If she had not been so distracted by the need to
run and by Harrigan, she probably would have noticed
George's infatuation back at the train.

"I can almost hear the plots hatching under that gor-
geous hair of yours," Harrigan murmured, smiling when
Ella glared at him.

"You have a vivid imagination," she said as sweetly as
she could. "If you heard anything it was the stiffening of
your stubborn backbone."

Harrigan grinned. "Now there is an image. Did you
learn your witty turn of phrase from your mad aunt?"

"My aunt Louise is not mad."

"The woman put her foot in front of a train."

"Which, if you could push aside your inclination to
ridicule everyone but yourself, you would see as a very
clever plan. She needed to stop the train, but did not want
anyone to be hurt. The safest obstruction she could put
in front of the train was herself, something that would
cause the engineer to stop if he was warned about it, but

which could also be immediately removed if the man ignored Joshua's warning.''

"The only way she could have removed that foot was to cut it off.''

"Well, I will admit that her plan went a little awry.'' She gave Harrigan a disgusted look when he laughed. "It was still a brilliant way to bring the train to a stop without hurting the machine or the passengers it carried. And, if you were not so arrogant, you would admit that.''

Very soon after he had been the victim of Louise's plan, he had been able to see the cleverness of it, but he was not about to admit that to Ella. He was certainly not going to admit that he was not sure he would have the courage to do such a risky thing. One thing he had become certain of was Louise Carson's abiding love for her niece. It told him that, for as long as she was able, the woman would continue to try to rescue Ella. He did not think the woman's injured foot would hold her back for very long either. Louise would soon be on their trail again and he intended to get as far ahead of her as possible.

"Well, that clever plan of hers has now put her out to pasture,'' he said, not believing it for a moment, but curious to see if Ella did.

"A little twisted ankle will not keep my aunt down for long,'' Ella said, praying that she sounded far more confident than she felt.

"Are you sure it was only twisted?'' asked George.

Ella almost smiled. That one shyly asked question proved that she was right about George's feelings for Louise. The way Harrigan scowled at his friend only increased her pleasure at gaining such knowledge.

"Yes, George,'' she answered politely, blatantly showing George the courtesy she refused to extend to Harrigan. "With a little care the swelling will subside and my aunt will be her old self again. Of course, you will soon see that for yourself, when she takes me away from you again.''

"As I have said before, Ella,'' Harrigan said, "I believe you have far too much faith in Louise Carson.''

"And as I have said before, Mr. Mahoney, you don't know my auntie."

"I can't believe some green, fancy dresser from back East managed to follow us and steal Ella back," grumbled Joshua as he struggled with the slowly loosening ropes that bound them all to the tree.

"Harrigan Mahoney may be from back East and he may dress well, but I don't think he's green," said Louise. "The man has skill, more than I gave him credit for. That was a mistake, one I will not make again."

"You're not thinking of running right after him, are you?" asked Manuel as he managed to squirm free of his bonds and began to help the others get loose.

Louise stared at her swollen foot and grimaced. "I was thinking of it, but I believe my foot has other plans for me. I hate it, but I have to concede to my injury for a little while."

"Then we have lost." Joshua crouched by her side and handed her the canteen of water. "They'll be too far ahead of us. We'll never be able to catch up with them."

"Harrigan may be a lot more clever than we thought, but he's still a stranger to this land." Louise took a long drink of water and handed the canteen to Edward. "He'll have to follow the well-traveled routes, if only out of a fear of getting lost. Taking a wrong turn would cost him time, and he won't want to risk that. Don't worry, we'll catch up with the bastard, and this time I will make sure he can't follow us."

Joshua grimaced. "I'm willing to give it a try, but I don't feel as sure as you do."

"That's because you didn't consider our Ella." Louise smiled. "She knows we'll need time to follow, and she'll do everything she can to buy us some."

Chapter Five

"I need to have a bath," Ella said the moment Harrigan ordered a halt to their long ride, and she dismounted.

"Shall I call the servants?" he muttered as he began to unsaddle his horse.

"Very amusing. There is a little creek over there." She pointed toward a thin line of trees. "That will do."

Harrigan looked at her and almost smiled. She was dusty and disheveled, her hair was untidy, and her face flushed. She looked adorable and Harrigan was very sure that, if he said so, she would probably threaten to cut his tongue out. Ella Carson looked so soft and sweet, like a tiny porcelain doll, yet, when she opened her mouth, she revealed a wit and temper as sharp as a knife. She was like a wild rose, beautiful but protected by some very sharp thorns, he thought, a little amused by his sudden fancy. Harrigan blinked, shaking himself free of the disturbingly tender thoughts, and forced him mind back to her request.

He could sympathize with her need to clean up, but it did present a problem. There was no doubt in his mind that, given half a chance, Ella would try to escape. She had made no secret of her intention never to return to

Philadelphia. Since he could not bring himself to deny
her a bath or embarrass her by standing right there while
she did it, he was going to have to think of a way to give
her what she wanted yet take away all chance of escape.
That was not going to be easy.

"What if I swear I will not try to run away?" she said,
tired of waiting and easily guessing why he was hesitating.

"I mean no insult, but I don't know you well enough
to know if I can trust in your promises. Go and clean up
then, but remember that we are keeping a watch on you."

"Watching me?"

"From a respectful distance. Don't worry, you'll have all
the privacy you need, as long as you stay right by the creek
and don't try to wander."

Ella was not sure how he could do that, but decided to
trust in his assurances. As she collected what she needed,
she knew part of her willingness to believe him was inspired
by a desperate need to get clean. She was not sure she
would be deterred even if she knew he was planning to
crouch behind the bushes and watch her every move.

When Ella reached the creek, she sighed with disappointment as she set her things down on the grass. It looked
refreshing, clear and cold, but it was also shallow. There
was not enough water for her to immerse herself completely and that was not only what she had hoped for,
but what she needed to feel that her modesty would be
preserved. Without the depth of water needed to hide
herself, she could not take all of her clothes off. It would
be as if she stood naked in the middle of an open field
and she knew she would feel that way even if Harrigan was
not lurking close by.

After a moment of thought, she decided to leave her
camisole and pantaloons on. They needed to be washed
anyway, and Louise had packed some clean ones for her.
It would only take a moment to change from the wet ones
to the dry ones and there was plenty of cover amongst the
trees and bushes to hide her while she made the quick
change.

The water was almost too cold, but Ella welcomed the refreshing chill. She felt as if she had been coated with dust and dirt for days. After she was done, she used her soiled gown as a drying cloth, then washed it out. Although she was sure Harrigan would not spy on her, she still checked for him before hastily changing her underclothes. She donned a blue gingham gown, found a black rawhide tie in her bag, and loosely tied her wet hair back. It was making the back of her gown wet, but it was still hot enough for her to find that pleasantly cooling.

Gathering up her things, she walked back to the campsite. Now that she was clean, her mood had improved, but she still felt a sharp pinch of anger when she looked at Harrigan. He was her uncle's hired man. Ella was beginning to believe that he had no idea of what Harold's plans for her were, but he was still taking her to Philadelphia, to her death, and she almost hated him for that.

"Enjoy your bath?" he asked as she sat down near the fire after draping her wet clothes on a nearby tree.

"The creek is very shallow, but it sufficed," she replied, watching George make the coffee.

"Good," he said as he stood up. "I think I'll have a wash too."

"Watch out for the snakes," she called after him, smiling sweetly at him when he gave her a doubtful look.

She had not seen one snake, but he did not have to know that. Some of the enjoyment of getting clean had been stolen by the knowledge that he was closely guarding her. Ella felt it served Harrigan right if some of his enjoyment was stolen by a need to look for snakes that were not there. And, she thought with a little smile, even though he did not really believe her, he would look.

Harrigan cursed as he caught himself carefully checking the ground before setting his clothes down. He really hated snakes, and, if he did not know better, he would swear that Ella had found that out. Until she had said something he had been blissfully ignorant of the possibility of meeting up with a snake. Her parting remark had reminded him that they were out in the wilderness.

He then softly cursed her as he shed his clothes and cautiously entered the cold water. Ella Carson was one tiny, beautiful bundle of pure trouble. He was going to make Harold Carson pay dearly for all of the trouble he had to endure.

His mind lingered on Harold Carson as he scrubbed himself clean. The man was as big a crook as some of the ones rotting away in the jails, but he walked among the elite. Power and money was what made the difference. A poor man could spend years of his life behind bars for taking a loaf of bread while Harold Carson stole thousands and was invited to parties. It was unfair, but it was the way of the world. Recognizing the injustice of it and feeling bitter was not enough to bring about a change.

What he had to decide was just how big a crook Harold was. Although he was not ready to believe everything Ella said, he could not discard it completely. Could the man stoop to the murder of his own niece just to add to his already full coffers? Deep in his heart, Harrigan knew the answer was yes, but was that answer inspired by his dislike for the man, or by fact? Or worse, he thought with a grimace, his growing attraction for Ella?

There was no profit in chewing over the matter, he decided as he stepped out of the creek and dried himself off. He could not decide Harold's guilt or lack of it based on such tenuous things as intuitions and Ella's accusations. He needed proof and that was in Philadelphia. Earlier, when he had said that he would look into the matter, he had not been entirely sincere. Now he was determined. If Ella was telling the truth, then Harold Carson was using him and George to help him commit a crime. He would see that the man paid dearly for that.

After rinsing out his dusty clothes, Harrigan hurried back to camp. He suspected that George would also like a bath and the light of day was rapidly waning. The moment he had tossed his clothes over some tree branches to dry and could turn his full attention on Ella, George strode off to the creek. Harrigan smiled faintly at the man's uncustomary haste as he sat down next to Ella before the fire. George was a very precise, tidy man and was undoubtedly finding the dust and heat of the journey a real trial.

Supper was going to be beans, biscuits, and coffee. Harrigan decided that was another inconvenience Harold would pay for. He was no wilderness man. He liked hearty meals of meat and potatoes, soft beds, and hot baths. Although he could ride, he preferred trains and carriages. When he had told Harold what the job would cost, he had not figured in all these inconveniences. The moment he saw the man again, he intended to make it very clear that the price for his services had just gone up.

"A bath obviously did not improve your temperament," Ella said as she poured them each a cup of the coffee George had made. She briefly wondered why she was doing that, then decided constant animosity was simply too exhausting.

"I was just thinking about how much I should add to the bill I will give your uncle," he replied as he accepted the cup she held out to him.

"You actually plan to collect money from the man?"

"We have an agreement. I get paid when you return to Philadelphia."

"You should have added a clause to that contract."

"Oh? What?"

"That you would get at least part of your earnings even if you fail. It will be a shame when, after all the trouble you have gone through, you find yourself penniless."

"I don't intend to fail."

Ella shook her head over the heavy tone of confidence in his voice. "Oh, I really think you must, if only so that you lose a little of that overpowering arrogance."

"Overpowering, is it?"

"Very. I am surprised you don't gag on it."

"And your unwavering belief that you and your lunatic aunt will win is not arrogance?"

"No, it is just simple fact. And my aunt is not a lunatic."

"The woman put her foot in front of a speeding train."

"Will you just forget that?" she snapped.

"I don't think I can," he murmured as he filled two tin plates with beans and biscuits, and set one down in front of her. "The image is seared into my mind."

"Well, at least something has settled there. The truth has obviously found it difficult to get a grip." She inwardly grimaced as she began to eat. She really did not like beans, but she was too hungry to be choosy.

"I have been told two different truths," he reminded her. "I don't know either you or your uncle well enough to know which one of you to believe. So, why don't we just cease to discuss that. I will search out the truth the moment we get back to Philadelphia."

She frowned and watched him covertly as she ate. There was the strong ring of a promise behind his words. It only comforted her a little, however. He was still implying that she was a liar and she deeply resented that. The fact that she was so attracted to a man who refused to believe her only added to her resentment.

There was a great deal of injustice in the world, she decided. It was unfair that she should suffer for her uncle's insatiable greed. It was certainly grossly unfair that she would have to die for of it. And, she thought sadly as she studied Harrigan's strong profile, it was painfully unfair that the man who was going to deliver her to that fate was so handsome, so intriguing, and so dangerously close to invading her heart.

Ella started, blinking in confusion. It was now dark and someone was gently shaking her by the arm. She absently swatted away the hand on her arm and looked around, slowly recalling where she was and why. George was missing and Harrigan was sitting next to her watching her with an annoying little grin on his face.

"Perhaps you ought to go to bed before you fall into the fire," Harrigan said.

"Where is George?" she asked, troubled by the man's disappearance.

"He offered to take the first watch."

"Aha! So you *are* worried that my aunt will find you."

"No. Despite all of your attempts to slow us down today," he almost smiled at the quick flash of guilt that crossed her face, "I am not worried that she will catch us up anytime soon, if ever. She can't ride with that foot and I don't believe she'll send those boys out alone. There are, however, a lot of other dangers to watch for. Bandits and Indians to name just two." He did smile when she made a poor effort to hide a big yawn. "Go to bed, Ella."

"Where is this bed?" She frowned as she looked around the camp and saw only one pile of blankets spread out on the other side of the fire. "I see only one."

"That's all there is. We are going to be very close tonight." He held up the shackles he had used on the train.

"Has anyone ever told you what an irredeemable bastard you are?"

"Not with as much feeling as you, Miss Carson."

It was embarrassing, but Ella managed to make her need for a moment of privacy understood. Harrigan called to George and then let her seek out a sheltered spot to see to her personal needs.

The moment she was done, Ella walked straight to the bed, not looking or speaking to Harrigan. She needed a little time to get over her embarrassment, one she knew would be revisited on her for as long as she was with the men. They were trying very hard to respect her privacy, but she did not feel very grateful at the moment. If they had not allowed themselves to be hired by Harold, none of them would be in such an awkward position, so, she decided crossly, her discomfort was all their fault.

Harrigan sighed as he banked the fire. He could not help but think that Harold Carson could have found a better way to retrieve his niece. In fact, although Louise was eccentric, he really saw no reason why the man could not have just left Ella with her aunt. Louise was Ella's family, more so than Harold, and she clearly loved the girl. Some arrangement could have been made with the lawyers who controled Ella's inheritance. It would appear that, at the very least, he had been dragged into the middle of a family squabble.

He walked over to the bed, sat down, and yanked off his boots. When he reached over to grab Ella's wrist, intending to shackle them together for the few hours of sleep he would be able to steal, she pulled away. He reached for her again and found himself in the middle of an undignified wrestling match. Although he tried not to hurt her, Ella obviously had no qualms about injuring him. He was panting and bruised by the time he got her pinned to the blanket, his right wrist securely manacled to her left one.

As he stared into her angry face, he became far too aware of her slim, soft body pressed against his. Instead of moving off her, he settled himself more comfortably on top of her, smiling faintly when her eyes widened. He had been thinking about kissing her since the first time he had set eyes on her and wondered if he might have a chance to satisfy that urge now. Although he admitted there was a chance he was deceiving himself, he thought he caught a flicker of interest in her lovely face, as if she was having the same thought he was.

"You've chained me now," she said, fighting to keep the huskiness out of her voice. "You can get off me." Ella prayed that the man could not sense how much she liked the provocative position they were in.

"I will in a moment," he murmured as he leaned closer and touched his mouth to her soft, flushed cheek.

"Mr. Mahoney, I do not believe this is what my uncle hired you for."

He just smiled. "Such a sharp tongue hidden inside this soft, sweet mouth."

When he brushed his lips over hers she trembled, and inwardly cursed the weakness her body was so gleefully revealing. "I don't want this," she said.

"Well, I could call you a liar, but that would be arrogant of me. And I'm not sure I really care what you want right now. That's wrong, I know, but I can't be right and honorable all the time. Right now I intend to steal something I have been thinking about far too much."

Ella murmured a half-hearted protest as he covered her mouth with his. His kiss was gentle, almost tender, and she felt all of her weak resistance vanish. It was flattering to know that he had been thinking about kissing her. Comforting as well, for it meant that she was not alone in suffering an inappropriate attraction.

He teased her mouth with enticing, nibbling kisses, as if he savored the taste of her. When he shifted his body on top of hers, lightly rubbing against her, the feeling that shot through her was so strong it made her gasp. Harrigan took quick advantage of her parted lips, slipping his tongue between them and slowly stroking the sensitive inside of her mouth. The only clear thought Ella could grasp was that a mere kiss should not feel so good, firing her blood and making her heart pound so hard she could hear it.

She lifted her arms to wrap them around him and a soft clinking noise yanked her out of the passionate stupor his kiss had sent her into. Even as she opened her eyes to stare at the manacle enclosing her wrist, she felt Harrigan tense. He slid off her, lying down at her side, as if he knew the moment of desire they had been indulging in was about to come to an abrupt end. Ella was not sure it was such a good thing that he could sense her change of mood so accurately.

"You are a complete cad," she said, a little surprised at how amiable she sounded.

"I know," he replied with an equal calm. "It is the cross I must bear."

Harrigan breathed an inner sigh of relief. It appeared that Ella was not going to be outraged or furious, both of which she deserved to be. That seemed to confirm his opinion that she had suffered from the same curiosity he had.

What he would really like to know now was if she had experienced any of the same feelings he had, but he doubted she would answer truthfully even if he had the courage to ask. He was also not sure he wanted to have that discussion, for he could inadvertently reveal some of what was deeply troubling him at the moment. That sweet, short kiss had sent him reeling. He had never wanted a woman so swiftly or so strongly before. Harrigan had been confident that it would be good, and it had been, dangerously so.

She had shared his passion. He was sure of that. He had felt it in her every breath and the way her body had welcomed the weight of his. It was hard not to see the promise of more in her response and he desperately wanted more. A small voice in his head told him he would be a scoundrel to try and take more when he had every intention of completing the job he had been hired for, but he forcefully silenced it. Harrigan had never wanted anything as bad as he wanted Ella Carson and he suspected he never would again. Right or wrong, he was going to try for a fuller taste of the sweet passion she held in every tiny, delicate inch of her.

"If you have quite finished mauling me," Ella said, forcing her eyes shut and wishing she could turn her back on him but restricted by the manacle, "I believe I will go to sleep now."

His soft laughter caused her to grit her teeth and she clenched her hands beneath the coarse blanket covering them. Ella decided it had been foolish to think she could make him think she had been disgusted by the kiss. Any man who looked like Harrigan Mahoney had to be experienced with women. He probably knew exactly what she had been feeling, or most of it.

Ella inwardly sighed. It had seemed such an innocent, only slightly naughty thing to do. She had thought about kissing him so often that the opportunity to satisfy her curiosity had been too tempting to resist. There was no question that she had completely satisfied her curiosity, but she had opened a whole new bag of troubles.

Although she was still a virgin, she was not totally innocent of what could occur between a man and a woman. Louise had felt it was important for women to know such things, if only so they could know what pitfalls to avoid. Ella had a feeling that she had just plummeted down a very deep pitfall.

She could still feel the warmth of his mouth on hers. Her lips still tingled softly and there was a gentle ache deep inside of her, an ache that grew stronger each time she recalled the feel of his body against hers. Ella knew that she wanted Harrigan, fiercely desired him. Lying by his side, she found herself recalling all Louise had told her and imagining Harrigan doing such things to her.

As subtlely as she could, Ella took several slow, deep breaths in an attempt to clear such thoughts from her mind. Harrigan was working for Harold and she would be an idiot to forget that. To give into her desires would be both foolish and dangerous. Every instinct told her that she would be opening herself up to a great deal of pain.

For a moment she tried to argue what her heart and mind told her. Because she had run away and was living with Louise and a dozen young, unmarried men on a ranch in what most people considered the wilderness, she had already been marked as *soiled*. Since she was already accused and condemned of the crime, why not commit it? She knew, without a doubt, that making love with Harrigan would be an experience she might never have again. A passion that siezed one so swiftly and so strongly had to be special. Surely she had a right to grasp at such pleasure? Who would it hurt?

Even as she asked herself that question, her heart loudly answered it. She knew she could not simply take the pleasure she craved and leave. The reason she felt such desire for Harrigan was because she cared for him. Ella suspected that she could easily love him. Becoming his lover would probably cinch it. And that, she thought sadly, would be disastrous for her.

Opening one eye, she cautiously studied him. He was a man any woman would desire. Ella dearly wished she was one of those women who could climb into his bed, take all she needed and wanted, and just walk away, but she knew she could never be like that. With her body would go her heart and Harrigan did not want that. She had no doubt that he desired her and would willingly take her as his lover, but that was all he would do. Her passion would be fed for a little while, but nothing else, and she suspected she would be left very hungry when he walked away.

And he would walk away, she reminded herself, right after he left her in Harold's deadly hands. It was now even more important that she remember that Harrigan Mahoney was Harold's man. For a while she could probably make herself forget that, even hope it would change and that Harrigan would start to believe her, but that would be naive. Ella knew it would cut her deeply if she was his lover, even for just a little while, but never had his love. But to be held in his arms one night and handed over to Harold in the morning could easily destroy her.

Ella stared up at the star-crowded sky and prayed. She prayed that her aunt would recover in time to save her. She prayed that something fatal would happen to Harold before he could get ahold of her. But mostly she prayed that she had the strength to keep resisting Harrigan Mahoney.

Chapter Six

It was very hard for Ella to resist the urge to kick at the door which connected the two rooms Harrigan had rented for the night. When Harrigan had announced that they would spend the night in a hotel, she had been delighted. She was chagrined to admit that an opportunity for escape had not been the first thing on her mind. The promise of a soft bed, a hot bath, and some time alone had been all that she could think of. Although they had spent only one night on the trail, she had not had a chance to clean up before he had captured her for the second time. The quick wash and change by the creek had not really been enough.

Harrigan had rapidly spoiled all of her plans, she thought sourly. She was stuck in a room with him, George occupying the second room. She would indeed get to sleep on a soft bed, but he would be right beside her. There was still the opportunity for the hot bath she craved, but it would not be the long, luxurious soak she had envisioned. Harrigan would never leave her alone for that long. The man had no sense of propriety.

"I believe I'll order your bath now," Harrigan said, eyeing her a little warily. "Perhaps that will sweeten your temper."

"My temper might improve if, on your way down to the front desk, you trip over your big feet, fall down the stairs, and break your thick neck," she said in a sweet voice as she rose from the chair she had flung herself into the moment they had entered the room.

The smile that had started to curve Harrigan's mouth faded abruptly when Ella stood in front of the cracked dresser mirror and began to undo her hair. For one brief moment he wondered if she was purposely trying to tempt him. She had to know that he wanted her and could easily be trying to use that weakness against him. It was a fleeting suspicion. The way she was brushing her long, glorious hair was indeed stirring his blood, but the cold, angry look on her face did not hold any hint of invitation. If she was trying to trick him through seduction, she would at least try to look coy. The expression on her face at the moment would warn even the stupidest man that he would be risking life and limb if he tried to touch her.

"I'll have your bath sent up," he said as he opened the door. "You'll have one hour."

"You are actually going to leave me alone? To show some respect for my privacy?"

He ignored the derision in her voice. "You will be alone within this room," he replied as he left.

Ella frowned and stared at the door after he shut it behind him. It took her a minute to understand what he had meant, then she cursed and slammed her hairbrush down on the dresser. He had told her quite clearly that he would have every exit watched. It was going to be very hard to escape if he kept guessing her plans even before she made any. Somehow she was going to have to lull him into a false sense of security. That was going to be very hard and not simply because of her own hot temper. Harrigan did not trust her as far as he could spit.

She started to set out what she would need for her bath, thinking of and discarding a hundred different ways to escape. It began to give her a throbbing headache. Ella fought the urge to just give up, to wait until she got to Philadelphia before she even tried to escape. She had slipped free of Harold before and could probably do so again. Shaking her head, she pushed aside that thought. It would not be wise to wait until the last minute to break free. Ella knew she could not allow her confidence to wane, that she had to keep believing that, somehow, she would escape. Harrigan Mahoney would not win this game.

Harrigan leaned against the rough clapboards covering the outside of the hotel, lit a cigar, and watched the people on the street. When he realized he was looking for Louise Carson or one of her boys, he cursed. He did not want to think that Louise was that good, but it was obvious that some part of him did. If nothing else, the woman was certainly determined.

"Shouldn't we be watching Miss Ella more carefully?" George asked as he leaned against the wall next to Harrigan and accepted a cigar.

"Those boys we hired will keep a close watch on the doors and the windows. I paid them well and promised a handsome bonus if they actually stopped her from escaping."

"They might find her very pretty, prettier than money."

"Not these boys. I picked hungry ones, ones who might indeed think Ella's pretty first, but then they will turn her over to me. Besides, I don't really think she will try to escape this time. I more or less told her that all exits would be watched before I left her to her bath. She is also very tired. My guess is that, this time, she will just take her bath, cursing me all the while. Ella will decide to take advantage of the comforts the room offers and return to her attempts to escape only after she has had a good night's rest."

"Which would give us a pleasant respite." George took a puff on his cigar, then asked quietly, "Are you sure it's wise for you to share a room with her?"

"If we leave her alone in her room, we won't get any rest."

"You could just manacle her to the bed."

"I could, but I don't think that will work. Those boys didn't get the key from me when they boarded the train to get Ella back, yet she was freed from the manacles and they weren't broken. I think little Miss Ella knows how to pick a lock."

George stared at Harrigan for a moment, then laughed and shook his head. "Harold Carson is definitely going to have to pay us more." He quickly grew serious, staring blindly at his boot tips before tentatively saying, "I still think we ought to consider what she says more seriously. I believe Harold Carson is cold enough and avaricious enough to commit any crime. Even murder."

Harrigan sighed, tossed the stub of his cigar onto the muddy road, and ground it beneath his boot heel. "I begin to think he might be as well. However, I still believe that all of the answers are in Philadelphia and it does us no good to speculate on who is telling us the truth. We can only get the answers we need back home, not here, and certainly not from Miss Ella Carson."

"But when we return home, we must hand Miss Carson over to Harold. If she's telling the truth, we could become partners in a murder."

The mere thought of that made Harrigan's blood run cold, but he told himself that it was a natural reaction. He was no killer and he certainly did not want to help Harold Carson kill his niece. If all Ella told him was true, it was greed that would cost her her life, the same sort of greed that had cost him his family's business.

"Harold would never kill her openly," Harrigan said, confident in his opinion. "If he does plan to murder her, he will do so deceitfully and cleverly, making damn sure that no one can ever blame him for her death. That sort of planning takes time. We will have the time we need to sort out what is the truth."

"I hope you won't object if I continue to keep a close watch on her until you find that truth."

"Just don't let Carson know you're watching her or, rather, him. Don't forget that she could be lying through her fine white teeth. We can't afford to anger a man like Harold Carson. He could destroy us and I really don't want to have to rebuild my life for a third time."

"Understood," George said, staring down the road as he finished his cigar.

"Louise isn't lurking out there. I already looked." Harrigan laughed at the disgusted look George gave him.

"The woman has a determined nature."

"Very. Why do you think I looked? Well, I'm going back to the room. I told Ella she had an hour and I've given her more than that." He handed George some money. "Pay the lads, get one or two of them to do the night watch for us, and then have some food sent up to our room, please."

Harrigan found himself approaching the door of the room with some caution a few minutes later, and muttered a curse. Ella Carson was a tiny, green-eyed girl. She did have spirit and more wit than some men thought healthy in a woman. Nevertheless, he should not be approaching her as if she was some hulking killer. This job was getting harder every day, he decided as he unlocked the door.

Ella took a deep breath to steady herself when she heard the key turn in the lock. She had managed to keep hold of the big metal jug brought up with her bath so that she could rinse her hair. It was not very heavy, the metal thin and already dented, and she doubted that it would knock Harrigan out, but she had found nothing else to use. She was not confident that she would get very far, either, but saw no harm in trying. If nothing else, it was going to really annoy Harrigan and that made it worth the effort.

As the door opened, Ella flattened herself against the wall. Harrigan stepped in, frowned, and looked around. Even as he turned his head toward her, she swung the jug as hard as she could, wincing a little when it thudded against the back of his head. He stumbled forward a few steps, clearing the doorway, and fell to his knees, clutching his head and swearing colorfully. Ella grabbed her bag and lunged out the door. There was one brief, heady moment when she felt the sweet thrill of success then a strong hand wrapped itself tightly around her ankle and pulled.

A curse escaped as she barely stopped herself from landing flat on her face on the hard wood floor. She twisted around to see Harrigan lying flat on the floor and reaching for her other ankle. Muttering another curse, she kicked out at him, hitting him square in the face. When she tried to kick him again he caught her by her free ankle, pinning her to the floor. Despite all of her attempts to inflict further injury with her fists and her bag, he finally won their wrestling match, holding her down by straddling her body and holding her wrists almost painfully against the wide plank floor. She looked into his face and inwardly grimaced. He looked a great deal more than annoyed.

"Damn it, woman, that hurt," he snapped, keeping a firm grip on her arm as he stood up and pulled her to her feet.

"It was supposed to, fool! Actually, it was supposed to knock you out cold. That was my plan, but I couldn't find anything heavy enough to make a dent in that thick skull of yours."

He pushed her back into the room, watching her closely as he locked the door and shoved the key in his pocket. The next time he felt reluctant to enter a room she was in, he would listen to the warning his instincts were trying to send him. As he glanced in the mirror to make sure that he was not bleeding, he inwardly confessed to some surprise that she would physically attack him. It was possible that he had allowed her delicate appearance to lull him into a false sense of safety from attack. It was clearly an error in judgement and one he did not intend to repeat.

"Don't worry," she drawled as she sat down in a chair near the window. "I didn't mar your pretty face."

"Not for want of trying," he said as he took off his coat

and hung it over the back of the chair next to the dresser. "This town is not that big. Just where did you think you would go?"

"Back to Wyoming." When he sat down in the other chair by the window, she glared at him across the table set between them.

"Know the way, do you? Or did you just plan to head west until you bumped into it?" He picked up the heavy crystal decanter on the table and poured each of them a glass of the brandy he had ordered it filled with. "Go on, drink it," he said, nudging the glass toward her. "Although I might wish it, one small brandy will not make you senseless. Didn't you learn to have a drink before the evening meal?"

"Aunt Louise prefers wine or whiskey. Joshua has been trying to get her to drink some tequila, but he hasn't succeeded yet."

Ella was not sure she ought to trust in his pleasant demeanor. She had just hit him on the head and kicked him in the face. He ought to be spitting nails, but the anger he had expressed as he had pinned her to the hall floor appeared to be gone. She wondered if he was trying to make her feel safe and relax, at which time he would strike. Ella sipped at her brandy and decided that she would keep a very close eye on him no matter how friendly he acted.

The meal was delivered and they were halfway through it when Ella realized she was not holding to her decision very well. She had to keep catching herself, reminding herself that this was not some social event. It was rapidly becoming clear to her that Harrigan Mahoney was a very dangerous man when he decided to be cordial and charming. He was now playing a game she was not really equipped to play.

"What game are you playing now?" she demanded the moment she ate the last bite of her meal.

Harrigan took a sip of his brandy to hide his smile. He had not really thought that he would get far with sweet

talk, flattery, and smiles, but it had been worth a try. It
had also been fun to watch her bounce from wary to cheer-
ful and unsuspecting and back again. She had not stayed
lulled by charm for very long.

One thing did trouble him and that was how much he
had enjoyed it when she was at ease. It had been delightful
to hear her wit used for more than insulting and threatening him. With her face softened by laughter and interest,
she was enchantingly lovely. He wanted her so badly he
ached. Harrigan hoped that need did not show in his face.
He suspected that she would run as far and as fast as she
could if she guessed what he was feeling.

"Game?" he asked, struggling to look innocent and
slightly confused. "What game?"

"All this pleasantness, the smiles, and the charming conversation."

"You found that troubling? I was always told that good
conversation is a must over dinner. Acrimony can trouble
one's digestion."

"Of course, and we wouldn't want you to suffer a bad
tum-tum, would we?"

"Why do you find my good humor suspicious?"

"Perhaps because I just hit you over the head and kicked
you in the face? Your temper cooled rather quickly. One
moment you're breathing fire, the next you're smiling
and offering me brandy. If I behaved like this, you would
certainly be eyeing me warily. If you think to woo me into
placidly following you to Philadelphia, you waste your time.
Even your Irish charm is not enough to convince me to
put my neck in Harold's noose."

Harrigan sighed mournfully and shook his head. "I but
try to make our time together a little more pleasant. I offer
the hand of friendship, and you bite it off."

"My heart bleeds for you."

When he grinned, Ella felt her heart skip. The man
was dangerously handsome and her attraction to him was
getting completely out of control. She knew that was one
reason she resented his feigned amiability. Her mind knew

it was only a game he played, but her heart softened at his every smile and greedily accepted his every practiced compliment. Worse, she kept recalling the kiss he had stolen. Suddenly, she remembered something else about that kiss. Harrigan had been all pretty smiles and sweet words then too. A rush of angry suspicion swiftly, and she feared briefly, killed all her attraction for him.

"Oh no," she said as she quickly stood up. "No, you don't. I won't stumble into that trap."

"What trap?"

"The let's be nice and talk sweet until Ella gets so stupid she lets you maul her trap."

"Maul you?" It was only the memory of how completely and warmly she had responded to his kiss that kept Harrigan from being deeply offended. "I had not realized that you viewed simple courtesy from a man as a prelude to seduction."

"Why shouldn't I? It usually is." She picked up her carpetbag and stepped toward the dressing screen in the far corner of the room. "I suppose you intend to stay in this room with me, whether I wish your company or not."

"You suppose correctly," he replied as he poured himself a little more of the brandy.

"It does not concern you at all that you are destroying my reputation, does it?"

"Ella, I think we both know that, fair or not, your reputation was destroyed when you ran away to live with your aunt." He spoke in a gentle tone, honestly sympathizing with the injustice of such attitudes. "Now, which side of the bed do you want?"

"Excuse me? You mean to share that bed with me?" Ella was not really surprised, but hoped that a display of shock and maidenly outrage might work to change his mind.

"Yes. Since I left Philadelphia I have had only one night of complete rest in a decent bed. I may not get another until I return to the city. There is nothing you can say or do that will keep me from enjoying my half of that bed."

"Cad."

Ella stepped behind the screen, set her bag down, and pulled out her nightgown. For a moment, she considered sleeping in her clothes, but only for a moment. The night-gown was prim, made of a heavy white cotton, and covered as much of her as any gown she owned. She only had two gowns with her and she did not want to add to the wear they would be suffering by sleeping in them.

As she stripped down to her pantaloons, carefully putting her clothes away, and then slipping into her nightgown, she wondered if it was wise to be so immodest in front of Harrigan. He had shown a few distinct signs of a budding desire for her. Few men saw a woman all prepared for bed unless they were married or lovers. It could be something men found very enticing and the last thing she wanted to give Harrigan was an invitation. Although, she mused as she looked down at herself, her slim form completely obscured by the voluminous nightgown, she did not think she looked very enticing.

The more she considered the matter, the more she decided she was being foolish. Every instinct told her that she did not have to worry about Harrigan, that he was a man who understood the word *no*. She smiled crookedly when she admitted that the danger was not in Harrigan's desire for her, but in hers for him. He would honor a no, but there was a good chance that she would forget to say it. The kiss they had shared had shown her that her desire for the man was not easily controlled. She shook her head, took a deep breath to steady herself, and stepped out from behind the screen.

Harrigan watched Ella as she walked to the bed and slipped beneath the covers. The sudden rush of desire he felt for her both disconcerted him and made him want to smile. In the large, crisp, white nightgown, with her hair lightly braided, she looked like a young girl. He decided that it was the intimacy of the attire that stirred him, for *adorable* was not usually something that fired his blood. What disturbed him was the strength of his desire for her. He had always prided himself on the control he had over his emotions. That control was hard to grasp when Ella Carson was around. The kiss they had shared had moved him in ways he had never experienced before. It had roused feelings he was not familiar with and made the ones he had thought himself familiar with so much more intense and complicated. It was difficult to look at Ella's sweet face and her big green eyes and think of her as dangerous, but Harrigan knew he had to.

After finishing his drink, Harrigan put their supper dishes on the tray and set it outside their door. He then checked the doors and windows to be sure that everything was locked up tightly. Turning his back on Ella, he undid his trousers and slipped the key into a little pocket in his drawers where he often hid some extra money. He smiled faintly when he thought that, if she managed to find the key, they would probably be engaged in an activity that would keep her from escaping anyway, at least until he had time to regain his senses. In fact, if her delicate little hand was wandering in that area, he would probably be willing to hand her the key just as long as she did not leave too soon.

He sat on the bed, hesitated a moment, then stripped down to his drawers. He carefully set his clothes on the chair next to the bed and slid under the covers. Harrigan briefly considered using the manacles to secure Ella to the bed, but decided there was no need. She could not get out of the room without the key and he would certainly know it if she took that away from him. There was no way to get out of the window and it would take time for her to pick the lock. A little smile touched his lips as he glanced at her stiff back. There was also the very alert pair of youths he had hired to watch for her. She might still try to escape, but he was confident she would not get very far. Crossing his arms beneath his head, he decided he could rest easy for at least one night.

When Ella shifted slightly on her side of the bed, one of her small feet fleetingly brushing against his leg, he grimaced. His body's reaction to that light, innocent touch was swift and fierce. He wanted her a lot more than he had realized. There was a good chance that having her so close yet so untouchable would prove to steal a lot of the rest he needed. He closed his eyes, took several slow, deep breaths, and tried very hard to convince himself that he was alone.

Ella murmured her pleasure and curled her body around the hard warmth she had bumped up against. The sunlight pouring in the window was trying to force her eyes open, but she ignored it. Beneath her cheek was smooth skin and around her shoulders was a comfortable weight that inspired a sense of security. It was not until she felt lightly calloused fingers stroke her cheek that she woke up enough to realize the precarious position she was in. Sometime during the night she had turned to Harrigan, either seeking out his heat or giving in to the attraction she fought so hard to deny when she was awake. Although it could prove to be embarrassing, her biggest problem was that she had no inclination to move.

When Harrigan threaded his long fingers into her hair and started to turn her face up to his, Ella knew what was going to happen. The smart thing to do would be to break free of his light hold and get out of bed as swiftly as she could. She caught the warm look in his grey eyes as he lowered his mouth to hers, felt her body respond, and decided she would be stupid for just a little while.

She had received a few kisses in her short life, stolen and freely given, some inexperienced or tentative and some very nice, but none like Harrigan's. The feel of his mouth against hers sent a thrilling warmth throughout her body. She welcomed his touch, the way he moved his big hands over her back. When he prodded at her lips with his tongue, she willingly parted them, shuddering as he stroked the sensitive inside of her mouth. It was not until he brushed his thumbs against the sides of her breasts that she began to come to her senses. The feelings that tore through her were so sharp, so exciting, they were frightening. She muttered a sharp "no" against his mouth and abruptly pulled away.

"No," she reiterated the word more clearly, as she got out of the bed.

"It didn't feel much like a no to me," Harrigan said a little harshly as he sat up and finger-combed his hair, frustration a hard knot inside of him.

"I don't care what you felt. You should just pay very close attention to what is said, and this time it was no. God, I can't believe I allowed you to kiss me again, that I was behaving so cozily with the man who's taking me to my death. What was I thinking of?"

Harrigan grew furious, tired of being accused of aiding Harold in her murder. "Probably of trying to seduce me."

"Seduce you? Are you actually daring to accuse *me* of trying to seduce *you?*" Ella could not believe what she was hearing.

"Yes, seduce me. If that is your newest plan of escape, you've got to do a hell of a lot better than you just did."

Even as the words left his mouth, Harrigan wanted them back. They were not only unkind, they were unfair. The tight look on her face and the way all the color had fled her cheeks told him he had hurt her and he felt ashamed of himself.

"Ella," he whispered, afraid he had irredeemably offended her. "Say something."

"I was just thinking that, after I kill Harold, I believe I will come looking for you."

Chapter Seven

Anger and hurt had formed a solid, painful knot in Ella's stomach. All the while she and Harrigan had packed up their belongings, eaten breakfast, and walked to where he had stabled their horses, she had not once spoken to the man. She had barely even looked at him. Even George had been made to pay for Harrigan's insult. She had exchanged only the barest of cool pleasantries with the man and he too had fallen silent.

She knew it was more than the pain inflicted by Harrigan's words that troubled her. The fact that his angry accusation had hurt her at all, let alone so deeply, was a cause for concern. So was the fact that she could still feel the warmth of his kiss, and, worse, knew she would greedily accept another without much hesitation. Beneath all of her pain and fury was a need that refused to be ignored or pushed aside by common sense and pride.

When Harrigan reached for her bag she jerked her hand away so fast, in a blatant attempt to avoid his touch, that the bag almost fell to the ground. Harrigan looked uncomfortable and embarrassed. Ella supposed it was a good sign that he was aware of how badly he had behaved, but she was still too hurt to be cheered by that. She just prayed that he thought her cold silence was born of a deep sense of insult and nothing else. The last thing she wished him to be aware of was how much he had hurt her.

Suddenly she realized that Harrigan was as immersed in his own thoughts as she had just been. He was not paying any attention to her, busily saddling his horse and pointedly avoiding her gaze. George was still at the far end of the stable settling accounts with the owner. There was a clear path to her saddled horse and a very good chance she could be in the saddle and riding away before either man was fully aware of what she was doing. Ella then realized that she was wasting precious time thinking about it and made her move. She ran to her horse and threw herself into the saddle.

Harrigan proved to be far more alert than she had thought. He cursed even as he turned and reached for her. Ella kicked him in the face and he stumbled backward into his horse. As she rode out of the stable, spurring her little mare to a fast trot the minute she was clear of the building, she was a little stunned by the violence the man stirred in her. She then smiled to herself as she admitted that she had not kicked him solely to expedite her escape, but also in payment for his cruel words. A quick glance behind her revealed that she had not stopped Harrigan for long either, for he was just emerging from the stable. She concentrated on getting out of town without hurting anyone and prayed that she could maintain the small lead she had.

"What the hell happened?" demanded George as he rode up next to Harrigan.

"What does it look like?" Harrigan replied, yelling to be heard over the horses. "I wasn't paying attention and she got away from me again. And I'm getting damned sick of being kicked in the face."

George said nothing and Harrigan was glad of it. He

did not want to try to explain things, especially not while they were chasing Ella. It still astounded him that he had said those harsh things to her. For one brief moment he had allowed his frustration and mistrust to control his mouth. One minute he was holding a passionate Ella who, quite rightly, had put a stop to their impromptu and very improper lovemaking. Then, with a few cutting words, he had turned her into a block of ice, a cold, furious woman who was doing a very good job of pretending that he did not even exist.

The moment they cleared the edge of town, Ella spurred her horse into a full gallop and Harrigan cursed as he did the same. It was not going to be easy to catch her. Her little mare was as swift as their horses and Ella had the lead. Harrigan soon realized that they could ride their horses to death if something did not change. The only way he could think of to bring about that change was to scare Ella into stopping.

Ella screeched with surprise when she heard a shot. A bullet hit the ground in front of her and her horse faltered slightly. She looked behind her and was stunned to see Harrigan aiming a rifle at her. Since he and George had stopped chasing her, she reined her horse to a halt and turned to look at them.

"Harold won't pay you for a corpse," she yelled, unable to believe that Harrigan was trying to shoot her.

"According to you, dead is just how he wants you," Harrigan called back.

That caused Ella a start, but she quickly shook aside a sudden attack of unthinking fear. Harrigan did not believe her tale of deceit and attempted murder. He was still sure that Harold was just trying to get his errant niece to come back to the family nest. And, no matter how furious she was with him, she simply could not believe Harrigan would hurt her, at least not physically. That left her wondering just what he was shooting at. She started to turn her horse, intending to go on her way, when he fired another shot. This one came very close to her increasingly nervous mare's hooves.

"Stop that!" she demanded. "You're scaring her."

"You're being particularly slow-witted this morning. I would have thought you'd have guessed my plan by now."

"Well, let's just accept that I haven't yet realized what depths you will sink to for your blood money and that you'll have to tell me what your grand plan is."

He found it a little amusing that he preferred her insults to her cold silence. "You see, I began to realize that we could keep this race going until our horses dropped, you never getting away and me never catching you. So, I came up with a solution to this rapidly moving stand-off."

"And I'm not going to like it one little bit, am I?"

"Nope. You stop running or I will shoot your horse." Harrigan prayed she would believe his threat, no matter how insulting that would be, or that she at least had enough doubts about him that she would not want to gamble with the life of her mare.

Ella gaped at him, not wanting to believe him, yet not sure she could trust her own judgment. Although she had been sure that he would have no qualms about seducing her, she had never thought that he could speak to her so cruelly. That miscalculation now left her unsure. Louise and all the young men at the ranch would never think of shooting a horse except under the most dire of circumstances, but Harrigan was from the city. He could well be capable of such a thing.

She considered the matter for only a moment longer as she patted the mare on the neck then began to slowly ride toward Harrigan. Polly was a good little mare and Ella could not bring herself to gamble the horse's life on the hope that Harrigan's threat was a toothless one.

Surrender was not as hard as it might have been, either. She knew she had had little chance of escape, that she had not had enough of a lead to elude him. The chase probably would have ended with their horses' exhaustion

and no winner. In fact, Harrigan would have won in the
end, she thought sullenly. Without a horse, she would have
had to run and she was very sure that she could never have
outrun the man. When he reached out and took her reins,
she cursed him, ignoring his feigned look of shock.

"Well, we have already covered more miles than I had
wanted to . . ." Harrigan said as he turned them around
and headed back east.

"Oh, shut up," she grumbled, deciding that she did not
have to be a good loser.

Harrigan ignored her, and continued, ". . . all of it in
the wrong direction. So I believe we will probably not get
much further than the next town today. Sure you're not
still trying to delay us in the vain hope that your aunt will
catch up?"

"The thought never crossed my mind."

Ella was a little chagrined that it had not, but Harrigan
did not have to know that. It was a small, unexpected gain,
however, and it cheered her a little. She was not even sure
if she had really been thinking of escape, at least not of
escaping Harold. Her only clear plan had been to get away
from Harrigan, from the hurt he had dealt her while she
had still tingled from his warm kisses. From the way he
was talking, he did not know that, simply thought it was
just another of her many escape attempts. She was relieved,
for she did not want the man to know what power he had
over her.

The fact that they were going to another town began to
worry her. A town meant a hotel, for they were springing
up along the railroad lines like weeds, and Harrigan was
staying very close to the railroad tracks at the moment.
And a hotel meant that she and Harrigan would be sharing
a room again, probably a bed too.

Still stinging from his insult, Ella felt confident that she
could resist his charms. The problem would come if he
apologized and convinced her that he was sincerely contrite. She fully understood how one could say terrible
things when angry, hurtful things that one did not really

mean. Ella also knew that her stiff resistance of the moment would fade like smoke on a windy day if Harrigan apologized with skill and sincerity.

And then, she decided, she would be in deep trouble. She wanted him, badly. It was definitely a strong, almost blinding, carnal need, but there was so much more, and that more was what made it so hard to resist. Ella knew it was also what made it dangerous. There was no doubt in her mind that, if she gave in to the lust she felt, she would give in to all the other feelings churning inside of her. Once those feelings were given free rein, she would never be able to pull them back. The tragedy would be that she would be giving her heart to a man who, knowingly or unknowingly, was going to give her to a killer.

Ella grimaced, wincing slightly as she eased her weary body into a chair near the window. Just as Harrigan had said they would, they had reached the next town and stopped for the night. The morning's race had exhausted the horses and them. Although there were several hours of daylight left, no one had wanted to go any farther.

As before, Harrigan had rented two rooms side by side, ordered a bath for her and left her alone. While her bath had been prepared, she had checked the doors and window only to find them all locked. She had also spied a couple of young boys below the window who were obviously watching out for her. Harrigan had probably hired them so that he and George could go to the barber's down the street, she decided. She strongly suspected that he had done the same thing the last time they had stopped, for he had been surprisingly clean and refreshed when he had returned to the room, yet she had never seen him wash up or change his clothes.

When Ella heard the key turn in the lock, she wondered if she should have prepared herself to try another escape instead of sitting around sulking. The door swung open and Harrigan stood just outside until he saw her, then stepped in and locked the door. Ella decided it was just as well that she had not made the effort. It was clear that she could not try the same trick twice on Harrigan. After so many failures, she was also feeling somewhat defeated, weary of trying to save herself time and time again only to keep drawing closer to Harold.

It was not until they were done with their meal and Harrigan had poured them each a brandy that he actually caught and held her gaze. Ella tensed, wondering what he intended to say, and praying she was not going to be dealt any more hard blows. The conversation since he had entered the room had consisted mostly of Harrigan attempting to draw her out of her cold silence and her responding with no more than an angry glare or an uninviting mumble. She was not sure she wanted to change that, then told herself not to be so timid. There was always the chance he would apologize. She was also sure she could not remain cold and quiet all the way to Philadelphia.

"Ella, I think we need to talk," Harrigan said, his tone of voice calm with a hint of reticence.

"Really? I'm not sure we have anything to say to each other, Mr. Mahoney."

He released one brief, dry laugh. "Now I am certain we need to talk. That's the most you've said to me since this morning and it was so cold I'm damned surprised there isn't snow upon the table." He reached across the table and took her hand in his, holding on tightly when she tried to pull away. "I'm sorry, Ella."

"About what?" She stopped trying to escape his touch, but struggled against softening toward him too quickly. One little *I'm sorry* was not enough.

"Don't play stupid, Ella. Strange, that coy ignorance that can be so attractive in some women is just annoying in you."

Ella blinked, wondering why she was so pleased with his words, for they hardly sounded like a compliment. "You are a true silver-tongued devil, aren't you?"

"Ella, the moment those words left my mouth this morning I wanted them back."

"They should never have been in your mind waiting to be said."

Her words were little more than a soft hiss, but Harrigan welcomed that show of fury. He knew he could deal with her anger far more easily than he could her cold silence. There was a small chance Ella was not the forgiving sort, but he needed to at least try for absolution. As long as she had refused to speak to him, he had not had any opportunity to plead his case. Harrigan just prayed that he could convince her of his sincerity.

"No, they should not have been there. They were indeed ill-thought as well as ill-said. Even though I knew you had every right to tell me no, I did not receive it well. I wanted to continue, Ella, and I grew angry when you put a stop to it." He sighed. "Eleanor's betrayal, and the behavior of other women I have known, has left me with a mistrustful nature."

"Ah, so, yet again, you condemn a whole group for the actions of a few."

He grimaced and nodded. "I know, and that's unfair. I have known some very good women too, but, fair or not, betrayal often leaves a stronger mark, twisting the way one feels things or views people and incidents."

"I have not betrayed you."

"No. Kicked me in the face, hit me over the head, and constantly tried to run away, but, no, you've never betrayed me."

"You think I'm a liar, though." She could tell by the pained look on his face that, despite his contrite demeanor and the honesty of his apology, he was still not ready to believe her claims about Harold.

"I think *you* really believe what you say."

"Very well said," she murmured.

Harrigan decided to ignore that little remark. He had felt the tension leave her body as he spoke. That gave him confidence. His apology might not be eloquent, but he was sure she was accepting it. She did, however, still look wary, and he wondered how he could soothe that away.

"Ella, we are never going to agree on Harold and what I should or should not believe. I want to believe you. I sure as hell don't want to give you to a killer. But I have no proof of what you say and, to be plain, I need the money Harold will pay me far too badly to take a gamble. Because of my stupidity, my family has no livelihood now. They had a damned good business, but now they scrape by working for the rich, scrubbing floors, doing washing, gardening, and every other menial chore the wealthy do not wish to dirty their hands with. The only thing that will put matters right again, or as near to right as they can be, is money. All I can do is swear to you that I will search out the truth the minute we return to Philadelphia."

It surprised Ella that Harrigan was being open, but it also saddened her. He would never listen to her. She had not realized it, but she was asking him to choose between accepting her word with no proof and getting enough money to start pulling his family back out of servitude. The fact that he clearly blamed himself for his family's financial straits made it certain that he would choose them over her. If nothing else, a deep guilt would force him to it unless he could prove without question that her very life was in danger and she did not have that proof to give him. He was right when he said that the answer to this dilemma was in Philadelphia. All she could do was pray that he would find the truth in time to help her.

"I can only hope that I survive until you get your answers," she said quietly, soothed somewhat by the look of doubt and concern that briefly crossed his face.

"Can we come to an agreement on this?"

"What? That I will cease to ask you to believe me?"

He grimaced. "Yes. I'm not going to change my mind in this and I think you know that. So what's gained by the constant arguing? Can't we just push the whole subject aside?"

"I hope you're not asking me to promise that I won't try to escape again."

"No, just that we cease to argue about who is telling the truth. I don't think I can make you understand how desperate I am to put my family back where they were before my ill-fated liaison with Eleanor Templeton."

"Probably as desperate as I am to stay away from Philadelphia and Harold." She held up her hand to silence him when he started to argue. "I detest being thought a liar or, worse, delusional, but, fine, we will set the whole matter aside. You're right, I can see that nothing I say will change your mind, that you need a sort of hard proof that I cannot provide. I can even honor and appreciate your need to help your family. So, I will agree that we will no longer argue the matter of what Harold will or will not do. I will silently acknowledge that I know the truth and you can silently continue on your way, believing what you wish."

Harrigan was too pleased to get the agreement to care how she worded it. He pressed his lips to her knuckles, inwardly smiling at the way she gently trembled. His cruel words had not killed her passion for him, he was sure of it.

"And can we agree that I was an idiot—"

"Very easily." She almost smiled at the mildly disgusted look her interruption drew from him.

"—who spoke before he thought?" he continued. "I swear that I do not really think you would try to seduce your way to freedom. You'd try just about anything else, but not that."

"I suppose. I just don't quite understand why the thought leapt to mind so quickly even though I certainly understand opening one's mouth and putting one's foot firmly inside. It is something I have occasionally been afflicted with."

"I was stirred by the kiss we shared," he confessed in a soft voice as he kissed the inside of her wrist. "Very stirred. I want you. Have done so from the first time I saw you. Holding you like that, kissing you, I fear I let that want gain too much control. One moment I am kissing you and thinking thoughts you should probably slap me for and then I'm alone in bed. I got angry. It's no excuse, just the truth. Since you were the one who put a stop to things, I visited that anger on you.''

"Fair enough," she said, gently extracting her hand from his grasp and standing up, stirred by his words and needing to put some distance between them.

"That's all you have to say? Am I to understand from that that you accept my apology?"

"Yes. I will admit that I had envisioned a little more groveling on your part—"

"I thought I had groveled."

"—but what you have said will do. It's the truth and who can argue with that?"

Harrigan frowned slightly as she stepped behind the privacy screen to prepare for bed. That little parting remark had a bite to it. He was certain of it. Ella was reminding him that he refused to believe her when she said she spoke the truth. He suspected he was supposed to notice that she was willing to believe him despite his mistrust.

Inwardly grimacing, he accepted what he was sure was a gentle reprimand. He had not lied when he had said he really wanted to believe her. More and more he was starting to believe that she thought she was speaking the truth. It was also more and more tempting to be completely on her side and tell Harold Carson to go to hell. Harrigan knew he was going to have to recall the plight of his family, and how much they depended upon him, with more frequency.

It was almost amusing. He truly believed that Ella had no plan to seduce him to her side, but she was doing it all the same. Everything about her pulled at him, not only to believe in her, but to do all in his power to help her. Her spirit, her wit, her constant and clever attempts to escape, and even the actions of her aunt all worked to make him wish he was in a position to forget the money and act solely on whim and high principle.

As he watched her slip into bed, he ruefully admitted that

everything about her appearance also seduced him, even when she was wearing her maidenly white cotton nightgown. There was unquestionably a womanly air to her looks, her wide expressive eyes, and her full mouth as seductive as any he had ever seen. Her slim figure with its gentle curves tempted him with every move she made. Holding her close and touching every inch of her warm silken skin was something he thought about with an almost alarming frequency. Despite that, he knew in his heart that she was innocent, and, although he had always avoided innocents, he admitted that he found that alluring as well. He ached to be the first man to fully awaken the passion he knew lurked inside of her, to savor the fire he had tasted in her kisses.

He finished off his brandy and rose to prepare for bed. His conscience told him to get control of himself and his desires, to leave her alone, but he knew he would not listen to it. Harrigan knew he was going to try to do exactly what he had so nastily accused her of, that he was going to do his utmost to try to seduce her. As he slid into bed beside her, he also knew that, until he succeeded and could make love to her, he was probably not going to get much rest.

"Time for you to get some rest, Joshua," said Louise as she moved to stand beside the young man.

Joshua glanced down at her bandaged foot. "I think that's what you should do. I can watch the hotel and the others can spell me when I need it."

Louise slouched against the saloon wall next to him. They had caught up with the train and ridden it into this town never really expecting to find Harrigan. Their plan had been to try to get to Philadelphia before him and stop him from handing Ella over to Harold or, if need be to try and take Ella back from her guardian. It had surprised all of them to see Harrigan and George leave the barber's and walk into the hotel. Since the moment she had realized how close she was to Ella, she had not been able to rest, despite the urgings of the boys.

"I have to do something. My foot is a lot better than it was. Sitting comfortably on a train has done a lot to aid its healing."

"But it ain't healed yet."

"Nearly so."

"Nearly ain't good enough."

"Joshua, I have to do something. I can't just lay about wondering what is happening." She scowled at the hotel. "I also keep wondering if we should be waiting at all. Maybe Edward is right, and we should just go and grab her."

"If you'll just look around, you'll see that I was right about those boys I saw. They've been paid to be Harrigan's eyes. Yeah, we might be able to get in and grab her, but we won't get far before a very loud outcry is raised. This is best. We wait until we can get one of them alone, even though that probably won't happen until the morning. I've got a gut feeling it will happen though, and then we have something to deal with."

"I hope you're right. I'm really worried about Ella."

"If we don't get her back this time, we'll keep trying. You know we'll do all we can not to let Harold get his filthy hands on her."

"I know. Actually, I was more worried about Harrigan."

"Harrigan? True, him working for Harold doesn't exactly shine the best light on him, but I can't believe he'd hurt Ella. Can't say what it is, but something makes me think he is a decent enough fellow who's been caught up in something he just doesn't understand. I don't think he knows what the hell is going on and he really doesn't have any reason to believe us or Ella over Harold. He's probably just anxious to get back to Philadelphia so that he can shed this mess. No, I can't really see the man doing anything to hurt Ella."

Louise smiled sadly as she stared at the hotel. "Not physically, no, but I think you'll know what I mean when I say that there are a lot of ways for a man to hurt a woman." She was not surprised when Joshua just grimaced and offered her no comforting words.

Chapter Eight

The touch of warm lips against her temple made Ella murmur with pleasure. She cuddled closer to the hard warmth that was gently wrapped around her. It was as if the heated dreams of the night had become reality. When she felt long fingers tangle themselves in her hair and her face being tilted upwards, she started to come awake. As she enjoyed the feel of soft kisses on her cheeks and forehead, she realized that this was no dream, that yet again she had ended up in Harrigan's arms.

She kept her eyes closed, feigning sleep, and only briefly wondered why, the answer to her question forming quickly in her mind. Harrigan's expression of desire had haunted her dreams all night because she felt the same way. She wanted him as badly and as blindly as he'd said he wanted her. It did not seem to matter what they said to each other or all that stood between them, their bodies were starved for each other.

It was all wrong, she mused as their lips met, which made it odd that it should feel so perfect. Everything she had ever been taught warned her to stop, but her body ached to continue. Her heart sent her conflicting messages. It warned her to pull away, to protect herself, even as it beat faster with delight, sending the mindless heat of desire racing through her veins.

When he slid his tongue into her mouth, she shuddered, pressing closer to him and gripping his shoulders. She tentatively touched her tongue to his and he groaned slightly, wrapping his arms around her almost too tightly. Those signs that he desired her made her head swim and her thoughts scatter.

"Ella," he whispered hoarsely as he kissed the pulse point on her neck.

"Mmmm?" She trailed her hands over his broad chest, savoring the feel of his smooth, warm skin beneath her fingers.

Harrigan gritted his teeth, fighting vainly to rein in his passion. Despite how badly he wanted her he was suddenly suffering a bout of guilt. He was the worldly one. He had also caught her off guard, at that moment when she was neither asleep nor awake and all of her defenses were down. She was warm, passionate, and welcoming, but Harrigan knew he had to give her the opportunity to retreat. He was sure that, if he took advantage of what could easily be a momentary weakness, he could turn that passion into an icy rage.

"Ella, I know you are awake now," he said.

"What a clever man you are." She frowned when he suddenly grasped her by the upper arms and held her away from him.

"Ella, are you fully aware of what we are doing?"

She blinked and studied him closely, wondering why he was interrupting their pleasure to ask such a stupid question. The dark warmth in his eyes, the taut lines of his face, and the light flush on his high cheekbones told her that he wanted her. It also told her what an effort it was for him to halt their love play. This sudden hesitation confused her.

"We're kissing," she replied.

"And if we do not stop now, it'll become a hell of a lot more than kissing."

Ella inwardly smiled, a little touched by what he was doing. Harrigan was trying to be gallant, giving her the chance to flee and save her chastity, and it was costing him dearly. In a way, it proved that his harsh words of the previous morning had indeed been a cruel blunder of words inspired only by anger and frustration. Ella felt the last of her anger fade.

For one short moment she considered accepting the chance to retreat. If she grasped at the passion he promised she would lose a great deal more than he would, her heart, her innocence, and, perhaps, any chance at marriage. Harrigan would simply have a good time then hand her over to Harold, collect his money, and walk out of her life. She could not base her decision on the chance that there would be any more than passion from him, because that chance was pretty thin. There was also the possibility that she would not escape Harold this time, that, in fact, her life was drawing to a swift and probably unpleasant ending.

That realization decided her. She had never fully understood why women were expected to be sweet, chaste, untouchable dolls while men could run about doing whatever took their fancy. It made even less sense to restrict herself so when she was in a fight for her life, a fight she could lose. If Harold did win, the last thing she wanted to be doing in her final few minutes on earth was to be thinking *if only*. It was reckless and probably unwise to make any decision while desire heated her blood, but she was going to take all Harrigan had to offer. She was going to satisfy her own desires without a thought to the consequences. Even the possibility that she was exposing her heart to pain was not enough to stop her. If she survived, she would deal with it. If she did not, a little heartache would be the least of her problems.

"How much more?" she asked in a soft husky voice as she reached out and trailed her fingers over his stomach, enjoying the way he trembled at her touch.

"This is a dangerous game you're playing," he said as he slowly pulled her into his arms.

"Who says I'm playing?"

"I know you're innocent, Ella, but I also know you're not stupid."

"How you flatter me, sir. I am quite overcome." She kissed the hollow of his throat, smiling faintly when she heard his breath catch.

Harrigan was beginning to get the feeling that he had lost control of the situation, but doggedly continued trying to make himself understood. "I want to make love to you, Ella. Kissing and this idle play is not enough. And once I get started I am not sure I'm going to be sane enough to even hear a no, let alone heed it. I want you that badly."

"Well, I shouldn't worry about that, Mahoney," she murmured as she straddled his body and brought her face close to his. "You won't miss me saying no because I have no intention of saying it."

A soft squeal of surprise escaped Ella when Harrigan held her tightly and rolled over so that she was sprawled beneath him. She smiled as she curled her arms around his neck, but when she tried to pull his mouth down to hers, he tensed. Ella wondered a little crossly what was holding him back now.

"If you have any desire to hold on to your chastity, you'd better get out of this bed now," he said, his voice husky and faintly unsteady.

"I have a desire, to be sure, and it has damned little to do with chastity." She almost laughed at the way his eyes widened in shock.

"Ella, I'm—"

"—talking far too much."

She yanked his mouth down to hers and kissed him. To her delight he gave up all resistance. Ella greedily accepted his fierce kiss, returning that barely restrained ferocity with her own.

When Harrigan began to kiss her throat, she curled her fingers into his thick black hair and tilted her head back.

Nothing had ever felt so good. She felt only a brief unease due to the strength of her own desire, but she easily pushed that aside. There was a good chance that taking Harrigan Mahoney as her lover could cause her some pain, but she was also sure that she would have some very sweet, fiery memories to treasure.

He slowly undid the small buttons on the front of her high-necked nightgown, tenderly kissing each newly revealed patch of skin. Ella trembled with a mixture of embarrassment and anticipation when he eased open her gown, exposing her breasts. When he touched her she lost all remnants of modesty, arching to his caress. He brushed his thumbs back and forth over her nipples until they were hard and aching. She cried out softly with delight and relief as he began to soothe that ache with slow, teasing strokes of his tongue. When he enclosed one hard tip in his mouth and began to suckle, she shuddered, tightening her grip in his hair and holding him close in silent, greedy encouragement.

It was not until he pulled his mouth away from her breasts and began to trail kisses down her midriff that she realized he had removed her nightgown. He untied her pantaloons, covering her legs with gently nibbling kisses and strokes of his tongue as he eased them off her. As he moved out of her reach, she clenched her hands at her side, her eyes closed as she let herself be completely caught up in the feelings washing over her. Her whole body trembled. Every part of her that he touched was warm and alive. There was an aching inside of her, an almost painful tightening low in her belly. Ella did not think she had ever felt so good.

The minute he was in reach again, she clutched at him. He slid his hand up the inside of her thigh to stroke her intimately and she jerked from the strength of the feelings that tore through her body. As he kissed her she slid her hand down his stomach, planning to touch him in the same way. Even as her fingers brushed the waist of his drawers he caught hold of her hand and pulled it away.

Ella experienced a brief check in her passion as she began to fear that she had done something wrong, offended him in some way. She cautiously looked at him but saw only an exciting look of desire and need on his face.

"I would like nothing more than to feel those soft, pretty hands touch me, but not this time," he said, his voice little more than a raspy whisper.

"I need to make an appointment?" Ella was a little surprised that she still had the wit left to make a joke, then realized that the invigorating feelings rushing through her put her in such a high good humor that she could not help herself.

Harrigan laughed shakily. Ella was a constant source of surprise to him and he realized that that only excited him more. Her humor also took away the small lingering doubt he had that she really understood what she was doing. She could not make jokes unless she was completely confident of her decision.

"No, you just need to wait. This time is for you, only you, although I will have a fine old time too. Don't doubt that. I barely have the control to do what I'm doing now. If you start loving me back, I will have none at all. I can't tell you how many times, as I have lain at your side, I have thought only of turning over and burying myself deep in your warmth. I still want to, but this is your first time and I know I have to go slowly."

"I don't think you have to go as slowly as you think," she said, touching a kiss to his forehead.

"I don't think I can wait much longer anyway."

"For once we are in accord."

He quickly shed the last of his clothes, easing his body back into her arms. They both trembled as their flesh met for the first time. Ella curled her body around his, moving her hands over his back as she tried to touch as much of him as possible. She did not think she had ever wanted anything as badly as she wanted him. Each touch of his hand, each kiss, made her ache until she was almost mind-less.

When Harrigan began to slowly join their bodies, Ella grew still, her body so filled with anticipation that she found it hard to breathe. Then, suddenly, after one quick sharp pain, they were one. Ella heard herself cry out yet did not really feel the pain. All of her thoughts were centered on how exquisite it felt to be so close to Harrigan, as close as any man and woman could be. It was a moment before she realized that he was not moving, just lying stiff -ly in her arms as he stroked her with unsteady hands.

"Harrigan," she said, her voice so thick and husky she barely recognized it as her own, "I may be innocent, but I believe there is a little more to this."

He laughed a little breathlessly and brushed a kiss over her mouth. "I hope it's more than a little," he murmured against her lips as he began to move.

Ella wrapped herself around him, trembling as he kissed her, his tongue imitating the movements of his body. She groaned his name as the aching knot inside of her tightened, then cried out as it shattered, passion washing over her with a blinding speed and ferocity. For a moment she retained enough of her senses to feel his movements grow rough, then he tensed, pushing himself deep within her as he shuddered and called out her name.

Harrigan was still feeling stunned as he gently extracted himself from Ella's grasp. He ignored her blushes when he returned to the bed with a cool, damp cloth and washed them both off. A little cautiously, he slipped back into bed, relaxing when she readily accepted him back into her arms. Despite her passion and her apparent readiness, he had still feared some sign of regret once their desire had been fed.

"Ella," he began, idly running his hand up and down her side.

"I hope you aren't about to ask me stupid questions or want to have a deep, serious discussion," she murmured as she rubbed her cheek against his chest. "I'm feeling quite lovely just now and that would spoil it. I think I would like life to just pass me by for a moment or two."

"That would be nice, but—" He smiled when she groaned softly. "It's getting late, and we have to get moving."

"And in one quiet little statement the man reminds us of all the reasons we shouldn't be here like this. I thought we agreed not to discuss Harold and Philadelphia."

"We aren't discussing him, but not talking about it doesn't mean it all ends."

Ella sat up and clutched the sheet to her breasts, almost smiling at the cautious look on his face. He was waiting for her to put an end to any chance that they would make love again or to cast aside their agreement and try again to talk him out of taking her back. They would be stealing moments out of time, but she did not want to do anything to stop that. The happiness they could find in each other's arms might be a false one, but it was too sweet to throw away.

"Just as our agreement and all that has happened here does not mean that I will cease to try to escape."

"Fine, but do you think you could stop kicking me in the face when you do try?"

She laughed softly as she bent to pick up her nightgown and pantaloons. "I will try, but that might depend upon my mood."

He slid an arm around her waist and tugged her close, kissing her on the shoulder. "Then I had best do my utmost to keep you in a very sweet mood."

"Yes, you had best do that."

Even as their lips touched a sharp rap sounded at the door. Ella silently cursed as reality intruded far sooner than she would have liked. Harrigan groaned as he sat up, pulled on his drawers and went to the door. While his back was turned, Ella hurried behind the privacy screen to get dressed. She felt herself blush when she heard George's voice recalling her to the fact that she and Harrigan were not really alone and might well have few moments when they could steal some privacy.

As she dressed, she wondered again if she was doing the right thing. Her innocence was irretrievably lost, but that did not mean she had to continue to be Harrigan's lover. She grimaced as she buttoned up her gown. There was little chance of winning him to her side in the fight against Harold and she would be a fool if she thought he had to fall in love with her now. Stopping now simply deprived her of a great deal of pleasure and the chance to pretend, at least for a while, that he cared for her as much as she did for him and that they could build a future together.

She loved him; she knew that for certain. As he had joined their bodies it was not only passion that had swept over her, but love. Freed from her heart, it had coursed through her veins as fast and as strong as her desire. Ella did not know whether to laugh or to cry. It was nice to be in love, but she knew it would bring her more pain than delight if Harrigan did not return that love. Since she did not have much hope of that happening, she decided to take all she could and pray that it would be enough to ease the pain when he left.

"Look there, Louise," Joshua said, nudging a dozing Louise awake and pointing toward the hotel. "Ain't that George?"

Yawning and rubbing her back, Louise straightened up from the wall she had been leaning against for hours and looked in the direction Joshua was pointing. "It is, and the little man is alone. Get the boys and try to corner the fellow."

"What about you?"

"I'll be hobbling along right behind you."

"What the hell do we do if we get the man?"

"I'll be thinking of a plan while I hobble." She nudged him to start him moving. "Hurry up. That big Irish fool could be right behind George."

* * *

George's soft whistle stopped abruptly as he turned the corner into a small side street and came face to face with a smiling Joshua. He took a cautious step back and bumped into someone. A quick glance over his shoulder revealed Manuel and Edward right behind him. They nudged him lightly in the back and he moved a little further into the shadows of the narrow side street. When Thomas appeared a moment later escorting Louise, who seemed to have trouble walking, George was not really surprised.

"Might I ask how you found us?" He almost smiled when he saw Louise's heavily bandaged foot peeking out from beneath the hem of her gown.

"By pure accident," Louise said. "We rode the train into town, stepped off for a bit, and there you were walking back to the hotel with that damned Irishman. Our plan had been to try to get to Philadelphia before you could."

"And what is your plan now?"

"Well, I think we will trade you for our Ella."

"It won't work."

"Why the hell not? You are that fool's friend, aren't you?"

"One of his closest."

"Then, if he is a true friend, he won't want to risk your life," Louise said coldly as she pulled her pistol and aimed it at George's head, a little disconcerted when he didn't even blink.

Her plan to use George to get Ella back had been hastily concocted, but she thought it had a chance to work. The calm way George was acting began to undermine her confidence. If he was not afraid, it was going to be difficult to make Harrigan believe her threats.

"What are you doing, Louise?" demanded Joshua. "I thought you were going to come up with a plan."

"I did. As I just said, my plan is to trade him for Ella," Louise replied, beginning to feel even less sure about her plan.

"What? Are you just going to walk up to Harrigan and say, 'Here's George, now give me Ella,' as if you're trading horses or something?"

"No. We'll confront Harrigan, hold a gun to this fool's head, and tell him to give us Ella or we'll shoot his friend."

"He's not going to believe us."

"Why not? He doesn't know us from a hole in the ground. For all he knows, we've left a trail of dead bodies all the way here." She glared at George. "And if you do anything to warn him or tell him we're lying, I just might shoot you."

"I cannot believe you could kill anyone, Miss Carson," George said.

He spoke so softly, an almost tender look on his face, that Louise nearly smiled, but she quickly sensed her weakness and softly cursed. "Maybe not, but that doesn't mean I can't shoot you. I could well have the stomach to commit a little maiming." She nodded when he eyed her a little warily.

"This plan is as stupid as the one you had to stop the train," grumbled Joshua even as he holstered his gun, and grabbed George by the arm.

"That plan worked," Louise complained as Joshua started to lead George toward the hotel, she and the others quickly falling into step behind him. "This one might too. I suspect that Harrigan Mahoney isn't the most trusting man in the world."

"Probably not," agreed Joshua. "And we could have one other thing to our advantage."

"Really? What's that?"

"That Harrigan undoubtedly thinks you are a dangerous lunatic."

Harrigan frowned as he stepped out of the hotel and gently took hold of Ella's arm. George should have joined them for breakfast. Although he had excused the man's absence then, George's lingering disappearance was beginning to trouble him. His partner had said that he was going to check on the horses and that he would meet them at breakfast, and it was not like George not to do exactly what he said he would.

As he started to walk toward the stables, Harrigan looked around. His gaze fixed on a group of people walking straight toward him and he stopped so fast that Ella walked right into him. Harrigan tensed as Louise and the others stepped up to him, a surprisingly calm George in their midst.

"We missed you at breakfast, George," Harrigan said pleasantly, glancing only briefly at the gun Louise held on his friend.

"Ah, sorry, Harrigan, but I was unavoidably detained," George murmured.

Ella tried to step toward her aunt, but Harrigan kept her firmly held at his side. "How's your foot, Auntie?" she asked.

"It's better, but you'll be able to see that for yourself when you come with us." Seeing the way some of the early morning passersby were eyeing her, Louise concealed her gun more carefully behind George's back.

"I fear Miss Carson has another appointment," Harrigan said, and he glanced down, almost smiling when he caught sight of Louise's thickly swathed foot.

"You will give Ella to us or I will shoot George."

Harrigan briefly wondered how seriously he ought to take her threat. He looked at George, caught the faintest of smiles on his friend's face and relaxed. Ignoring Ella's gasp of shock, he stepped around the group and started to walk to the stables.

"Where the hell are you going?" demanded Louise.

"Well, I fear I don't have the stomach to watch George meet his untimely end, so I thought Ella and I would just be on our way." When two men stepped up to him, their badges shining brightly as the morning sun glinted off them, Harrigan was unable to believe his luck. "Morning, Sheriff, Deputy."

"You having trouble, sir?" the older, heavier set one of the pair asked, looking at Louise and her friends with narrowed eyes.

"Just a small disagreement, sir," Harrigan answered.

For a moment Harrigan wondered if he now had a perfect solution to the problem of Louise and a way to free George. One long look at the sheriff's face, however, decided him. Even though he knew Louise's threat to shoot George was an empty one, he did not wish to push the woman into too tight a corner. If there was a confrontation between Louise and her friends and the law, George could easily be hurt in the ensuing battle. There was something about the way the sheriff and the deputy looked at Louise and the four youths, as if they were something nasty dirtying up their fine streets, that made Harrigan very reluctant to set them on the group. He had seen prejudice before, still suffered from its sting from time to time, and he saw that poison glittering in the two men's eyes. If he turned this particular branch of the law on Ella's erstwhile rescuers, they could be in far more danger than George ever was or would be. Harrigan also knew that, if he did anything that brought harm to Louise, George would probably never forgive him.

"Sure you don't need any help?"

"This young lady's guardian has asked me to bring her back home and I fear the girl's aunt disagrees. It is no more than a complicated family matter. However, if you would be so kind as to escort us to the stables, I believe it will expedite our leave-taking."

"They going to be leaving too?"

"Oh, yes," Harrigan replied as he started toward the stables, the sheriff and his deputy falling into step behind him. "I believe they will be leaving on the next train, or the stage."

"I could always make sure they don't follow you."

"No need. Trust me, sir," he assured the man as they stopped at the door to the stables. "This is little more than an annoyance, a game that, at times, becomes a little tedious.''

"Well, I think I'll keep a close watch on them until they leave.''

"Now you've gotten them all in trouble,'' Ella complained as soon as the two lawmen left them alone.

"Saddle your horse,'' he ordered as he nudged her toward the little mare.

"Harrigan!''

"Saddle your horse,'' he snapped, the unease the sheriff and his deputy had roused in him making him a little short-tempered. "The sooner we get out of here, the sooner Louise and her little band will leave. And, trust me in this, Ella, the best thing your aunt can do at the moment is to get the hell out of this town.''

Ella hesitated only a moment, then did what he said. She had seen the hatred in the eyes of the two men. They would like any excuse to hurt her aunt's boys, the object of their scorn. She suspected Louise would suffer as well simply because she traveled with Joshua and the others. Harrigan was right. The best thing to do was to get out of town and thus draw Louise and the others after them. She could argue with him later.

Chapter Ten

"He just left you here," Louise said in a shock-softened voice as she watched Harrigan walk away with the two lawmen.

"I told you it wouldn't work," George said, fighting back a smile.

"I should shoot you just to spite the bastard."

"Those lawmen are coming back," Joshua said quietly, as he watched the sheriff and the deputy lean against the wall of the saloon only a few feet away. "They're watching us closely, Louise."

"Do you think Harrigan has set them on our trail?" she asked, covertly holstering her gun and frowning at the men.

"No," George said firmly. "Harrigan would never set that pair on your trail."

"Oh?" She glared at him. "And what makes you so damned sure about that? Harrigan doesn't want us hunting him down. Setting the law on us would solve that problem real fast."

"It would, but he would never set those lawmen after you. Those two are eyeing you as if measuring you for a noose. Harrigan wants you gone, not dead."

"He's right, Louise," Joshua said as he took her by the arm and started walking toward the train station. "Don't forget that Harrigan's an Irishman."

"What the hell does that have to do with anything?" Louise asked.

"He knows hate," George said quietly as he fell into step beside her. "I'm sorry, but those two men hate you."

"Not your fault," Louise muttered as she glanced behind her and saw the two lawmen shadowing them. "Damn. I was so concerned about Ella and getting her free, I didn't see it. I'm usually quick to pick up on that nonsense."

"Fine. You've seen it now," Joshua said. "Let's get the hell out of here."

"Going on the train?" George asked as they all paused by the station.

"Yes," Louise answered, then frowned at him. "And what the hell are you still doing hanging around? Why aren't you following your friend?"

"I haven't got the money to get another horse and Harrigan took mine with him. I can't be sure which way he went, either, and I'm not much of a tracker."

"You mean we're stuck with you?"

"I fear so."

"I could just leave you here." She sighed when he just stared at her. "Well, I suppose we're all headed to the same place, anyway." She took some money out of her purse and handed it to Edward. "Get the man a ticket and find out when this lump of metal leaves." She waggled her finger at George. "You had better behave yourself. If you try anything to help Harrigan or stop us from rescuing Ella, I will shoot you."

George caught her hand in his and kissed her knuckles. "I'll be the most well-behaved prisoner you have ever had, Miss Louise." He smiled when Joshua started to laugh.

* * *

"I still cannot believe you just rode away from poor old George," Ella said for what she knew had to be the hundredth time.

"I have a feeling that poor old George is quite hale and hearty and probably very content."

"Content? How can he be content? You didn't even leave him a horse." This was the first time he had really answered her, and she prayed he would say something that would make her understand his actions.

"He won't need the horse, but we need the supplies on it."

"If he doesn't have a horse, how is he supposed to catch up with us?"

"I think he'll catch up with us in Philadelphia exactly when your aunt does." He smiled at her. "Did your aunt really think I would believe her threat?"

"It was worth a try."

Ella silently admitted that she thought it had been a weak ploy on her aunt's part. Harrigan was a pretty astute judge of character from what she had seen, and he saw through Louise's act very quickly. Although she could accept that Harrigan had not feared for his friend's safety, it still did not explain how he could just ride away from the man.

"Are you saying that it didn't make you hesitate for even a moment?" she asked.

"Not even that long. If Louise was the type of woman to kill a man, she would have shot me long ago. And George's expression told me that he was not worried at all."

"You saw an expression on George's face?"

"Briefly." He laughed at her doubtful look. "Trust me, Ella. George is safe."

"Well, I will concede that my aunt won't hurt him, but she might leave him stranded in that nasty little town."

"No. He'll get himself on the train or the stage she and the others are riding in."

"Oh, no. Is he going to cause trouble for them? He's a spy now, is he? A spoke in their wheel?"

"Ella, where is your faith in your fellow man?"

"I don't think we ought to have that discussion."

"You're probably right. I think your aunt will get him to promise that he'll behave and, if George promises something, he will do it."

"He's going to be mad at you." It troubled her that Harrigan did not seem concerned about that.

"No, I don't think so."

"There's something you're not telling me."

"Oh, I think if you ponder the matter a while, you'll figure it out."

"I don't feel like doing any pondering just now. It's too hot. So, why don't you just explain it to me."

"George now gets to spend a great deal of time with your aunt. I believe you will agree with me when I say that that will not trouble him in the least."

"Oh." Ella suddenly remembered her suspicions about George's interest in her aunt and grimaced. "Well, at least they will be well chaperoned." She ignored Harrigan's guffaw as she recalled how and why they had left so quickly. "Do you think they'll all get out of town safely?"

"Yes. Your aunt is a smart woman. She and the others will quickly see what I did. So will George. I suspect Louise has confronted this problem before."

"Far too many times."

"Good. And, don't forget George. He'll see that there's no trouble. He can be very imposing and persuasive when the need arises."

Ella nodded, accepting Harrigan's assurances about his friend's abilities. She had seen a hint of that strength in George and instinct told her that the man would do everything he could to protect her aunt. It saddened her to think that George might be the right man for Louise. Because he was working for Harold, any romance between the two could well be hopeless. Ella knew her aunt would never forgive the man if anything happened to her niece.

It seemed that the Carson women were doomed to care for men they could not have, she mused as she glanced at Harrigan. He had once told her that George would never work against him and she suspected he was right. That meant that, although George might not hinder her aunt's rescue attempts, he would never join forces with her. Just as it was with her and Harrigan, that meant that there was an insurmountable hurdle between them. Unless Harold was defeated and she escaped him unharmed, there could be no future for any of them.

For one brief moment, she suffered a few pangs of jealousy. Unlike Harrigan, George would love her aunt if given half a chance. Ella was sure of that. She quickly pushed aside those ill feelings. In a way, it would all be worse for her aunt than it was for her. When Louise turned away from George she would be giving up a lot more than a delightful bed partner. She would be walking away from a man who would care for her, marry her, and cherish her. Ella silently prayed that Louise kept a firm grip on her heart. She did not want her aunt to suffer the kind of pain she herself was courting.

The sun had almost set by the time she and Harrigan made camp for the night. She knew he had hoped to reach the next town. It was not that far down the road, but they agreed that it would not be wise to ride a trail neither of them knew in the dark of night. As she dismounted and began to unsaddle her horse, she suddenly realized that he was watching her very closely.

"Is something wrong?" she asked.

"Maybe." He poured a little water from the canteen into his hat and gave her mare a drink. "I don't suppose I can get you to promise that you won't run away."

She stared at him for a moment while she weighed her answer. It would be nice to forget where he was taking her and what awaited her there, but she knew she could not. Although it was easy enough not to talk about Harold and his threat to her, it was impossible to forget it completely. She knew that, even though it might feel as if she had just ripped the heart from her chest, she would run from Harrigan if given half a chance. She also knew that standing out in the middle of nowhere, with no idea of which way to go, was not one of those chances. Harrigan might know where the railroad tracks were, for she guessed that he was still following them closely, but she did not.

"I will promise it for tonight," she finally said.

"Only for tonight?"

Watching him as he moved to make the fire, she found it odd that he would believe her promise yet not her accusations about Harold. "Only for tonight."

"And why is that?" he asked as she sat down beside him.

"Because I have no idea of where we are."

He laughed and handed her the bundle of blankets he had taken from George's horse. "As good a reason as any. Make yourself useful then and lay out the bedding."

"Bedding is a grand name for this collection of scratchy blankets," she murmured as she spread them out on the other side of the fire, careful to keep them a safe distance from the flames yet within the circle of warmth and protection the fire provided.

"I prefer hotel beds as well, but those are a little better than the hard ground."

"Only a little." She sat down next to him again and watched as he prepared their supper of coffee, beans, and biscuits. "Where did a lad from the city learn to do that?"

"My father sent us off hunting with my uncle, Michael, from time to time, with strict instructions that we were to learn how to survive out in the woods."

"And who was we?" She knew she was showing, perhaps, too much interest in his life, but she was unable to quiet her curiosity about him.

"Me and my three brothers."

"How nice."

"Four Irish kids stomping about in the woods driving their uncle mad with their questions and mistakes is hardly nice," he drawled as he sat down next to her, idly draping an arm around her slim shoulders.

Ella smiled at the image, a little jealous of his family, which sounded large, happy, and loving. "It is nice. I only have my aunt. Such a large family sounds like a very good thing."

"Sometimes it can be the best there is. Other times, not so good. There's ten of us. Eight children and my mother and father. Then there are cousins, uncles, aunts, and all the rest. Sometimes one feels as if there's just a little too much family around."

Especially when one now feels obliged to support them, she thought, but said nothing. That touched a little too closely on a subject they had agreed to ignore. It made it all the more painfully clear, however, that he would not listen to her because he dared not. He could not allow one person's apparently baseless accusations to make him turn his back on what sounded like a few dozen family members. Harold could not have picked a better man to go after her, and she wondered if her guardian had known that.

She continued to press him for information about his life and family. It amused her a little that she was so deeply fascinated by what most people would consider very mundane facts. She was also saddened by the certainty that she would never be a part of that life, not even if she survived Harold's plots.

As soon as they had finished eating, she collected her bag and went to the creek to wash. She frowned a little as she stripped down to her camisole and pantaloons. Harrigan was doing a good job of staying close to any good source of water, but this creek looked unusually low. It should still be full with the winter runoff and spring rains, yet it barely covered the rocks that peppered its bed. That meant that it had been very dry, and she knew that could cause them some trouble as they continued on their journey. As she rinsed out her hair, she decided she would make a concerted effort to keep their canteens full.

The moment she returned to the camp, Harrigan hurried to the creek. She smiled faintly as she sat by the fire and combed out her damp hair. It was nice not to be watched constantly. For a little while she could pretend that they were just on a pleasant journey together. She prayed she could keep deluding herself so successfully, for she did not really want to spoil what little time she and Harrigan had together.

Harrigan rubbed his hair dry with his shirt, then rinsed the shirt off in the shallow water of the creek. He wondered briefly if he was a fool to leave Ella alone and unguarded with the horses, then shook his sudden attack of suspicion aside. She had said she would not try to escape tonight and he believed her. He suspected that he found belief easier to grasp than he might have because of the reason she had given for her promise. What was the point of trying to escape when she did not know where she was thus could not know where to flee to?

He collected up his things and started back to camp, smiling faintly when he realized how eager he was to return to Ella. What troubled him about that eagerness was that it was not simply for the passion he knew he could find in her arms. He was also eager to look at her and talk with her. That hinted at a depth of feeling that he did not want to have.

As he hung his damp clothes over the branches of a gnarled tree, he glanced at Ella and felt his heart skip. She sat before the fire in her thin camisole and lacy pantaloons, slowly combing her long hair. He did not think he had ever seen a prettier sight. Bathed in the glow of the fire, its lights enhancing the red in her hair and the soft paleness of her skin, she looked almost ethereal, and he felt desire course through his veins with a heady speed.

He struggled to rein in his passion for her as he sat down next to her. She was still new to the game of love. Even if her body did not need much time to recover from its introduction to desire, he suspected her mind and heart needed a little time to adjust to the fact that she was no longer innocent, that she had accepted a lover. Harrigan did not want to frighten her with his eagerness and the heady strength of his desire for her. He told himself to go slowly, to wait for some sign from her that she was interested in tasting more of the pleasure they could share, and then prayed that he had the strength to abide by that decision.

Ella idly brushed her hair and listened halfheartedly to Harrigan murmur inconsequential nonsense about the weather. She covertly watched him, catching him glancing quickly at her from time to time with hunger in his eyes. He did not act upon that hunger, however, and she wondered why. It was a moment before she thought she had an answer. She had been an innocent. There was a very good chance that he was waiting for her to, if not ask outright, at least show some hint that she shared his need.

She tucked her brush back in her bag and turned to face him, a little smile touching her mouth when she saw how difficult it was for him to move his gaze up from the low neck of her camisole to look at her face. His caution was touching, stirring a gentle warmth in her heart that she knew had more to do with affection than desire. There was no way she could bring herself to bluntly ask the man to make love to her, but she felt sure she could make her interest clear enough. In fact, she mused, the idea of conveying her aching need for his lovemaking without words was an exciting one.

Slowly, she leaned closer to him and touched the whisper of a kiss to his mouth even as she trailed her fingers across the taut skin low on his belly. He trembled and enfolded her in his arms. He felt so good, so alive, beneath her fingers that she was sure she would be content to touch him for the rest of her life if given half the chance. She resisted his subtle attempts to pull her down onto the blankets. Once there she knew he would lead their intimate dance and, suddenly, she was intrigued with the chance of finding out just how daring she could be and how much she could stir his blood despite her lack of experience. When she was done with him, he would no longer have any doubts about whether she wanted to continue to be his lover.

As he kissed her, she moved her hands over his body, carefully exploring every inch of his broad back and muscular chest. She boldly battled with his tongue, occasionally invading his mouth and savoring his soft groan of approval. The moment he released her mouth she began to cover his strong throat with kisses. He tilted his head back. Ella took quick advantage of his passivity, caressing his smooth chest with her lips and her hands.

She moved her hands to his thighs, gently kneading them before she inched her hands up to the waist of his drawers. He trembled as she undid them and eased her hand inside. His whole body jerked when she curled her fingers around his erection. For one brief moment, Ella's passion dimmed as she feared she had been too bold, and she started to pull her hand away. Harrigan grabbed her by the wrist and held her hand in place.

Ella closed her eyes as she intimately stroked him, her passions heightened by the way he trembled beneath her touch and whispered heated flatteries and encouragements against her skin. When he unlaced her camisole, opened it wide, and tenderly caressed her breasts, she breathed her pleasure. She could feel his gaze on her and that only fed her desire. At the first touch of his mouth against the aching tip of her breast, she curled her free hand in his hair and held him close, inviting him to taste his fill.

A murmur of regret escaped her when he finally pulled her hand away. He grasped her by the hips and pulled her up on her knees. She curled both hands into his thick hair as he kissed and licked her midriff while he undid her pantaloons. Only for a minute did she worry about how much of her he was seeing as he urged her to her feet and tugged her pantaloons down, following the descent with tiny nibbling kisses. The sure knowledge that the sight of her was stirring his blood simply enhanced her own pleasure.

The moment she had stepped out of her pantaloons, she started to move toward their bed of blankets, but he held her in place. He smoothed his hands over the back of her legs as he covered the front of them with soft kisses. Ella was shaking so much by the time he reached the top of her thighs that she was surprised she was still standing. A cry of shock and pure delight escaped her when he suddenly moved his kisses from the inside of her thighs to the softness between them. She started to pull away, but he held her there, and with one slow stroke of his tongue had her captured. Ella clenched her hands in his hair, steadying herself even as she held him in place, opening to the intimacy of his kiss.

Too soon she could feel the rapid advance of her release and she called out to him, trying to pull away, but he held her firmly in place. She cried his name as the culmination of her passion tore through her body and he seemed to feed on it. He caught her as she sagged in his hold, and placed her on the blankets. Ella watched him as he shed his drawers, her body limp yet feeling almost painfully alive. She held her arms out for him, but he eluded her grasp. Before she had time to recover from her release, he set about reviving her passion. Ella closed her eyes as he stroked and kissed his way down her body and back again, from the hollow in her throat to the far too sensitive soles of her feet. This time, when he touched a kiss to the inside of her thigh, she opened to his touch, welcoming his intimate caresses, and he took full, greedy advantage of it. He left no part of her untouched or unkissed, and Ella did not care what he saw or what he did, so long as the feelings he stirred did not stop.

The tightening low in her belly began again, and, recognizing what that meant now, she called to him a little desperately, clutching at his broad shoulders and trying to pull him into her arms. He acquiesced, but slowly, hungrily, tasting every part of her he could reach as he eased into her arms. Even as he touched his mouth to hers, he joined their bodies, and Ella groaned with the sweet pleasure of it. She slid her hands down his back, clutched his taut backside, and, as she wrapped her slim legs tightly around him, pulled him as deep within her as she could. Harrigan cried out and finally lost all control, much to her delight.

Harrigan grimaced a little as, after washing them both off, he slid beneath the blanket at her side and watched a blushing Ella pull on her clothes. The lovemaking had been hot and wild, but now he feared he might have pushed her too far too fast. Even as she finished tying her camisole, he pulled her into his arms, inwardly sighing over the slight tension he could feel in her slim body.

"God, you are enough to drive a man mad," he murmured as he lightly hugged her and brushed a kiss over her shoulder.

Ella blinked and chanced a peek at Harrigan. He was smiling and looked almost annoyingly smug, yet there was a hint of wariness in his expression as well. What she did not see was contempt or disgust. As soon as her passion had begun to cool, she had started to fear that she had done far too much and allowed him far too much freedom. She feared that she had behaved like some whore and that Harrigan would begin to see her as one. About all she could read in his face was pure satisfaction and a touch of wary concern. He was concerned that he had gone too far, she suddenly realized, and relief made her smile faintly.

Always, in the back of her mind, lurked the knowledge that her time with Harrigan was going to be short and that there would be no second chances whether Harold won or not. She liked the idea that she could be free in her passion. Although she did not know much, she realized that she was more than willing to explore every delightful aspect of lovemaking. Embarrassment and an innate modesty might pinch at her from time to time, but she now knew how quickly passion could eradicate such hesitation.

If she was not so tired, she mused with a silent chuckle, she would begin her exploration of the art of lovemaking immediately.

"I have you courting madness, do I?" she asked, then hastily covered a yawn.

"In more ways than you know." He tucked her up against his side, smiling faintly as she sleepily curled her body around his.

"I will admit that I don't know many ways. I was a little afraid, for just a moment, that I might have disgusted you with my greed to learn more."

"Ah, that explains the silence."

"Worried you, did it?"

"Some. Your passion is so free and so hot, I forget that it's still newly awakened. I was also a little afraid, afraid that I had demanded too much of you."

"If I wasn't so tired I could ease those qualms."

"Well, then you had best get a lot of rest. I intend to remind you of that remark when we camp tomorrow."

He smiled when she gave a sleepy chuckle. As he combed his fingers through her soft, lightly tangled hair, he felt her breathing grow soft and even and her body grow lax. He sighed and stared up at the stars. Right beside the delight he had in her passion was the painful knowledge that he would not be able to savor it for long. With each kiss they shared he knew he was making it harder and harder to give that passion up. His desire for it was like a knife held to his throat, but he would never turn away from the pleasure they shared.

He touched a kiss to her forehead. The way she murmured his name in her sleep both thrilled and pained him. Harrigan briefly contemplated turning away from her before he sank any deeper under her spell, then grimaced. He would not and could not. She was a sweet, heady addiction and he knew he would keep coming back for more until they were face to face with Harold and he was forced to give her up.

Chapter Ten

"A town at last," Ella said, shifting in the saddle and wondering how soon she could crawl into a hot, soothing bath.

For three long, torturous days they had ridden from dawn to dusk. They had only stopped briefly in one dusty little town. It had been crowded with cowhands on a spree. Harrigan had paused only long enough to replenish their supplies, then gotten her out of there. Although she had clearly seen the dangers there, as one day and then another had passed with no sign of a town big enough to have a hotel, inn, or boardinghouse, she had begun to heartily regret their hasty departure.

She glanced at the way Harrigan held the reins of her little mare and sighed. The moment they had drawn close to the railroad tracks again, she had lost her small sense of freedom. He had not even asked if she would promise not to try to escape. Ella decided that was probably a good thing. If he had dangled the carrots of a hot bath and a soft bed in front of her, she just might have promised to behave herself all the way to Philadelphia.

"Let's just hope that this dust bowl has a decent inn," Harrigan said.

"I'd be happy to sleep in a lean-to as long as it had a tub and some way to heat up some bathwater," Ella said, her voice exposing the weariness she could not deny any longer.

Harrigan laughed softly as he reined in before the stable. The hotel he could see up the road looked very new and very rough, just like so many of the others that were springing out of the ground all along the railroad tracks, but it would suffice. It would have the two things he wanted as badly as Ella did—a bath and a bed. Ella seemed to be no more than hot, tired, and dirty, just as he was, but he was worried about the toll such a hard journey could take on a woman as small and as delicate as Ella. He knew she was a lot stronger than she looked, but that did little to ease his growing concern for her welfare.

He dismounted, then helped Ella down, keeping a light hold on her arm as he talked to the owner of the stable. The total lack of resistance Ella revealed to his subtle but firm control of her every move troubled him a little. It was a clear sign of just how exhausted she was and he knew that could be dangerously unhealthy. She needed a few of the comforts they could not find on the trail in order to recoup her strength. Although he hated to miss any chance to make love to her, he decided she also needed a full night's sleep with no distractions.

The stable owner demanded almost a full night's keep for the horses before he would even take them. Finally, realizing that arguing was a waste a time, Harrigan paid the man, and started to lead Ella toward the hotel. After yet another concerned glance at the strangely silent Ella, he looked toward the hotel and his steps faltered. The small group of people he watched walk out of the hotel caused him to curse viciously. He could not believe that Louise and the others had stopped in the same place as he yet again.

For one brief moment he considered hiding out, then trying to sneak into the hotel, but he quickly realized that was a foolish idea. Louise would be keeping a close watch for him and, as soon as Ella knew her aunt was near at hand, she would do her utmost to alert the woman. The only real chance he had was to get back to the stables and ride out of town, hopefully before Louise or any of her compatriots spotted him.

Ella cried out in surprise and annoyance when he clapped a hand over her mouth, picked her up, and ducked down a dark, filthy alley between the saloon and the jail. She caught one brief glimpse of her aunt and cursed. Try as she might, she could not break free of Harrigan's grip. He carried her along like a rag doll as he crept back to the stable. It was not until he was inside the doorway of the stable, the man who was just beginning to unsaddle their horses staring at them in open-mouthed surprise, that he set her back on her feet. He still kept a tight grip on her arm, but cautiously took his hand away from her mouth, then hastily drew his gun.

"If you call out to any of them, I will shoot the first one who comes close enough," he threatened.

The scream Ella had planned to make caught in her throat, but she scowled at him. "Like you were going to shoot my horse?" she asked, her voice weighted with scorn.

"Guessed that was a lie, did you?" He briefly looked toward the owner of the stable. "Saddle them back up. Do it fast enough and you can keep the money I gave you." The man quickly did as he was asked.

"If you couldn't shoot my horse, you certainly can't shoot Louise or any of the others."

"If you wound a horse, you have to kill it, and, you're right, I was lying then. I couldn't have killed your mare. One can, however, shoot a person without killing them and knowing that they will heal. No, I have no intention of shooting any of them dead in the streets, but I will cause them a great deal of pain if you push me to it."

Ella cursed and, straining against his hold, peeked out of the stable, tensing a little when she realized her aunt was headed straight for them. "What will you do if they come in of their own accord?"

"I plan to be out of here by then."

She could not fully repress a startled cry when he grabbed her around the waist and tossed her into her saddle, grabbing her reins and swiftly mounting his horse. Ella barely had time to grab hold tightly before he was urging the horses out of the stable. When she heard her aunt cry her name, she cursed, knowing that she had just lost another chance to escape. It was growing harder to ignore Harrigan's part in her fate. She loved him and desired him, but, as he galloped out of town, she decided that she could also hate him.

"Damn it," Louise cried as she watched Harrigan ride away. "That man is too damned lucky."

George moved to stand beside her. "I don't think he is feeling so very lucky at the moment. Harrigan prefers a more comfortable mode of travel to horses and campfires and you have managed to keep him out of town, out of hotels, off the train, and riding hard."

"Our horses are on the train," Joshua said. "Do you want us to get them off and chase him down?"

"No," Louise replied. "By the time you get them off and saddled, he'll be too far ahead of you. You'll never catch up to him. I can't believe I was so stupid. I should have been more careful, stayed out of sight."

"You couldn't have known he would be in this town."

"One of the reasons we are riding the train and stopping in these towns is to try and catch him. I guess I just got too used to *not* seeing him. I wrongly assumed that this was going to be just another missed opportunity." She shook her head and muttered a curse. "I should have just shot the bastard when I had the chance."

"I am not sure your niece would approve of that plan," George said quietly.

Louise sighed. "I know it. Ella's not as bloodthirsty as she sometimes sounds. I am also not a child. I know those two have now spent more time together, alone, than is wise, especially since Ella is a pretty little thing and she is far too aware of what a fine-looking man Harrigan is. Oh, hell, and I saw the way they looked that day we caught you, George. I'm no fool. I know what went on that night they were alone in that hotel and what's been going on since. I ought to blow his head off for that alone."

Hearing the increasing anger in her husky voice, George reiterated, "Don't forget your niece's feelings in your anger. I am sure she is a woman who must feel some sentiment toward the lovers she takes."

Joshua's softly laughed *"Oh, my God"* was not really necessary to tell George that he had made a serious error. Louise turned to face him fully and, when she took a step toward him, he warily retreated a step. He did not think he had ever seen a woman look so furious. As he squared his shoulders and prepared for the onslaught of her temper, he briefly thought that at least he had taken her mind off of killing Harrigan. All he had to do now was keep her from killing him.

"I think you can stop running now," Ella yelled, desperate to be heard over the galloping horses.

She breathed a heavy sigh of relief as, a minute later, Harrigan began to slow the pace of the horses. As covertly as she could, she raised herself up in her saddle a little and rubbed her aching backside. At the moment, her discomfort bothered her more than the fact that, yet again, Harrigan had been one step ahead of her aunt. She was tired of riding, eating biscuits and beans, and sleeping on the ground. A small part of her resented her aunt for ruining her chance to spend a comfortable night in a hotel, to have a hot bath, eat a hearty meal, and sleep on a real mattress.

"It seems that we have to find a campsite again," Harrigan said, annoyance roughening his voice.

"I suppose there is little chance of finding a feather mattress among the bushes," she murmured.

"Some good fairy trots ahead of us scattering such largesse, does she?"

"What a pleasant thought. I was, however, just wishing that some settler tossed one off his wagon to lighten his load. I've heard that it is a common practice."

"So have I. And, perhaps, along with some soft bedding, he discarded a tub and a slab of bacon."

"The true necessities of life."

Harrigan just smiled, relieved that she was not going to discuss Louise and yet another lost opportunity of escape. He briefly wondered if, now that they were lovers, her urge to flee had lessened, even disappeared entirely, then told himself firmly not to be a fool. There was no doubt in his mind concerning the depth of her passion. It was hot and strong, as strong as her desire never to see Philadelphia or her guardian again. The reason Ella was not talking about the lost chance to escape was because it could easily lead to a discussion about Harold and the man's plans for her. Ella was simply holding to her agreement not to discuss that any more.

He frowned as he reined up to what should have been a good source of water and dismounted. Still holding the reins of the horses that eagerly moved to drink, he walked down the riverbank to the narrow rivulet of water that still flowed down the middle of the riverbed. Harrigan crouched down and dabbled his fingers in the shallow water, then lightly splashed some on his face. When he heard Ella do the same, he turned to see her at his side looking as solemn as he was sure he did.

"Another low river," he murmured.

"Yes." She dampened her handkerchief and wiped her face as she looked up and down the river. "This should be three times this size."

He hesitated to speak his thoughts aloud, then decided he would not be telling her anything she had not seen for herself. Ella had spent several years on a ranch. She probably knew more about seasons, rainfall, and the signs they were seeing than he did. The look on her face told him that she was already seriously concerned.

"There is less and less water the further east we ride."

"Then perhaps we should ride west," she suggested and shrugged at his brief look of disgust. "If there is no rain soon there will some very hard times in this area."

"And I'm sorry for those who will suffer, but my main concern at the moment is us and these horses. If the water keeps diminishing at the rate it has been, it'll only be a day or two before there is none to be found."

"We could stay close to the railroad tracks. Trains need water and keep a supply all along the tracks."

"And your aunt will be riding the train on those same tracks. If that woman catches sight of us, I would not be surprised if she leaps out of a window or a door of the moving train."

Ella vainly tried to bite back a laugh, then giggled when he caught her at it. "Sorry, you make my aunt sound so formidable."

"She is." He stood up, tethered the horses to the stunted brush on the riverbank, and started to unsaddle them. "You kept telling me so. I finally listened."

"That is not exactly to my advantage." She frowned out at the grassland that encircled them as he set their things down and started to make a fire. "I would make that fire very small and very carefully contained," she said.

"I'm always careful with a fire," he murmured, glancing up at her.

"I know. I just felt a need to ask you to be especially careful tonight. This is wildfire weather."

"Wildfire?"

"I suppose they don't have that problem in Pennsylvania. Everything is dry, dangerously dry. We're sitting in the middle of a field of tinder. One stray spark and this will all catch alight and burn like an old barn full of dry hay."

Harrigan shook his head. "I really didn't need something else to worry about."

"Sorry," she murmured as she took the blankets and

spread them out. "I'm just nervous. This land we're cross-ing is clearly in the middle of a serious drought. That trickle of water that used to be a river is not enough to protect us from fire. And, although it pains me to admit to it, fire is one thing I have always been deeply afraid of."

"Were you caught in one?" he asked as she sat down next to him while he prepared their meager supper.

"No, but I have seen a few and remember a little too clearly what a fire can do to animals, people, and property. I also recall how hard the fires were fought, yet the fire still won."

She fell silent and Harrigan concentrated on fixing them a meal, not eager to break the solemn quiet. Despite how hard it made cooking, he kept the fire so low it barely reached the tops of the rocks he had encircled it with. He had fought a fire or two in his time and knew what she meant. When a fire reached full strength it roared over everything and everyone in its path. Glancing around, he realized she was right. They were sitting in the middle of miles of tinder with no place to escape a fire if one started. Although he intended to be very careful, Harrigan knew he would not be able to shake the fear she had unwittingly instilled in him. It was made worse by the knowledge that there were many other ways a fire could start besides care-lessness with a campfire.

They were both yawning by the time they finished their meal. As Ella went to the river to wash up before bed, Harrigan worked to make the fire as safe as possible, piling a second layer of stones around it and dampening the ground. He could not bring himself to douse it completely for, although they did not need its warmth, they still needed its protection. Harrigan was sure there were wild animals roaming the vast open grasslands they crossed and he did not want one sneaking up on him. The fire would make any animal keep its distance.

Ella barely spoke when she returned, stripped to her camisole and pantaloons. She carefully placed her clothes on her bag and crawled beneath the blanket with an obvious weariness. As he moved to clean up for bed, Harrigan was glad that he shared her exhaustion, for she was in no state to satisfy any urge save for sleep.

When he joined her in their rough bed he gently pulled her into his arms. Her body was already heavy with approaching sleep and he found it easy to push aside his desire for her in deference to her need for rest. He idly stroked her hair as she curled her body more comfortably against his.

"There is a heaviness to the air. Perhaps it will rain soon," he said in a soft voice, unable to completely dismiss the concern about fire from his mind.

"Out here there can be a heaviness in the air, but the storm never appears, or it thunders and crackles with lightning, but no rain." She closed her eyes, part of her telling her to stay alert for danger, but a greater part demanding sleep.

"And the lightning starts the fires."

"I fear so. Go to sleep, Harrigan."

"You put such thoughts in my head, tell me that I'm lying down in nature's fireplace waiting for a match to strike, then tell me to sleep?" He smiled when she chuckled.

"I always feel it's best when worries are shared."

"Worry doesn't seem to steal away your sleep, however."

"No sense in both of us being awake."

He just laughed and fell quiet, letting the soft sounds of the night relax him. Ella close at his side, her gentle breathing, and the light weight of her warm, slim body also worked to soothe him. Harrigan grimaced when he realized that he would find it hard to sleep alone once she was gone. He closed his eyes and tried to push those thoughts from his mind. Fate had thrust them together and the needs of his large family would ensure that they had to part. There was nothing he could do to change that.

* * *

"I think you should take the gag off George now, Louise," drawled Joshua, smiling at the couple seated across from him on the train. "The other passengers are beginning to talk."

Louise tore her gaze from the troubling scenery passing by the window of the train and looked at George, who sat next to her. A sigh holding both resignation and irritation escaped her as she yanked off the gag she had stuffed in his mouth then undid the ropes binding his wrists together. She gave Joshua a look that cried "traitor" when the youth handed George his canteen. When she heard the other three young men seated across the aisle laugh softly, she sent them a brief glare as well.

"You can't gag everyone who says something you disagree with," Joshua said as he relaxed in his seat.

"Sounds like a good idea to me," Louise replied, then grimaced when she heard the somewhat childish petulance tainting her voice.

"I did apologize for my hasty judgment," George said as he gave Joshua back his canteen.

"It was not so much the insult you gave Ella, who did not deserve it, but that tone of stuffy moral outrage that set my teeth on edge."

"Stuffy?" George murmured, but Louise ignored his interruption.

"I had my fill of that when I was in Philadelphia. Half or more of the women who acted so righteous, shook their well coiffed heads, and clucked their busy tongues, were far from sainthood. They judged me on rumor and innuendo and cast me out of their little society as fast as they could. I know it was not because of the murder I was falsely accused of, either. They pushed me out of the nest because they wanted to, because I did not fit their ideals. I was not *one of them.*"

"I'm sure it was unpleasant to have friends turn against you."

"Unpleasant?" Louise could not help herself, she giggled. "George, you do have a way with words." She quickly grew serious again. "I don't miss a one of them. Truth is, although I counted them as friends, I realized I was never close to any of them. It is the injustice of it all that still angers me. The pettiness of those people is still a sore spot on my skin. They treated poor Ella in a like manner. True, they never cast her out completely, but they never allowed her in either. It can leave one feeling as if there is nowhere that she belongs. The younger one is, the harder that is. I thought the new lands out west would be different, and they are a little, but I still didn't fit." She winked at Joshua. "So I made my own little society and only the best can join."

"And you intend to keep Ella as part of that little group," George said quietly.

"I do. I know you and that fool Harrigan do not believe it, but Harold means to kill her. Even if he didn't, I would still fight to keep her from being taken back to Philadelphia. There is nothing there for her, no family, no friends. Even Harold barely tolerates the girl's presence in his house."

"It does sound a very sad situation, but the law says Harold Carson is her guardian, not you. The only way you can win this is to have her rightful guardian changed, to depose Harold from the position."

"That is never going to happen. Harold owns too many judges and lawyers and others of prominence in that city."

"Then you must wait until she is of age to do as she pleases."

Louise cursed softly. "You don't listen, do you? Harold will never let Ella reach that age. Why do you find that so hard to believe?"

"Actually, I don't."

"Then why are we even playing this game? Why don't you just let her go?"

"I am not the one who makes that decision. I work for Harrigan. There is also still the law to consider. It says she belongs with Harold. Perhaps I am a coward, but I do not feel comfortable breaking the law, no matter how unfair that law or ruling may be. Now, you may be able to convince me that Harold Carson means her only ill, but the law needs a great deal more than your word. So, I fear, does Harrigan."

"You know, you have a very annoying skill of always sounding so reasonable." She felt a definite softening within her when he gave her one of his fleeting smiles and quickly turned her attention to what was passing by the window. "Of course, none of this may matter."

"What do you mean?"

"Harrigan and Ella may not ever make it to Philadelphia," she replied, finally putting her growing fear into words.

"Harrigan is not without skill," George said in his friend's defense.

"I am sure he is a clever fellow. He cannot, however, make it rain, can he?" When she glanced at George and saw the faint look of confusion on his face, she pointed at the passing scenery. "It's dry out there. Bone dry. Miles and miles of parched grass and dirt. There is a drought going on in this land. I'm sure of it."

"It does look bad," agreed Joshua. "There is still time for some rain before the summer sets in hard, though."

"True, but I think this land needs a lot more than a few late-season showers," said Louise.

"If Harrigan needs water, he'll go into town or find one of the railroad's water holes or water towers," said George. "He'll understand the danger of getting too low on water."

"Yes, but the way you're talking tells me that he might not understand the dangers a parched land can present. There's the danger of wildfires. They can decimate miles of grassland and all that is in their path in the blink of an eye. Animals desperate for a drink can lose their natural reticence around man."

George frowned as he stared out her window, trying to see all that she did. "Harrigan will do all he can to be sure your niece is safe. And, as Joshua says, the rains could still come."

"They could, but the storm that brings them can be just another threat. You haven't been out this way before, have you, George?"

"No. I haven't done much more traveling than to move from Boston to Philadelphia."

"Well, the storms out here can be fierce and deadly. They can put down a wind that rips apart everything in its path. The more I look out there, the more I study the skies and the ground, the more I worry."

George lightly patted her hand where it lay clenched tightly in her lap. "They won't be in this land for long."

"I hope not. In truth, I could almost wish Ella was in Philadelphia. At least she can fight Harold."

Chapter Eleven

Ella took a small sip of water from her canteen then poured some into a battered tin bowl and gave her little mare a drink. An idle shake of her canteen proved her worst fears. They were rapidly running out of water. Despite his reluctance to draw near any towns, Harrigan was slowly veering back toward the railroad tracks. The trains needed a constant and ready supply of water and there would be some at various points along the tracks. For two days Harrigan had resisted doing that, certain that they could find sufficient water elsewhere, but it was proving impossible. Each place he went to, places where his charts, maps, and notations had promised water, they had found little more than mud. Now he had no other choice, for, if they did not find water soon, they would not have a drop left and no guarantee of replenishing their supply, and that was a peril Ella had no wish to experience.

She slumped against her placidly grazing horse and watched Harrigan gently remove a pebble from his horse's hoof. They had halted the moment his mount had developed a slight limp. The man took very good care of their animals and obviously valued them. Ella thought again of the time he had threatened to kill Polly. She knew for certain now that he would never have carried out that threat. She was annoyed that he had tricked her, but mostly she was annoyed that she had fallen for the ruse.

Taking out her handkerchief, she dabbed at the perspiration on her face. The air was almost chokingly heavy. Some very black clouds were rolling toward them from the west and Ella prayed that they would hurry up. Not only would a storm clear the air for a while, but it would bring some much-needed rain. And a little rain would serve to tamp down the invasive dust, she thought, as she brushed off her skirts.

"I'll have to ride George's horse for now," Harrigan said as he took the rope lead off George's horse and fixed it on his own mount. "How are you feeling?" he asked her.

"Hot, tired, sore, and uneasy," she replied.

"Uneasy? About what?"

"Water and weather. Too little of the first and too much of the second."

Harrigan cast a brief, wary look toward the black clouds chasing them. "It does look like a bad storm. It might not catch up to us, though. We still have fair skies over our heads."

"True. Hot and weighty fair skies. The air is so heavy I sometimes feel we'll need to push it out of our way as we ride through it."

He smiled wearily and nodded. "A little rain would clear the air some, probably be very refreshing."

"Very. Although, if that grey haze I can see beneath the clouds is not just a vision caused by the heat, that storm is carrying more rain than we might want." She grimaced, wondering if her unease was a product of her exhaustion and nothing else. "Part of me wants that storm to hurry up and get here even if it is tossing rain down by the bucketful."

"But? There is a definite *but* in your voice."

"The *but* is that I don't like the look of those clouds.

They are fierce and very alive. You can see the lightning they're are spitting out from here. If that touches a dry patch, even the rains won't stop the fire it can start. I do not claim to be very knowledgeable about such things, but those clouds look like ones that could set down a killing wind, the kind that rips up and smashes everything in its path."

"A tornado," Harrigan said in a soft voice, a little relieved that she held the same concerns he did, for it meant he did not have to hide them.

"Have you heard of such things?"

"Heard of them and seen one. You must know that they occasionally do their deadly dance over parts of Pennsylvania. You lived there long enough." When she nodded, he continued. "One descended upon a part my uncle called home. We survived as did the house. Well, all except the windows. But the destruction it left behind was indescribable. George and my uncle occasionally have friendly arguments about which is worse, hurricanes or tornadoes. Personally, I don't care which is worse. I would prefer never to have to deal with either." He grasped her by the waist and set her in her saddle. "Going to stay with me? If you swear not to try and escape today, you can hold your own reins."

"I swear it. You'll be blessed with my best behavior until midnight." She exchanged a brief grin with him as he handed her her reins then mounted George's horse. "I would prefer to have control of Polly if we suddenly feel a need to run for our lives."

"Thought you might."

As they rode, Ella could not stop herself from periodically glancing behind her. The threatening clouds appeared closer each time she looked. She seriously considered spurring her little mare into a gallop and trying to outrun the storm, then inwardly told herself not to be foolish. The horses were suffering from the weather as badly as she and Harrigan were. A mad gallop now would quickly sap their strength and, quite probably, gain them nothing at all. It was almost impossible to outrun such a huge, fast-moving storm. Considering the risks such a storm held, Ella knew it was wiser and safer to conserve the strength of their horses. There was still the chance that they would have to make a run for their lives.

When the wind suddenly picked up, pushing hard against Ella's back, she tensed. The first plump drops of cool rain were refreshing, but she barely had a minute to savor their gentle cooling when the deluge began. Despite the lingering greyish light of day, it was nearly impossible to see through the heavy curtain of rain, and their pace slowed. Knowing how hard Harrigan was working to keep them on their chosen trail and try to find them some shelter, Ella hunkered down, struggled to stay close to him, and said nothing. Then, suddenly, she was alert, fighting to pick out one particular sound mixed in with the noise of the storm.

"Harrigan," she shouted, relieved when he turned his rain-soaked face toward her. "Are we near the tracks?"

"The railroad tracks? No. Why do you ask?"

"I'm sure I hear a train. Although, it's not exactly the right sound for a train. More a roar than a chugga-chugga."

"Oh my God."

Even in the bad light Ella could see how Harrigan paled as he looked behind them. She felt the chill of the rain enter her veins as fear clutched at her heart. Although she did not really want to see what had a strong man like Harrigan looking so afraid, she also glanced behind them and felt her heart almost painfully skip a beat.

"We're dead," she yelled, her voice hoarse and unsteady.

"There's one slim chance for us," Harrigan shouted back.

"We can't outrun that."

"Nope, but we might be able to get the hell out of its way." He slapped her mare on the rump. "Ride south as hard as you can."

Ella did not need to be told twice. She clung tightly to

her horse and gently spurred the mare on. Polly needed
no encouragement, apparently relieved to be given full
rein to run for her life. All Ella had to do was direct the
terrified animal so that the mare continued to try and
outflank the storm, not outrun it. She could hear Harrigan
and the other horses keeping pace, and concentrated on
staying in the saddle.

"Head toward those rocks," Harrigan yelled as he rode
up beside her and pointed to a circular mound of boulders.

"Are we far enough away from that thing?" she yelled
back.

"Let's hope so, because by the time we reach those
rocks, we'll have run as far as these poor beasts can take
us."

The moment Ella reached the boulders, she flung herself out of the saddle. A narrow passage cut into the rocks
and she dragged her exhausted mare into the center of
them. Harrigan and his two horses quickly followed her.
It was crowded, but Ella slumped against the rain-slick side
of one boulder and felt a little safer. A small voice in her
head told her that the tornado could reach her even there,
but she ignored it, preferring to accept the security of the
thick, solid rock, even if it was a false one.

"Where are you going?" she asked Harrigan as he cautiously started to climb to the top of one of the smaller
boulders.

"I want to see where that cursed thing is going," he
answered.

"If it's headed straight toward us, I don't really think I
want to know it."

Harrigan kept climbing and, after taking a deep breath,
she moved to follow him. He caught her by the arm and
held her steady when she reached the top and crouched
beside him. When she saw that the tornado was already a
goodly distance away from them and looked as if it was
beginning to lose its power, she was almost glad that she
had made the climb.

"Do you think it will produce any more?" she asked as he helped her back down the rock.

"Could be. I think we should stay right here until the weather clears."

"That could take all night."

"I know, so I'll try to make us some kind of shelter. Wait here."

"As if I have any place to go," she muttered as he slipped away.

For a brief while she sat pressed against the rocks, shivering as the rain poured down on her. When she began to feel as stiff as she was cold, she stood up and searched through their supplies for anything that could hold water. By the time she had set their bowls and cups on the rocks, even tenuously balancing their canteens in a small trench at the base of one boulder to catch the runoff, Harrigan had returned.

She stood out of his way, hugging herself in a vain attempt to stay warm, and watched him fashion a rough lean-to against the rocks using sticks and his and George's trail coats. The moment he was done, she ducked inside, relieved to be out of the rain even though she was already soaked to the skin. Harrigan quickly joined her, carrying their bags and the blankets, which had been kept dry by an outer wrapping of oiled canvas. As he struggled to build a small fire, she shed her wet dress and wrapped herself in a blanket. As soon as Harrigan had stripped down to his drawers, he draped another blanket over both of them, and tucked her up against his side. Ella wondered why, after such care, she was still cold.

"Sleep, Ella," Harrigan urged her. "We can't do anything in this downpour, not travel, not even cook, so you might as well get some rest."

"This was far more rain than I wanted," she murmured as she tried to press even closer to his warmth.

"I don't think even this is enough to end the drought. This land will need several more storms like this to revive."

"Please, God, let me be away from this place before they

arrive." She yawned and closed her eyes, still chilled to the bone, but suddenly too tired to care. "I also pray that I never see one of those tornadoes again," she added in a tremulous whisper.

"I heartily echo that prayer. We were fortunate today. I'm not really sure how we eluded it. I suspect it turned a little to the north even as we rode south. We just made a damned lucky guess as to which direction to run."

"I'm very sorry I don't have some sugar, or an apple, or something. Those poor animals deserve something a little special. Are they alright?"

"Yes. Unsaddled and securely tethered. The rain won't hurt them." He rubbed his hand up and down her arm when he felt her shiver. "I'm not so sure it's good for you, however."

"I'll be okay once I'm dry. It's nearly summer. It should not be this cold."

"As soon as the rain and the wind die down, it'll warm up."

"I think I'll cease wishing so hard for a bath."

Harrigan laughed softly, then frowned when he looked at her and realized that she had fallen asleep in a heartbeat of speaking. She was sleeping soundly too, and, although her breathing was even and quiet, it troubled him. He picked her arm up a few inches and dropped it, but she did not stir. It was as if she had been knocked unconscious. Harrigan was sure that falling asleep that quickly and that deeply was not right.

What Ella needed, he decided, was a good long rest in a soft bed, a few hearty meals, and a little pampering. The journey on horseback over a hard land, sleeping on the ground, and a steady diet of beans, biscuits, and coffee had to be taking a toll on her. It was certainly wearing him down.

He was astounded that she did not want to kill him simply for making her travel so roughly, especially when he was taking her somewhere she did not want to go. Instead, she rode along with few complaints, made sweet love to him in the night, and held to her promise not to discuss Harold and the right or wrong of returning her to her guardian. At times she even readily promised not to try and escape and held firm to that promise. While it was true that, most of the time, she had no idea of where they were or where she could run to, he suspected that she might still try to flee if given a chance.

It suddenly occurred to Harrigan that, in word and deed, Ella continuously revealed an innate sense of honesty. He grimaced when he realized that she probably saw his refusal to believe what she said about Harold as a deep insult. It was certainly a plausible tale she told, but he could not allow himself to accept any more than the fact that she honestly believed what she said. Too many people relied on him to finish the job he had been hired for and to collect the money owed him.

He closed his eyes and rested his cheek on the top of her head. It was a good thing she had agreed that they would not discuss Harold. Simply thinking about the matter both confused and discomforted him. There had to be a solution that would give her what she wanted and give him what he needed. Once they reached Philadelphia he was determined to find it. But first, he mused, as he prepared to go to sleep, he was going to find Ella some place comfortable to rest and recoup her strength. Harold and all of the questions and troubles that went with him could wait.

Harrigan cried out in alarm when he saw Ella sway in her saddle then slump forward. She had been groggy and somewhat disoriented since they had woken up, but she had insisted that she was fine. In the ensuing two hours he had grown progressively more concerned about her. She had not said a word and had continually started to fall asleep only to jerk herself awake again. He flung himself out of the saddle and caught her in his arms even as she started to slide off her horse.

"Ella," he said, shaking her slightly as she lay in his arms, but she did not even open her eyes.

He cursed and sat her on his horse. As quickly as he could, he hitched Polly to the same lead George's horse was on. Holding Ella's limp body steady, Harrigan remounted and enclosed her securely between his arms as he took up his reins again. He saw no outward signs of fever or of any other illness, but something was wrong, and he knew he had to find shelter and aid.

As he rode, Harrigan tried very hard to find someone to blame for Ella's condition, someone besides himself, but to no avail. He was the one who had dragged her from her secure, happy life with her aunt to take her back to Philadelphia. He was also the one who insisted they ride the open trail like cowhands or prospectors because he dared not stop in a town where he might have to elude or do battle with Louise. Harold may have started the game, but it was he, Harrigan Mahoney, who was the key player. He decided that, if he could find no one else to help Ella, he would hurry to the nearest town where the railroad passed through and find Louise.

Harrigan was already following the road to a town by the time he saw a small homestead. He nudged his horse into a trot. Once at the gate of the rough-hewn rail fence, he dismounted and took Ella into his arms. Pausing only to loop his mount's reins over a post, he walked to the front door and knocked.

It did not surprise Harrigan to be met by a man armed with a rifle. People in such desolate places had to be cautious. A young, plump brunette warily peered out from behind the tall, burly man facing Harrigan. It was hard to push aside his concern and recall his manners, but Harrigan managed a small nod of greeting for the woman before fixing his gaze on the black-bearded man blocking the doorway.

"I hate to impose, but I desperately need some help," he said.

"Is your wife sick?" the man asked, relaxing a little as he looked the unconscious Ella over carefully.

Harrigan barely stopped himself from correcting the man's false impression. A man and his wife traveling together would be welcome. A man dragging a young, unwed woman back to a place she did not want to go to would be met with suspicion, perhaps even anger. If these people found out the truth about him and Ella, he could easily find himself on the wrong side of the big man's rifle again. Harrigan decided to let the man believe that he and Ella were married and pray that, when Ella was sensible again, she would allow him to continue that lie.

As succinctly as he could, Harrigan told them everything that had happened in the last twenty-four hours. He was not really surprised when he was immediately invited inside. As the man went to tend to the horses and get their bags, the woman showed him to a seat then hurried to freshen the linen on her bed. She ignored Harrigan's protests over putting the couple out of their own bedroom.

Willie Lindon and his wife Rose proved to be far more helpful than Harrigan could have hoped for. Rose was certain that Ella had no real illness, that she was simply exhausted from her ordeal. At the woman's insistence, Harrigan helped her bathe Ella, Willie dutifully heating up the water they needed. They dressed Ella in her modest white nightgown, dried her hair, and tucked her up in the Lindons' bed.

Ella roused herself only a little throughout it all. Harrigan found it somewhat comforting that Ella stayed conscious enough for long enough to eat a small bowl of Rose's hearty venison stew. Although Ella did manage to say a few things, to Harrigan's relief she said nothing that could expose his lie to the Lindons. She murmured no more than a few confused questions and well-practiced expressions of gratitude.

Harrigan put aside his concern for Ella long enough to have a meal and visit with the Lindons. Hungry for information, they asked him a disconcerting number of questions. He answered everything carefully, not wishing to lie too profusely. It not only seemed an ill return for their kindness, but he did not want to tangle himself up in so many half-truths that he was unable to remember everything he had said. Ella could be sicker than Rose thought and they might end up being guests of the Lindons for a few days.

"I can't thank you enough for all your kindness," Harrigan said to Willie as he sat on the front porch with the man, enjoying a neatly rolled cigarette as Rose cleared away the remains of the meal.

"Glad to help," Willie replied, handing Harrigan a cup of homebrew. "Nice to have visitors. We don't get into town much since it takes most of a day to get there, and the town ain't grown enough yet so that folk have moved out closer to us. It'll happen soon. People coming here all the time. Have a lot of folk who just get weary of traveling and stop here rather than going on to California or some of them other far-off places."

"After all of the traveling I've done, I can easily understand that."

"Haven't seen too many folk headed the other way, going back East to them crowded cities."

Harrigan smiled and took a cautious sip of the strong liquor, struggling not to cough as it burned its way down his throat. "Wyoming doesn't have much use for what I'm skilled at and I need to make a living."

"Not a farmer or a cowhand, huh?"

"No. Born and raised in the city. Perhaps I just need to learn a few things before I try to be a pioneer."

"I don't mean no disrespect, but maybe your wife ain't one of them women who can set out from all she knows and start anew. She's just a little bit of a thing."

"She is, isn't she?" Harrigan laughed softly. "She's a lot stronger than she looks, spirited, determined, and quick-witted." He shook his head. "Hell, I was getting tired and sore. It's no surprise that she collapsed. I just hope that your wife is right, that Ella is simply very, very tired, that running from that tornado sapped the last of her strength."

"My Rose is real skilled at healing folk. If she says the girl's just tired, that she just needs a good rest and some good food, then, mark my words, that's exactly what ails your wife."

"I really hope so. Guilt has a very sour taste."

"Don't feel so bad. She made her choice."

Harrigan inwardly winced, but managed a brief smile for Willie. "I'll remind her of that when she starts to complain."

It took Harrigan longer than he liked to finish Willie's eye-watering liquor, and he was already feeling its potency by the time he excused himself to go to bed. He held the door open so that Rose could step out and sit with her husband, then lingered just inside for a moment as he tried to shake free of the homebrew's grip. When Rose and Willie began to talk, he knew he ought to move away, at least far enough away so that he could not eavesdrop on their conversation, but then he heard his name.

"You know, lovey, there's something not right about Harrigan and Ella," Willie said. "Not bad, mind you, but just not right, either."

Rose laughed softly. "You probably sensed that they're not really married."

"You mean we've been lied to?"

"Not really. We said *wife*. He didn't."

"Not sure we oughta have given them our bed then, sweetie."

"Oh, they aren't bad folk, dear. Fact is, I wondered if maybe they're running away to get married. I think that little lady is of society, born and bred. Now, Harrigan's a gentleman, sure enough, but I think it's newly learned."

"Still not sure it's right."

"It's perfect, dear. Those two are in love."

"Didn't hear it said."

"Didn't have to. It was there in the way Harrigan looked at little Ella, in his deep and very real concern for her, and in every word he said about her. They aren't married by law, but they're married in spirit and that's good enough for me. Now, hush, enjoy the company, and give me a sip of that poison you call Willie's Brew.''

Careful not to make a sound, Harrigan moved away from the door, and tiptoed into the bedroom, silently shutting the battered door behind him. As he undressed, he could still hear Rose's words in his mind. He wanted to chuckle at the endearing romantic fancies of women, but he couldn't.

Standing at the side of the bed, he watched Ella sleep. The word *love* stuck in his mind and he found himself wondering if Rose could be right. An attempt to blame such thoughts on Willie's potent brew failed. He found that he was both afraid and deeply curious.

He slipped into bed and gently pulled Ella into his arms. When she cuddled up to him, mumbling his name in her sleep, he grimaced. He could not deny that he felt something for her, something a great deal deeper and more complicated than anything he had ever felt for a woman. Cautiously, he admitted that he cared for her, liked her, enjoyed her company, and desired her more than he had ever desired a woman. He dared not call it love.

Love meant commitment. Love meant marriage and children. Love of Ella meant that he could not possibly give her to Harold Carson, he could not collect his pay, and he could not help his family. He closed his eyes and tried to convince himself that Rose was wrong, that she had just misread the depth of his feelings for Ella.

Chapter Twelve

"Where the hell are we?" Ella asked in rising panic as she started to sit up in the bed.

Harrigan quickly pulled her back down, retucked the worn blanket around her, and tugged her back into his arms. "Hush, you'll wake the Lindons."

"The who?" Ella warily looked around the small, roughly plastered room.

"The Lindons. You were very unsteady yesterday, the day after the big storm. I didn't realize just how unsteady until you nearly fell off Polly's back. I set you in front of me and brought you to the first house I could find. The Lindons graciously took us in, Mrs. Lindon helping me tend to you, and even gave us their bedroom to sleep in."

"I don't recall any of that." She frowned and cautiously stretched, feeling only slightly weakened. "I couldn't have been too sick as I don't feel very bad now."

"I believe it was mostly exhaustion that felled you. You have slept soundly for almost fourteen hours and that doesn't include all the time you slept while we traveled here."

"I've never slept that long," she whispered, her voice weakened by shock.

"You've never been so exhausted before."

She frowned as she considered the matter and decided he was probably right. Even in her flight from Philadelphia she had not been subjected to such continuous strenuous activity. She had gone by train, eaten well, and occasionally enjoyed a comfortable night in a hotel. For a brief moment, Ella was disgusted by what she saw as weakness, then told herself not to be such a fool. What she and Harrigan had been doing required a little hardening. It was not something one just up and decided to do. She could hardly be blamed for not preparing herself to ride across the country on horseback.

Concerns about her stamina or lack thereof were quickly pushed aside by other questions. She suddenly realized that she and Harrigan were sharing a bed in someone's house. This was not a hotel where their scandalous behavior would go mostly unnoticed. Beyond the battered door of the room were the Lindons. She did not know who they were, could not even remember meeting them, but she could not believe they would allow a couple to climb into bed together if they were not married. Ella was suddenly afraid that Harrigan had slipped into the room unseen and an embarrassing confrontation with the inhabitants of the house was imminent.

"I think you had better go now," she whispered. "It's almost dawn. Someone will be stirring soon."

"Don't worry. They know I'm in here." Harrigan grinned at her look of horror, then decided to put her at ease. "Ella, the Lindons think we're married." He felt sure that neither Rose nor Willie would let their suspicions become known, so there was no need to tell Ella about them.

"They think what?"

"That you and I are man and wife."

"You lied to people who were kind enough to shelter us?"

He grimaced, for that still troubled him a little. "Not exactly."

"Harrigan, they think we're married. We're not. So, you had to have lied to them."

"When I knocked on their door, Willie Lindon asked if my wife was sick. I just didn't disagree with him."

Ella rolled her eyes. "Well, we have to tell them the truth."

"Go right ahead," he said, hoping she didn't take him up on the dare. "Go on out there and tell that kindly couple that the man you have just spent the night with in their only bed is not your husband."

She blinked, then muttered a curse, but was not ready to fall in with his lies that easily. "I could remind them that I was in no position to argue with you or what you let them think."

"And what happens if that isn't good enough?"

"I think you're giving me the headache."

It wasn't easy, but Ella ignored his soft laughter as she tried to decide what to do. She was thoroughly disgusted when she finally had to concede that the best thing to do was to play along with his lie. Although she had no real qualms about being Harrigan's lover, she didn't really want the world to know. There was always the chance that she could survive her battle with Harold, so it was wise to at least try to protect her good name.

It would be no secret that she had spent many long days riding the countryside, alone, with the man, but everything they had done so far was easily denied. She could act offended if her honor was impugned and no one could find any proof that she was not still as innocent as when she had left Philadelphia. All anyone could do now was whisper rumor, damaging enough, but able to be fought if she had a mind to do so. It would be no more than the kind of nonsense she and her aunt had been fighting for years. The Lindons, however, had undoubtedly seen her in bed with Harrigan, as she knew she had not undressed herself or put herself to bed. She also knew it was not only her good name she sought to protect. Since Harrigan had shown no inclination to be any more than a temporary lover, she really did not want people to find any proof that she had been such a fool as to bed down with one of Harold's hirelings.

"Fine then. Have it your way," she finally said. "I don't like it at all, but I think the truth would cause more trouble than the lie at the moment."

"Such a gracious concession."

"So I'm not a good loser. Arrest me. Now tell me what other lies you've told them, and don't try to deny that there are some. You would have to tell a few just to support the first one."

He sighed and nodded, then proceeded to tell her everything he had said to the Lindons. "I tried to keep it as simple as possible."

"I'm impressed." She wasn't sure she liked knowing how skilled he could be at weaving tales. "Don't look so concerned. I won't march out there and tell them that you're a kidnapper."

Harrigan prepared to complain about how she and Louise insisted on calling him a kidnapper, but then Ella yawned. He suddenly noticed that she was still somewhat pale and her eyelids were still heavy. The fact that she had woken up and had a long, rational conversation with him eased a lot of his concerns about her health, but he realized that she was not fully recovered yet.

"Go back to sleep, Ella," he ordered softly.

"After so much sleep, how can I still be so tired?" she asked even as she closed her eyes.

"It takes a while to recoup your strength when you've used it all up."

He waited until he was sure she was asleep and then slipped out of bed and got dressed. The Lindons were moving around in the other room and he wanted to give Willie a hand with the chores. It was a small repayment for their kindness and, he confessed, a salve for the guilt he felt about lying to them.

* * *

Ella cautiously opened the door of the bedroom. She was not sure how long she had slept after she and Harrigan had talked, but one peek out of the window revealed that the sun was high in the sky, hinting that it was at least the middle of the day. For a little while she had lingered over dressing herself, nervous about confronting her hosts. Finally she could not tolerate sitting by herself. She just prayed that she had the ability to hold up Harrigan's lies and that the Lindons did not ask any pressing questions.

As she stepped into the big room that made up the rest of the cabin she caught sight of a plump brunette scrubbing a long plank table. She nervously cleared her throat. The smile the woman gave her was so open and friendly, Ella relaxed a little even as she felt a pinch of guilt. It seemed a real shame to lie to such a woman.

"I'm Rose," the woman said as she hurried over, put an arm around Ella's waist, and urged her toward a rocking chair set before a huge stone fireplace. "You just make yourself comfortable over here."

"I'm fine, really," Ella protested, even as she sat down. "I have had more than enough sleep."

"And that's good," Rose agreed as she slapped a lump of dough on the table and began to knead it. "Your color is much improved. However, you shouldn't try to do anything today."

"I really do feel quite hale."

"It's still more false strength than a true healing. When a body gets so worn out it forces you to fall asleep even though you're on a horse, it's sending you a mighty powerful message. Heed it. Better to sit and rest now than to get a few miles down the road and feel all weak again."

"I just feel that I ought to be helping you. You've done so much for us."

"Your man is outside helping Willie do his chores. You know, some of those things that require an extra pair of hands to do properly. He'll be doing us a great service by helping my Willie do some much-needed repairs."

The thought of Harrigan doing hard, menial work was intriguing, and Ella wished she could slip outside to have a peek. "I'm not sure how much help Harrigan will be. He's no homesteader."

"He can't be doing too badly. I've been outside once or twice and didn't here any cussing, so things must be going smoothly enough."

"There must be a few things that you need to have done."

"Not truly, but, if you begin to look as if you want to pull out your hair from boredom, I might have some darning you can do."

Ella smiled faintly. "I do have some skill with a needle, if you'll pardon my boasting."

"If we don't occasionally boast about our housewifery skills, who will?" She exchanged a brief grin with Ella then put the dough back into the bowl and covered it. "Now, I'll get you something to eat."

"There's no need to trouble yourself. I'm not really very hungry."

"It's no trouble. Just some bread and cheese. Simple, soothing, and filling," Rose said even as she cut some bread and cheese and put it on a plate. "Food is as important as sleep to build up your strength. And, while you eat, we can talk about those things your man knows so little about."

As she accepted the plate of food, Ella watched Rose a little warily, not quite sure what the woman referred to. "Such as what?"

"Female things." Rose pulled up a stool, grabbed a bowl of potatoes, a bowl to catch the peelings, and a sharp knife, and then sat down facing Ella. "Fashions, scandals, all that sort of thing."

"I'm not sure how much I can tell you, as I've been living in the wilds of Wyoming for almost three years. It's been a long while since I sipped tea and gossiped with the ladies in Philadelphia."

"Something I've never done. I don't care how old the news is. I'm just powerful eager to hear some."

Ella laughed softly. In between bites of the tangy cheese and thick bread, she told an avidly listening Rose everything she could think of about fashion, manners, and society. They shared a few chuckles over some old scandals and a couple Ella recalled left Rose wide-eyed and gaping. Rose finally allowed Ella to shuck some peas as she told the woman about the theater. It was while they were giggling over the foibles of the fashionable at the theater that Harrigan and Willie arrived.

The speed with which Rose had some food on the table astounded Ella, then she realized that they had been preparing the evening meal, not the midday one. Rose had fixed the hearty meal she now served the men much earlier and had simply kept it aside until they left their work long enough to eat it. It was what she and Louise had done back at the ranch, but her mind had been so consumed with thoughts of Harrigan and her guardian for so long, she had nearly forgotten about such simple, everyday events. As she walked to the table to sit next to Harrigan, Ella suddenly and fiercely missed the uncomplicated life she had been leading at Louise's ranch.

Harrigan watched Ella closely as she ate. He was briefly concerned over how little she consumed, but then Rose assured him that Ella had already had a plate full of bread and cheese. He finished his meal and rejoined Willie at his work, confident that Ella was in good hands. That confidence grew even stronger when he returned at the end of the day to enjoy a hearty supper, and found Ella quietly sewing. A little smile curved the corners of his mouth, for he knew she must be finding such enforced rest galling. She looked as if her strength had fully returned, and she undoubtedly wanted to do more than Rose was allowing her to.

"You look much better," he said as he walked over to where she sat and bent to kiss her cheek.

"Strong enough to beat you back to Wyoming," she whispered, smiling sweetly at him.

"I can see that there is some advantage to your being so exhausted you can neither think nor speak."

"Many regrets, sir, but I have returned to my endearing old self."

"Well, bring your sweet little self over to the table and have something to eat."

"I am not sure I can," she said softly as he tugged her to her feet and led her over to the table. "Rose has been feeding me all day long."

Harrigan laughed softly, set her down at the table, and filled her plate. Throughout the meal she cast him surreptitious looks of irritation, but he just continued to smile at her in what she obviously considered an annoyingly doting manner. As soon as the meal was over, he retired to the porch with Willie, bracing himself for another drink of the man's brew as he went.

Ella tried to help Rose clear away the remnants of the meal, but was politely and firmly pushed aside. She was beginning to feel more irritated than grateful even though she knew that was unfair. When Harrigan returned, she was delighted to see him, but it was a fleeting pleasure. There was a slight flush to his cheeks and a glitter in his eyes. Ella grew a little suspicious as he approached her. When he leaned close to her, she grimaced, smelling the liquor on his breath.

"Are you drunk?" she asked.

"That's a distinct possibility," he replied carefully. "Willie's homebrew is heady stuff, but I couldn't think of a polite way to refuse."

"Perhaps you should have discreetly poured it over the porch rail when he wasn't looking."

"He'd know. I think it'd kill the grass." He smiled crookedly when she giggled. "Are you strong enough to take a little stroll? I could use a walk to try and work this brew out of my system and I thought you might need one to calm yourself enough to go to sleep."

She did not hesitate, standing right up, and hooking her arm through his. A quick peek around the room revealed that they were alone, that Rose had already slipped away to sit with her husband. A well-taught sense of courtesy made her pause, however.

"Don't you think we ought to stay and visit with our hosts?" she asked as he led her out the back door of the cabin.

"They know where we're going. They even suggested that we take a walk. Rose thought it would be good for you. She said you were beginning to look itchy and might not be able to go to sleep. Willie told me about a pretty little water hole just on the other side of those trees."

Ella smiled faintly at the careful way he walked. She knew it was not done solely out of consideration for her. He was getting better, the fumes of Willie's homebrew obviously clearing out of his head, but he was still a little unsteady.

The moment they stepped through to the other side of the trees, Ella abruptly halted, stilled by the beauty of the place. There was a creek running down the rock-strewn hillside and that created a small waterfall. The trees, grass, and shrubs grew lushly all around the water's edge. A full moon added a soft glow to the little glade and an inviting sparkle to the water. She released Harrigan's arm and skipped down the hillside to the water's edge.

"What are you doing?" Harrigan asked as he sat on the soft grass and watched her carefully inspect the area.

"Just checking for snakes." She laughed at the way he hastily looked all around him. "You aren't fond of snakes, are you?"

"Is anybody?" he muttered. "Well, if it's safe, you can come and sit down next to me now."

"Nope. I intend to enjoy this water."

Ella was not sure what had suddenly possessed her. It could have been the haunting romantic air of the glade, or the fact that she was full of energy after such a long rest, but she felt alive, sensual, and daring. She wanted

Harrigan to make love to her. Even more, she wanted to enflame him. Dozens of exciting possibilities sprang to mind and she was a little surprised at the boldness of some of them. Casting Harrigan a faintly taunting look she began to undo her gown.

"You're going to have a swim?" he asked.

"Yes. It looks lovely and cool and very clear."

"That's nice, but you've been ill."

"Not ill, tired." She wiggled out of her gown and placed it carefully on the grass, then tugged off her shoes. "I've slept for a day or so and have done little more than sit in a chair for a whole day more. I don't believe a little paddle in the water will do me any harm." Setting her foot up on one of the many rocks littering the banks, she slowly unrolled her stockings, knowing that Harrigan was watching her and finding that very exciting.

Harrigan drew in a slow, unsteady breath as he watched Ella take the pins from her hair and let it tumble free down her slim back. "If you want to take a swim, fine, do so, but I think you ought to be a little more careful. You're tempting fate with the way you're carrying on."

Ella kept her back to him as she undid her camisole. She slipped it off, held it out to the side, and let it drop onto the pile of her clothes. Her heart pounding, she tugged off her pantaloons, savoring the feel of the cool night air on her body.

"Tempting fate, am I? I had rather hoped that I was tempting you."

She heard Harrigan stand up and walk to the edge of the pool even as she eased her body into the almost too chilly water. Keeping her body submerged, she turned to look at him, knowing full well that her modesty was only partly preserved by the clear, moonlit water. Ella found it a little amusing that she could want him so badly, so quickly, when he had not even kissed her yet. Passion, she decided, was a very curious thing and apparently had a mind of its own.

"I'm trying to figure out if you're playing some game," he said, his voice thick and husky.

"I might be," she replied, smiling faintly at her own vagaries. "I'm not sure why, but when we arrived here, I looked at this place and decided there was something I wanted to do. Odd, but I felt almost compelled to do it."

"What? Swim?"

"No. Enflame you."

"Oh, you've more than succeeded at that."

"Have I? Then why are you still dressed?"

She giggled when he began to shed his clothes with a speed that threatened to damage them. Within seconds he was in the water and pulling her into his arms. She sighed with pleasure as their flesh met and, curling her arms around his neck, she kissed him, meeting the ferocity of his kiss with one of her own.

Ella slid her hands down his sleek body to intimately stroke him, finding him hard and eager despite the chill of the water. She realized that she wanted him now, that she needed no kisses or caresses. Simply undressing in front of him and thinking about making love had stirred her passion to the point where she did not wish to waste any time. She wanted to be one with him immediately.

"Ella," Harrigan gasped as he tore his mouth free of hers and began to kiss the rapid pulse point in her neck. "What the hell has gotten into you?"

Using her arms around his neck for leverage, she jumped up and wrapped her legs around his waist. "Damned if I know, but I think it might be one of those times when talking about something could ruin it." She shuddered as he slid his hands down to gently clutch her backside and rubbed her against him.

"Now?" he asked, his hoarse voice holding both a demand and surprise.

"Yes, now," she whispered and cried out with pleasure as he lowered her down on him, the feel of him entering her enough to bring on a blinding release of her mindless desire. She was faintly aware of how quickly he joined her in the sweet depths of passion.

Ella murmured with a lingering pleasure as Harrigan laid her down in the soft grass and held her close. They were both still breathing heavily and she smiled with a mixture of delight and surprise. She rubbed her cheek against his smooth damp chest and trailed her fingers up and down his thigh. There had to be something in the air of the little glade, for she was still feeling very hungry for him, and very daring. Hot, fast, and furious was very nice, but now she wanted slow, gentle, and lingering.

She sat up, picked up her camisole, and used it to lightly rub dry her hair. Her nudity only bothered her for a second. Harrigan had made it very clear that he enjoyed looking at her, and tonight she felt inclined to let him look his fill. She idly wondered if it was the soft touch of moonlight that made her feel beautiful enough to be so brazen.

He sat up behind her and gently covered her breasts with his hands. Ella leaned back against him and watched as he used his fingers to tease the tips of her breasts until they were taut and aching. She offered no resistance as he turned her to face him. When he lowered his mouth to lathe and suckle her breasts, she curled her fingers in his thick, damp hair and held him there, wishing she had the strength to linger at that precise stage of her passion. It felt so good she wanted to enjoy it for hours, but knew that was impossible.

When he started to trail kisses down to her midriff, she knew what he was planning to do. Scandalous though it was, she liked it, and it was an effort to gently stop him, tugging his face up to hers so that she could kiss him. He had given her that pleasure several times and she decided it was time she returned the favor.

The moment she ended the kiss, she began to move her mouth down his body. She licked and nipped her way down his chest, the taste of him, the feel of his warm skin beneath her lips, heating her blood. He threaded his hands in her hair as she moved to kneel in front of him, caressing every inch of his strong thighs with her mouth and her hands. When she touched her mouth to the tip of his erection the groan that escaped him startled her. Fearing she had erred, she started to pull away, but he pulled her back.

Harrigan closed his eyes and shuddered as her tongue stroked him. He sought the strength to enjoy the pleasure she was giving him, but it was so intense he knew he could not last for long. When she enclosed him in the moist heat of her mouth, he doubted he could last longer than a heartbeat or two.

Knowing he had to cool his blood a little or he would not be able to give her any return for the delight she had gifted him with, he pulled her away even as he fell back onto the grass. He tugged her on top of him, gritting his teeth when she straddled him and lightly rubbed herself against him. With her passionate nature running wild and free, Ella was almost more than he could handle.

Harrigan felt his competitive nature flicker to life a small voice in his head scolding him for letting her rule in passion's game. It was obvious that Ella was taking great pleasure in driving him mad, and he decided to steal a little of that for himself. Slowly he eased her further up his body until he had free access to her firm, ivory breasts.

Delicious,'' he murmured as he licked each hardened tip.

Ella shivered and tried to move against him, but he held her by her hips, keeping a little distance between their bodies. "Harrigan, I thought—''

He nuzzled his face against her breasts. "God, you even smell like roses. And I begin to believe that you have been doing a little too much thinking.''

"I have?'' She gasped when he drew the tip of her breast deep into his mouth and pulled on it in a slow, rhythmic manner as if they had all the time in the world. "Maybe I have, but I don't think I can do much more of this."

"Well, we'll just have to see, won't we."

Her soft gasp of pleasure as he turned his attention to her other breast was like a caress to his ears. He took his time and savored the freedom she was allowing him, using his hands and his mouth to stir her, pausing between each leisurely caress to view the results of his handiwork. His body began to protest his meandering, and he edged her up a little further, turning his attentions to the smooth skin of her stomach.

It was not until he touched a kiss to her navel that he felt the first hint of resistance. He ignored it, pulling her that last inch forward. She tried to pull back, to close herself to his look and his touch, but he would not allow it.

The feel of Harrigan's mouth on the inside of her thigh stole away Ella's hesitancy. The only tension she felt was her body's anticipation of what he would do next, its aching eagerness for the intimate kiss he was about to give her. She breathed her acceptance when his lips touched her, opening to him in eager welcome at the first slow stroke of his tongue. Ella allowed him complete freedom, not caring what he did so long as the exquisite feelings racing through her body continued.

He kept her teetering on the edge of release and she both cursed and blessed him. Finally, she knew even his skill could not forestall the need of her body any longer and she called to him. He suddenly pulled her down his body, sitting up as he did so. Ella gasped with the sharp pleasure that tore through her as he joined their bodies. He leaned her back and slowly took one nipple deep into his mouth even as he began to move her body against his. Ella felt her insides explode as wave after wave of delight ripped through her. Even as she sank beneath the weight of her own desires, she felt him press her down tightly against him as he cried out her name and greedily accepted the warmth of his release as it poured into her body.

When Harrigan finally eased out of her arms, Ella shivered from the chill of his absence. She hurried to the edge of the water, cleaned up, and began to put her clothes on. A quick glance at Harrigan revealed that he was also getting dressed. It was as if they had both decided at the same time that the magic of the glade had fled.

"Rose and Willie will wonder what's happened to us," she said as she finished buttoning her gown and began to pin up her hair.

"I think they know exactly what this place can do to a person," Harrigan said, and smiled faintly. "Willie had a little grin on his face when he told me how to get here." He laughed when she frowned, then blushed. "Don't look so concerned. They'll be asleep by the time we return. We can sneak into the bedroom by the window. I opened it before we left, thinking to let some of the cool night air in."

"Creeping to bed like sneaky children," she murmured as he took her by the hand and started to walk toward the house.

"I would prefer to curl up on that soft grass and sleep right there, but I don't think it'd be good for you. And you need your rest, because we have to get an early start in the morning." He inwardly cursed when he felt her steps falter slightly, knowing he had destroyed the last lingering pleasure of the glade, and wishing he had found another way to tell her they would be leaving in the morning.

"Back on the trail to Philadelphia?"

"Yes."

Ella took a deep breath and fought down the urge to rail at him. He had never faltered in his determination to do the job he'd been hired to do. A few special moments in a moonlit glade could not change his mind. She told herself to savor those moments, that they would make a very pleasurable memory, and then inwardly sighed. Memories were nice, but she knew she was going to spend many a night wishing she had the man instead.

Chapter Thirteen

"Please say there's a town just up ahead and that you intend to stop in this one," Ella said, afraid she had not kept all hint of a whine out of her voice.

Although Harrigan had been taking it very slow since leaving the Lindons, stopping for plenty of rest periods, it had been three long days on horseback and she wanted a few extra comforts. If nothing else, it would break the monotony. Riding mile after mile after mile had to be the most boring thing she had ever done. Since they were not racing across the country like pony express riders, they were crossing a certain area for a couple of days at a time, which meant she saw far too much monotonous scenery.

The only change there had been in day after day of grasslands was the sighting of the mountains that loomed just ahead of them. They made a change, but they were not a welcome sight. She knew they were the last barrier to Philadelphia.

She and Harrigan still did not talk about Harold and Philadelphia, but that little game was getting harder and harder to play now that they could see the mountains. At times she had the urge to shake him until his teeth rattled, but even if she found the strength to do it, it would not change his mind. What annoyed and hurt her more now was that he also knew their time together was severely limited, yet he said and did nothing. There was still no hint of anything more than passion from the man. She knew that, if it was not a case of cutting off her own nose to spite her face, she would stop giving in to her desires and let him finish the ride to Philadelphia gaining nothing more than cold silence from her. Ella knew that the minute he handed her to Harold she would have more cold silence than she wanted and it would last for the rest of her life.

"We should ride into a town by evening," he answered, breaking into her dark thoughts. "I did think I would try one last time to spend a comfortable night in a hotel."

"There should be a fairly good one in the next town because we're getting closer and closer to established areas of settlement, older towns with far more amenities."

She watched him closely to see if he had any reaction to her reminder that they drew near to their final destination. There was only a faint tightening of his features. It was not an easy expression to read. He could be feeling as downcast as she was or simply fearing that she was about to break her promise and start to plague him about Harold again. She sighed and firmly told herself to stop trying to guess what he was feeling. It was impossible.

They approached the town cautiously and Ella knew Harrigan was looking for her aunt. She was able to find a small touch of amusement in the fact that a big, strong man like Harrigan was going in fear of her tiny aunt. It also showed her that he feared she could succeed in rescuing Ella and that raised Ella's hopes a little. After all, if Harrigan believed it was possible, why shouldn't she?

They stabled their horses, but Harrigan did not begin to relax until they were secured in their hotel room. He ordered her a bath and then left to go to the barber's for a bath and a shave. Even though she knew it was a waste of time, Ella checked the door and window before she settled down to the business of enjoying a nice, hot, relaxing bath. Once she discovered that she was securely locked in her room, she knew there would also be a boy or two watching the hotel from the outside and she saw no point in wasting valuable time and energy trying to find an escape route that did not exist.

While her bath was being prepared, she stared out the window. To her utter dismay, the mountains were clearly visible. For the duration of their stay in the hotel she would be reminded of how close they were to the end of her journey, and, whether Harrigan chose to believe it or not, the possible end of her life. She shook away a sudden chill and hastily climbed into her bath the moment the maid left the room. If she had to, she would close the curtains. Harrigan and she did not have many nights left together and she did not want a view of the mountains to spoil them.

Harrigan took one last check of his face, decided the barber had done an excellent job, and paid the man more than he had asked. A hot bath, clean clothes, and a good shave had put him in a very good humor. He strolled back to the hotel, paid the boy who had been standing guard, and then lit a cigar.

As he slowly breathed out the rich smoke of the cigar, he caught himself carefully surveying the street again and cursed. He was beginning to see Ella's aunt around every corner. If anyone found out how hard he was trying to elude one tiny woman, how constantly he watched for her, and how fast he ran from her, he could easily become the object of ridicule. The woman had the distressing habit of popping up where and when one least expected her.

Harrigan found himself wondering what George's fascination with Louise stemmed from. George was a quiet, controlled, steady, level-headed man. Louise seemed to be all emotion. George always spoke precisely and softly. Louise said whatever popped into her head and often said it very loudly. If he had been presented with a dozen young

women, including Louise, and told to pick a match for
George, Harrigan would never have chosen Louise Carson.
George, however, had been immediately and forcefully
struck by the woman, unable to get her out of his mind
from the moment he saw her. Harrigan could not see how
it could work out for George, but he did wish the man the
best of luck.

He rather envied George, even though the man might
not get the future he craved with Louise. George knew
what he wanted and had no doubts, no fears, no complications. In fact, the only hindrance George suffered from
was the one created by Harrigan. As he ground the cigar
butt beneath the heel of his boot, Harrigan dearly wished
that his life was so simple.

"There he is," Joshua whispered as he peered around
the corner of the saloon and watched Harrigan put out
his cigar. "You have some luck, Louise. You find the fool
every time you step off the train."

"But I don't catch him, do I?" Louise frowned when
George peered around her to look at Harrigan. "You better not warn him. I still have that gag."

"I gave my word that I would not help him," George
said.

"No need to puff up with insult. I was just reminding
you." She frowned again, lightly rubbing her hand over
her chin as she watched Harrigan enter the hotel. "At
least he hasn't seen us this time. I was starting to fret about
that. Thought I had lost my touch." She grinned when
Joshua laughed softly.

"Never, m'dear," Joshua drawled. "No one can be as
sneaky as you are."

"I suppose I'm to take that as a compliment. The best
way to go about this may be to seek Harrigan out in his
hotel room. We'll just go to his door, knock on it, and
grab him when he opens it."

"That's your best idea?" Joshua shook his head. "Why,

that's almost as clever as sticking your foot in front of a train."

"It could work."

"There are a few dozen people in that hotel. We'll be seen and they'll probably call in the law. You know they always think me and the boys are just coming to steal things or cause trouble. I doubt they'll even let us start up the stairs before someone begins screaming for the sheriff."

"I know it may be tricky." She ignored Joshua's scornful laugh. "I do, however, believe it holds the best chance for success. Every time we've tried to grab him out in the open, he's gotten away. This time, if we can catch him inside of that room, we can corner him. Where can he go? Out the window?"

"How do we find out what room he is in?" asked Manuel, standing behind the much shorter George and peering over the man's head.

"I already know," replied Louise, pointing to the middle window on the second floor. "I've seen Ella in the window several times already. She was probably trying to see just how trapped she was."

"She could just be looking for Harrigan to return," George murmured, smiling faintly when Louise whirled around to glare at him. "It was just a thought."

"You're treading on dangerous ground, George," Louise warned him.

He shrugged. "Merely a suggestion."

"Well, keep that kind of suggestion to yourself. Now, Manuel, you can stay here with this fool."

"I've said that I will neither help nor warn Harrigan."

"Yes, for as long as you're my prisoner. If I leave you alone, you could easily desert our little camp. Once you're back with Harrigan, you don't have to hold to that promise any longer."

"I would never desert you, Louise," George said softly, smiling briefly when the four young men laughed.

Louise blushed, glared at all five men, and turned back toward the hotel. "It seems I've finally found a use for

you, George. We failed in trying to make a trade of you
for Ella. But, by keeping you with us, we deprive Harrigan
of your assistance. It's a lot easier to corral one stallion
than two."

"You've not had much success in corralling that particular stallion."

"Oh, shut your mouth."

"When are we going in?" asked Edward. "We might as
well do it now, don't you think?"

"No. Harrigan will be getting them a dinner soon. Let
the poor girl have something decent to eat first. When I
think they have had enough time to eat, I'll go in and
charm the room number out of the desk clerk. Joshua,
while I have him distracted, you, Edward, and Thomas slip
up the stairs. I'll join you as soon as I can and then we'll
finally get that scoundrel."

"You dismissed the boy early tonight," Ella said as Harrigan entered their room and locked the door.

Harrigan eyed her a little warily. "So you know about
the boys, huh?"

"Of course I do. You didn't think I would just sit here
all sweet and complacent when you left me alone, did you?
I checked and rechecked every possible means of escape.
I noticed the boys the first time you hired them."

"I thought it would give me and George a little rest from
time to time. Now that George is gone, it's a necessity."

"This little trip is costing you a lot of money."

He cast her a mildly disgusted look as he hung up his
hat and coat. "No need to look so pleased with that. I was
given money before I left to defray my expenses. At the
time I thought it was far too much, but saw no point in
correcting the man's assumption about travel expenses.
The rich travel differently. I decided it wouldn't hurt to
benefit from that a little."

Ella could not help herself, and she giggled. "You tiptoe
so carefully around that name."

"Well, we agreed not to talk about him."

"I hadn't realized that meant we could not even say his name."

"Supper's here," Harrigan said when there was a soft rap at the door.

He was glad of the diversion. It was suddenly uncomfortable to even think about Harold and Philadelphia. Harrigan did not want Ella to know that.

As he set their food on the table, he idly glanced out of the window and inwardly winced. The sight of the mountains had been troubling him since they had first appeared on the horizon. He did not like the idea that he would have to see them every time he looked out of the window.

It struck him as very contrary to work so hard to take Ella to a place he did not even want to think about. The closer they had drawn to Philadelphia and Harold the harder he had worked to keep both the place and the man out of his thoughts. Deep down he was very troubled by what he was doing, yet he saw no way to get off of the path he was treading. It was childish just to ignore it all, to push it all out of his mind, but he began to think it was the only way to keep his sanity.

"It feels a little odd to be sitting here having a quiet meal," Ella murmured in between bites of hot, buttered carrots.

"We have had one or two before this," Harrigan replied before taking a drink of his beer.

"Only in the beginning and at the Lindons. Every other time we stopped in a town my aunt appeared." She was a little surprised when Harrigan laughed. "You think that's funny?"

"It is. I was standing outside enjoying a cigar and realized that I was looking all around for Louise. She looms large for such a tiny woman." He was relieved to see Ella smile.

"Louise is a very determined woman and she loathes that man whose name we can't say."

"That's been clear from the beginning. What amused me a little was what others would think if they knew how hard I was working to avoid her. They would look at Louise, a delicate, pretty little woman, then look at me, and laugh heartily. I could almost hear the ridicule.''

"If it happens, just find some way to set my aunt on their trail and they won't be laughing for long. Most of the townsmen near her ranch go softly around her. When I first went to live with her, I did think she rather overdid the tough and sassy woman role, but I soon saw that it was necessary. The men out there do not like a woman owning land and ranching. That's a man's job. That she does it well only annoys them all the more.''

"Is that why she has such a mixed group of workers?''

"Very politely said,'' Ella murmured, and silently toasted him with her glass of lemonade before taking a sip. "Half-breeds and outcasts is what everyone else calls them. It is true that Auntie had trouble getting any of the white men to work for her. They wanted her to fail. Anytime a man considered accepting a job at her ranch, he was quickly discouraged. Then she rescued Joshua.''

"Rescued him?''

"Yes. He was beaten badly by a group of cowhands and left in the road just outside of town. Seems he had the audacity to ask for a job. Auntie found him when she was returning from getting some supplies. She took him home, healed his injuries, and offered him a job. She now has twelve young men working for her and only two are what most people would consider white men. They're bastards, and their mothers were whores. People seem to think they're somehow responsible for the bad behavior of their parents, or that they'll act the same way.''

"And they're all incredibly loyal to her, correct?''

"Correct, but that's not just because she helped them in some way. She didn't spit on them, didn't treat them like they were dirt, or as if she was doing them a big favor by letting them clean the muck from her stables. She treated them all like equals. It was a new thing for most of them and they've decided that they like it.''

Harrigan nodded. "That's something I can easily understand. The Irish were not welcomed with open arms when they arrived by the boatload. It's gotten a little better, but the prejudice isn't completely gone.''

"Auntie's boys, as they are not so affectionately called, see her as their mother, their aunt, their sister, even their guardian angel. She's the family they've never had or lost at too young an age.''

"And Joshua is the smart-mouthed child.'' He smiled when Ella laughed.

"He does feel a little responsible for her.'' She caught him glancing out the window at the mountains and wondered if they affected him in the same way they did her. "It won't be long now before you're home.''

She smiled faintly at the quick, guilty look he gave her. Although she knew it was a mistake to do so, she tried to guess what he was feeling about the rapidly approaching end of their journey. The possibilities were wide-ranging and few of them were comforting or encouraging. Harrigan could simply be eager to get back to Philadelphia, back to his work, and his family. A little voice told her not to do it, that she could be asking for additional hurt, something she did not need, but Ella decided to try and get some hint about his feelings from him.

"You don't look exactly pleased to see those mountains.''

"Ella,'' he said, a warning note in his voice, because an answer to her statement would bring them dangerously close to the very kind of discussion they had agreed they would not have.

"It was just a simple observation.''

"Sometimes I wonder if you ever say anything simple.'' He pushed aside his plate, sighed, and dragged his fingers through his hair. "If we start talking about how close we are to home—''

"Not my home.''

He ignored that and doggedly continued, ''—we will be edging very close to that topic we said we wouldn't talk about any more.''

"We'll be face to face with that *topic* in just a few days. We've reached the point where we don't even dare to say the man's name. Maybe it's time to stop that game. It seems clear to me that, even though we do not talk about it, it's on our minds a lot. And the moment those damned mountains came into view, it began to weigh more and more heavily on our minds."

"I don't know what you want me to say. In truth, I can't think that you'd really want to hear anything I have to say about how near the end of the journey we are, about Philadelphia, or Harold. You won't agree with me and I can't afford to agree with you. So, what's the point of talking about any of it?"

"Probably none, but I think I'm just tired of trying to pretend the whole mess is not hanging over our heads like a big, black rain cloud."

Harrigan nodded, a somewhat bitter laugh escaping him. "I've felt like that too. Perhaps I'm just afraid of hurting your feelings."

"I think we're far past the point where that can be avoided," she said quietly, then briefly feared that she might have revealed too much about the state of her heart.

"Yes, seeing the mountains bothers me. Knowing that we only have a few days left before we ride into Philadelphia also bothers me. And I am damn well not looking forward to seeing Harold Carson."

"And the part of all that which you fear will trouble me is that you still intend to do it all, to cross the mountains, go to Philadelphia, and see Harold."

"Well, doesn't it?"

"Of course it does. You've known from the start that I don't want to go to him and why I don't. My aunt is taking time away from her ranch at the busiest time of the year and spending a small fortune to come after us and stop you. I would praise God for one good chance to get away." She shook her head. "That's been the way of it from the very first minute, so, how can talking about what you feel now make any difference at all?"

"It can't make anything better, true enough, but it could make it all worse."

Before she could say anything, there was a sharp rap at the door. The look of blatant relief on Harrigan's face was almost amusing. He leapt up to answer the knock so quickly he nearly knocked over his chair.

"You're having some very opportune interruptions today," she said as she watched him go to the door.

Harrigan did not bother to reply to her gentle sarcasm. He started to remove the door chain, then hesitated and wondered why. Recalling how badly things had gone the last few times he had ignored a sudden uneasiness, he left the heavy chain on and eased the door open. A harsh curse escaped him when he saw who was in the hall and he hastily slammed the door shut.

Chapter Fourteen

"What's the matter?" Ella demanded when Harrigan began dragging the dresser in front of the door.

"This interruption is not as opportune as I had thought," he replied as he began to throw their things in their bags.

"Open this damned door, Harrigan," yelled an angry female voice as the door shook beneath the pounding it began to receive from outside.

"Auntie!"

Harrigan quickly caught Ella as she ran to the door. Although she fought him, he managed to get the wrist shackles on her. Ella stared at the shackles then at him and Harrigan felt like the very worst of scoundrels.

"We're getting out of here now," he said sharply, more angry with himself than with her or the persistent Louise.

"There's nowhere to go."

He started to tell her what he planned to do, then realized that would be stupid. Ella could tell her aunt and, unless he gagged her, he would be hard put to stop her. He began to drag her toward a door that connected the room they were in with the room next door. When he had first asked for connecting rooms, his main thought had been to give Ella's much-damaged reputation some protection. Now he was grateful for that brief moment of chivalry.

It did not surprise him to hear Ella curse him as he unlocked the door to the other room. He knew she was wondering what else she might have done while she was alone if she had known about the second room. One sharp look and a brief touch of his handkerchief was enough to make her keep her mouth closed. He did not want to gag her and he was very glad that she understood his silent threat, that she obviously did not want to be gagged.

Once inside the other room, Harrigan crept toward the door. Even as he pulled out the key, he looked at Ella and sighed. He might not want to do it and she was going to hate it, but he was going to have to put a gag on her. There would be very little time for him to get out of the door and start running before Louise and her boys spotted him. One little sound from Ella and that tiny window of opportunity would be slammed shut and there was a look on her face that told him she was preparing herself to make that sound.

Ella's eyes widened when he pulled out his handkerchief and wrapped it around her head. She muttered a curse as he knotted it, tightening it so that it forced itself between her lips. It would not completely silence her, but she would not be able to make any clear, understandable noise. It was going to be really hard to forgive him for this, she decided as he slowly eased open the door.

Harrigan hesitated only long enough to grab their bags in one hand and her by the other before he bolted down the hallway. As he had feared, an outcry was raised by one of Louise's boys before he had even reached the top of the back stairs. Praying that Ella could keep her feet, he scrambled down the stairs and out the back door of the hotel. The workers in the kitchen were so startled they dropped a few things but no one got in his way.

Once outside, Harrigan ducked down a shadowy alley,

and quickly removed Ella's gag. "Are you going to be quiet or shall I put it back on?"

"When and if we get out of here, the first time we stop on the trail, I am going to make you eat that."

"Shall I take that as an agreement to behave yourself?" he asked, even as he began to lead her in and out of a tangled series of alleys and narrow passageways.

"Fine, I agree. It won't make any difference. This time you can't get away."

"I made a close study of this place while you were having your bath. I know it far better than Louise and her little gang. I think I've got a chance of slipping away from her." He glanced at her as he edged into a store, walked brazenly through and out the back. "And, if worse comes to worst, I will just sic the law on them."

Ella gasped, wondering if the man ever listened to a word she said, or if he was really so consumed with his need for the money Harold had promised him that he did not care what he did to get it. "You can't do that," she protested. "You know how people treat her and the others. It won't be just an inconvenience; it could be a real danger."

Although Harrigan did not like her to think that he was so heartless, at the moment it served a purpose. "Then you had better be a very good girl, hadn't you?"

For a while Ella just let him drag her from place to place, shove her in dark little corners, and pull her across open spaces so quickly she was in danger of tripping. She was not really sure if she was being quiet to save her aunt and the others, if she was just sulking over such ill-treatment, if she was struggling to decide how she felt, or all three. Being an uncooperative participant in the chase made it difficult for her to get a firm grip on her thoughts and feelings. It was not until Harrigan stopped at the corner of the saloon and peeked around the corner at the stables, just one building away, that she finally decided to push aside her confused feelings and concentrate on what was happening now.

"Auntie will have a guard on the horses," she said, and recognized the strong hint of gloating in her voice.

"I'm aware of that," he snapped, not really angry with her, but unable to completely suppress his annoyance over being forced to run yet again.

"I think you had better just give up," said a deep voice from right behind them.

Harrigan turned even as he drew his gun. He cursed when he saw Manuel standing next to a relaxed George. The youth had his gun out and Harrigan wondered how he was going to get himself out of this confrontation. He did not want to put George or Ella into any danger and he did not really want to hurt Manuel.

"Do you think you might lend a hand here, George?" Harrigan asked, wondering why his friend and partner was just standing there.

"I wish I could," George said, subtlely keeping his body between Manuel and Harrigan. "Unfortunately, Louise has extracted a promise from me and you know how I feel about promises. I'm not allowed to help or warn you."

"So you're just going to stand there and let the kid shoot me?"

"Ah, well, probably not. I didn't promise to let them hurt you."

"George, I think you've been out in the sun too long." Harrigan looked at Manuel and could see the uncertainty in the youth's eyes. He inwardly thanked the powers that be that he was not facing Joshua. "There's only one answer to this standoff," he said.

"And you have it, of course," drawled Manuel.

"We both just back off and go on with what we were doing before we met."

"Sounds like you're asking me to let you win again."

"No, just trying to forego some stupid tragedy. I don't want to hurt you and I sure as hell don't want any harm to come to George or Ella. If either of us makes a move they'll be caught in the middle."

"Oh, just shoot him, Manuel," snapped Ella.

"I'm truly devastated at this apparant lack of affection, Ella," Harrigan murmured, keeping a very close watch on Manuel and beginning to feel confident that the youth would just let him leave.

"Now you have to shoot him. Such nonsense deserves to bring a little pain."

"You won't get very far even if I let you go," Manuel said.

Sensing the youth's hesitation, Harrigan replied, "I know that. I suspect there's someone in the stable just waiting for me." The way Manuel furtively glanced toward the stable told Harrigan that he was right. "So, let him get me."

For one long tense moment, Harrigan waited as Manuel considered the situation. Each time he tried to step away from George, George suddenly appeared directly in front of him. The youth then looked toward Harrigan and Ella. Harrigan was not using Ella as a shield, but he could tell that Manuel was nervous about her even being there.

"Get out of here," he finally snapped. "I can't see how either of us can disarm the other one without someone getting hurt. Louise won't be happy that I let you go, but she would be real unhappy if Ella got hurt while you and I fought it out." He looked at George and smiled crookedly. "Begin to get the feeling that she wouldn't really want this slippery devil hurt, either."

After checking to be sure the way was clear, Harrigan began to back toward the stable. "You'll have to show me how you did that, George."

"Did what?" George asked with a blatantly feigned air of innocence.

"Kept moving without appearing to take a step."

"I'm not quite sure what you're talking about."

"Of course. Well, say hello to Louise and tell her I'll see her in Philadelphia."

"I think you'll be seeing her before that," said Manuel.

Harrigan just smiled, determined not to reveal his own uncertainties to the youth. With a firm grip on Ella, he made a dash for the rear of the stables. One swift peek inside revealed a pacing Thomas keeping a very close eyes on the horses. He edged back and looked at Ella.

"You'll stand right here, say nothing, and do nothing," he ordered her, watching her eyes narrow as she grew even more angry with him.

"You demand an awful lot of a prisoner," she said.

"I ask you to remember how much the law loves your aunt and her friends. If you leave or warn them, I'll go to the sheriff. They won't be able to get you out of town before the law is after them."

"Fine. Not a word, not a move. I'll be like a statue."

He knew that what she had not said was more important. He was going to pay dearly for this, for his threats and the faint possibility that he might have actually meant them. The rest of the journey to Philadelphia was going to be a long, cold one if he couldn't placate her.

Silently he crept into the stable, keeping close to the shadows. He sent up a silent prayer of thanks when Thomas began to roll a cigarette, all the youth's attention fixed on the chore. Hoping Thomas was one of those who was slow and meticulous, Harrigan slipped up behind him. Thomas seemed to sense his presence, but Harrigan was ready. When the youth turned toward him, Harrigan delivered one clean uppercut to the jaw, knocking the boy unconscious. He caught Thomas as he started to fall and gently laid the boy on the floor.

He went and collected Ella, who grimaced when she saw Thomas. "He's not dead, for God's sake," he grumbled as he pushed her toward their horses.

While Harrigan saddled the horses, Ella crouched next to the unconscious youth. She could tell at a glance that Harrigan had only knocked Thomas out, but she was still angry. Thomas and the others were only trying to save her life. They didn't deserve this kind of treatment.

Just as she was about to make her opinion of Harrigan's actions clear, he pulled her to her feet and tossed her on the back of the mare. She clutched the pommel of the saddle as Harrigan cautiously led them out of the stable. It didn't surprise her when, just as they entered the street, there was an outcry. Harrigan immediately spurred their horses into a gallop and headed toward the mountains. She decided it was far more important to hold on and stay in the saddle than to argue with the man. They could talk later.

"Damn it all to hell," Louise snapped, and she gave in to the childish urge to stamp her feet, only to stir up the dust on the street so badly that she coughed. "So much for my good luck," she said as Joshua moved to stand beside her.

"We almost had them," Joshua said in a weak attempt to console her.

"I am getting very tired of almosts."

"I suppose there's still no real point in getting our horses and chasing after him."

"None at all. Yet again, by the time they're off the train, saddled and ready, he'll have too big a lead. Also, there's now a wider choice of trails he can follow."

"True, but he would leave tracks to tell us which way he went."

"Somehow I don't think so."

"Sorry," Manuel said as he walked up to her, George ambling along beside him.

"It's not your fault," Louise said as they all moved out of the street.

Manuel grimaced. "It might be. Met up with him and Ella in the alley. I let him go. Just couldn't see how we could settle the standoff we had ourselves stuck in. He was aiming a gun at me and I was aiming one at him, but we really couldn't start shooting. Don't think I would've won a punching contest with him either."

"George," Louise said, eyeing the man suspiciously.

"He didn't help him or warn him," Manuel said in the man's defense.

"Didn't help you though, did he?"

"I didn't promise to do so, Louise," George said quietly.

"Oh, you are a sneaky fellow." She shook her head then did a quick head count and frowned. "Where's Thomas?"

"He was watching the horses," answered Edward.

"The horses Harrigan and Ella just galloped out of town on?" Louise asked.

She did not wait for anyone to answer, but hurried to the stable. A cry of alarm escaped her when she saw Thomas's prone body, but her first flash of terror faded when the boy groaned. She quickly knelt by his side, put her arm under his shoulders, and raised him up a little. When George knelt on the other side of Thomas and gently held a cold, wet rag to the boy's chin, she directed all of her anger at Harrigan toward him.

"Some friend you have. He beats up children," she snapped.

"Children?" Thomas muttered, glancing from Louise to George and back again.

"Harrigan simply knocked him out," George said, his calm voice a marked contrast to Louise's emotionally charged one.

"He punched someone smaller and a lot younger than he is."

"You would rather he had shot him?"

"Er, Joshua, maybe you could take me out of the line of fire," Thomas said and a laughing Joshua helped him stand up. "It was just one light punch, Louise," he said in an attempt to calm the woman.

"It couldn't have been that light," she argued as she stood up, slapping away George's helping hand. "You were flat out on the floor."

"I was between him and the horses. Like George said, he could've just shot me. It couldn't have been easy to creep up on me like that."

"I cannot believe the way you all defend him. He's taking Ella to Harold. I don't care if he does it gently or politely or any other way. He shouldn't be doing it at all.'' She muttered a curse and strode out of the stable.

George looked at the four youths who were watching the rapidly disappearing Louise as if she was a stick of dynamite that was about to go off in their hands. He started to laugh, the looks of surprise on the faces of the others only adding to his amusement. Louise Carson was more woman than most men knew how to handle. George sobered as he realized that he might never be given the chance to try.

''I can't believe you hit that boy,'' Ella said the moment Harrigan slowed their pace enough for her to talk.

''That 'boy' is as tall as I am and probably as strong,'' Harrigan said, inwardly relieved to hear little more than a hint of shock and annoyance in her voice.

''That still didn't give you the right to knock him down. He's only trying to help me.''

''Careful, you're edging close to that forbidden topic.''

''Tough. We are just a few days from a big, fat piece of that forbidden topic. I'm real tired of the game of let's pretend we're just strolling through the countryside.''

''I was rather enjoying that game,'' he muttered, realizing he was not going to be able to completely avoid an argument.

''Of course you were. It was very nice and pleasant for you. You got to do just what you wanted without the annoyance of constantly having to explain yourself.'' He just shrugged when she cast him a look of irritation.

''Discussing the matter is much akin to banging our heads against a brick wall. What's the point?''

''Probably none.'' She sighed. ''It's just I that look at those mountains and the whole game seems a little silly now. We're riding right in Harold's shadow now. I did try. Believe me, I was enjoying the game too. I just can't do it any longer.''

"So you intend to try and talk me out of taking you to the man? Do you really think I've changed my mind?"

"No. I begin to wonder if you will change it even if Harold grabs me and drags a knife across my throat right in front of you. You'd probably tell yourself that he just slipped while trying to cut my hair."

"Ella!" The image she painted chilled him even as he was distressed by her lack of faith in him. "I've told you that I will look into the whole matter."

"You sound like a damned lawyer."

He slowed his pace so that he was riding right next to her and eyed her warily. "You don't like lawyers?"

Something about the way he asked the question told Ella not to say the derogatory words that immediately sprang to mind. "Don't have much against them really. It was just an expression of sorts. Everyone knows that lawyers are clever with words. It's what they're trained to be. That's why people rush to hire one when they're in trouble. Why? Have a close friend who's a lawyer?"

"You might say so. I went to Harvard and trained to be a lawyer."

Ella gaped at him. "A lawyer *and* a Harvard man? What the hell are you doing taking work as a bounty hunter?"

"I am *not* a bounty hunter," he snapped.

"You are paid money to find people and bring them in. Sounds like a bounty hunter to me."

"You're in a particularly contrary mood at the moment, aren't you? Are you looking for an argument?"

Ella studied him for a moment then gave him a slightly contrite smile. "I think I might be."

"Why?"

"Because I almost got away and, as always, you ruined the opportunity."

Harrigan sighed and shook his head. He could understand how she felt. This time rescue had been very close. He was still surprised that he had eluded Louise. It was probably foolish, but he began to wonder if fate had a hand in it all, if it was pushing them toward some destiny of its own choosing.

"You have a very strange look on your face," Ella said, breaking into his thoughts.

"Sorry. I didn't mean to interrupt your tirade." He grinned at the almost petulant look that briefly crossed her face.

"You have a true skill at taking all the joy out of a good temper."

Harrigan laughed, then quickly grew serious again. "I know that everything that stands between us, what you want and what I must do, are totally incompatible, and I guess that's why I try so hard to keep you off of the subject. I don't mind a good argument, rather fond of them actually, but there is so much between us, I'm not sure we can have one and still be speaking when it's over. Nothing will be resolved."

"Are you afraid I might be able to change your mind?"

"Maybe. The closer we get to Philadelphia and Harold, the less I like this. I don't want to do this, but I have to. It's that need that will make it hard for you to change my mind. If I let you talk me out of this, I let down my whole family. The money I'm being paid is already earmarked for things, much-needed things. It also puts us all closer to making a new start. Perhaps building a business as good as the last one, and one that can't be stolen away."

"And you're not going to fully recover from what Eleanor did until your family has a good business again, are you?"

"Probably not. That shipping business was everything to us, a future for me, my brothers, cousins, the whole lot. It meant a comfortable life for my parents as they aged. It means nothing to the Templetons except for one more possession, and a little less competition. I think that angers me more than the fact that I was completely duped and tricked. It wasn't needed. They could have lived in grand splendor without it. In fact, I have kept an eye on it, and there is no sign of improvement in it, no changes at all.

Maybe if they had thought we were not bringing it to its full potential and were doing good things with it now, I could somehow understand. Instead, it just sits there putting money in their pockets.''

She felt a strong wave of sympathy for him. A lot of people were fooled in love. Heartache was an acceptable risk in the game. Total destruction of a family's life was not. Even after Harrigan got over his stung pride and hurt feelings, the damage of his relationship with Eleanor Templeton continued.

''I think they did not like the competition,'' she said quietly. ''It was the grandfathers of both the Templetons and the Carsons who built the fortunes. The last two generations, the sons and the grandsons, have done little except live off the labors of their forefathers. They're very good at deception and all of that, but I don't think they have what their grandfathers did. They don't have the wit and skill to build a business of their own or strengthen the ones they have. They don't compete because they don't know how.''

''So they steal.''

''Yes, they steal or, in a few cases, they completely destroy what they fear is threatening them.''

''Are we back to you and Harold again?''

''I don't believe Harold sees me as a threat, or even competition. He sees me as a way to add to his fortunes without even breaking a sweat. In truth, except for his precious Margaret, I do not believe Harold could ever see any woman as a threat or a competitor. He simply does not see us as strong enough, smart enough, or even worth his time.''

''He obviously hasn't had much to do with you or Louise,'' he drawled, and was pleased to see her smile. ''Still, he and Templeton used women to get the businesses they've stolen over the years.''

''Yes, their daughters. Both men think of those women more as sons. They've raised them to walk in their footsteps. Even so, it's still a matter of Eleanor and Margaret getting orders from Papa and doing exactly as they are told. They're not given the run of the businesses after they help steal them, are they?''

"No. Well, none of that matters, except that it might help me put a stop to it all before any other families are ruined.'' He looked ahead at the slowly rising rock-strewn trail. "If you are still of a mind to have a roaring good argument, I think it had better wait for a little while. The trail ahead gets tricky and it'd be best if we keep all of our attention on it.''

"I think I can save it for a while.''

She smiled at him when he chuckled, then held herself more firmly in the saddle. As soon as they were too far away from town and her aunt for her to run right back to the woman, she would remind Harrigan to unshackle her. The trail through the mountains was only going to get worse, and she wanted to have control of her horse. If he asked for a promise that she would not try to run away while they rode the treacherous roads, she would give him one. She did not want to go to Philadelphia and end up in Harold's grasp, but she did not want to miss the confrontation because she had plummeted down a ravine in the mountains.

Chapter Fifteen

A small pebble slipped out from beneath Ella's boot, and she stumbled. As she righted herself, she silently and heartily cursed Harrigan. There had to be a better trail through the mountains, perhaps one well worn by thousands of pioneers. When they had first started up the trail late yesterday evening, she had thought it might be a poor choice. Now she was sure of it. She began to suspect that Harrigan was purposely taking the worst route he could find to discourage any pursuit. It also meant that they had little chance of meeting up with anyone, even the people who called the mountains their home.

What Harrigan seemed to be oblivious to was the danger they were courting. She doubted he knew the trail they were on any better than she did. It was madness to walk along a rocky path over a ravine that neither of them had ever explored. Ella could not believe she was worth that much money or that Harrigan was that desperate to win. She cautiously leaned to the right, so that she could see around him, and breathed a sigh of relief when she saw a wider path several yards up ahead of them.

Just as she prepared to demand an explanation, she saw

Harrigan make a strange sliding step sideways. Ella cried out in alarm as his foot slipped over the edge. That unbalanced him enough to make him fall. There was not enough room on the narrow path for him to land safely. Harrigan scrambled to catch himself, but the ground was far too unstable, and there was not enough of it. She moved to try and grab him, but it was too late. Ella screamed his name as he disappeared over the edge of the ravine.

For a moment, Ella knelt on the rocky path, shaking and struggling to catch her breath. She did not want to look down, terrified of seeing Harrigan's body broken on the rocks at the floor of the ravine. Then, taking several deep, slow breaths to try to calm herself, she finally peered over the edge, and felt her heart skip painfully. Harrigan was not a sprawled mass of broken bones at the bottom. He was half sitting, half lying on an outcrop of rock that was barely wide enough to hold his large body.

Ella considered leaving him there only for the space of a heartbeat. He was alive, and looked to be no more than bruised and battered. She would be free. Unfortunately, she didn't have the heart to do it. He had no supplies and no protection. Although she could lower such things down to him, the real problem was that she could not count on someone coming by who could help him. If she walked away from him, he could well rot on that ledge.

"I don't think anything is broken," he called up to her, a little unsettled by the way she was staring at him without saying a word.

"This was not one of your better choices," she called back.

"Ah, so you can speak. I was a little afraid that you had gone into a state of shock or something equally unhelpful."

"No, although I was briefly contemplating just leaving you there, turning the horses around, and riding back to that last town."

Harrigan wondered how long she had considered that idea, heartily relieved that she had decided against it. It had occurred to him too. He had already begun planning his arguments to make her help him. He knew that if she left him where he was he would be as good as dead. What had terrified him about the possibility was the sure knowledge that his death would have been a long, slow one of starvation, thirst, and deprivation.

"I'm very glad you had a change of heart," he said.

"I just might have left you there if this path showed any signs of being used by humans. It is clear, however, that no one with any wits at all comes this way."

"Alright, I concede that it was a damned poor choice of road. Now, can we get to the business of getting me the hell off this ledge before it decides it can't carry my weight any longer?"

Ella smiled, pleased to have his agreement about his bad taste in trails. She moved to take the rope off his horse, then frowned. He was too big a man for her to pull up.

"Do you think your horse can tug you up without plummeting down the ravine?" she asked.

"Yes, especially if I don't make him do all the work. Just tie the rope securely to the saddle."

The way he stressed the word *securely* made her a little nervous. She had no real knowledge of knots, of which was the strongest and which had the least chance of coming undone. Harrigan was a big man and would put a lot of strain on it. Trying to recall what little she had learned at Louise's ranch, she tied the rope to the saddle, then moved to the edge to look down at him again.

"Any suggestions on how I should make the horse help you?" she asked.

"Just lead him forward slowly."

She nodded and went back to his horse. Taking the animal by the reins, she began to tug him along inch by inch. She could hear Harrigan's boots scraping the rock wall as he climbed even while the horse pulled him, but she didn't dare leave the animal to check on Harrigan. One wrong move and she suspected Harrigan would definitely land at the bottom of the ravine. It was not until she saw the top of his head edge up over the rocks that she began to relax.

The moment Harrigan was back on the narrow path, he

leaned against the high far wall and closed his eyes. He
did not think he had ever been so scared. Pure good
fortune had saved him and he swore he would find a way
to thank God for that. He heard the soft rustle of skirts
and opened his eyes to see Ella crouched at his side.

"Well, that harrowing experience has probably added
ten years to my life," he said, briefly taking her small hand
in his and gently squeezing it.

"You owe me your life," she said quietly, smiling faintly
when he grimaced.

"And I bet I can guess what reward you will ask for that."

"Set me free. Tell Harold you failed. Hell, tell him I
died. That would make my life a lot easier."

"Would it?" He slowly got to his feet, delighted at how
close the end of the narrow part of the trail was, because
he no longer had the stomach for tiptoeing along the edge
of a deep ravine.

"Yes. Then he would cease hunting me or having me
hunted down."

"He would also have your money."

"True, but I think I would prefer to be poor and alive
then briefly rich and quickly dead."

"Well, much as I would like to repay your kindness, I
can't," he said as he grabbed the reins of his mount and
started to move again.

Ella moved to grab the reins of her horse as quickly as
she dared. The man was impossible, she decided as she
followed him. Anyone else would do as she asked if she
had just saved their life, but not Harrigan. He still went
blindly on doing what Harold wanted him to, and ignoring
what she wanted.

"I don't know how you can sleep at night," she grumbled
as, the moment they reached the wide part of the trail,
they mounted their horses.

Harrigan was not sure either, although bringing Ella
almost all the way across the country with Louise Carson
on his trail was an exhausting business. At the end of the
day, Harrigan doubted anything could keep him awake,

certainly not a guilty conscience. Now, however, he was not sure even the bone weariness he felt at the end of the day was going to help much.

It was hard to convince himself that he was still doing the right thing. There were still a lot of doubts in his mind about Ella's talk of Harold's murderous plans, but whether he believed her or not did not really matter. She had just saved his life and all she asked in return was that he did not take her to Harold, a man she hated and feared. It seemed a small return for giving him his life, but he was going to refuse her, and he was disgusted with himself.

To his relief, she said nothing more. He did not want to discuss the matter for fear he would weaken. He was also too full of self-loathing to have a reasonable discussion about anything. Harrigan knew it would never happen, but he found himself hoping that she was so furious with him that she would not say another word all the way to Philadelphia.

It was still early in the day when Harrigan decided to make camp for the night. The near tragedy on the cliff path had exhausted both of them. Ella looked as if she was about to fall asleep in the saddle. He was also feeling every one of his bruises and scrapes.

And, deep inside, there was still the bitter taste of fear, that gut-wrenching terror he had felt as he had fallen. He needed to rest so that he could banish it, hopefully before Ella saw any hint of it. Harrigan knew that a fear of falling to one's death was not something to be ashamed of, but he ruefully admitted that he did not want Ella to know, that he was worried she would see it as a weakness. He had always been confident, sure of his own strength. This uncertainty was uncomfortable and hard to bear.

"I think we will stop here for the night," he announced a moment later, turning off the rocky path they followed into a small, well-shaded glade.

"It's a little early in the day, isn't it?" Ella asked, then cursed silently, praying he would not now feel compelled to go on, for she was bone weary and eager to rest.

"You began to look as if you would fall asleep in the saddle again."

"I guess I am a bit tired."

As they stopped and dismounted, Ella inwardly shook her head over her own foolish pride. She *was* tired. What was the harm in admitting it? And yet, there was a part of her that rebelled against revealing that weariness, a lurking fear that Harrigan would see it as a weakness. Ella ruefully admitted that she was indeed a great deal like her aunt, for Louise always fought hard to be, or at least appear to be, equal to any man.

After tending to her horse, she sat down before the fire Harrigan was making and struggled not to sigh aloud her exhaustion. As soon as he had begun their meal, he rose, and she roused herself enough to frown up at him. The way she had been staring blankly into the fire had probably revealed how weary she felt, but she was starting not to care if he saw it.

"Where are you going?" she asked.

"Just into the wood a ways to see if I can find us any meat to have with our beans and biscuits," he replied.

"That would be nice."

"Can I trust you to stay right here?"

She hesitated only a moment before nodding. Not only was she too tired to run, but she knew her poor mare was in sore need of a rest as well. The minute he disappeared into the trees, she allowed her body to slump, crossing her arms on her knees and resting her head on her forearms.

A soft noise yanked away the clouds of sleep sweeping over her mind. She sat up straighter, wondered how long she had dozed as she rubbed her itching eyes, and tried to listen for a repeat of the sound that had ended her little nap. When she heard her mare snort nervously, she tensed and looked around. It was hard to see beyond the fire, to discern anything in the grey twilight and the shadows cast by the trees all around her.

The sound of a twig snapping brought her to her knees. She opened her mouth to call for Harrigan, but instinct told her it was not him, and she pressed her lips together. Two men stepped out of the shadows and she leapt to her feet, her heart pounding. Even in the dim light, the grinning pair looked threatening. Their gap-toothed smiles were predatory, not friendly.

"Well now, my pretty, what are you doing out here all alone?" asked the taller of the two men.

"And why should you think I am alone?" she asked.

Ella silently cursed when the men flanked her. Because of her weariness, she had missed a perfect opportunity to avoid them. The shadows of the surrounding trees would have provided her with plenty of hiding places, but she had been too slow to see the threat and lost the chance to run deep into the forest. Neither did she have any weapon to fight them with. Ella fought a choking fear as she debated the wisdom of screaming for Harrigan. He might be close enough to hear her, but if he came running blindly back to camp, that could cause even more trouble. The men would either drag her off into the night or shoot Harrigan.

"Oh, you're alone, alrighty," said the man as he inched closer to her. "Only a fool would leave such a tender bit as you all alone in the night."

"Or a man who felt a need to water the trees."

"There are two horses here, Johnnie," said the shorter, stouter man.

"Could just be her supply horse," replied Johnnie, looking Ella over in a way that made her skin crawl.

"And it could belong to her man."

"We can hold our own agin one man, Pete."

"Maybe we should just take her and run."

"I ain't of a mind to wait till I find a different place. I be thinking I need a taste of this right now."

Pete scratched his shaggy black beard, still holding his rifle on Ella, as he peered into the shadows all around them. "You do that now and you'll be leaving your backside bared for anyone who wants to take a shot at it."

Johnnie spit, the black tobacco juice only partly clearing his mouth, most of it trickling down the thin greying beard on his chin. "I be counting on you to watch my backside, Pete."

"I'm to just stand here and watch you have at it, eh?"

"You can have a piece when I'm done and I'll watch your ass."

All the while they talked they paced around her, closing in on her warily, watching both her and the woods at their backs. Ella was both amazed and infuriated at how well they did it, one of them always looking at her while the other checked their backs. The indication that they were not as stupid as they looked was almost as chilling as their words.

"If you touch me, you will die," Ella said, amazed at how hard and cold her voice sounded, for inside she was shaking with fear.

"And just who be going to kill us, my pretty? You?" Johnnie laughed.

"Yes. Maybe not now, but some day."

Her soft threat only held them back for a moment. Johnnie suddenly laughed again and lunged for her, leaving Pete to stand guard. Ella tried to dodge him, but he caught hold of her skirts, yanking her toward him. She kicked at him, but gained only curses for the pain she inflicted, not her freedom. A soft cry of fear escaped her as he flung her down onto the hard ground. Even though a voice in her head reminded her that she could be putting Harrigan in danger, she screamed his name as Johnnie pinned her to the ground and began to tear at her clothes.

Harrigan heard Ella scream his name and immediately ran toward the sound. He had already gone several yards before good sense returned. There had been fear behind that scream, which meant Ella was in danger. If he charged into camp without thought, he could easily get her or himself killed.

He stopped and took several deep breaths, fighting to

calm himself enough so that he could approach with some semblance of caution. After securing the rabbit he had caught to his belt, he carefully checked his weapons, making sure that both his pistol and his rifle were loaded. Harrigan began to creep toward the camp, struggling to be as silent as possible and to remain out of sight. Both proved almost impossible as he drew close enough to see what had prompted Ella's scream of terror.

Easing himself down on his stomach behind some shrubs, through which he had a clear view of the camp, Harrigan clenched his teeth as he subdued the urge to roar out his fury and go for the throats of the two men threatening Ella. The sight of one of the men mauling her and tearing at her clothes while the other watched, grinning broadly in amusement and anticipation, enraged Harrigan so much that he felt short of breath. Guilt was a sour taste in his mouth. He should never have left her alone.

Carefully, he aimed his rifle at the man sitting on Ella and pulling at her clothes. That was the one he needed to kill first and not just because he wanted to. If he shot the other man first, the one attacking Ella could easily have time to put her between himself and the bullet he so richly deserved. It was going to be a difficult shot, one that required as much luck as skill. Although he was not concerned about hitting Ella, for the roughly clad man on top of her was sitting in a way that allowed a clear shot, Harrigan was concerned that he might miss. He had to kill the man with the first shot.

Harrigan licked the sweat from his upper lip as he steadied his aim. He fired and for one tense instant, thought he had missed. The man jerked but did not fall, sitting there and staring at Ella. Then he began to slowly crumble on top of her. Harrigan quickly turned his attention to the other man who was wildly looking around. Even as the second man began to fire his rifle blindly into the dark, Harrigan shot him.

In one clean move Harrigan was on his feet and running into the camp. It took only a quick glance at the second man he had shot to know that he had killed him. He then hurried over to Ella, who was struggling to push the dead man off her body. Harrigan pulled him aside and reached for her, frowning when she made an odd strangled noise and scrambled away from him.

"Ella, it's Harrigan," he said in a soft, calm voice, and he slowly held his hand out to her. "You're safe now."

Ella blinked, clutched her torn bodice together and looked around. Her stomach clenched as she saw the bodies. When she glanced down at herself and saw the dark stain of the man's blood on her gown, she moaned, turned away from Harrigan, and was violently ill.

A small, rational part of her mind was aware of Harrigan as he held her while her body shook from the violent retching. She sat limp, unable to think clearly, as he washed her face and helped her into her nightgown. Harrigan wrapped her in a blanket and urged her to sit near the fire. Ella clutched the blanket close and stared at the flames, listening to him remove the bodies from their campsite.

It was not until he sat next to her and put a rabbit on a spit over the fire that she began to break free of the shock that had such a stranglehold on her. She found it difficult to grasp what had just happened. One minute she had been dozing peacefully by the fire, the next she was being mauled by a filthy man, and then it was over, the enemy dead and supper on the fire. It seemed like a very bad dream.

"Where did they come from?" she asked, not really expecting an answer.

Harrigan tentatively put his arm around her shoulders, tightening his hold slightly and pulling her close to his side when she did not resist his touch. "Probably just out on a hunt. I found no horses, just an odd sledlike contraption loaded with animal skins. I think they were just walking by and saw the fire."

She shook her head. "I think that might be the most frightening part of it. It was all just evil chance." Ella looked at him, a little startled by the tenderness of his expression.

"I saw no sign that he got what he was after," he said quietly, the statement holding a hint of a question.

"No, he didn't." She shuddered. "He just touched me, mauled me some," she whispered, shivering with remembered horror. "I wish I could have a very long, very hot bath."

Harrigan touched a kiss to her forehead. "After we eat, I might be able to heat a little water for you so that you can wash up, if that will help."

"Yes, thank you." She looked at the rabbit, then gave him a shaky smile. "Your hunt was successful."

He briefly hugged her. "It was not worth the price you had to pay."

"You couldn't know that would happen. We haven't seen a single sign of a person since we entered these mountains. You couldn't know that two pieces of filth would appear the moment you left. It was the first time you left me alone in these hills, too. I was so at ease that I was half asleep. That's how they were able to slip up so close without me seeing them."

"You're just trying to talk me out of my sense of guilt."

"Yes, because you carry no guilt for this. It was just one of those things that happen, that cannot be planned for or protected against."

"Why didn't you scream when they first arrived?"

"Because I was already trapped. I was afraid that you would just come running and then be shot. They had seen that there were two horses here and were watching for a companion. I couldn't warn you and I could do nothing to help you."

Harrigan poured her a cup of the strong coffee and handed it to her. "Were you hoping that I would just stumble by and see them before I got too close?"

"I guess I was," she replied, feeling the heat of the coffee warm her chilled insides. "They just wandered by, didn't they? Oh, hell, in truth I wasn't thinking too much at all. I saw that I couldn't get away, that I had no weapon, and knew that you couldn't rush blindly back to camp without putting your own life in danger. Once that creature grabbed me, I didn't do any more thinking, which is why I screamed then."

"Well, you were probably right to think what you did. I did start to run blindly back to camp when I heard you scream. I was halfway here before the voice of reason returned. It was not easy to cling to, either. Not when I saw that pig on top of you," he added in a soft harsh voice, strong emotion roughening his tone.

Ella stared at him, suddenly wishing she could see him more clearly in the firelight, hearing the feeling behind his words and wanting to see if it was reflected in his eyes and his expression. "I will recover."

"Are you sure?"

"Yes. I'm alive. I don't believe they intended to leave me that way."

"Well, I dearly wish I could have saved you from all of the indignities you just suffered, but I can find comfort in the fact that I did save your life."

She blinked and pulled away enough to look him full in the face. For one brief moment he looked as if he was considering his right to claim that, then he smiled. "There is no need to look quite so pleased with yourself."

There was the hint of tartness to her voice, and Harrigan welcomed it, for it meant that she was beginning to recover from her ordeal. "I do not like to be in debt."

"Especially to me."

"Ashamed as I am to admit it—yes, especially to you."

She frowned at him for a moment, then shook her head, making a soft noise of disgust. "Men can be so pigheaded." Before he could reply to that insult, she added, "I think the rabbit is done."

Ella was a little surprised that she had any appetite at all, but decided that a change from beans and biscuits was enough to stir her hunger. As soon as they had finished eating, Harrigan heated up a small stewpot of water. He allowed her some privacy to wash up, keeping his back to her the whole time. It was not until she crawled beneath the blanket of their

rough bed that he began to watch her, and Ella quickly felt
uncomfortable beneath that steady, intent gaze.

"I will be fine, Harrigan. Truly, I will," she assured him.

Even as she said the words, she realized that they really
were the truth and not just said to comfort him. It would be
a while before the horror of the incident faded, but she was
confident that she would recover from the attack. There
were two things she could tell herself to ease the horror—
the rape had not been completed, and she was alive.
Repeating these things to herself over and over had already
begun to work. She had washed all trace of the man's unwel-
come touch from her skin. Now she just had to push the
chilling memories from her mind or, at least, end their power
to leave her afraid and trembling.

When Harrigan slid beneath the blanket at her side, she
tensed, then cursed. She refused to allow those men to
make her afraid of any man's touch. As Harrigan cautiously
slipped his arm around her waist and tucked her up against
him, she forced herself to relax and welcome his closeness.
A lot of people might consider Harrigan nearly as great a
cad as her attackers, because he had seduced a woman he
had been hired to find, but Ella knew he would never treat
a woman as those two men had. She had always had the
option to tell Harrigan no.

"Where did you put their bodies?" she asked softly.

"Tossed them into a gully and shoved some leaves over
them," he replied in a flat voice. "Don't worry. They're a
safe distance away. They won't draw any unwanted visitors
our way."

She shivered a little, knowing he referred to the beasts
who were drawn to the scent of blood and death, and
snuggled up against him. "And are they *really* dead?"

"Those two will never maul another woman."

"Do you know, I find that a great comfort," she murmured, and closed her eyes, praying that she had the
strength of will to stop the memory of those men from
stealing her sleep as they had so roughly and abruptly
stolen her peace of mind.

Chapter Sixteen

They would be in Philadelphia tomorrow. Ella still could not believe how Harrigan had announced that chilling fact, coolly, as if he was mentioning that it might rain in the morning. She shifted slightly in the saddle, and surreptitiously rubbed her backside. There was at least one part of her that would be heartily glad to stop riding, she thought wryly. All she had to do to stop that pain was to get off her horse. She wished she could cure the hurt Harrigan was about to deliver as easily.

When he had saved her from her attackers last night, Ella had thought she had sensed some deep emotion in him. Now she was not so sure. If he did care about her, or her well-being, as strongly as she had suspected then, he would now be offering her some chance of escape. Instead, he held her reins tightly, leading her down out of the mountains and straight into Harold's lethal hands. That look that had softened his eyes last night could easily have been a look of triumph, she decided. Harrigan had made no secret of how pleased he was that he had fully repaid her for saving his life.

"Ella, you haven't said a word in hours," Harrigan said

as he led them through the thickly growing trees toward
the stage route that would lead them straight into Philadelphia.

"I don't think you want to hear the words that are
churning about in my head right now," she replied.

Harrigan sighed, looking around for a secure place to
camp for the night. "Do you want to plead your case
again?" he asked with obvious resignation.

"Actually, that snake coiled and waiting in Philadelphia
was not really in my thoughts. Mostly, I was defaming your
character." She smiled faintly when he chuckled.

"Something you do with great skill and wit."

"Thank you kindly. I do my best."

"Does that look like a good place to camp for the night?"
he asked, pointing to a small grassy knoll set among a thin
stand of trees.

"Actually, there is one other I would prefer."

"Where?"

"Wyoming."

"Not very amusing," he muttered as he reined in and
started to dismount.

She eased her travel-sore body out of the saddle and
stretched, rubbing her lower back as she looked around.
"I didn't realize it was my job to entertain you."

Harrigan mused that it might have been better if she
had remained silent and distant. "I suppose it would be
useless to ask you for your word that you will not try some
foolish escape."

"Escape from Harold is not foolishness, but survival."

She ignored his muttered curse as she considered her
options. Refusing to swear that she would remain with him,
would not try to flee, seemed silly when she was so close
to her enemy, so near to losing her battle against Harold.
Ella knew she should be trying her best to run as fast and
as far as she could in the other direction. She also knew
she would not do it. The attack last night had left her with
a deep fear she could not shake that easily.

"I believe I will stay put," she finally said.

"Is that a promise?" he asked, eyeing her warily.

"Yes. You have left me alone in these woods only once. Once was enough. I don't want to go to Harold, but I also don't want to meet with any more men like those two last night. Harold is at least a danger I know."

As Harrigan prepared the fire, Ella tended to the horses. She then took a quick survey of their campsite. The sound of trickling water drew her to some thickly growing scrub brush at the far edge of the clearing. When she saw the small creek, she knew she would be unable to resist its temptation.

"Ella," Harrigan called, a hint of trepidation in his voice.

Ella realized she had started to leave his sight, edging closer to the water. "There is a little creek right here and I believe I will have a bath."

"I can understand your wanting to have a good scrub down, but I hope you can understand my reluctance to let you out of my sight."

"I told you I wouldn't run away."

"That's not what concerns me. These hills now seem a lot more dangerous than they did when we rode into them."

Ella grimaced, suffering a swift return of her fear, then tightly grasped at a scrap of common sense. "I will be just on the other side of this brush. It puts me only steps away, yet allows a little privacy."

"Alright then. Just don't take too long or I might feel compelled to infringe upon that privacy."

"Understood."

Ella grabbed some clean clothes and their rapidly shrinking bar of soap, and went to the creek. It was shallow and cold, but she wasted no time in sinking her body into its chilly depths. The wash she had had last night had helped remove the stench of her attacker, but she knew that a good scrub in these clean waters would finish the job.

After rinsing her hair and squeezing out the excess water, Ella stepped out of the creek. She rubbed herself dry with her spare petticoat, dressed in her pantaloons and camisole, and sat down to gently rub her hair dry. She had to decide what to do about Harrigan. It was their last night together and, even if she was able to escape Harold's deadly plans for her, it could well be the last night they would ever share. Harrigan had never talked of his feelings or of a future together, and the only promise he had made was to investigate her claims about Harold.

It was far past time to stop trying to guess what he thought or how he felt and face some hard, cold facts. The only thing she knew for sure about Harrigan was that he desired her. Despite all the time they had spent together and all they had shared, she had not been able to convince him of the danger she was in. He now believed that *she* felt all of her tales were the truth and had enough of his own doubts to want to investigate Harold, but none of that did her much good. He was still going to hand her over to Harold tomorrow.

Ella sighed. All the facts added up to one truth. She should tell Harrigan and herself a resounding *no*. No, she would no longer be his lover. No, she would no longer play the game of *let's pretend Harold isn't lurking on the horizon*. And, no, she would no longer love him or try to win his love. If she did not stand back and start treating him like the enemy, she was a fool.

She stood up, picked up her clothes, and started back to camp. A fool was exactly what she intended to be, she decided, as she looked at Harrigan, who had been standing guard on the other side of the scrub brush that sheltered the creek. Pride told her to push him aside, but there was a little idiot voice in her head too and it was louder than the voice of pride. It told her to try one more time, take one more chance.

As if something will miraculously change this time, she mused. *As if, while he holds me in his arms for what might be the last time, some lightning bolt will strike him between the eyes and fill him with some wondrous revelation. Suddenly he will know that he loves me. Suddenly he will see Harold for the murderous, greedy scum that he is. Right. And, suddenly, I will become a tall, buxom blond who turns all men's heads.*

"It doesn't look as if your bath relaxed you very much," Harrigan said as they sat by the fire and he served her some beans and biscuits.

Ella smiled crookedly. She was tempted to tell him that she was carrying on a glorious argument in her head. Unfortunately, she would have to tell him what it was and that would reveal far too much about the sorry state of her heart. It would also make him question her sanity.

"I was just a little disappointed that some meat had not miraculously appeared on the spit to add itself to the beans and biscuits," she replied.

Harrigan smiled, then began to eat. He did not believe her, but was too cowardly to press her for the truth. Whatever had put the dark frown on her face was probably not something he wanted to discuss in any depth. Tomorrow he would complete the job Harold had hired him to do and he hated it. He was not too fond of himself either. He was sure she was thinking of the same things.

This would be their last night together, and Harold loomed between them like some unbreachable wall. They did not have to talk about him; he was just there. Harrigan knew it was selfish, but he wished that wall was not there, because he ached to make love to her. After tomorrow, he might never have another chance.

The thought of never holding Ella again, of never tasting her passion again, was deeply painful, but Harrigan shied away from examining the why of that. He shrugged it aside as a regret for losing something he so enjoyed. It was a price he had to pay to help his family, and he would recover. If there was one woman who could make him feel so good, so fulfilled and sated, there had to be another. When he had regained all that had been stolen from him, he would look for her. Harrigan ruthlessly silenced the little voice that tried to tell him he was seriously deluding himself.

His problem at the moment was how or even if he should

approach Ella. There was a good chance she would react to any advance with pure fury, and he did not want their time together to end that way. Neither did he want to lead her to believe there was still a chance he would change his mind about what he had to do. He ached for her, however, and he was not sure he had the strength to be wise or considerate.

Confusion still reigned in his mind as they cleaned their supper dishes and banked the fire. He watched her lightly braid her hair before she slipped beneath the blanket, then he stripped to his drawers and crawled in beside her. When he realized how closely she was watching him, he inwardly grimaced. He was torn between saying a calm goodnight then pretending he was going to sleep, and kissing her, reaching out unthinkingly for one last taste of the passion they shared.

"Ella," he said, then choked, not sure what he should say next.

"I know," she murmured as she reached out to stroke his cheek.

Harrigan had the sinking feeling that she did know, knew far more than he wanted her to. "I should leave you alone."

"Yes, you should."

"You can't change my mind." He began to unbraid her hair, combing his fingers through its silken depths.

"I've known that for a long time."

"You mean you haven't been trying to change my mind?"

"Not with this, and you are very lucky I am in the mood to ignore the implied insult."

He laughed shakily, closing his eyes as she smoothed her small, soft hands over his chest. "I feel like a cad."

"You should." She began to follow the route of her hands with her mouth, slowly, tenderly kissing his skin. "However, I am neither stupid nor naive. I also have a voice. I could say no. In fact, I know I should say a very loud no tonight."

"But you're not going to."

"No. I fear greed has silenced the voice of my pride."
She undid his drawers and slid her hand inside, watching
the lines of his face tighten as she stroked him. "Tomorrow
you will do something I may well find impossible to forgive.
I may even grow to hate you, if I live long enough. But
tonight I believe I can push all that from my mind. No, I
am certain I can. I will deal with my offended pride another
day."

Harrigan did not have a chance to reply. Ella removed
his drawers, kissing her way down one leg then back up
the other. When she replaced the enticing strokes of her
hand with her mouth, he could only groan his approval
of her daring. He slowly sat up, watching her as she plea-
sured him. He had always preferred to control the lovemaking, but with Ella, he felt no need, was in fact delighted
when she was bold enough to take the lead.

Finally he knew he could not continue, that he would
reach his release before she did if he did not stop her. He
pushed her back until she kneeled in front of him. The
soft look of desire on her face, the visual proof that she
was stirred simply by making love to him, was almost his
undoing. It took all of his willpower not to lie her down
and immediately possess her.

He slowly undid her camisole and kissed the tip of each
breast as he slid it off her. Then he untied her pantaloons,
easing her to her feet as he pulled them off her. She started
to sit down again, but he grasped her by her slim hips and
pulled her closer, determined to repay the delight she had
just gifted him with. The way she welcomed his intimate
kiss, opening to him with no hesitation, giving him free
will of her body, was intoxicating.

The moment he sensed that her release was near at
hand, he pulled her back down, easing their bodies
together. Ella's gasp of pleasure as they were joined was
like a caress. Harrigan leaned her back over his arm and
began to give her taut breasts the attention he had thus
far denied them. When he felt her body begin to squirm

against him, he held her tightly against him and kissed her. Their cries of release blended in their mouths when, as one, they reached the crest their bodies craved.

Ella sighed and curled up by Harrigan's side. They had washed up and returned to bed, yet she was only just starting to return to her senses. When he trailed his fingers down her spine and began to caress her backside, she murmured her appreciation and snuggled closer to him.

"Ah, my wild mountain rose, I don't think we'll get much sleep tonight," Harrigan said, a little astounded at how quickly his desires were returning.

"And were you thinking of sleeping, my dark Irishman?" she asked.

"No, not once you let me know there was something else we could do."

He smiled when she chuckled. Ella had a sense of freedom he had rarely found in a woman. She was open in her dealings and in her passion. Somewhere in her upbringing there had been a lack of the lessons taught other well-bred young women. He had no doubts about her morals or her ability to be faithful if she promised to be, but she put few restraints on her passion, and held none of the strange notions planted in the heads of so many young women. It would be a very fortunate man who finally put his brand on her.

The knowledge that it would not be him both hurt and angered Harrigan. He almost laughed at his own contrariness. He was not going to claim her, but he was already jealous of the man who would. The only way to stop himself from thinking about tomorrow, or any day beyond that, was to lose himself in the fire he and Ella could ignite, he decided. He would just keep making love to her until the sun came up or they both collapsed from exhaustion.

"Your strength has returned already, has it?" she asked, laughing as he suddenly pulled her on top of him.

"I believe mine will hold longer than yours will," he

drawled as he trailed his tongue along the pulse point in her throat.

"Ah, a challenge. I do so love a challenge."

"Going to try and prove me wrong?"

"Most definitely," she whispered as she kissed him.

The first hint of dawn's brilliant color was tinting the sky as Ella opened her eyes. Her first clear thought was that neither of them had won the challenge. She was pretty sure they had both fallen asleep at the same time.

Careful not to disturb him, she slipped from their bed and, throwing on her camisole, hurried to the creek. After quickly seeing to her personal needs, she scurried back to bed, smiling faintly to find Harrigan still sound asleep. There was a certain amount of pride to be felt in knowing she had exhausted such a strong man.

She sat beside him, watching him sleep. For one brief moment she suffered a strong urge to weep. She loved him deeply and, she feared, would do so forever. It seemed a cruel twist of fate that it was Harold, a man who wanted her dead, who had sent her the love of her life. It did not seem strange that it would also be Harold who would tear that man from her arms.

What made her even sadder was that she could not tell Harrigan how she felt. Love was something every woman longed for, to feel and to share, yet she had to swallow the words, hide them deep inside of her. Ella could not foresee any time when she would be able to reveal all that was in her heart. That, Ella mused, was the cruelest cut of all.

Afraid she was about to start dripping tears all over Harrigan, she went to stir up the fire and make the coffee. For a little while longer she would pretend that everything was fine. She knew that the minute they got on their horses and started down the road to the city that pretty little dream would be shattered. It would hurt no one save herself if she clung to it for another hour or two.

When she returned to their blanket bed, she gently

nudged him, laughing when he muttered and rubbed his hands over his face. "I made you some coffee," she said, holding the cup out when he finally sat up and looked at her.

"Thanks," he said, watching her cautiously as he took the cup.

Harrigan sipped at the coffee, mildly annoyed that it was a lot better than his own, and eyed her over the cup. She looked especially tempting as she sat there by his side. It was obvious that she wore nothing but her thin shift and that she had just tossed it on. The front was unlaced, but not fully opened, the edges caught against her nipples, which were hardened by the cool morning air. He glanced down and thought idly that, if she took a deep breath, the bottom edge of the lacy shift would rise enough to reveal all of her secrets.

He looked back at her face and the sweet smile she gave him made him a little uneasy. Today he was taking her to Harold. She should not be so pleasant. Harrigan wondered if this was some form of revenge, if she planned to torment him with all he could no longer enjoy.

"It's morning," he said.

"Not quite yet," she murmured as she set down her empty coffee mug.

"The sun will be up soon. You can see its light on the horizon."

"Only if you keep insisting on looking at it."

"Ella, at times you can be the most confusing woman," he muttered, and finished off his coffee in one gulp.

"And what am I doing that is so confusing you?"

"Being nice to me. Today is the day—" His eyes widened when she suddenly placed a finger against his lips.

"Don't speak of it. I have decided that the day has not yet begun. It would be imprudent of you to argue with me."

"I see. So you're saying that it is still yesterday."

"Yes, poor deluded child that I am."

"And just when does the new day start?"

"Oh, in about an hour or two, when one can actually see the sun."

Harrigan tossed his cup aside and reached for the front of her camisole. He hesitated just a moment to see if she would pull away, then opened it. The last of his doubts about what she was saying disappeared as he bent to drag his tongue across one hard tip. Ella sighed in that way he had come to delight in, threaded her fingers in his hair, and held him close.

Their love-making quickly became intense, almost frantic. Ella reveled in the way he kissed and stroked every inch of her, then greedily returned every caress. They reached the heights they both so enjoyed, rested, then reached for each other again.

They tried to go slowly the second time, to linger over every touch, every kiss, but the rising sun would not let them ignore the passage of time. Its light pushed its way through the surrounding trees. Ella settled herself on top of Harrigan, watching him as she eased their bodies together. When he reached for her, she put her hands on his shoulders and lightly pressed him against the ground. This time when their passions were spent, there would be no resting in each other's arms. Reality would be waiting for them, and before that completely stole away their little dream, she needed to know something.

"I want you to tell me something, Harrigan," she said. "I want you to answer one little question."

Harrigan tensed, the clouds of passion clearing from his mind as suspicion snaked its way in. "What do you want to ask me?"

"Such mistrust I can see in your eyes."

"It's just that you have me at a bit of a disadvantage."

"I do, don't I?" She smiled faintly. "It's only a little question, Harrigan."

"And it can't wait until later?"

"No, because I believe it might be best if we don't talk much later."

"You're probably right."

"Harrigan," she whispered as she bent down to brush a kiss over his mouth, "I swear I am not asking for any great promises or commitments."

"Ella," he began, unsure of what to say, but deeply regretting more than he cared to think about.

"I just want to know one little thing. Will you miss this, Harrigan?"

"What?" Harrigan was so startled by the question, he was not sure he had heard it correctly.

"I said, will you miss this?" She slowly moved against him to try to silently make it clear what she referred to.

"You mean the passion we share?" He broke free of her light hold, and grasped her by the hips.

"Yes, this." She closed her eyes and sighed with pleasure as he sat up and pressed her body close against his.

"Oh, God, yes. No one has ever stirred the fires higher and hotter than you. No one has ever felt as good wrapped around me as you do. No one has ever tasted as good, smelled as good, or looked as good as you. Hell, I even delight in those soft sighs and gasps you make. Yes, I will certainly miss this."

"Good," was all she could manage to say as he began to move her against him, forcing them to the completion she had tried to hold back.

Harrigan watched Ella dress even as he pulled on his own clothes. When their passions had been spent she had silently pulled away from him. He did not think he had ever felt so chilled, the cold reaching down deep inside him. This time there was no doubt that he would never return to her arms.

As he cleaned up their campsite, he briefly wondered if he could go to see her later, once she was settled in at Harold Carson's house, then shook his head. That was pure madness. Even if Harold was not the killer she claimed he was, Ella had made it clear that he would be cutting all ties to her the moment he handed her over to Harold.

If he showed up at her door, she would probably try to shoot him.

That's if Louise hasn't already put a bullet in me, he mused as he saddled his horse. The certainty that Louise would be waiting for him in Philadelphia was just another black cloud on his horizon. This was probably going to be the worst day of his life. He suspected it might even prove to be worse than the day he discovered Eleanor's treachery.

He reached out to lift Ella into her saddle and grimaced when she neatly avoided him, mounting without his assistance. She had barely even looked at him. It was for the best, yet it saddened him. He did not want to part from her with such a cold distance between them, but there was nothing he could do to dispel it. After one last look at her, he mounted and picked up her reins. It might only be a few miles to Philadelphia, but it was going to be a very long trip.

Ella stared at Harrigan's back as he led them out onto the road. She wanted to argue with him, to plead with him, but she pressed her lips tightly together. It would do her no good and she decided her pride had taken enough of a beating.

She felt the aching in her body that their long night of lovemaking had left her with and sighed. For a moment she was deeply ashamed of herself, but she quickly pushed that aside. She loved the man. The fact that he did not love her or have an inkling of how she felt did not really matter. She had gone to his bed out of love and that was enough to banish her brief bout of shame.

It would be nice if she could retrieve her pride as easily, she thought, a little sadly. That was going to take a little longer. She had loved and lost and was not finding it poetic or romantic at all. It made her sad, angry, and frustrated. It also made her feel foolish.

Ella reminded herself that, in a few hours, she would be faced with something that should take her mind off all of her hurts and disappointments concerning Harrigan Mahoney. Harrigan had only taken her chastity and her love. Harold wanted her life. She needed to concentrate on that, to clear her mind of all the other clutter. When she faced her guardian, she wanted to do so calmly and with her back straight. Ella did not want Harold to sense any weakness in her.

Harrigan Mahoney was a big weakness, she mused. It was vital that she push all of those feelings down deep within her where Harold could not sniff them out. When Ella realized that part of the reason she wished to do that was to protect Harrigan from Harold, she cursed. She was an even bigger fool than she had thought. In a few hours she would be involved in a fight for survival. Harrigan showed no inclination to help her in that fight, so she was stupid to worry about him. He could take care of himself. It was time to push the man right out of her mind and heart, no matter how temporary that reprieve might be. There was only one person she should be thinking about now—herself. It was the only way she could win against Harold, and Ella was determined to come out of this fiasco alive. She would worry about lost loves and heartbreak later.

Chapter Seventeen

"There's the city," Harrigan announced as he reined to a halt on a small rise in the well-rutted road.

Ella's little mare came to a sedate stop right next to his gelding, blithely ignoring Ella's wish to keep some distance between herself and Harrigan. She looked down the road at the city she had fled nearly three years ago and felt her insides knot up with fear. It was not the city itself which caused her such terror. There was a lot to appreciate in Philadelphia. There were also a lot of bitter, sad memories. And, at the moment, Philadelphia was a death trap for her.

She opened her mouth to try to talk Harrigan out of handing her over to Harold, then closed it again. She had repeated herself until she was sick of hearing the words. While it was true that he no longer thought she was lying or trying to trick him, he did not waver in his intention of completing the job he had been hired for.

It annoyed her a little that she could sympathize with his unwavering sense of purpose. He blamed himself completely for his family's losses and was determined that they would not suffer too badly. That required money, and Harold was paying him handsomely. Even if he felt inclined

to, he could not throw that away when he had absolutely
no proof that she was telling the truth. It hurt to think
that her word was not good enough, but, if their situations
were reversed, she was not sure she would act any differently. When family was involved, there came a point where
they had to take precedence, and all one could do was
pray that others understood.

"I suppose it's pointless to restate my case against Harold," she said quietly, not able to give up on one last
chance of changing his mind.

"I've explained why I have to do this."

"Yes, you have, and a part of me understands. I hope
that you understand that another large part of me still
feels betrayed."

He sighed and nodded. "I swear to you, Ella, I won't
just leave you there and do nothing else. I'll do all I can
to prove what you say and get you away from the man."

"And who will you be finding that proof for, yourself
or the law?"

"I can't do anything to stop Harold without proof," he
answered, and inwardly grimaced when she gave him a
mildly disgusted look in return for his vague response.

"I suppose Harold is informed of our impending arrival."
She smiled at the look of guilty surprise he was unable to
suppress. "I'm not stupid, Harrigan. You know my aunt is
doing her best to be here waiting for us, to stop you from
completing this job. The easiest way to insure that you have
any help you might need is to warn Harold. Now, I might
be able to come to some understanding about why you are
doing this to me, even forgive you, but if Louise is harmed
in any way, that is something I will never be able to forgive
or forget."

He just nodded, and started into the city, tugging her
along with him. From the moment he had wired Harold of
their impending arrival, he had begun to regret it. It had
meant that he had no choice about what he could do once
he rode into the city. Harrigan was sure that there would be
people watching for his arrival, probably even someone at

the edge of town ready to ride back to Harold with the news
that they were on their way.

As they started through town, he looked toward the railroad station, but had no idea which one of the many trains
there was the one Louise might be on. After running from
the woman across miles of countryside, he found it odd that
he now wished to see her. If Louise arrived and stole Ella
out from under Harold's nose, however, it could solve his
problems. He would have met his part of the bargain, so
Harold would have to pay him, yet Ella would not be given
to the man.

A moment later, he inwardly shook his head. It wouldn't
work. Louise would never get out of the city. The woman
would not only have the law hot on her trail, but every
crook and bully Harold could hire. Now that they were
actually in Philadelphia, it was probably safer to quietly
hand Ella over to the man. Rescue could come later, a
well-planned, unanticipated rescue. He just hoped Louise
had the sense to know that. It was going to be hard enough
to hand Ella over to a man she was so afraid of. Harrigan
did not want that trauma compounded by her aunt getting
into a losing battle or being taken away by the law.

"You can't do this, Louise," Joshua warned as they
lurked in the shadows of a narrow alley between two fancy
brick houses and watched Harrigan approach with Ella.

"Why not?" she asked. "He's alone, isn't he?"

"He was alone every other time you tried to get him
and you failed each time."

"So I'll either win this time or suffer another failure.
Failure only hurts Ella."

"Not this time. I'm sure that he's being watched, that
Harold knows he's coming in today. You show your face
and there's no telling what will happen."

"I believe he may be right, Louise," George said gently
as he moved to stand next to her. "Harrigan will have told

Harold that he's coming, and the man will be ready for him."

"That doesn't mean he'll be ready for me," she protested.

"I think it does and I think you know it. Harold is well aware of how you feel about him and you have been fighting him for three long years. He knows you're the reason that he hasn't been able to get his hands on Ella for all this time."

"Well, I can't just stand here and do nothing," she snapped.

"Fine then," said a deep, gruff voice from behind Louise and her friends. "You can go to the jail with me. It ought to be easier for you to control yourself once you're secure behind them bars."

"Now, Thompson," George began when he recognized the sheriff, but Louise was already turning on the man.

"There's no use trying to talk sense to this pig," Louise said, glaring at the potbellied man. "He oinks for Harold."

"Here now, you watch what you say," Thompson yelled after glaring his two chuckling deputies into silence.

"He's actually said something you should listen to, Louise," George advised, leaning close to Louise so that only she could hear what he said.

"This fool wouldn't know a wise word if it jumped up and bit his bulbous nose."

"That's just about all I'm taking from you, missy," Thompson scowled as he grabbed Louise by the hand and pulled her toward him. "You and this range scum are all under arrest."

"Arrest? For what? Telling you what an idiot you are? You'll have to arrest the whole damned city."

George inwardly groaned. He adored Louise's spirit, but her mouth could be a source of unnecessary trouble at times. He waited until the sheriff's deputies had collected all of the weapons. It gave him a moment to think of what to say, although he had the sinking feeling that nothing was going to help Louise or her boys now.

"Sheriff, I assume you know who I am or you would be arresting me as well," George began.

"Yeah," growled Thompson. "You're that fool who let this little slut capture you."

It took George a moment to decide what angered him more—being called a fool or hearing Louise called such a low name. They were almost equal, but he decided that an attack upon his intelligence was of less import than one on Louise's morals. The fact that both insults were delivered by a man who was no more than the lackey of anyone who paid or threatened him, made it all the worse.

"I believe I will hesitate to shoot you today," George said in a cool, polite tone that caused Thompson to take a step away from him. "I realize that some things may be difficult for you to understand. In fact, I suspect many of the most elemental facts are difficult for you to grasp, but do try to listen carefully. This woman, whose morals you feel so free to slander despite your own craven turpitude, has commited no crime. I believe you may well be commiting one if you incarcerate her." He glanced toward Louise and caught her grinning at him.

"As I keep saying, George," she murmured, "you do have a way with words."

"Well, he can talk as fancy as he wants, but it ain't getting him nowhere," Thompson said. "This lot is being arrested because they threatened the life of one of Philadelphia's most important citizens."

"I haven't threatened anybody in this city for so long, I challenge anyone to remember it," Louise snapped.

"You've threatened Harold Carson."

"I have only offered to give the man what he deserves," Louise began.

"Louise, hush," George said, surprising everyone into silence, including Louise. "Right now the man has no good reason to arrest you. Do not give him one. Do not give Harold what he needs to get you out of his way for a very long time. And try to think of the lads for a moment. They will not find jail a pretty or a friendly place." He nodded when she pressed her lips together, looking an odd mixture of sullen and contrite.

"If you're done talking, mister, we'll take our prisoners to the jail," Thompson said, pushing past George as he started to leave the alley.

"Don't worry, Louise, I will get you out of there," George promised, aching to do something but knowing that joining Louise in jail would be no help at all.

"I'll be fine," she called back to him as Thompson dragged her away, his deputies pushing the four youths ahead of them. "You go watch out for my niece."

He sighed and shook his head. "I told you—"

"Damn it, George, I didn't ask you to break your word or go against Harrigan. All I ask is that you watch out for her. I need to know what's happening with her and exactly what that bastard is doing."

"That I can do," he replied, needing to yell because Thompson had already taken her across the main street. "And I will do what I can to get you out of there."

Muttering soft curses under his breath, George began to walk toward Harold Carson's house. He hoped he would meet up with Harrigan before the man gave Ella to Harold, even though he doubted he could halt the transaction. What he wanted to see was how Harold acted as he took hold of his niece and all that was said. Harrigan was far better at deciphering such things, able to understand the true meaning behind the smallest gesture and expression. George was not sure Harrigan was at his best at the moment, and wanted to be able to tell the man everything as clearly as he could when he finally started thinking straight again.

Harrigan recognized several of Harold's men as he rode down the street. A gasp from Ella stole his attention from counting them. He followed the direction of her wide-eyed gaze and inwardly cursed. There would be no aid from Louise. Thompson was roughly pushing the woman into his jailhouse, her boys being urged after her by Thompson's deputies. Harrigan briefly looked around for George, but saw no sign of the man. His only consolation was that he had not seen George being dragged into the jail along with the others. Since he was confident that Louise had not injured the man, he knew George would be along shortly.

"He's had Louise arrested," Ella cried in outrage.

"Considering some of the things your aunt does and says, that arrest might not have anything to do with Harold," he replied, wondering why he was still so quick to defend such a man.

"We both know that Harold had a hand in that. He had Thompson lying in wait for my aunt."

"There has to be some reason for an arrest to be made, especially of a woman."

"The reason is that Harold told Thompson to do it."

Ella made her last statement just as Harrigan reined in in front of Harold's huge brick house. Harold was standing on the walk in front of the house, clearly expecting them, and he gave Ella a very condescending smile.

"What have I instructed our duly elected sheriff to do now?" Harold asked, his air of innocence almost more than Ella could stomach.

"You sent Thompson after Louise," Ella accused. "You had him put her in jail."

"I don't know where you get such strange ideas. Why should I do such a thing to a member of my own family?"

"To get her out of your way so that you can finally have a chance of winning this little game. She's been a thorn in your side for years, but you haven't been able to reach her in Wyoming."

Harold shook his head and adopted a look of innocent sorrow that made Ella want to gag. When she looked at Harrigan, he was wearing an expression that was tight and closed, and she wondered if he was finally seeing Harold for the deceitful, dangerous man that he was. That Harrigan could see the danger in her guardian was of the utmost importance to her, even if he couldn't keep her out of the man's house. Somewhere, somehow, Harrigan had to begin to see the truth. It was all she had left to hope for.

She tensed as Harrigan dismounted and picked her out

of her saddle. Ella had talked to herself about this moment from the time she had ridden away from Wyoming. Time and time again she had told herself that she would not let it hurt her, that Harrigan had his reasons, and she had to respect them or how could she truly love the man? It had been easy to decide that she would be calm and mature, understanding and forgiving. Harold had still been many miles away.

Now she trembled, her heart skipping painfully in her chest. She felt afraid and betrayed. She saw George walk up to them and was anxious to ask the man a few questions about what had happened to her aunt. He had to have been with Louise when Thompson appeared. Then she realized that, if he had been, he had obviously not done anything to stop it.

It was hard to suppress a cry when Harold grabbed her by the arm, then shoved her toward one of his huge guards. Ella saw Harrigan's face tighten and his hands clench, but he did nothing. He just wanted his money, she thought sadly. That was all that really mattered to him.

"Ella and Louise tell a different tale than you do, Harold," Harrigan said, his voice tight as he fought to control his anger.

"I warned you about that," Harold said smoothly, waving his guard away. "Take the girl into the house, Matthew," he ordered.

Harrigan watched the big, dull-faced Matthew drag Ella away. It took every ounce of his will not to go and yank her out of the man's rough hold. Harold was certainly not acting as if an errant child had been returned to the fold, more as if a prisoner was being returned to her cell.

"I just found it odd that both of them told the very same story," Harrigan murmured.

"Well, of course they would. They've had several years to concoct it and perfect its telling. I fear Louise is mostly at fault. She wants the child to stay with her and has slowly turned Ella against us."

"If you say so, sir. My next question concerns the money owed me."

"You'll be paid," Harold said and briefly shook Harrigan's hand before disappearing into his house.

George stepped up next to Harrigan. "I believe the man intends to try and cheat us out of that money."

"Well, he can think again."

Harrigan looked up at the windows on the second floor. One glimpse of a small, pale face was enough to tell him which room Ella was in. He was not sure what he could do, or how useful that knowledge might be, but he was pleased to have it. Even if he decided not to do anything, he was determined to let Louise know which room her niece was in. Harrigan was still not quite sure how dangerous Harold was, but he was sure that the man deserved every drop of aggravation Louise could deal out.

One other thing he was sure of was that he hated what he had just done. The look of hurt on Ella's face was burned into his mind. He felt wracked with guilt and self-loathing. Right up until he had handed her to Harold he had convinced himself that he could do it, even that it was the best way to handle matters. Now he felt as if he had been kicked in the gut, and the one who had delivered the blow was himself.

"Why was Louise arrested?" he asked George as, knowing there was nothing he could accomplish by standing outside of Harold's house staring up at the window, he grasped the reins of the horses and started to walk toward his office.

"Because Harold ordered it," George replied.

"Are you sure that is the reason?"

"Very sure. That fool Thompson nearly said so himself. There was no outright confession that he was taking a totally innocent group of people to jail simply because Harold Carson told him to, but he was too stupid to think of a good excuse to cover himself."

"Louise must have been furious."

"Yes, but not surprised."

"And how was your little journey with the group?"

George smiled faintly. "You aren't really interested in that, at least not now."

Harrigan grimaced and shook his head. "Sorry, old friend, I was just trying to make conversation."

"There are other things you need to do besides try and be pleasant."

"Such as make sure that bastard pays us for the dirty work we did for him?"

"There is that. I was thinking more of what you can do to take that load of guilt off your shoulders."

"That noticeable, is it?" Harrigan released a short, bitter bark of laughter. "I'm still not sure the man means to kill her, but I do know it was wrong to bring her back here. He means her no good. I do, wholeheartedly, believe one thing she accused him of, and that is wanting her money. I just have to decide if he's capable of murder to get it."

"I believe he is," George said quietly.

"Then help me prove it. Perhaps I should go and talk to Louise."

"If you're in the mood for a great deal of abuse, go right ahead."

"Even if she feels like spitting in my eye, don't you think she'll answer my questions if it might help Ella?" Harrigan paused across the street from the jail and worried his bottom lip with his teeth.

"Yes, I think she will. I do not, however, think she will believe that you are going to help Ella until you actually do so. Go on then," he urged. "I'll wait here and hold the horses."

"Not going to come with me?" Harrigan felt a little hesitant about going on his own.

"I believe I'll give her a little time to calm down before I go to see her. Just ask her what she wants me to do with her horses."

"Alright, but there is a chance the answer will be profane."

George briefly grinned. "A very big chance, but then she will tell you what I should really do."

Harrigan followed Thompson to the cells. He winced a little under Louise's glare then noticed that she redirected her anger to something behind him. A quick glance revealed that Thompson had no intention of allowing them any privacy. Warily, Harrigan stepped closer to Louise's cell, nodding briefly to the four youths in the next cell. Thompson was far enough away, trying to act as if he was not listening, so Harrigan hoped that if he and Louise talked very softly they might actually be able to exchange a few bits of information.

"You have a lot of nerve coming here to face me after what you've done," Louise said. "You've already delivered my niece to that bastard, haven't you?"

"Yes. I made a bargain with the man."

"A devil's bargain."

"I begin to think so."

"If you were having doubts," she whispered, suddenly lowering her voice, "then why did you bring her here? Why didn't you just set her somewhere safe until you were sure which one of us was telling you the truth?"

"I don't think we'll be allowed the time to really discuss this in the depth it needs. I promised Ella that I would now look into Harold's affairs." He kept his voice very low, forcing Louise to lean against the bars. "I need names."

"It's a little late now, don't you think?"

"She's still alive. I thought you might have a few pieces of information you would like to share, things that might shorten the time I spend finding the truth."

To his relief, Louise began to tell him names, incidents, and anything else she could think of. Since he did not dare write it all down, he struggled to remember it. Once she began, however, he knew he would have to come back again or have George do so. She was giving him far more than he could remember. He finally asked her to stop, promising her he would be back for more as it was needed. He then asked her what George was to do with her horses, not surprised by her first, very painful suggestion, but then she sighed and gave him some instructions to relay to George. Once he returned to George, they shared a brief smile over her first suggestion about the horses, then went to see that the animals were properly cared for. George was a little intimidated by the number of people they would have to check, but he was more than willing to be the one to go visit Louise and get more information as needed. They had no proof of anything yet, but the wealth of information Louise was ready to provide made Harrigan uneasy. He desperately wanted to find out just what the truth was, but he was beginning to fear that the truth was exactly what both Ella and Louise had been trying to tell him from the start.

"What do you want me to do first?" George asked as they returned to Harrigan's office, opening a window to air the place out, and then sitting down in his chair to face Harrigan directly.

"I think you should keep a close watch on Harold," Harrigan replied as he sprawled in his chair.

"That's what Louise asked me to do. She wants to know whatever happens at that house, whatever Harold does, and any news of Ella."

"And I want our money. I may have just sold my soul for it and I'll be damned if that bastard will cheat me out of it."

"The man will be tripping over me each time he tries to leave his house."

"Good. If he's planning to do something illegal, he'll pay you off just to get you out of his way. He certainly won't want someone constantly watching him. Once you get the money he owes us, you can continue to watch his house, but do so covertly."

"And what will you be doing?"

Harrigan looked at the list he had been making, trying to write down as much of what Louise had told him as he could before he forgot it all. "I'll be trying to find someone, anyone, who will tell me something I can use against Harold. I may be slow to do what I should, but believe me, it will be done thoroughly. If Harold has used us to give him a victim, he'll pay dearly for it."

Chapter Eighteen

Ella paced her room, pausing only to try the door, find it locked, and curse. After catching herself at that fruitless endeavor for the fifth time, she clenched her hands at her side, and took several deep, slow breaths to try to calm herself. She wanted to hurl herself at the door until it fell open, but told herself firmly that that would be stupid. The door was solid oak with heavy iron hinges. She would just hurt herself.

She felt torn apart by fury, pain, and fear. Despite all that had passed between them, Harrigan had handed her over to her relatives without hesitation. He had muttered some vague promises about keeping a close watch on her, but she refused to have any faith in his promises. With that one traitorous act he had shown her that he had never believed her, so she refused to believe in him. Her brief bout of understanding had faded the minute she had been given into Harold's hands. Ella found it hard to believe that Harrigan would ever take Harold's word over hers. He had his blood money and she had been fool enough to let him enjoy the use of her body. There was no reason for him to stay around and certainly no profit in it.

"And you have far more important things to worry about than some handsome, grey-eyed rogue," she grumbled, and kicked over a footstool. "Idiot," she cursed herself as she hobbled over to her bed, sat down, yanked off her slipper, and rubbed her sore foot. "You will not get far if you break your foot."

"Ella?" called a tremulous female voice from the other side of the door. "Are you in there?"

"No, I'm waltzing down the promanade," Ella snapped as she limped to the door, wondering if some miracle was about to happen and her cousin Margaret was going to set her free.

"There is no need to be pert. It is I, your cousin Margaret. Eleanor is here too. We wished to talk to you about Harrigan Mahoney."

Ella slumped against the door, cursed, and shook her head. She was locked in a room facing death at the whim of her relatives, and these two women wanted to gossip about Harrigan. He was the last person she wanted to talk about. There was, however, a slim chance that she could fool or cajole her cousin into setting her free, a very slim chance, but one she had to try for.

"We could talk more clearly and freely if you would open this thick door," Ella suggested, not really surprised when the two young women giggled, but thinking that it was a particularly cruel thing for them to do.

"Come, cousin, do you think we are stupid?"

Deciding it was best if she did not reply to that, Ella sighed. "I had thought that you might not wish to be party to a murder."

"Murder? Carsons do not spill the blood of their own."

"No, they hire others to do it for them."

"Ella! Eleanor and I have come to visit, to have a pleasant chat, and all you can do is spit accusations at us. If you do not wish to talk about Mr. Mahoney, you need but say so. There is no need to be so unpleasant."

For a moment, Ella stared at the heavy door and wondered if Margaret was truly ignorant of her father's deadly

plans, then shook her head. Margaret had helped her
father destroy the lives of half a dozen men and their
families. She was also very close to her father. In fact,
Harold and Margaret's love for each other was sometimes
so obvious and intense it was uncomfortable to see. The
woman knew exactly what her father wanted and just how
far he would go to get it. Under Margaret's genteel, pretty
face, the woman was as cold and as avaricious as her father.

"Many pardons. I fear the thought of my impending
death has made me ill-tempered. What do you wish to
know about Mr. Mahoney? I am not certain I can tell you
very much. I was merely his prisoner." Ella realized that,
despite her hurt and anger, she did not want to tell these
women anything they could then use against Harrigan.
Their families had hurt him enough.

Margaret laughed, a high, light, trilling sound she had
practiced long hours to achieve. "Cousin, you are modestly
fair of face and Mr. Mahoney is a rogue. Would you have
us believe that nothing passed between the two of you?"

"Yes, because nothing did."

Ella subdued the urge to tell Margaret and Eleanor that
she and Harrigan had made wild, passionate love all the
way from Wyoming to Philadelphia. She might yet escape
her dire situation alive and she did not want that little bit
of news to be spread far and wide. Giving Eleanor's haughty
pride a little tweak was simply not worth the price she
might have to pay. She wavered slightly in her decision
when she heard Eleanor say, "I told you Harrigan would
never touch such a thin, plain mouse like Ella." The woman's vanity certainly deserved a thorough bruising. Ella
hastily pushed aside all thought of how intimate Eleanor
and Harrigan might have been during their courtship.
That was something she neither should know, nor wanted
to know, anything about.

"But Ella, you were alone with him," Margaret began
in a too sweet voice.

"Not often. And Margaret, you may deny that I have
been brought here to die, but I certainly believe it. Do you

really think I would stoop so low as to become romantically involved with the man who is dragging me to my own execution?" Margaret did not need to know the depths of her stupidity, Ella thought glumly.

"Well, you could have thought it would help you gain the freedom you so crave."

"Harrigan was fooled once by close friends of this family. He is too smart to be fooled twice."

"Any man can be fooled by a woman," Eleanor said, her voice heavy with scorn. "They are easy to blind with sweet words, promises, and passion. One simply must know how to stroke their vanity and stir their passions. A man caught tight in the net of his own desires cannot think clearly."

Ella was a little shocked at the cold, cynical way Eleanor spoke of men and then wondered why she was. The woman thought nothing of winning a man's affections so that her family could more easily steal all he owned. Despite all her efforts not to, she also wondered just how deeply Eleanor had stirred Harrigan's passions and if the woman had then satisfied them in any way. The images that that thought brought into her mind were painful and she shook her head, fruitlessly trying to fling them aside. What Harrigan had done before they had met was not her concern, not even if they had shared more than a fierce passion. She knew what troubled her most was not that he had been some other woman's lover once, but that he had been Eleanor's. That realization angered her, for it made her feel even more the fool than she already did.

"And that is when you steal all that is important to him, isn't it, Eleanor," Ella said, forcing herself to concentrate on Eleanor's crimes and to try to forget the woman's love affairs.

"If the man does not have the strength or the wit to cling tightly to what is his, he deserves to lose it."

"No man deserves the treachery you visited upon those poor fools you wooed, won, and discarded."

"How high-minded you are. If all you mean to do is preach to us, I believe we will leave you alone."

"I am prostrate with grief."

"You have more than earned your fate," snapped Margaret. "If you had tried harder to be more amiable, more pleasant of nature, you would not have stirred Papa's anger."

"I have not stirred his anger, Margaret, only his greed."

"Curse you and the fates that made you stay behind the day the rest of your family went boating. You ruined many a good plan."

Ella stared at the door as she listened to the two women walk away. A coldness gripped her, sweeping through her body until she shivered. She told herself that Margaret's parting words were simply meant to be hurtful, no more than a spiteful child's wish that she had died years ago so that she could not plague the woman now. It was not an assertion she could make herself believe, no matter how often she repeated the words. The words Margaret had spat out were little more than a curse; it was the cold, hard way Margaret had spoken them that troubled Ella so.

She gritted her teeth, forced herself to walk to the bed, and sat down. Her hand shaking slightly, she clutched at her locket, running her thumb back and forth over the embossed rose on the front. There had been knowledge weighting Margaret's words, the strong insinuation that she knew something about the boating accident that had stolen away Ella's family that warm summer day seven years ago. Ella was certain that Margaret knew it had been no accident.

"How could I have been so blind, so utterly stupid?" she whispered, fighting back a grief she had thought she'd conquered years ago.

There was no doubt in her mind now that her family had been murdered. She was also certain that no one would believe her if she made the accusation. She had no proof, and, if she repeated what Margaret had said, she would be thought foolish or mad to have read so much

into one angry statement. There was no clear admission
in those harsh words, but Ella knew that was exactly what
it was.

Fear became a hard knot in her stomach. She had known
for a long time that Harold wanted her dead. Knowing
that he had already committed murder, however, made it
all the more starkly certain, and much more terrifying.
Anyone who could kill three people, including a babe in
arms, would not blink an eye at killing her. A small part
of her had always hoped that she could change Harold's
mind or continue to elude him. Now she knew she had
never had a chance.

The sound of the door being unlocked yanked her from
her dark thoughts. She struggled to push aside her fear,
to adopt an expression of anger and derision, as her uncle
by marriage and two of his hulking men entered the room.
As she held Harold's cold stare one of his men set a tray
of food and drink on the small writing desk in the corner
of the room.

"Food for the prisoner? How kind," she drawled.

"You brought this trouble upon your own head,
m'dear," Harold said in a soft, cold voice.

"Odd, I do not recall requesting that I be dragged back
here and locked in this room." Ella could see that she was
angering Harold and knew that was dangerous, but a cold,
cynical voice in her head said that it did not really matter.
The man intended to kill her, and being sweet and obedient would only make it easier for him.

"This treatment is necessary because of your constant
attempts to run away."

"Not attempts—successes. You would never have pulled
me back here without help."

"Which cost me dearly," he said, his voice slightly
rougher as his anger grew stronger.

"Good." She resisted the urge to lean back when he
took a step closer to her. "I should hate to think that my
life was bought cheaply. I just hope you used your own

money and not what you anticipate gaining from my death.''

"Child, I am your guardian—"

"Only because you killed my parents before they could alter their will.''

It was hard not to stare at him in surprise when he visibly reacted to her accusation. His too-narrow face hardened, the bones standing out with an ugly clarity. His cold eyes narrowed and he clenched his hands so tightly that his thick knuckles turned white. Obviously there was proof of his crime somewhere, or he thought there was, and he now believed that she had found it. Ella knew she had just given him another reason to kill her.

"You clearly need more time alone to reflect upon your errant and foolhardy ways." He signaled the two men with him to go out the door even as he backed toward it. "You have not yet recognized your own faults and weaknesses in character.''

"My only fault was in trusting you, and my only weakness was in allowing you to keep breathing,'' she snapped, racing toward the door even as he shut it behind him and locked it.

Ella fruitlessly yanked on the door latch, then kicked the door, cursing when she hurt her foot again. Part of her fury was bred of fear, but a greater part was born of the injustice of it all. Even if she escaped, or her Aunt Louise made the man pay for whatever he did to her there would never be any retribution for the death of her family. Even if Harold feared there was proof, Ella doubted there was any, not after seven long years.

She limped over to her desk and sat down, staring morosely at the meal in front of her. Although she was not hungry, she knew it would be foolish to weaken herself through hunger. There was always the slim chance that she could escape or be rescued and she needed her strength so that she could grasp whatever small opportunity might come her way.

The food was tasteless to her, her mind too clogged with

thought for her to appreciate the cook's efforts. She had let her anger take control again and it had cost her. Not only had she made Harold even more determined to kill her, but she had neglected to find out what had happened to her aunt and the others. Ella was not sure how much trouble Harold could make for them, and she needed to know if they were free.

She stared out of the barred window as she drank the tart lemonade, thinking morosely that Harold had planned well for her return. So well that she might not be able to escape even if Louise and the others were free to help her. It took more effort than she thought it ought to to push away the sudden sense of defeat that swept over her. She would not let it take root, however. It just did not seem right that a man like Harold could continue to commit such crimes and never have to answer for them. It certainly did not seem right that she should have to die simply because she had money.

As she set the glass back on the desk, she frowned, wondering why that simple act had suddenly seemed so difficult. Ella shook her head. There were still a lot of thoughts swirling about in her head, but they were no longer clear. It was hard to center her mind on any one of them. She fiercely blinked her eyes as the objects on the desk became less distinct, but that only made her dizzy. Suddenly, in one brief flash of clarity, she stared at the now empty glass. The lemonade had held a lot more than a refreshing tartness. Ella struggled to stand up, then cursed Harold as blackness flooded through her mind and she slid to the floor.

"I wasn't really sure that would work," Harold said as he tossed Ella's limp body onto the bed.

Margaret stared down at her unconscious cousin. "I think my slip of the tongue might not have been as ill-advised as we thought. I suspect it made her a little less sharp and cautious than she usually is. It was probably completely occupying her mind."

"True. It has, however, made killing her far more necessary. She is clever. I don't think she can find any proof that I murdered her family, but if there is some out there, she is one who could find it."

"And she is stubborn enough to never stop looking for it." Margaret grimaced. "Sorry, Father."

"No real harm done, dear. I understand how furious the bitch can make a person. We will just have to move a little faster than we planned. It's probably wise, anyway. Mahoney is still poking around in our business, and Thompson is getting nervous about keeping Louise and her mongrels in jail when he has nothing substantial to charge them with."

"Louise could be charged with Robin Abernathy's death."

"Not any more. Not only has it been eight years, but not many people still believe the tale we so assiduously put about back then. It did what it was intended to—got rid of Louise before she could get her brother to change his will. I remained the heir."

Margaret lightly chewed on her bottom lip. "Louise could be trouble."

"Not if we're careful. Everyone thinks the woman is mad, an embarrassment. And now that they have seen the sort of people she travels with, many think she is little better than a whore." Harold put his arm around his daughter's shoulders and led her toward the door. "I am a little more concerned about Mahoney. It's time to come up with a way to completely destroy his credibility." Harold paused outside the door to speak to the muscular, bearded man standing just outside. "The minute she shows signs of growing clearheaded, make her drink some more of the lemonade."

"What if she won't drink it?" the man asked.

"Then pour it down her damn throat." He shook his head as the man shuffled into the room and shut the door behind him. "Once I have Ella's money, I think I'd better loosen my purse strings enough to hire a few men with some brains."

"Brawn is also important, Papa," Margaret said as they headed down the stairs.

"True, but just once it'd be nice to give an order without having to explain it or repeat it."

"How long are you going to hold Ella in that room and pour opium down her throat?"

"A few days, just until she is so filled with it that it'll take a long time for her mind to clear, and long enough for a few select people to notice her problem before we take her to the river." He smiled. "People will shake their heads and murmur *poor girl.* They'll recall what an emotional little thing she was and the ones we allow to see her will speak of the opium, the glazed eyes, and the incoherence of the girl in her last days. They will all think it a tragic suicide."

"Ah, yes, the poor thing never really did recover from the death of her family, did she?" Margaret laughed along with her father.

A voice in Ella's head warned her not to swallow, but she had already done so. She looked up at the bearded, homely man who had poured the drugged lemonade down her throat and wished she could think of some curse to spit at him. Tiny flashes of memory poked through the haze enveloping her mind. There had been people in her room, tsking, and shaking their heads as they had looked down at her. That should worry her, but she was not sure why.

Her uncle's face came into her view and she felt a sudden strong wave of hatred and fury, but it faded as fast as all other feeling and thought. "How long have I been like this?" she asked, fighting to cling to the tiny scrap of rationality she had grasped, before it was swept away by the new dose of opium forced upon her.

"Only three days, Ella." He sighed and shook his head, looking at someone behind him. "I do not understand such mental disorders, Mr. Stanton. I just do what I can. She is either like this, or raging and thus a danger to us as well as to herself."

Ella looked at the man who moved to stand next to Harold, and heard herself laugh, a strange giggle that alarmed even her. Harold was lining up his witnesses. Who would question the minister of their church when he said that poor Ella Carson had lost her mind? Ella wished she could think straight so that she could figure out how spreading the tale that she had lost her mind would help her uncle.

"It's the lemonade," she said, and could tell by the way Mr. Stanton shook his head that her words made no sense to the man, simply worked to confirm Harold's claim of madness.

"Has there ever been insanity in the family?" asked Mr. Stanton.

"Well, we have often wondered about poor Louise," Harold replied. "We always tried to explain away her wild actions by saying she had too much spirit, or that her upbringing was unusual, but now, I confess, I begin to wonder. Right now Louise is in jail, alongside the four half-breeds with whom she's been galloping over the countryside," he added, as if revealing some confidential family shame.

"Only two are half-breeds," Ella said, but no one paid her any heed.

When the two men moved away from the side of the bed, Ella struggled to lift herself up enough to watch them. Neither man paid any attention to her, talking as if she was not even in the room. It was clear that Harold's tale of madness had its believers already. When the men walked out of the room, shutting and locking the door behind them, she flopped back down onto the bed.

There was a faint hint of clarity in her mind and she fought to hold onto it. Lethargy held her body in a tight grip. She knew she was in danger, but each time her mind tried to tell her to save herself, she either did not heed it or she forgot the warning the minute it had sped through her mind. Her strength and will were still there but it was as if they were held captive in hundreds of layers of heavy batting. The opium was making her more of a prisoner than the locked doors and the bars on the window.

All the doses forced upon her after the first one had been weaker, she realized. Harold did not want her unconscious. He wanted her to be awake enough to confirm his tale of insanity with the strange way she acted and the odd, disjointed things she said. This was the clearest of mind she had been in a long while, although it was still not enough for her to plan an escape and enact it. She could feel the newest dose of the drug intruding upon her mind and trying to steal away her thoughts.

There was no way to fight it, she thought with a flash of alarm that was immediately soothed by the drug. That inability to be afraid, that sweet blind compliance now infecting her, was the worst, she thought as she slowly closed her eyes. She was going to walk to her death with a smile on her face and there was nothing she could do to stop it.

Chapter Nineteen

Harrigan scowled at the papers spread on his desk. They blended with all the testimony he had gathered to paint a very grim picture. His blood ran cold as he finally conceded that everything Ella had told him was the truth. In fact, he suspected Harold was even worse than she had ever imagined. He had given Ella over to her executioner just as she had tried to tell him so many times.

There was no doubt in his mind that he had let fear overcome his true instincts. The closer they had gotten to Philadelphia, the harder his common sense had tried to tell him to listen to Ella, to at least hesitate before handing her over to Harold. He had refused to listen to those instincts, too alarmed by the strength of his feelings for Ella to be impartial or analytical. All he had been able to think of was putting some distance between them before he was unable to, before he gave himself over to her, heart and soul. Now he was not sure he had even accomplished that goal.

He cursed and swept everything from his desk, then reached for the crystal decanter that held his dwindling supply of strong whiskey. The question he had to answer now was what he should do with all he had discovered. Harrigan cursed again and took a long drink of whiskey as he realized there was not much he could do. It raised a hundred and one questions, but answered very few. It roused a lot of strong suspicions but held no real proof of a crime. Even if, by some miracle, his information proved to be enough to get Harold before a judge, the man needed only a mediocre lawyer to get it all laughed right out of court. About all he could do was spread a lot of nasty rumors around and maybe hurt Harold Carter's business. If he was going to help Ella, he needed a great deal more than that.

Louise and her friends were in jail, so they could not help him unless he could come up with some way to set them free legally. Thompson really had no crime to charge them with, but Harrigan did not think he had the power to make the man go against Harold's orders. That was just another problem he had to solve.

There was always the option of just taking Ella away from Harold, he mused, then shook his head. That would only help Ella for a little while. Harold would simply hire men to come after them and they would all be on the run again. Harrigan knew it would be impossible to find proof of Harold's crimes if he was in hiding, constantly watching his back. And if Harold caught them, this time he would be the one in jail, charged with kidnapping and anything else Harold could think of. Ella would then be completely alone.

The only thing he was sure of was that George would readily help him if he could come up with a plan that would remove Ella from her guardian's deadly grip, yet not set the law on their trail. That, he decided as he sipped at his drink, would not be easy. He was not sure how much time he had to come up with something, either.

"You look very dark spirited," came George's voice next to his ear.

Harrigan started and nearly spilled the last of his whiskey, then slouched in his chair and watched George pour himself a drink. "Just trying to think of a way to clear up some of the mess I've made." He was glad when George did not press him to be more specific. "I have all the information I need to call Harold a snake, but not one thing I could take before a judge."

"Harold is a smart thief."

"He's worse than that, my friend. He's also a clever killer."

"Who has he killed? Not Ella? I've been watching and I haven't seen anything yet." George helped Harrigan pick the papers up off the floor and restack them on his desk.

"No, he hasn't killed Ella. Not yet, but I now believe that that is his plan. Why should he hesitate to kill her when he has already murdered the rest of her family?"

"That drowning seven years ago was no accident?" George asked in a soft voice, as he pulled a chair up to the desk and sat down.

As he piled the papers that had roused his suspicions in front of George, Harrigan replied, "No, and I'm almost certain of that. Harold may not have murdered them with his own hands, but he might as well have. And Ella should have died with the rest of her family, but for some reason she was not with them that day." He waited a moment for a frowning George to finish looking over the papers. "That scowl on your face tells me you reached the same conclusion I did."

"None of this is the hard proof needed to convict him of the crime."

"Exactly. You'll also see my little notations that reveal that very few of these people will repeat such things in court. They will deny it all, in truth. There are a lot of people who are scared of Harold Carson or so caught up in his net that they would hurt themselves as much as they would hurt him. And that's if they even considered testifying against him, for, if Harold caught wind of it, he could destroy them. Those who suspect him of murdering his own family would fear even worse than financial ruin.

Their consciences might urge them to speak out, but every-thing else tells them to shut their mouths."

"Then what use is all of this?" George asked as he tossed the papers back down on to one of the many piles littering the desk. "If we have no hard proof of his guilt, how can we stop him now?"

"That's what I've been trying to figure out."

"Well, I'm more than willing to lend my assistance."

"I was hoping you would say that," Harrigan said even as he stood up and walked toward the door.

"Oh. You have to leave now? I had wanted to have a little talk."

"Soon as I get back, George." Harrigan stuck his hat on his head and stepped through the door. "I need to get away from that pile of papers and walk. It often works to clear my head. I'll walk and you can read and maybe, when I return, one of us will have found a way to bring Harold down."

"Ah, and that will allow Ella to escape his hold."

"That's the plan. Dig away, George, and, hopefully, you will find some tiny, useful gem I have overlooked."

Ella struggled to sit up on the bed and heartily cursed her body for its inability to obey her commands. Her mind was beginning to clear and she desperately wanted to make use of that, but her body was still held tightly in the grip of the opium. Even her hands felt heavy and awkward.

Something was about to happen, she was certain of it. Although she was not sharp-witted enough to know why she felt that way, something told her that Harold would act against her today. It was also the first time in days that she had been left alone. She was sure there was not even a guard at the door, a door she seemed totally incapable of getting to. When she heard the door open, she just sughed, knowing she had lost any chance she might have had.

"I told you it was silly to leave her alone," came Margaret's sharp voice even as a hard push against her shoulder sent Ella tumbling back onto the bed.

"She wasn't getting very far, was she?" snapped Harold as he scowled down at Ella.

"Dissension among the troops?" Ella said, dismayed at how slurred her words were, for it proved that she was still held tightly in the grip of the opium.

"I also think it was a mistake not to give her more of that stuff," said Margaret. "She seems dangerously clear of mind to me. What if we meet up with someone before we get her to the river?"

"I believe we have convinced enough people of her unsteady state of mind, the kind of people who have probably spread the tale all over the city by now. Add to that the fact that no one thought she was quite normal before, and that she has spent nearly three years with the mad Louise, and I don't think anyone will listen to her. If we give her another dose she may well be so unclear that people will question why we are taking her for a carriage ride."

Margaret glared at Ella and grumbled, "I suppose, but I do not like it. This means that we will have to listen to her all the way to the river."

"A small price to pay for what we shall soon gain."

Ella cried out softly in protest when one of her uncle's hulking men suddenly appeared at her bedside and scooped her up in his arms. In her mind she was putting up a glorious fight, but her body refused to move, lying limp in the man's thick arms. Ella decided that it might have been better if she was still completely under the spell of the drug. At least then she would not be so aware of what was happening to her.

As they started down the stairs, Ella managed to gain enough control of herself to grab the railing, but it was a short-lived resistance. Harold's burly guard just kept walking and a smirking Margaret punched her hand, forcing her to release her weak grip on the highly polished wood. Ella stared at her cousin and found herself wishing that the woman would suffer some horrible, painful, and lingering death. She was a little surprised at her bloodthirsty thoughts, but decided that Margaret had earned them.

"What is your clever little plan, Harold?" she asked, struggling to make her words clear. "Are you going to toss me out in the woods and leave me for the wild animals? Or perhaps you mean to shoot me and try to claim that I was accosted by thieves as I staggered down the road?"

"I mean to take you to see your family, m'dear," Harold replied coldly as they all paused at the front door.

"You're taking me to the cemetery?"

When Harold and Margaret laughed, Ella cursed. She hated the way the drug slowed her ability to think. Her wits were what had kept her alive so far, and the opium had stolen them away. She felt totally defenseless. Then a brief flash of clarity gifted her with an understanding she almost wished she had not had. Harold was going to take her to the river and drown her, just as he had done to her family.

"People won't believe I went boating, Harold," she said.

Margaret cursed. "She needs more of the drug, Papa. She understood you far too quickly."

"It's fine, Margaret," Harold reassured his daughter, then patted Ella on the head. "They'll believe a poor, mad girl would throw herself in the river thinking she could be with the family she had lost. Ah, yes, poor little girl just couldn't bear their loss any longer; she missed them so much."

The man carrying her stepped outside and Ella saw Harold's ostentatious carriage waiting at the foot of the brick steps. She thought about screaming, but doubted she could get that much power behind her voice. She also doubted it would do much good. Harold had made sure that everyone thought she was mad. Screaming in the middle of the day as she was put into a carriage would simply make the neighbors shake their heads in pity.

"Aunt Louise," she began.

"Can't help you this time," Harold said.

"You can't really believe that she will let you get away with this."

"Louise might work her way out of jail in the primitive land she now calls home, but she has no power in Philadelphia. Here she is just an embarrassment. People see her as a mad woman with no morals. They will believe anything I say against her. Hell, if she gets to be too much of a problem I might just give Margaret what she wants and kill the bitch. I could always blame it on her little pack of mongrels."

Ella swayed as Harold's man set her on her feet by the carriage door. She could think of nothing to say and that infuriated her. Fear was a sour taste in the back of her throat, fear for herself and her aunt. That she could feel anything at all was proof that she was slowly crawling out from beneath the influence of the opium, but she was too concerned about her aunt to be pleased by that. Her recovery was not fast enough to do her any good anyway.

"Hello, Harold, Miss Margaret, Ella," said a deep voice that caused Ella's heart to skip.

She slumped against the man who still kept a firm grip on her arm and looked at Harrigan. There was only a little flicker of the anger and pleasure she always felt when she saw him. His expression was cold, his grey eyes dark and hard. Something had made him very angry and she wished she could ask him what. Ella dared not hope that he had finally found out the truth about Harold. There was a small chance, however, that she could give him some hint of what was about to happen. If he had begun to believe in her, he might act on a clue and do something to help her. Even if he figured it out too late to save her, it could serve to warn Louise about the danger she was in.

Harrigan stared at Ella, and she smiled sweetly. She looked achingly lovely in her soft green gown, yet something was not right. There was glazed look in her eyes and the soft look on her face reminded him of the look on a witless child's face or a happy drunk's. Gone was the spirit and the wit that had always given her lovely face such life and character. Also missing was the anger he had expected and now knew he deserved.

He fought the urge to knock down the man holding Ella and take her away. She looked as if a part of her was missing, and that alarmed him. Harold and Margaret looked tense and were clearly not pleased to see him. The scene before him was telling him something, but he could not figure out what, and that infuriated him. Ella would tell him, but there was no chance of a private word with her.

"Hello, Mahoney," Ella said, praying that her cloying sweetness would give him some hint that something was very wrong. "It's so nice to see you again."

"I'm glad to see that you have sorted out your problems with your guardian," he said, fighting to hide his uneasiness and act as if this was no more than some casual, polite meeting.

"Oh, Uncle Harold and I have spent many pleasant hours together. I have learned so much."

"That's good to hear. A family should get along."

"Yes, we are as close as the grave."

Margaret laughed as she moved to take hold of Ella's free arm and try to urge her up the steps of the carriage. "What a strange choice of words."

"You're going somewhere?" Harrigan asked.

"Dear Uncle Harold is taking me to see my family. He says that soon I won't miss them any more."

"Your family? But I thought . . ."

Harold gave his guard a sharp signal as he interrupted Harrigan. "I am sure you have a lot to do, Mr. Mahoney, and we are running a bit late." Seeing that Margaret and his man had gotten Ella into the carriage, Harold started to climb in after them. "If you are here about your pay, I suggest you speak to your man George Morgan."

As Harrigan watched the carriage disappear down the road, he heard a soft tsking to his right. He turned and nodded a restrained greeting to the Jensons, an aging couple who lived next door to Harold. Even as he started to turn and walk away from them, his curiosity got the better of him. They looked as if they were both concerned and filled with pity.

"Is there some trouble at the Carsons'?" he asked them.

"Well, I suppose there is no harm in telling you," said the plump Mrs. Jenson. "It's no secret. I fear the poor girl is suffering from some fever of the brain."

"A what?" Harrigan whispered, shock stealing the strength from his voice.

"Aren't you the fellow that brought the girl back from that heathen land she had run away to?" asked Mr. Jenson, stroking his long, well-oiled moustache as he frowned at Harrigan.

"Yes," Harrigan replied. "I noticed no fever of the brain in the girl."

"These things can come on suddenly," said Mrs. Jenson. "Maybe what troubles her was simply not clear to see while you were traveling together."

"I should have seen something," he muttered, struggling to continue the conversation even though his mind was feverishly trying to figure out what Harold could gain by spreading such a tale.

"Perhaps you just do not know enough about how young ladies should act to realize how oddly she was behaving."

"What do you mean?"

"Well, she ran away from a very comfortable life to go live with her aunt in the Wild West. Who knows what sort of rough life that woman lives out there, yet Ella wanted to stay. No young, well-bred lady would wish to remain in such an uncivilized place, but little Ella fought every attempt to bring her home. Poor Harold was quite distraught."

"I'm sure he was." Harrigan realized his anger was evident in his voice, for Mrs. Jenson eyed him nervously. He forced himself to smile at the woman. "And what is Mr. Carson doing for the poor girl? Has there been any explanation of her illness?"

"Harold thinks she's just succumbed to grief. She lost her whole family, you know."

"That was seven years ago."

"True, but the child has always been a bit, well, odd. And he thinks madness might run in the family. After all, just look at how her aunt behaves." The woman shuddered, and her husband patted her on the shoulder. "There are those who believe Louise Carson murdered Robin Abernathy. A brutal murder it was, too. And just look at who the woman travels with. I think Harold might be right. There certainly seems to be a weakness there, some wildness in the blood."

Harrigan wondered idly what would happen if he slapped the silly woman. "Harold must believe the illness can be cured or he would have had her locked away."

"He may yet have to do that. The doctor has been to see the girl, as has the minister, and neither sees much hope. They have no answers."

It was an effort to do so, but Harrigan bid the couple a very courteous farewell and started back to his office. The uneasiness he had felt earlier had been transformed into a hard, cold fear. Harold had done a good job of spreading the tale that Ella was insane. Harrigan suddenly recalled a few odd remarks made by some of the people he had spoken to in the last few days, but he had mostly ignored them. Ella had always told him that people in Philadelphia thought she was odd. She could also be playing some game in the hope of gaining a chance to escape the man. Now he realized that Harold was the one spreading the tale and that the man had most of Philadelphia believing that Ella was completely mad.

What troubled him even more was that a part of him started to wonder if there was any truth to the tale. Ella had been acting strangely. He had put her through a lot as they had traveled across the country. It could have been too much for her. She was delicate, a tiny, well-bred woman, not some pioneer.

Those thoughts had barely finished going through his

mind when he shook them away, cursing himself as a fool. Ella was indeed tiny and delicate of appearance, but she had a backbone of pure steel and a very sharp mind. She may have been acting oddly just now, but he refused to believe that she had gone mad. Harold wanted the world to believe she had, however. Harrigan knew he had to figure out why Harold would spread such a lie and what the man could gain from it. Instinct told him he had to find those answers soon, that there was very little time left for him to guess Harold's game and put a stop to it.

Ella forced her body to move, turning just enough to look out the back of the carriage as it pulled away from Harold's house. She watched Harrigan, not sure what she expected or wanted to see, but deciding it was better than looking at Harold and Margaret. Before they turned a corner and she lost sight of his tall, lean form, she saw him stop and begin to speak to the Jensons.

No sign of him having a revelation or rushing to her rescue, she mused as she slumped back down in her seat. *What did you expect? That he would suddenly pull a gleaming sword, leap on a white charger, and ride hard after you, screaming for Harold's head on a pike?* a voice sneered in her mind. She did think he could have showed some hint of concern. There was a very good chance that she would be dead in a short while, and it would have been nice to have seen some hint of feeling in him, some soft look that she could have recalled fondly in her last few minutes.

"I do not suppose we can stop by the jailhouse so that I might say goodbye to Louise and my friends?" Ella asked, thinking that her voice sounded a little stronger and praying that she was not deluding herself about the progress of her recovery.

"Very amusing, m'dear," Harold said. "I will let Louise know that you were thinking of her in your last days when I go and tell her of your unfortunate demise."

Margaret glared at Ella. "I noticed you were looking

back at that Mahoney fool. Did you really think he would understand your babbling and rush to your rescue?"

"My babbling was obviously clear enough to make you nervous," Ella said. "You practically threw me in the carriage to shut me up."

"Listen to her, Papa. I'm telling you, she is far too clear-headed. The opium is leaving her body."

Harold patted Margaret's clenched hand. "You worry too much, child. True, her mind and her mouth seem to be working again, if a little slowly, but it won't be a problem." He smiled at Ella. "You still can't move much, can you, m'dear?"

"Enough to dance the jig on your grave," Ella said, fighting to hide how sick with fear his cold smile made her feel.

"Oh, I don't think so. If you had any strength in your body or could get it to do what you wished it to, we wouldn't be sitting here having this pleasant conversation. I recall clearly how the opium affected a man I knew. He could, at times, carry on the most intelligent and rational conversation, yet he was so incapable of movement he would urinate where he sat, even as he kept on speaking. Much like some drunks."

"You obviously have a high class of acquaintances."

"You are very much like your father. When he realized what was happening and knew he could not save himself or his wife and child, he still cursed me with great skill. When you people get scared, you obviously turn nasty."

"You watched my family die?"

"From a safe distance, of course. Actually, I believe you and Louise might be a little cleverer than he was, a little less trusting and naive. It has been much more difficult to deal with you as I must."

"Tsk, such a pity." Ella found herself praying that God would give her back her strength for just a minute or two, just long enough to kill Harold. "I find it a marvel that you think you can continue to escape any punishment for your crimes."

"And who will make me pay? You? You can barely stand up. Louise? If she has any sense she will bury you and flee back to her pathetic little ranch. Louise lost all power and credibility in this city many years ago. Perhaps it is the opium that makes you so slow to see the truth. You have lost. I have neatly removed all allies from your side. You are alone, and alone you cannot beat me. I suggest you accept the fact and make your peace with God."

"Oh, I am not so deluded that I think I can save myself, but I do believe that you will have to pay the penalty for all the evil you have done. Although I hate it, I even accept the fact that you might well live to a ripe old age without ever having to pay for the deaths and destruction you have caused. But even you know that you cannot live forever, Harold."

"What do you mean?"

"Obviously you have been too busy destroying people to go to church. I refer to the punishment that comes after one has lived his life. Hell, Harold. I believe you've heard of it? We all pay for our sins in the end. Your comeuppance might take a lot longer than I like, but it will come. Yes, you are probably right to believe that no one will be able to save me." She leaned back against the plush carriage seat and closed her eyes, finding a little pleasure in the fury and fear she had seen in Harold's eyes. "But guess what, dear Harold? No one will be able to save you either."

Chapter Twenty

"Sounds like they've given her some drug. Mayhap opium?"

Harrigan turned slowly from the window he had been staring out of to look at his friend and partner, unsettled by George's response to his tale of his brief meeting with Ella. It had been barely fifteen minutes since he had seen Ella, had the strange conversation with her and the Jensons, and returned to his office. Every one of those moments had been spent trying to deny what his heart and mind were telling him—that Ella was in great danger.

"Ella would never use that poison, George," he finally said. "And she's too smart to let them give it to her."

"Oh, she's smart, and she's a fighter, but she's also just a tiny woman." George rose from the chair he had sprawled in and moved to the desk. "I need a drink," he said as he opened the crystal decanter set there and poured himself a large whiskey. "You could probably use one too."

"You think I need to stiffen my backbone or clear my head?" Harrigan asked as he helped himself to a drink.

"A little of both maybe." George ignored Harrigan's scowl. "I feel sure they have drugged her. A girl doesn't fight tooth and nail against coming here as long as she has and then suddenly grow all sweet, quiet, and accepting. Whether you believe her relatives want her dead or not, you can't doubt that she believes it wholeheartedly. She was also spitting mad at you, yet, barely four days later, she smiles sweetly and says hello? Something is wrong."

Harrigan swore and finished off his drink in a few swallows, then carefully poured himself another one. "I've been trying to ignore that truth."

"I thought so, but damned if I can understand why."

"Because it means I have to admit that I have been horribly and consistently wrong. And maybe, for Ella, fatally so."

George grimaced, took a sip of his drink, and then, reluctantly, nodded. "You have been wrong, but that's not completely your fault."

"No? I'm the one who refused to believe her and blithely handed her over to that swine Harold."

"Well, I would not go so far as to say you did it blithely." George ignored Harrigan's angry glance. "Your only real fault is how hard you fought to ignore the truth of what Ella was saying. I understand your anger and mistrust of her class. I even share it to some extent. The fact that the ones who caused your family's downfall are close friends of her family only added to all that hard feeling. I fully understand that too. But—"

"Ah, the great *but.*"

"But," George doggedly continued, "I would have thought that those same feelings would have made you more inclined to believe her tale of treachery and murder."

"Exactly." Harrigan nodded as George's eyes slowly widened. "Right from the beginning I have mistrusted my own instincts concerning Ella and everything she said. I would look into those damn big green eyes and want to accept every word she said as pure gospel. The fact that she was telling me that her family and their friends were more corrupt than even I had imagined just made her words all the more tempting. I had to believe that she was a big, clever liar and as corrupt as her family. At least, that is what I kept telling myself."

"And, yet, believing that, you made love to the girl?" George could not fully hide his shock.

"She could have put a knife to my throat and it probably would not have dimmed my passion for her. I was so hungry for her that I was past thinking straight. Hell, I don't think I've been in full possession of my wits since I first set eyes on her. And I do not recall telling you that I had made love to her."

"You didn't have to tell me. It was obvious."

Harrigan frowned. He was not sure he liked that, for it meant that his emotions were not as controlled as he thought. Briefly, all the fear he had suffered while he had been with Ella returned in force, but he easily pushed it aside. He would be willing to bare his soul to the world if it would buy her even one more minute of life.

"It could not have been that obvious or Louise would have shot me," he said.

George flushed, and took a steadying drink before carefully setting his glass down on the dresser. "She wanted to, the very first time we caught up with you after she took me prisoner. I convinced her that Ella might not appreciate it. I thought that the girl might have some affection for you since she had become your lover. I fear the doubts I then held about Ella's morals and chastity weighted my words. Louise was distracted from her urge to kill you by the implied insult behind my words."

It surprised Harrigan that he still had the ability to do so, but he laughed at the image of George trying to deal with an enraged Louise. "Poor George. This has not been an easy job for you."

"No, and it's not yet over."

"George, if you're implying that we should do something for Ella, I ought to remind you that we still work for Harold. We have no proof yet that he will kill Ella and, if we now act against him, we could destroy all chance for further employment. Hell, we could even face charges." He raised one brow when George pulled a fat envelope from inside his coat and tossed it on the desk. "What is that?"

"Our pay. Harold finally coughed it up. I believe he grew weary of me squatting at his doorstep. After what you have just told me, I now think he was scared of what I might see or hear. We no longer work for the man."

Harrigan briefly weighed the packet in his hand, then set it back down on the desk. "So, you suggest we now work against him? We may yet have to stay in this business, George. Going against Harold could well end our chances of working in this town, and probably a few others." He smiled faintly when George looked at him with an even mixture of anger and disappointment. "I merely point out the possible consequences. After all, Ella is his legal ward and, despite all our efforts, we have no hard proof that he intends to do her any harm."

"He's given her opium."

"She is unruly, highly emotional."

"He's locked her up."

"She habitually runs away."

George cursed softly and ran a hand through his hair. "You still don't believe she's in danger."

"I do. I think I've always believed. As I said, I just didn't want to."

"Then why are you hesitating? Why are you arguing this with me?"

"Because you're ready to ride off on your white horse, your sword of righteousness raised high, and rescue the damsel in distress. I just want you to realize, to completely understand, that you probably won't return from this grand adventure to be showered in rose petals and honors. Even if Ella is telling the truth and that bastard Harold is trying to kill her, such an action could still cripple our business. Our livelihood greatly depends upon people with fat purses and those people do not like to think that the men they hire might turn their dark little secrets against them. It will be seen that we have betrayed a confidence, acted on something we would never have known about if we had never worked for Harold Carson."

"I think a young girl's life is worth the risk, don't you?"

"Yes. I just wanted to be sure that you did. There's one other thing. I hope you understand that Louise might still want nothing to do with you. Saving her niece may not be enough to make her forgive and forget."

George winced. "I know. I won't say that there isn't a part of me that wants to try and win her favor, but my biggest concern is for Ella's safety."

"So is mine, even if that hasn't been too obvious to everyone, especially Ella."

"I just wish we had had more success in finding out about Harold's dealings. If we could prove him guilty of some crime, we could get help. We could at least get Louise and the boys out of jail so that they could help us."

"Oh, I think we have enough for that," Harrigan said as he donned his hat and headed out the door. "Thompson is not only nearly as stupid as Sheriff Smith, but he's a coward to the bone. All we need to do is convince him that we have enough to bring down Harold Carson. Thompson will be so scared that we'll bring him down with the man that he'll do whatever we want."

"How did you do that?" Louise asked, wincing a little as they stepped out of the jail into the full light of a summer day.

"I just made Thompson think hard of all the things he's guilty of," Harrigan replied as he led Louise and the four youths to the horses he had obtained for them, trying to hide his sense of urgency, but knowing he was failing by the intent way Louise was watching him. "I might not have found out enough to put Harold in jail, but I had enough to make Thompson think he was in danger. Those two have been working together for a long time. That much I'm sure of."

"I could have told you that," Louise snapped. "It was Thompson who helped to make me look like a murderer."

"Thompson just repeated what Harold told him to." Harrigan smiled faintly when Louise stopped and stared at him, but gently touched her arm and silently urged her to keep moving.

"Harold was behind my being accused of murder?"

"I can't believe you're as surprised as you sound."

"Maybe not. I haven't let myself think of that incident too much. It was not only embarrassing and infuriating, but painful. Every time I thought about it I had to recall how so many of the people I thought of as friends turned their backs on me."

"And made you decide to leave Philadelphia, to go as far away as you could," he murmured as he mounted his horse, the others quickly doing the same.

"Exactly. It is because of him then that I was not here when my brother, his wife, and my poor little nephew drowned. I will never forgive him for that, or the ones who believed him."

"Oh, I think if you consider the matter for a while, you will realize that there's an even bigger crime hidden there."

"Who was the stronger one in your family, Miss Louise?" George asked quietly. "Who spoke out against Harold?"

"I did, of course," Louise replied. "My brother said the man was not as evil as I thought, that he was family. I was the one who reminded him that Harold is only a Carson because of a strange twist of marriages and name changes that were so convoluted that I can't even recall all of them. I'd almost convinced him to change his will and name me the children's guardian, despite my youth."

Harrigan watched Louise as she tensed the moment the words left her mouth. She stared at him as her eyes widened and she paled slightly. He knew she had finally figured out what he had begun to suspect more and more the deeper he had dug into Harold's affairs. Sadly, though, a growing suspicion was all he had, and he was increasingly sure that he would never find the proof to convict the man of those murders.

"He killed them," she said in a voice so cold and hard it was barely recognizable.

"If he did, he did it in a very clever way."

"You know he did or you would never have steered me toward the suspicion."

"True, the suspicion. That's all I have. Ever since I returned to Philadelphia I've studied the man, gathered all the information I could. There is no proof, none that I have uncovered, leastwise."

"So, now you begin to believe Ella."

"Enough so that I believe we should stop talking and go find her."

"We're supposed to ride with you? I'm still deciding whether I want to kill you or just maim you," Louise said, even as she nudged her horse to follow his. She glared at George, who rode up next to her. "Both of you."

Louise studied the two men as they rode through the city. She was not sure what to think. Both men were so tense that the feeling began to infect her. A small voice suggested that they might be working hand in fist with Harold and were leading her into a trap, but she easily silenced it. Harold would gain nothing with her death. She did not have enough money to rouse his interest and he knew no one would listen to anything she had to say. It just bothered her that the same men who brought Ella to Harold would now work to free the girl.

She struggled not to look at George, who smiled softly every time she glanced his way. Despite what she saw as his betrayal, she could not believe he would do anything to hurt her. Louise knew she had not been wrong about his increasing reluctance to do the job he had been hired to do.

"How do we know you ain't just leading us to Harold so he can get rid of us?" asked Joshua, putting Louise's own suspicions to voice. "Harold would probably like to see Louise dead too."

"There's no probably about it," said Harrigan. "I can only assure you that I am not helping Harold. The man gains nothing by killing Louise except to shut her mouth." He winked at Louise. "I suspect there's a few people who might think that reason enough, but not Harold. He knows no one will listen to her and she doesn't have enough money to tempt him." Harrigan looked at Louise, who was clearly still trying to make up her mind about trusting him. "I know you're not poor, that you have enough to live comfortably and survive several lean years at your ranch, but it's barely enough to keep Harold's three mistresses in dresses for a month."

"Three mistresses?" asked Louise.

"Three. They're all very young and bear an uncanny resemblance to Margaret."

Louise shook her head. "Well, that doesn't surprise me. I always thought those two doted on each other in an unnatural way. Still, it might mean that he hasn't committed the abomination I once accused him of. Margaret would never allow one of her lovers to have a mistress."

"You have a true skill at endearing yourself to people, don't you?" Harrigan drawled, easily imagining how furious Harold must have been to be accused of incest.

"It's a gift." Louise briefly exchanged a grin with a chuckling Joshua.

"So, do you trust me enough to work with me now?" Harrigan asked quietly.

"I think you've seen the error of your ways, but I also think I'll keep an eye on you. Although I didn't agree with them, you had a lot of strong reasons for not believing a word Ella said. Why the sudden change of heart?"

"Not really a change of heart, simply a cleaning out of my ears so that I listened to what my heart was saying." He smiled faintly when Louise's eyes slowly widened. "I was not trying to believe Ella, I was constantly trying very hard not to believe her." He shrugged. "I cannot correct past mistakes, except for the last one. I stupidly gave Harold his victim, and I damn well intend to take her back."

"Fine. Where are we going?"

A little disappointed that Louise offered neither forgiveness nor a declaration confirming her belief in him, Harrigan answered, "I think we need to get to the river." It had taken him longer than he liked to get Thompson to let Louise and her boys go, and Harrigan began to fear that they would reach the river only in time to search for Ella's body.

Louise tensed. "Harold wouldn't try to kill her in the same way he killed her parents, would he?"

"No. It might make people look a little too closely at the earlier deaths. No matter how well Harold has hidden his guilt, he'll worry about that." He sighed and carefully told Louise about the whispers of Ella's insanity and the meeting he had had with her and Harold. The fury he could read in Louise's face almost made him lean away from her. "He's laid the foundation for a suicide. At least that's how I look at it."

"It's how I see it too," she agreed, in a voice roughened by the anger she fought to control. "The poor mad Ophelia scene from Hamlet. The man is more clever and more sinister than even I imagined. If you watched this game being played out, why didn't you stop it before now?"

"I still doubted he would kill her. I had no real proof that the man had ever done anything violent, not even the hint of it until recently."

"And you once called Ella delusional, so maybe you believed the stories," said Joshua.

"No, never," Harrigan replied. "I was just not sure how Harold would use it. After all, if he got people to believe Ella was insane, he could take complete control of her money legally. I began to hope he had found another way to steal from her, one that meant he did not have to kill her. It would have given me more time to find some proof of his crimes. I even wondered if Ella was playing some game in an attempt to, say, make them relax their guard, so that she could escape."

"What changed your mind?"

"The way she was when I finally saw her again. That was no game. It was Ella, but it wasn't. There was an unsettling distance in her expression, as if her mind was miles away. Now I realize that it was clouded by the opium. There was still a spark of the old Ella left, however. She told me they were going to the river, even told me why."

"I can't believe Harold would let her speak so openly. With others he could shrug it aside with talk of madness, but he must have known he couldn't do that with you."

"Oh, she didn't say it so clearly. That's why I knew it was the real Ella peeking through for a brief moment. She told me that her uncle was taking her to see her family, that he was going to make it so she would not miss them any more."

"That was clever. Just like my Ella. But there's always the possibility that it was just nonsense caused by the opium."

"I considered that possibility. Harold's reaction made me certain Ella was trying to give me a message. The man couldn't get her away from me fast enough and almost babbled as he tried to give me some explanation for her words. No, he's taking Ella to the same place her family drowned. It makes perfect sense. Everyone will see it as a fitting place for a poor, sad, confused girl to end her life."

Louise cursed. "I realize that it would be best to take Harold alive, certainly less trouble to deal with afterward, but it is going to be damn hard not to kill the bastard."

George murmured a few words meant to soothe Louise and drew her immediate attention. Harrigan concentrated on getting to the river as swiftly as possible and tried to concoct a few plans. He could not be sure what they would find when they got there so it was difficult to come up with any firm plan of action, but he was able to imagine a few possible complications and decide how to react to them.

Harrigan inwardly cursed when that was not enough to keep his mind off Ella. He did not really want to think about her, about what she might be enduring, and what she had already suffered. Such thoughts left him choking on his own guilt.

There were so many reasons why he had not wanted to believe her, but reminding himself of them did not do much to ease that guilt. He had made her pay for his confusion and his prejudices. Ella had done nothing to deserve that.

Their time together had been too brief, their passion too strong to allow for any clear thinking. In many ways he had been afraid, afraid to trust her and afraid to allow her to get too close to him. The first time they had made love he had been so lost to the passion they shared that he had been terrified. All that had kept him from running away from her as fast as he could was the fact that she had not guessed how lost he was when he was in her arms. He knew that the gnawing fear that she would discover his weakness and use it against him had caused him to treat her unkindly at times.

It was that cowardice that had made him hand her over to Harold so quickly. The moment he had done so he realized that there were many ways he could have handled that. He had not really thought about the money or his business, just about getting Ella away from him before she could discover how badly he wanted her, how deeply she had touched him. She might never forgive him for that. Harrigan was not sure he could forgive himself.

In that one desperate act, in that unthinking attempt to protect his own heart, he was certain he had ended whatever future he might have had with Ella, something he now admitted he wanted. Although he had every intention of rescuing her, that did not mean he would succeed. And if he did free her and end Harold's threat to her life, Harrigan doubted there was anything he could say to make amends for all the mistakes he had made.

Chapter Twenty-One

Ella desperately wanted to kick her smiling uncle in the face, but could not seem to make her body obey that small, still angry part of her mind. She meekly let him lift her out of the carriage and turn her toward the river, the same deceptively beautiful and deadly Susquehanna that had drowned her family. She knew she should be furious and terrified, and a small, still rational part of her was, but mostly she felt nothing at all. It was as if she watched someone else, as if she stood apart from the woman Harold removed from his opulent carriage.

"The same river," she heard herself say. "The bodies were found on these banks."

"Yes. I felt it was appropriate," Harold said with a chilling glee. "Where better for a disturbed, brain-fevered child to go to die? Most people will remember that your poor family's battered, river-bloated bodies were found here. I fear yours will quite probably wash up further downstream, but don't worry, we'll bury you next to the others."

"And maybe Louise will soon join the little family gathering," Margaret said as she stepped up on the other side of Ella.

"Louise can't hurt you," Ella whispered.

Ella felt a sharp pinch of fear and welcomed it. She reminded herself that it had been a long time since they had poured any of the tainted lemonade down her throat. There had been signs of her returning strength before she had dozed off in the carriage. If she could stay out of the water just a little longer, she might actually regain enough of her clouded senses to have a fighting chance.

"I fear my sweet child has developed a fierce dislike for Louise," Harold said as he began to tug Ella down to the river's edge, two of his muscular guards falling into step behind them.

"Louise will be devastated." Ella was almost as surprised by her tart remark as Harold looked.

"The drug is loosening its grip on you a little faster than I had expected. You could almost walk on your own now. We've gotten you to the river just in time. I'll have Louise freed from jail just in time to find your body and give you a decent burial. It would be wise if she understood her own precarious position and swiftly fled back to her wilderness with her mongrels."

It would indeed be wise, but Ella knew Louise better than that. She could only pray that Joshua and the others saw the danger Louise was in and were able to talk some sense into her aunt. Although the thought of someone avenging her death was tempting, even comforting, Ella much preferred that her aunt stay alive.

"And I still think it would be wise to get rid of Louise," Margaret said.

"We will consider the matter later, child. Perhaps as a present for you on your birthday." Harold smiled at his daughter.

"Thank you, Papa."

"And people think that I am mad," Ella muttered. "You know, Harold, you are rapidly depleting your cache of wealthy relatives. Soon you might actually have to work in order to keep your purse full."

"Oh, do shut her up, Papa."

The way Harold was staring at her made Ella so afraid that she worried it was showing in her face. She did not want to give Harold the satisfaction of seeing the terror that was rapidly pushing its way through the lingering fog the opium had encased her in. In order to better hide her expression, she stared down at the river and decided that that was not much better.

The muddy embankment was not too high, but the murky waters looked deep. Heavy spring rains had made the river run swift and high. She knew the drug was seeping out of her body faster with each passing moment, but she doubted she had the strength needed to fight the current of the river. Harold had been pouring that poison down her throat for several days, and she suspected it would work to sap her wits and strength for quite a while yet. Unfortunately, she thought, as she sighed inwardly with defeat, she had but minutes left. Very soon she would be swirling downstream like the rest of the debris the river had captured in its strong current.

It did not really surprise Ella when she suddenly thought about Harrigan. It was certainly one of the biggest unfinished pieces of business in her too short life. What was saddest of all was that she knew she could have loved him so well, and now he would never know that. She didn't really find much comfort in the fact that he would soon realize just how thoroughly wrong he had been. If he was going to be humbled by regrets, she dearly wanted to be alive to reap the benefits of such humility.

"Why are we crouching here in the bushes?" demanded Louise as she crept up beside Harrigan. "The man is about to toss Ella into the river."

"Which he will do immediately if he catches sight of all of us," George said.

"Exactly," agreed Harrigan, fighting to harness the blind rage that had siezed him when he had seen Harold and Margaret at the river's edge, holding an unsteady Ella between them. "My first instinct was to race over there and kill the bastard, but Ella would probably be miles downstream by the time I got my hands around his throat."

"At least you're not just sitting here waiting for him to actually push her in before you finally believe that he means to kill her," Louise said, scowling at George when he gave her a gentle, punitive nudge.

"It's alright, George." Harrigan almost laughed at the way the couple was poking at each other like petulant children. "I deserve the derision." He turned to the four young men crouched behind them. "Manuel, Thomas, can you two take care of the two men by Harold's carriage?" When they nodded and slipped away, he looked at Joshua and Edward. "We have to encircle the five people down by the river. Harold and his two thugs are the most important, the most dangerous. We need to get as close as possible without being seen."

"Understood," Joshua said. "Me and Ed will circle around on the left and take care of Harold's guards. If we can't reach them before we're spotted, we can sure as hell shoot them. I just hope that someone here can swim," he said as he and Edward crept away.

Louise looked from Harrigan to George and back again. "I hope one of you can. I can't."

"Harrigan is a very strong swimmer," George replied.

"Good, because Ella might still end up in the river. If she wasn't filled with that poison, I wouldn't worry so much. She's a strong swimmer too and could probably hold on until we could help her. She's not herself though. For all we know, she doesn't even realize the danger she's in."

"Oh, I think she realizes exactly how precarious her position is," Harrigan said as he started to circle around to the right side of Harold and the others, Louise and George quickly following. "Don't forget that it was Ella herself who told me where they were going."

"Yeah, but did she mean what she said as a clue, or was she just so stupid with opium that she really thought she could see her family again?"

George tried to hush Louise, but she was not feeling very obedient, although she lowered her voice to a whisper so soft that Harrigan could barely hear her. Harrigan understood and sympathized with Louise's fears and concerns, but he was glad that he no longer had to listen to them. He had too many of his own to deal with. Despite her fear, he knew Louise would still do whatever was needed to help Ella, would be able to push her concerns aside the moment she had to, so that she could concentrate only on saving Ella. Harrigan was not so sure he had that skill, and now would be a very poor time to test it, so he fought to bury his fear and anger. It was the only way he knew of to remain clear of mind and steady of purpose.

Louise's concerns could not be fully ignored, however, for he shared a few of them. There was no way of knowing how firmly Ella was held in the numbing grip of the opium. Her rescue would be a lot easier, with a better chance of success, if they could depend upon her helping them and herself, but they could not. The very fact that Ella was standing at the river's edge not fighting the light hold Harold and Margaret had on her told Harrigan that she was definitely not in possession of her customary spirit. He would have to act as if she were unconscious and, depending upon how much of the opium still lingered in her blood, she could well be nearly so.

Guilt and remorse filled him as she saw how helpless Ella was. He had put her in the hands of her killer. If he could not save her, he would be as guilty of her murder as Harold was. He had always prided himself on his instincts, but this time he had scorned them, and yet again he ruefully admitted that it was simply because he had been scared. Instinct had also told him that, if he had allowed himself to believe in Ella only to discover that she had lied, it would have cut him in a way from which he never would have recovered. Eleanor's betrayal had hurt his family, his purse, his vanity, and his pride. Ella's betrayal could have destroyed him. That knowledge had kept him running from the truth. Harrigan prayed that he would have the skill to save them all from the results of that cowardice.

When he finally reached the point where they would have to step out into the open, Harrigan stopped and took a deep, steadying breath. He glanced toward the carriage and saw Manuel and Thomas there, carefully sheltered from Harold's view, but keeping a close eye on the scene by the river. Their speed and skill astounded him. He briefly wondered how he had managed to continue to escape them as they had all raced across the country. He looked to the other side of the clearing and saw Joshua and Edward. The youths were just leaving the more secure cover of the trees, and dropped to their stomachs. Only the movement of the grasses and wildflowers told Harrigan that they were still there and headed straight for Harold's two thick-necked guards. That left him with only Harold and his daughter to worry about.

"Why are you hesitating now?" asked Louise.

"Just trying to figure out the best way to reach Harold before he can shove Ella into the river," Harrigan replied, even as he decided he didn't have the time to come up with a perfect plan.

"Ella might have just given us a chance. She obviously still has wit enough to infuriate Harold. The argument she's started has distracted him. It might be enough to keep him from seeing us until it's too late. Should we wiggle through the grasses like Joshua and Edward?"

"No. They'll get to the guards before we can get within reach of Harold," said George as he crouched beside Louise.

"So, we charge him," said Harrigan. "Let's pray Ella has him so angry he can't see straight and that we can run faster than he can think."

"Prepared for a little swim, m'dear?" Harold asked, placing a hand on her back.

"You are a complete bastard, Harold," Ella said, glad

to hear how strong her voice was, but wishing that strength would hurry up and reach her arms and legs. "There's something you might like to know first."

"I don't believe there's anything you can say that I would care to hear."

"I've made a will." She almost cried out when he grabbed her by the arm and yanked her around to face him squarely.

"You're lying," Margaret snapped as she moved to stand next to her father.

"Maybe. Maybe not. You can't be sure, can you?"

Ella prayed that she had regained enough of her wits to keep the argument going and be convincing enough to make Harold believe what she said. She was not sure time would gain her anything, for Harrigan had never believed her, her aunt was in jail, and Harrigan had not shown any sign of understanding the clues she had tried to give him before being shoved into the carriage. There would be no one rushing to her rescue. One swift glance at the turbulent river convinced her that even a few minutes of delay was worth the effort. Her mind was freeing itself of the drug more and more. Soon her body would as well. All it needed was a little time.

"It will never stand firm in court," Harold said, but his statement lacked the weight of conviction.

"It was witnessed by a sheriff and a judge," Ella lied. "I think it'll be strong enough to survive all your tricks."

"Where is it?"

"Even soaked in opium, I'm not so stupid as to tell you."

"She's left everything to that bitch, Louise," Margaret said. "Now you have to kill the woman, Papa, or everything else we have done will be for nothing."

For one brief, heart-stopping moment, Ella thought the drug had swept over her again in force. The vision she saw over Harold's shoulder had to be a delusion caused by the opium. Then her senses returned and she realized that Harrigan, George, and Louise were indeed racing up behind Harold and Margaret. There should have been some outcry from Harold's guards, but Ella resisted the urge to look and see why Harold's faithful watchdogs were silent.

"I didn't leave it to Louise," she said.

"Liar. Who else could you leave it to? I know it wasn't me."

Just as Ella believed she would be successful in holding their attention long enough, a bee decided it had to investigate Margaret's heavy scent. Margaret hissed a curse, and swatted at it, turning just enough to catch sight of Ella's rescuers.

"Papa! Look out!" cried Margaret even as she turned to run back to the carriage, deserting her father without hesitation.

Harold took one look at a grim-faced Harrigan, who was almost close enough to grab him, and lunged for Ella. Ella tried to get out of Harold's reach, but her body responded far too slowly to her mind's sharp command to run. She cried out in frustration as Harold roughly grabbed her, held her in front of him, and pulled his gun. Harrigan, Louise, and George stumbled to a halt. Ella was a little shocked at how furious Harrigan looked, as if he would like nothing better than to tear Harold apart with his bare hands.

"How the hell did you get out of jail, Louise?" demanded Harold.

"Unlike you, Thompson can be made to feel guilty and afraid concerning his crimes," Louise replied. "Let Ella go, Harold. It's over. You've murdered enough of my family. Now it's time to pay the piper."

"I don't think so. I still hold a trump card," he said, tightening his grip on Ella. "Where's Margaret?"

"She obviously has your sense of familial loyalty. She ran, trying to save her own skin. My boys have her trapped in the carriage. She's not going anywhere."

Harold chanced a brief glimpse around and realized he stood alone, that neither his men nor Margaret could come to his aid. "You'll free Margaret and she and I will leave. I'll release Ella when my daughter and I are safe."

"You can't expect me to believe you."

"Let Ella go, Harold," demanded Harrigan, trying to edge a little closer without alarming the man. "You can't possibly win this standoff. You at least have a chance to survive this. You own enough people in this town to escape hanging for your crimes, probably even to elude jail. But if you hurt Ella, you're a dead man."

Joshua had moved to stand behind Harold, but Harrigan knew the youth would not shoot the man until Ella was safely out of the way. There was always the chance that the bullet could go through Harold and hurt Ella. Harrigan began to think that Harold was not going to calmly surrender even though it was the sensible thing to do.

"No, I'll have no chance at all," Harold said, his gaze darting from Harrigan to Louise and back again. "I've made a mistake here and mistakes are weaknesses. The wolves will move in fast now and tear me to pieces. Now they'll have something they can use against me. I haven't got any life left here, none at all."

"So start one somewhere else," snapped Louise. "Just let Ella go and leave us the hell alone."

"No, you won't let this rest. You know it all now, though I'm damned if I can figure out how." Harold slowly smiled. "I've lost, but I think I'll make sure you have too."

Harrigan knew what Harold planned to do, but was too late to stop him. He watched in horror as Harold shoved Ella over the embankment. As he moved to help her, Harold tried to shoot him, but Joshua was quicker. Harold got off only one wild, harmless shot before Joshua's bullet slammed into his back. Harrigan spared barely a glance at Harold, looking only long enough to reassure himself that the man was really dead, then rushed to the edge of the river. He did not see Ella and his heart froze.

"Over here!" cried a weak, shaking voice.

Ella had to call twice before the four pale faces peering over the riverbank turned her way. She was not sure how she had kept herself from falling into the river. She could only recall scrambling, tumbling, and clawing her way through the mud until she grasped the thick branch of a dead tree. It hung so low over the water that she could feel the currents tugging at her skirt and her hair. Ella prayed that her rescuers could reach her soon, for the branch she clung to like a monkey, with her legs and her arms wrapped tightly around it, did not look sturdy enough to hold her out of the water for very long. If she was any judge, its tumble into the river was long overdue.

"How the hell did you get over there?" Louise demanded.

"I was just wondering that myself." Ella screeched in alarm when the branch cracked, dipping her a little lower into the swift water. "I don't think I'll be here much longer."

"Joshua's going to get a rope," Harrigan said as he yanked off his boots and socks and began to edge his way down the slick embankment.

"Maybe you ought to wait. The footing here is very treacherous."

"Quiet, woman. I'm determined to be a hero. You should be encouraging me instead of trying to dampen my pretensions."

"Those pretensions will be well soaked if you slide into the Susquehanna."

"You need someone to help you with the rope. You can't let go without being swept away. What did you plan to do? Catch the rope in your teeth?"

Ella decided that piece of nonsense did not deserve a reply, and inwardly breathed a sigh of relief when he reached the tree. At least he had something to hold onto now. "Where are Harold and Margaret?"

"Harold is dead and Margaret is tied up in the carriage."

"Margaret won't be pleased about that."

"Margaret can go to hell. Her father will undoubtedly be waiting for her there."

Harrigan caught the rope Joshua lowered down to him

and cautiously edged closer to Ella. After closely inspecting
her situation, he decided to secure the rope around his
own waist. There was no way to safely tie it around her,
for any added weight on her precarious perch could easily
send her tumbling into the river. He might be able to grab
her, but without the rope to anchor him they would both
be swept away. One look at the cloudy, rushing water was
enough to tell him that even the strongest swimmer would
have to fight hard to survive. Edging as close to her as he
dared, he grasped her by the wrist.

"You're going to have to let go, Ella," he ordered her.

"If I do, the river will take me. It has a pretty strong
grip on me now."

"I can hold you. Let go and then throw yourself in my
direction."

For a moment, Ella was not sure she could release her
grip on the branch. Fear and the cold of the water, seeping
through her body, made her feel as if she was locked in
place. She realized she trusted Harrigan to grab her and
hold on tight. She was just not sure she trusted herself to
do as he asked or the river to allow them to escape its
hold.

Just as he wondered if Ella was still too soaked in opium
to understand him, Harrigan saw the fear in her eyes. "I
can hold you, Ella, even if you end up neck deep in the
water. And George and the others have a damn firm grip
on the other end of this rope. The minute I've got a good
hold on you, they'll pull us back up the embankment."
He gave a faint tug on her wrists, heard the wood crack
ominously, and felt his heart skip with fear. "We're running out of time, woman. Just toss yourself over here."

Ella took a deep breath, released the branch, and lunged
toward Harrigan. She could not fully subdue a cry of fear
as she felt her legs hit the cold water and be pulled by the
strong currents. But Harrigan pulled harder. The moment
she bumped up against him, she wrapped herself around
his strong body as tenaciously as she had clung to the tree
branch. She paid little attention to how he got back up

the slick riverbank except to notice that it was a rough ride. Ella did not ease her grip on Harrigan or open her eyes until she felt other hands tugging at her.

"You'll be fine now, Ella," Louise said as she wrapped Ella in a thick blanket Manuel had hastily retrieved from Harold's carriage. "This was not really how I wished it all to end, but at least it has finally ended."

Once glance at Harold's body was more than enough for Ella to assure herself that the man was dead. There had been numerous times over the last few torturous days that she had prayed hard for Harold's death. She felt no real sense of victory or joy now, although she did feel safe. After so many years of fear and hiding, she decided that was good enough. And perhaps, she decided as she meekly allowed her aunt to wipe the mud from her face, Harold's death was the only way to insure that she remained safe.

"What about the others?" Ella asked, wondering if her voice sounded as slurred to the others as it did to her.

"We'll take them to the sheriff," replied Harrigan.

"Thompson? He was hand in glove with Harold," said Louise. "He won't do anything."

"Oh yes he will," Harrigan assured her. "After all, he doesn't really want anyone to know for certain that he was no more than Harold's lackey. And I believe that, even if he lets Margaret go, she won't have the power to do anything to you. As Harold said, the wolves will circle soon, so I suspect that very shortly Margaret won't have any money left either."

"From some of the things I heard Margaret say," said Ella, "she was not the complete, simple follower you might think she was."

"No, she wasn't," agreed Harrigan, aching to say a hundred different things to Ella, but knowing it was not the time, and fearing it might never be. "She was not the leader either. When I was playing the fool for Eleanor, I had the misfortune of coming to know Margaret pretty well. She is venemous and can even see the threat someone could pose to her wealth or standing, but she lacked the wit and the patience to plan anything or enact a plan all on her own. Every step she took was directed by her father. You need not worry about her. It's truly over now.''

Harrigan stared at Ella for a moment, then gently brushed her cheeks with his knuckles, and turned away. As he enlisted the help of the younger men and George in moving Harold's body and securing Harold's men, Ella struggled to think of something to say to him. She wanted to say something clever which would invite him to express his feelings yet not reveal too many of her own.

When Harrigan returned, only to ask her aunt if she could ride, Ella decided that she must look as slow-witted as she felt. She then suffered another of his long, silent stares before he left with George in the carriage, leaving her with a simple, curt *"Good luck."* A soft curse escaped her as her aunt helped her to her feet. The opium was obviously still numbing her mind, her recovery probably set back by the chill of the river. A strong sense of self-preservation had been all that had cleared it enough to help her fight to survive. As Louise led her to a horse, Ella fought the urge to weep. She knew she might well have just lost her last chance of having more with Harrigan than a brief tempestuous affair and some sweet memories.

''You need to rest and recover for a few days,'' said Louise as she rode up beside Ella and took control of her reins. ''Then we can make some decisions about what to do.''

''We can go back to Wyoming,'' Ella said.

''Are you certain?''

Ella glanced in the direction the carriage had gone and sighed. ''Yes. There's nothing here for me now.''

Chapter Twenty-Two

The bright sun made Ella wince and she briefly massaged her temples, trying to rub away a persistent headache. She was not sure if it was a lingering effect of the opium, her own sometimes overwhelming sense of unhappiness, or facing the bright summer sun after spending too much time in a shaded hotel room and, now, several tedious hours in a dark lawyer's office. A quick glance at her aunt revealed Louise receiving a tender, modest farewell kiss from George, and Ella winced over her own spasm of jealousy. George had been a tremendous help since the rescue at the riverside three days ago, but Harrigan had completely disappeared.

"Shall we return to the hotel and have some lunch?" asked Louise even as she hooked her arm through Ella's and tugged her niece toward the hotel.

"Shouldn't we go to the jail to see if there's any news about Margaret?" Ella frowned a little and glanced toward the jail. "The woman deserves all she gets, but I think I'd like to know what that is."

"George is tending to the matter."

"So, you've completely forgiven George, have you?"

"Just as you have completely forgiven Harrigan."

"If that is so clear for others to see, how come Harrigan has not even stopped by to see how I am faring after my ordeal?" The fact that Harrigan's absence hurt her deeply annoyed Ella. "George doesn't even mention the fool."

Louise sighed as they entered the hotel and she steered them toward the dining room. "I've asked George about that and he just says that it's not his place to say anything. No amount of cajolery or scolding changes his mind. If he knows anything, it's been told to him in confidence, and he'll never tell anyone, not even me."

Ella shook her head as they sat down at a table near the front windows of the hotel and her aunt ordered each of them a meal. She was not really surprised at George's reluctance, but had hoped for a clue or two that would explain Harrigan's conspicuous absence. The only advantage to George's courtship of Louise was that it provided Ella with some time alone, a little time now and again to give in to her hurt and her sadness. Ella was sure that, if she had had to put up a brave front continuously for three days, she would have gone mad. She just wondered when those cleansing, exhaustive bouts of crying would begin to wash away her pain. She also wished they would cool the desire she still had for Harrigan, but they only made her tired.

When the waiter stuck a plate of steak and pan-fried potatoes in front of her, Ella blinked, realizing that she had been lost in her thoughts for a long time. She sent her aunt an apologetic smile and began to eat. The knowing look Louise gave her told Ella that she was not doing as good a job of concealing her emotions as she thought. Louise's look also hinted at a heart-to-heart talk and Ella inwardly sighed. For a little while, they ate their meal in complete silence, but then Louise finished, patted her lips with her napkin, and looked squarely at Ella. Ella swallowed the last bite of her steak and tensed.

"Perhaps, if you want the man as sorely as you seem to, it is time to swallow your pride," suggested Louise.

"I hadn't realized that I'd shown any pride in my dealings with Harrigan," Ella said, then scowled when her aunt briefly grinned. "I don't see my degradation as an appropriate source of amusement."

"Oooh, Miss Haughty rears her prim, pinched-lip face." Louise reached across the table and patted Ella's clenched hand. "Your words and the way you spoke them made me laugh, not your situation. Have you thought of some way to let Harrigan know that you've forgiven him?"

"I didn't try to shoot him that day by the river. That should have told him enough." Ella smiled weakly when her aunt chuckled. "He was the one who didn't believe me, the one who handed me over to Harold. I would think that it's up to him to speak to me, to apologize."

"Something no man likes to do. Yes, he should have been on his knees at your bedside, begging your forgiveness, but that didn't and never will happen. So you must decide how badly you want this man. Maybe he needs a little nudge, a little hint from you that you will receive him cordially. Perhaps you could send him a brief note of thanks for saving your life."

"He damn well should've helped me," Ella said, causing the plump woman who was clearing away the dinner plates and setting out the dessert to look at her in wide-eyed shock. "I wouldn't have been in any trouble if he had just listened to me, had put just a little faith in me."

Louise smiled her thanks to the woman who had served them and took a moment to savor the apple crumble smothered in thick cream. "Lovely," she murmured, then fixed her gaze on Ella. "Yes, he should have, but he also had some good reasons to mistrust women of society and wealth. I think a deep guilt for the loss of the family business made it even worse. When he explained himself, I thought they were all good reasons to believe the worst of Harold. He said that was exactly why he tried so hard not to believe you. It made sense to me."

"I wish it made sense to me."

"Oh, I think it does. You're just feeling contrary. The

man knew Harold was a liar and a thief. You were not only the man's niece, but you moved freely within the circle of society that had so blithely destroyed him and his family then cast him aside. Why should he believe you? And he did all he had promised he would. He sought out the truth and came to help you."

"For all Harrigan knew, Harold could have planned to put a bullet in my brain the moment I was in his hands."

"That was not Harold's way and Harrigan knew it."

"If he knew Harold was such a dog, why did he work for the man?"

"For money, plain and simple. Are you going to write that note, or just argue the truth with me all day long?"

Ella muttered a curse and concentrated on her dessert for a moment as she struggled to sort out her thoughts and feelings. It was not easy to look beyond her pain and, she reluctantly admitted, her badly bruised pride. All she had ever asked of Harrigan was that he believe her and he had refused to do so. Now her aunt was asking her to accept Harrigan's convoluted reasoning for that lack of trust, one he had not even seen fit to give her directly. She had forgiven the man, but the longer he stayed away, the more tenuous that forgiveness became.

"I grow weary of holding out my hand only to have it slapped away," Ella finally said.

"Can one more time make you feel any worse than you do now?" Louise asked quietly.

"Perhaps I have already begun to feel better and do not wish to risk a relapse."

"No, it's too soon. A simple note of thanks for what he did will neither expose your feelings nor endanger your pride. It simply lets Harrigan know that you might be approachable. Do it, Ella. I promise you that, if you don't, it'll be something you will regret for the rest of your life."

"Then I'll send the damned letter. You do realize, however, that if this fails, or if I only reap another harvest of hurt from this, I will feel free to blame you."

Louise smiled. "Yes, dear. I believe I am strong enough to bear that burden."

Ella paced her hotel room, paused in front of the window, and had to clench her fists tightly to resist the urge to look out for what seemed to be the hundredth time. Immediately after lunch she had penned a polite little note to Harrigan, stiffly thanking him for his aid. She knew he had received it, for George had told her so when he had arrived to take Louise to the theater an hour ago. Harrigan had now had a half day to decide what to do and there was still no sign of the man.

She flung herself onto the bed and stared up at the ceiling. It annoyed her that she had allowed a flicker of hope to spring to life in her heart. Harrigan's lack of response had brutally crushed that and she wondered why she continued to allow the man to hurt her. No man could be worth such pain or the continuous subjugation of her own pride.

What she wanted to do was blithely consider Harrigan as no more than an error in judgment and return to Wyoming with her head held high. She both loved and hated the man, both ached to hold him and ached to beat him senseless. Those conflicting emotions were almost as painful as Harrigan's rejection. She also feared that the wounds he had dealt were too deep to heal, that he had scarred her heart so badly she would never love again.

A sharp rap at the door yanked her from her dark thoughts and she felt her heart leap into her throat. She scrambled off the bed and hastily tidied her appearance as she strode to the door. It was not until she had flung open the door that she realized she should have at least inquired who was there. The fact that a solemn-faced Harrigan filled the doorway was not necessarily a reason to be so blissfully welcoming.

"Shouldn't you have found out who was knocking first?" he asked, then cursed himself for beginning their first meeting in days with a criticism.

"You should be glad I didn't," she said even as she allowed him to walk in and shut the door behind him. "If I had known it was you, I might not have opened the door."

"Why not? You invited me."

Ella silently cursed her aunt, but calmly said, "No, I didn't."

"You sent me a note."

"A polite word of thanks for saving my life. I felt it was only courteous to do so, despite the fact that you helped to put my life in danger." She moved to a dresser where a decanter of wine and several glasses had been set out for their use. "Would you like a drink?"

"Yes, a little wine would be nice," he murmured as he glanced around the room, then moved to sit in one of a pair of armchairs set in front of the window.

Ella took a deep breath to still the shaking in her hands then carefully poured out two glasses of wine. Praying that she looked calm and dignified, she served Harrigan his drink and sat down next to him. There was a tense distance between them that made her want to weep. She had no idea of how to cross it or even if he wanted her to try.

"George said you've sorted through all of Harold's twisted affairs," Harrigan said with a stiff cordiality. "It was good of you to try to restore all that he and Margaret had stolen."

"I'm just sorry I couldn't do the same with what the Templetons have taken," she replied.

"Oh, I think they'll soon fall. Not everything lost can be regained, but at least there will be some justice. And you heard what happened to Margaret?" Ella nodded, and he continued, "I was a little surprised that she would hang herself. I thought she was stronger than that."

"Her strength was Harold, her place in society, and her wealth. She could see that they were all gone now."

"I wonder which one of those things mattered the most?" he murmured, then finished off his wine, abruptly stood up, and paced the room for a moment before turning to stare at her. "And now you plan to return to Wyoming."

"Yes," she answered and knew that, at least for the moment, she would not waver in that decision. "I cannot stay here. There's nothing here for me save bad memories. This place has never welcomed me. And Louise is all the family I have now. I need to be with her."

"I understand. And I need to remain here. Not just for business reasons either. My family is here. I also intend to try to bring down the Templetons."

"And maybe, if good fortune smiles on you, regain the family business." She did not like the idea that he would have any contact with Eleanor, but knew he had to grasp at any chance there was to regain what he had lost.

"Exactly. I have to try."

"I understand. Is that what you came to tell me?"

"I don't know why I came." He softly cursed and gave her a crooked smile. "Yes I do. I wanted to see you before you left. Hell, I wanted to do a lot more than just look at you. I guess I hoped there would be a small chance that you would want the same."

Ella stared at him and wondered why she was not deeply insulted and furious. She decided it was because he was being painfully honest despite the discomfort it so clearly caused him. There was so much more she wanted from him, so much more she wanted him to say, but it would gain her nothing. He would still have to stay in Philadelphia and she would still have to go to Wyoming. Despite the pain she would carry with her, she knew it was the only place she could find the peace she needed. What harm could there be in gathering up a few more memories to take with her?

"That was very arrogant of you," she murmured.

"Probably damned rude too."

"And uncivilized. Well, if you intend to behave like a savage, you had better lock the door first."

She almost laughed at the way he stared at her with an interesting mixture of shock and hope. He tentatively moved toward the door, watching her closely every step of the way. When she just smiled, he moved a lot faster. A cry of surprised

laughter escaped her when he locked the door, nearly ran
back to her side, and scooped her up into his arms.

"Which one is your bed?" he asked in a hoarse, unsteady
voice as he took a step toward the two beds against the far
wall.

"The one on the right."

He placed her on the bed with more haste than gentle-
ness and started to yank off his boots. Ella briefly wished
she could savor the sight of his lean, strong body, but he
was moving too fast. Infected by the fever he made no effort
to hide, she tugged off her slippers and stockings and then
begun to undo her gown. She found this display of raw,
blind need exciting, and, when he finally flung himself into
her arms, she welcomed him eagerly. Their bodies trembled
from the strength of the hunger heating their blood.

"Are you sure?" he asked.

"Sometimes, Mahoney, you talk too damn much," she
said as she cupped his face in her hands and pulled his
mouth down to hers.

Ella looked down at the man sprawled in her arms and
slowly threaded her fingers through his thick hair. They
had made love twice; furious, greedy love, and she was
surprised to realize that she hungered for more. A quick
glance at the clock on the mantel over the tiny fireplace
told her that that was a need she would have to suppress.
George and Louise would soon return from the theater.
Both of them knew that she and Harrigan were lovers, but
she did not think they needed to see it. Neither did she
want any witnesses when Harrigan rose from her arms,
pulled on his clothes, and walked out of her life forever.

The pain she knew she would have to deal with was
already trying to claw its way through the lingering warmth
of their lovemaking. She bit back the sudden urge to bare
her heart to Harrigan. Even in the blind heat of their
passion they had not spoken of love or a future together,
only of need and of the beauty of what they shared. Speak-

ing of love would change nothing, not even if Harrigan
returned her feelings. It would only add to the pain she
would feel later. What good did it do to know all she could
have when she had to walk away from it?

For one brief moment, she considered staying with him
if he would just ask her to, but everything within her
cringed at the thought of remaining in Philadelphia. If
Harrigan truly loved her, it might help, but she was certain
even he could not cure her of the dread she had for the
city. Philadelphia had brought her nothing but sorrow and
loss. She knew it was not the fault of the place, that Harold
had commited the crimes, but her pain and fear did not
choose to be rational. Everywhere she looked she saw
reminders of all she had lost, and of how close she had
come to dying. She had to leave and she was not sure she
would ever be able to return.

"Ella," Harrigan whispered, propping himself up on his
elbow, and kissing her cheek. "You've gone very quiet."

"I was just realizing how late it's become. George and
Louise will return soon. I think our little interlude of self-
indulgence must come to an end."

If he had not been looking at her, Harrigan knew he
would have felt as if she had just slapped him. Her words
were cool, a calm invitation for him to leave, but her eyes
were dark with feeling. He had a sudden urge to tell her
all he felt, but he quickly sat up, busying himself with
getting dressed until it could be subdued. When he turned
back toward her, Ella sat in the middle of the bed wearing
a prim, white cotton nightgown. She looked very young
and fragile.

"I shouldn't have come here," he said as he stood up.

"Oh, I think it would be unwise for us to begin talking
about regrets and mistakes." She smiled sadly. "I think
it's best if we just leave this simple. We fed the passion we
seem to have no control over. To call it any more than
that or to try to do some heart searching will do neither
of us any good."

"You're probably right." He grabbed his hat and walked

to the door. "Ella," he said in a tight voice as he opened the door and looked back at her, "if you ever return to Philadelphia—"

"I know. And the same is true if you ever come out to Wyoming."

"I hope you can find the peace you need."

"And I pray you find the justice you need."

Harrigan stepped out of the room and slowly shut the door after him. He stood in the hall staring at his hat and wondering why he felt so devastated. Only a door separated him and Ella and yet he felt as if she was already thousands of miles away.

He looked at the door and seriously considered marching back in there and saying all the things she had said they should not speak of. There was a deep need in him to know that she felt more for him than passion, that she had truly forgiven him. He took a deep breath and fought the inclination. It would be cruel. He could offer her no future, no promises. She needed to flee the place that had brought her nothing but grief and misery, and he needed to stay. He slapped his hat on his head and walked away, wishing that following the correct path was not so painful.

Ella stared at the door until her eyes stung. She knew he would not return, but a small part of her still hoped. As the minutes ticked by, the clock on the mantel sounding unbearably loud in the silence he had left behind, she felt that tiny hope die. A shudder went through her as she collapsed onto the bed. Her body was still flushed and warm from their lovemaking, yet she was utterly alone.

She knew she was going to cry and she fought the urge even though she was certain she would lose the battle. What she wanted to be was calm, accepting, and mature. She had loved and lost. It had happened to thousands of people. It did not have to destroy her. It was not fatal. As the tears began to roll down her cheeks, she clutched at her pillow, curled up into a ball, and decided that, for a little while, she could allow herself to give in to the pain. She just prayed that she could indulge her grief and then compose herself before her aunt came home. Although she loved Louise dearly, she didn't really want her aunt to know how big a fool she had been.

"Oh dear," murmured Louise, stopping so abruptly that she caused George to stumble at her side.

George quickly regained his balance and unhooked his arm from hers just in case she decided to make another sudden, unexpected move. "Oh dear what?" he asked.

"That's Harrigan shuffling toward his office, isn't it? Just down the road on the other side?"

Looking at his friend, George grimaced as he saw Harrigan's bent head and hunched shoulders. "Ah."

"You do have a way with words, George. *Ah* is right. Damn, I had hoped he would go to see Ella, but I thought it would go better than it obviously did."

"Perhaps she decided she could not forgive him."

"No, she had forgiven him, although she did want to hear him apologize and explain his actions." Louise frowned and put her hands on her slim hips as she watched Harrigan disappear into his office. "I really thought they just needed to see each other again and talk to each other a bit. I thought I'd come home to hear about a wedding. Instead I think I will need to tend to one very upset girl."

"There is one problem I believe you did not consider. Harrigan feels he needs to stay here. This is where his business is, where he can watch the Templetons in hope of bringing them to justice, and where his family is."

"A family he feels deeply responsible for since he blames himself for the loss of their livelihood." Louise muttered a curse and shook her head. "And Ella must leave here. There are too many dark, painful memories here. I should have left well enough alone. I've probably just caused Ella more pain."

"You could not be certain how firm they would be in their

decisions." He took one of her clutched hands in his and brushed a kiss over her knuckles. "Maybe Ella doesn't love Harrigan, at least not as much as you thought."

"Oh, she loves him, more than he deserves. She also desperately needs to get away from here. I was a little naive in thinking love was enough."

"Will it be enough for you?" George asked softly.

Louise stared at him for a moment, completely forgetting her niece's troubles. "What do you mean?"

"If I come to you in Wyoming, I will have to start all over again. I will have nothing to offer you except love and a willingness to work."

"Which is more than enough, George." She placed her hand on his cheek and lightly kissed him. "Are you sure you can give everything up for a woman like me?"

"Very sure." He took a small box out of his pocket and placed it in her hand. "I had hoped to do this slowly and as romantically as I could, probably over a quiet glass of wine." He blushed a little. "I fear it is not a ring as I could not guess what size you would wear and now I fear you may be insulted." His eyes widened as Louise gently touched one finger to his lips.

"Hush, George, and let me look." Louise opened the little box, saw the small silver pin inside, and started to laugh. "A train. Why, George, I never knew you had such a delightful sense of humor. Here, pin it on me, and the answer is yes." She laughed softly when he hugged her then fumbled as he pinned the little brooch to her dress. "I will treasure it."

"I am not sure when I can come to Wyoming," he said quietly as he held her hand. "I have to try to help Harrigan."

"I understand. I'll wait." She sighed. "I would love to share my news with Ella, but I do not think tonight would be a good time. I really believed those two belonged together."

"Love may yet win out."

"What do you mean?"

"Maybe Harrigan has to believe he's lost her before he realizes exactly what he wants and how badly he wants it. Perhaps, after he takes care of the Templetons, he will decide Wyoming could use his skills."

"That would be nice." She kissed him on the cheek. "I thought it'd be nice to spend this evening together since I might not see you again for months." She idly smoothed her finger over her new pin, smiling briefly in spite of herself. "However, I think we each have people in sore need of a friendly voice and a strong shoulder."

George gave her a slow, tender kiss then smiled when he saw her blush. "I will see you soon and maybe I will not be traveling to Wyoming alone."

"Well, if that fool decides to come with you, let me know," she said as she hurried toward the hotel.

"I suppose you plan to interfere."

She paused in the doorway of the hotel and blew him a kiss. "Now, George, you can't expect me to just sit back and let nature take its course."

Laughing softly, George shook his head and strode toward his office. Louise sighed and entered the hotel. Part of her was still delighted with George's little gift, a token of all they had promised each other. His word had been good enough for her from the beginning, but she knew she would always treasure the pin. For a while she had to put aside her own happiness, however, and try to help Ella.

The moment she stepped into the room and saw Ella's huddled shape on the bed, Louise prayed that George would bring Harrigan to Wyoming. The pain she could hear in Ella's sobs tore at her heart. She moved quickly to the bed and took Ella into her arms, wondering just how much more the girl could endure before she broke beneath the weight of it all.

Chapter Twenty-Three

Louise scowled as she stared out of the kitchen window at Ella, who was weeding the kitchen garden. "Two months we've been home and that girl still walks around sunk in gloom."

Joshua rolled his eyes and took a sip of coffee, setting the cup back down on the well-scrubbed table with a distinct thud. "You staring at her all the time isn't going to cure her."

As she walked to the table, Louise paused to give Joshua a light slap on the back of the head before she sat down across from him. Joshua was always the last one to eat his morning meal and, she thought fondly as she studied his slender build, always ate the biggest meal. Knowing how often he had suffered from hunger, she enjoyed seeing him eat so heartily. He was the first one she had taken in and they were close. She could not blame him for finding her incessant fretting over Ella an irritation. She did too. Time and time again she had tried to stop herself from worrying about the girl, for she knew it did no good. But for all that, she would quickly return to it, for she could not bear to see Ella so unhappy.

"You can't mend this wound, Louise," Joshua said in a gentler tone of voice.

"I know." Louise sighed and poured herself a cup of coffee.

"Ella's the one who fell in love with that Irishman and she's the one who has to stop loving him."

"I know that too. I just begin to fear that she never will."

"Ella's too smart to cling to a lost cause and too strong to let it beat her."

"So I thought, but Ella feels things very deeply. She and I have talked, but I don't believe she's told me half of what she's feeling." Louise studied Joshua for a moment as she nervously bit her bottom lip, then decided she could trust him to keep what she was about to say between them alone. "There is something else I worry about."

"That will be a nice change."

"Not really. It still concerns Ella. I think she may be carrying Harrigan Mahoney's child." She smiled at the way Joshua gaped, then grew a little nervous when his shock gave way to look of hard anger.

"You just say the word, Louise, and me and the boys will ride east, hogtie the bastard, and drag him back here to marry Ella."

"No, you can't do that. It wouldn't help Ella much at all."

"What are you saying? She needs a father for that child. Think about what people will say about her, how they will treat her, if she has a child but no husband."

"Probably not much worse than they treat her or me now. We're two young, unmarried women living on a ranch with a dozen young, unwed men. It can't come as any surprise to you that most people in town have marked us as little more than whores." She smiled faintly when Joshua looked uncomfortable, even blushing slightly.

"I had hoped that you hadn't heard any of that talk."

"Joshua, there are always those women who feel it is their Christian duty to tell you what's being said. They claim they are just trying to get you to change your ways.

I'm afraid Ella and I don't make things any easier for ourselves by responding to such nonsense with the derision it deserves." She briefly laughed along with Joshua.

"Louise, all that does not change the fact that it would be best if Ella was married, if the child had a father," Joshua said as he split the last of the coffee in the pot between his cup and Louise's.

"What Ella needs is a man who loves her. Harrigan has to come to her. Anything else will slowly kill her. Yes, it will be hard for her, but not as hard as living with a man who married her simply to slap a name on his child. Hell, he could even come to resent the child."

"So, if we're not going to force Harrigan to the altar, why did you tell me about this?"

"Because she either does not suspect it yet or is trying to keep it a secret. I need someone to help me keep her from doing anything that could endanger her life or the child's. For instance, if she wants to go riding, she gets the old mare that probably wouldn't bolt even if a cougar popped up in front of it."

"I understand," Joshua said and nodded, then helped Louise clear the dishes from the table. "Sure she ought to be out there yanking weeds?"

"She's not working too hard, since she spends a great deal of her time staring off into the distance. And I intend to get her back inside the house before the sun gets too hot. Once I know for sure that she's with child, or once she tells me she is, we can be more obvious in our concern."

"Agreed. Am I to keep this a complete secret?"

"If you feel you must tell one of the boys in order to keep Ella from doing something dangerous, go ahead and do so. However, I would like to keep this as much a secret as possible. After all, I could be wrong. What I see as signs of a coming child could simply be symptoms of a deep melancholy." Louise suddenly smiled. "And it would deeply annoy Ella if she discovered that everyone knew her secret before she chose to tell it." She laughed along with Joshua.

* * *

Ella blinked, wiped the thin sheen of sweat from her face with her hands, and looked around her bedroom. She then looked at Louise, who sat on the edge of the bed, and blushed when she finally met her aunt's steady, knowing gaze. At Louise's insistence, she had finally given up the chore of weeding the kitchen gardens only to walk into the oven-heated kitchen and faint. Her aunt had called Joshua to carry her upstairs, and a few snatches of conversation she had overheard as she had wavered in and out of consciousness told her that Louise had just recently shared her suspicions with the young man. Joshua had cheerfully complained about having had only a few hours to savor knowing something the rest of the men did not. It would be amusing if it were not so embarrassing, Ella thought. It was no real secret on the ranch that she had been Harrigan's lover, but Ella did not see why she must now be put into the position of constantly reminding people of her slip in etiquette.

"Well, that was a surprising turn of events," she murmured, still hoping that Louise did not really know, but only suspected, and might still have a few doubts.

"Was it?" Louise drawled as she handed Ella a cool, damp cloth to wash her face with. "You don't eat enough."

"I eat far too much."

"You do too much work around here."

"Not that much."

"You don't get enough sleep."

"Ah, well, I think I might have to agree with that one for, although I go to bed early and even nap in the middle of the day, whether I want to or not, I still feel tired."

"That's because you are carrying Harrigan Mahoney's child. The symptoms are clear for any woman to see."

Louise's blunt statement left Ella speechless for a moment. She struggled to think of something to say to deny what they both knew, then wondered why she was bothering. Denials and lies could not hide the truth for very long. It was also a little foolish to keep such knowledge, no matter how embarrassing, from a woman who would willingly and lovingly help her. Despite all that good sense, there was still a part of Ella that did not want to accept what was happening to her. Once she confessed it to Louise, she would have to.

"They could be symptoms of something else," Ella said, her tone sounding sullen even to her own ears. "I have been through an exhausting ordeal. Maybe the opium still lingers in my body. Why, I could even have a summer fever." She inwardly grimaced at the mild look of disgust Louise gave her. "Harrigan and I were lovers for only a short while."

"And in that brief time, how often did you make love?"

"I don't know. I didn't keep a tally sheet."

"It doesn't matter. It only takes one time. Hell, some women are so fertile they claim it only takes a twinkle in their man's eyes. But, if you wish to keep it a secret for a while longer, perhaps deny it for a while, that's your choice. I don't much see the point of it really, but if it pleases you—"

"It doesn't please me. None of this pleases me. It's all grossly unfair." Ella sighed, struggling to rein in an anger that had nothing to do with Louise. "You must think I am incredibly stupid and thoughtless."

"No." Louise smiled and patted one of Ella's tightly clenched hands. "You are young, passionate, and in love."

"And, as you so correctly guessed, with child." Ella slowly sat up and began to tidy her hair. "I am also alone, unwed, and miserable."

"If you really want a husband, I could send the boys after Harrigan."

"Oh, God, no. Please don't. Yes, I would love to be married to the fool, but I don't want him dragged to the altar. The thought of having a child alone and unwed terrifies me. It breaks every rule I was ever taught. However, the thought of marrying Harrigan when he did not choose me himself, willingly, and because he loved me, terrifies me even more."

Louise leaned closer and briefly hugged Ella. "I understand completely. We will take care of you and the child. In truth, the child will probably have more love and attention than it knows what to do with."

"And what happens when George arrives?" Ella asked quietly, glancing at the little silver train brooch her aunt wore every day. "He is Harrigan's closest friend."

"Nothing will change. I promise you."

"He might insist on telling Harrigan and then I would have to deal with a man who only wants to do what is right."

"George will say nothing. Don't look so doubtful. He may be Harrigan's friend, but he will be my husband. Now, what is of more interest to me is how you feel about this baby."

"Right at this moment, if I answer that, I won't sound much like a mother. A part of me is deeply ashamed of all the harsh thoughts and bad feelings I have, but none of those are really aimed at the child. I don't want to destroy the child, I just wish it wasn't there. There's no doubt in my mind that I will keep this child, love it, and raise it, yet I wish to God it wasn't on its way. I am angry, and sad, and scared to death."

"There's nothing wrong with any of that." Louise stood up, took Ella by the hand, and tugged her to her feet. "Now, we're going down to the kitchen, where you will sit and have some tea and something to eat. And then we're going to make plans for this child, nice, happy, keep-Ella's-hands-busy kind of plans."

Ella laughed as she followed Louise to the kitchen. If anyone could make her look forward to the birth of her child with calm, hope, and love, it was Louise. There was one thing she had not told her aunt, but Ella suspected Louise knew that too. Upon her return to Wyoming, Ella had planned to banish Harrigan Mahoney from her mind. It both depressed her and infuriated her that now she

would never be able to do that. Each time she looked at
her child, she would be reminded of the tall, dark, and
very distant Irishman who had fathered it. Ella prayed that
somehow, in some small way, her memory would torment
Harrigan.

Harrigan tried to smile as he watched his family celebrate. It had taken over two months since Harold's death,
ten long weeks of constant work, but he had finally brought
down the Templetons. People had grown braver once Harold Carson was gone, and the witnesses and information
needed to crush the Templetons had been easier to obtain.
Although it had galled him to have to pay Eleanor's family
one copper penny for what they had taken with deceit,
Harrigan had taken advantage of the Templetons' desperate need for money and regained the family business. By
combining the hard-wrung savings of everyone in the family, there would be only a small loan from the bank left to
repay. He was proud of what he had done, but he did not
feel the joy the others did. Harrigan knew who was to
blame for that—Ella Carson. No matter how hard he had
worked, he had not been able to push her out of his mind
or his heart.

He was abruptly pulled from his thoughts when his father
Liam pushed a glass of whiskey into his hand. A quick
glance around revealed that everyone else had quietly
slipped away, leaving him alone in the parlor with his
father. The way Liam was eyeing him as he sprawled next
to him on the worn settee made Harrigan nervous. He was
not sure he was prepared for a man-to-man talk, or that
he wanted to indulge in any confidences. One look into
his father's grey eyes, however, told Harrigan that he would
be given no choice.

"Now, lad, I couldn't help but notice that you weren't
as gleeful as the rest of us," Liam said, his voice deep due
to the emotion he was still swamped with. "You should be.

We are all right proud of what you've done. I never thought I'd regain all I had lost.''

"All *I* had lost, you mean,'' Harrigan said, a hint of the lingering guilt he felt roughening his voice.

"Aw, now, we never blamed you for that.'' He laughed when Harrigan just cocked one dark brow and stared at him. "Well, at times, when things were hard and anger ruled o'er common sense, we might have, but our hearts weren't in it. We all felt shamed by the thoughts when the anger had passed.''

"I just wish I could have gotten your business back without costing us all so much.''

"It wasn't that much. Fact is, it was almost as big a theft as the Templetons committed. The man added a lot to my shipping company, improvements I didn't have the money or the acquaintances to accomplish.'' Liam ran a hand through his silver-dappled black hair, then straightened his broad shoulders and looked his eldest son square in the eye. "What I need to know is the why of your grieving, and don't deny that you are in a black, solemn mood. I can see it clear as a black cat on the snow. I hope it isn't caused by Eleanor Templeton. She deserves all she has to suffer now. She's as guilty as her father.''

"Good God, no, I'm not grieving for Eleanor or feeling one drop of guilt or remorse for the troubles I've brought her and her father. As you say, she is as guilty as her father. She was more than happy to help him commit his crimes; she can pay for them. To be completely honest, Da, I never loved the woman, although I tried to. I desired her, for she was beautiful, and I believed she was a lady. Hell, I had some lofty aspirations, and Eleanor Templeton seemed like the perfect wife to help me achieve them.''

Liam nodded. "Then I won't be hurting your feelings too much by saying I was glad she was gone before you could wed her. Even if it meant I had to lose the business. I didn't like her and I didn't trust her as far as I could spit.''

"It might have been nice if you had told me that *before*

she robbed us blind,'' Harrigan drawled, and smiled faintly when his father chuckled. ''Well, I'm glad I've been able to put your mind at ease,'' he said as he started to stand up.

''I'm settled in my mind about Eleanor Templeton, but that makes me even more curious about your dark moods.''

''It's just exhaustion.''

''Ha! And I'm Saint Patrick's saintly mother. Sit.''

Harrigan sat. ''It's nothing you can mend, Da.''

''No? Why don't you just spit it out and I'll decide. This old man might surprise you.''

After a moment, Harrigan began to tell his father about Ella. He intended to be circumspect, but soon found himself confiding everything—from how he had treated Ella to the vast confusion of emotion he suffered from. When he was done, he felt exhausted yet oddly relieved. He was still not sure his father could solve any of his problems, but it had felt good to talk to him.

Liam was silent for several minutes and Harrigan began to get nervous. He had not acquitted himself well with Ella, yet he felt he was too old for a scolding or a lecture. Harrigan also realized that, despite his doubt that anyone could fix the mess he had made, there was still that small boy inside of him that believed Da could fix anything. The longer his father remained silent, the more that childish faith withered. He idly toyed with one of his mother's prized porcelain ladies on the marble-topped table next to the settee as he waited for his father to concede defeat.

''Well, son,'' Liam finally said, ''I fear I just don't know what to say to you.''

''Not to worry, Da.'' Harrigan smiled a little sadly at his solemn father. ''I didn't think the problems I've made for myself could be solved so easily.''

''Oh, they're not as complicated as you think. I have plenty to say about that mess. What held me speechless there, a rare thing your Mam will be sad she missed, is that I don't recall raising you up to be such a cad.''

''A cad?'' Harrigan choked out, blindly holding out his

glass as his father poured them each a little more of the whiskey.

"Did you or did you not seduce the girl and then walk away from her?"

"It's not quite that simple. Even if I wanted more, it couldn't be. I had to stay here and she couldn't."

"Can't blame the lass for wanting to get as far away from this place as she could. It holds nothing but black memories for her. Not sure the wilds of Wyoming are safe, but she clearly feels secure and happy there. That poor, sweet child will probably never feel safe or comfortable here."

"If you had ever met Ella Carson, you wouldn't use the word sweet to describe her," Harrigan drawled, then sighed, quickly growing serious again. "I never said I didn't understand why she had to leave. I do understand, completely."

"Then explain to me why you're still here."

"I had to get the Templetons, to try to right the wrongs they've done, maybe return some of what they had stolen to the rightful owners. We weren't the only ones they and the Carsons deceived and cheated."

"Very noble, but the job's done now. So why aren't you telling me that you're headed out to Wyoming to get that little girl, marry her, and start a family?"

"My work is here. My family is here," Harrigan replied, suddenly wondering if he had made his troubles seem far more complicated than they were.

"You can do your kind of work anywhere, or do some other kind of work. Now that the trains run all over the country, even to places that aren't states yet, seeing your family is just a matter of scraping together the money for a passage." Liam patted Harrigan on the shoulder. "Go to her, son. Everything you've said tells me that you want her. You stay here and you'll never be truly happy. Yes, you might find some nice girl and settle down, even have a family, but you'll be cheating her as well as yourself, because there will always be a piece of you in Wyoming. Most of us have only one great love in our lives. Unless you do everything possible to hold onto it, you can never be fully satisfied with your lot in life. Yes, you could still lose, but unless you've done all you can do to win, then you'll spend the rest of your life wondering what you could have done differently."

Harrigan stared into his drink, gently swirling the amber liquid around in the glass. "I may have already lost. I haven't done one thing right since I set eyes on Ella."

"Well, you must have done at least one thing right or she would never have bedded down with you." Liam exchanged a fleeting, very male grin with his son. "Go to her."

"You don't even know her, haven't even met her."

"And I'm sorry for that. I'm also hoping that we'll be meeting before too long. Distance doesn't need to make us strangers. But I listened to you talk about her and know you need her, want her, and love her, even if you still hesitate to use such strong words. I also heard of a girl who has spirit, wit, and strength. You've got my full-hearted approval and many good wishes for success."

"If I'm going, I'm going far sooner than you might think. George leaves to join Louise in two days."

"Ah. A bit abrupt, but that may be best." Liam stood up and started to leave the parlor. "We'd best go tell your mother and the others. My Mary will be sad you're leaving, but very pleased that you have found someone."

Harrigan stood up and followed his father, but protested, "Da, I haven't said I'm going yet."

"Uh-huh, that's fine, son. Just be sure to tell us all when the train is leaving so that we can bid you a proper fare-thee-well."

After staring at the papers on his desk for the second hour in a row, yet not seeing one word, Harrigan tossed his pencil down on the desk and swirled around in his chair to look at George. That man was quietly clearing out his desk, his usually calm face holding an odd expression, a contradictory combination of sadness and anticipation. Harrigan reconsidered his father's words of that morning and smiled crookedly.

"When does the train leave, George?" he asked.

"I thought you knew. Two days from now, Thursday at nine in the morning."

"Do you think there's a seat left?"

George slowly turned his seat all the way around until he faced Harrigan squarely. "If you're thinking of riding with me so that you may attend my wedding to Louise, I thank you kindly, but I do not think it would be wise."

"Why not?"

"It could open a lot of wounds."

"Mine or Ella's?"

"I am inclined to believe that both of you would suffer."

Harrigan smiled at the irritation coloring George's voice. "I couldn't resist pinching at you, old friend. Sorry. And yes, I would regret not seeing you marry your Louise and start down that road of blissful marital confrontation." He held up his hand when George began to protest. "George, if you try to tell me that you will have a calm union with Louise Carson, you will deeply insult me. And disappoint me, for I have always had a deep respect for and faith in your honesty." He chuckled when George grinned, then grew serious. "I have settled the business with the Templetons and now see that I need more than this business and even more than the closeness of my large family to make me happy."

"You need Ella Carson."

"Yes, curse her. Even when I was working nearly every night and day, I still thought about my wild mountain rose. No matter how hard I tried to convince myself otherwise, Ella is what I want. And I find I must agree with my father when he says that I have to do all in my power to get her or I will regret it for the rest of my life. So, now I'm prepared to concede defeat. I'll go to Wyoming and see if I can mend some fences."

Chapter Twenty-Four

Muttering a curse, Ella swatted at a fly. She had been banished to the shaded front porch to sit on the swing and sip cool lemonade like some frail parlor doll, she thought angrily. The news of her approaching motherhood had been announced within hours of her faint in the kitchen, nearly a month ago. She had not fainted again, but then no one let her lift anything heavier than a feather pillow or let one ray of the summer sun touch her skin. The only thing she got much pleasure out of any longer was a ride in the afternoon, but they had managed to make that tediously safe as well. She was only allowed to ride Muffin, an old mare who plodded along at a steady, very slow pace no matter what one did to her or what happened around her. The most daring thing they allowed was to sometimes, though rarely, let her ride alone, but only if she told them exactly where she was going and how long she intended to be gone. Although, she mused, the few times she had been out alone, she had always felt as if someone was watching her, but she had not yet caught them at it. This pregnancy, she decided, was going to be a very long one.

The door creaked and Ella scowled at her aunt even though she knew she would be glad of a little company. Louise looked radiantly happy, almost skipping over to the swing to sit down beside her. Although Ella usually liked to see her aunt happy, in her current mood it only irritated her more. Since she was so miserable, she felt it only just that everyone else should be too. Louise's euphoria was like rubbing salt in her wounds.

"George is coming," Louise announced, smoothing out the piece of paper she had inadvertently crumpled in her hand. "He sent me this message."

"Oh? When did that arrive?" asked Ella.

"Joshua brought it back with him when he returned from buying supplies in town."

"So? When is the groom to arrive?" Ella pushed aside all thoughts of her own unwed state, as well as the lack of any word from Harrigan, and struggled to be happy for her aunt.

"In about an hour. Probably less, as he said an hour when he wrote this, and Joshua delivered it about half an hour ago." Louise laughed softly at Ella's shock. He arrived too late to ride out here yesterday, so he took a room in town."

It took Ella a moment to overcome her surprise, and then she asked, "So now you'll start planning the wedding?"

"Yes, if George is still of a mind to marry me."

"Auntie, I do not think he would travel all this way just to tell you he's changed his mind."

"No, of course not. Then again, he is a very honorable man. He might just feel that he needs to say such things to my face, not with a letter or a telegram." Louise lightly chewed on her bottom lip as she studied Ella.

"Ah, I see," Ella murmured after enduring her aunt's stare for a moment. "You wish to be alone with George."

Louise grimaced. "Yes. I just didn't know how to ask you to, well, go away for a while. The boys are all off doing their chores. I just had to ask them not to return unannounced or too soon.''

"But I presented you with a rather large problem." Ella leaned over to kiss her aunt on the cheek, then stood up. "Not to worry. I'll just take my plod on Muffin a little early today. I'll get my bonnet and be on my way." As she started into the house, Louise right behind her, Ella added, "By the time I get myself ready I'll have decided where I will be riding and tell you before I leave."

"Never mind, dear. I know," Louise said, distracted as she hurried to the kitchen. "Muffin rides the same trail every time she leaves the stables."

Ella gaped after her aunt, torn between laughing and screaming. Louise's unusual agitation was amusing, but the revelation that even the small freedom she thought she had was a lie angered her. Muffin had been sold to her aunt with the ranch and had probably been plodding along the same path for years. As soon as she returned from her ride, Ella intended to remind everyone that she was pregnant, not an invalid, and she would repeat it incessantly until someone listened to her.

Louise blushed and pulled free of George's passionate greeting to look at Harrigan. As she studied him while he grinned and slouched against the porch railing, she prayed she was not setting Ella up for more pain. George was sure that Harrigan loved Ella, and Harrigan had said so himself, but Louise was still uncertain. Harrigan had not treated Ella well, yet suddenly he walked away from his family and his work to offer the girl his heart. It seemed far too good to be true.

"Decided yet?" Harrigan asked quietly, a little unsettled by Louise's intense stare, but determined not to show it.

"Not really," she replied. "I just find it hard to understand how you could walk away from her in Philadelphia, then, a few months later, toss aside all you have back there to walk back to her. However, we don't have the time to

discuss this as thoroughly as I would like. We've stuck Ella
on an old mare that walks the same path every time she's
saddled and does it in a pretty regular amount of time.
You have to go now if you're going to catch Ella alone."
Louise gave him the directions to a shady spot near the
creek where Muffin always stopped for a drink. "Ella always
dismounts to wash her face and hands. Just remember one
thing, Harrigan Mahoney. If you hurt that child again,
even George won't be able to stop me from making you
pay for it."

"Understood."

Harrigan hurried down the steps, mounted his horse,
and immediately set out after Ella. He easily pushed aside
a sense of insult caused by Louise's mistrust. He knew he
had earned it and that he would have to work hard to gain
that trust now. Louise was wrong to worry about Ella being
hurt, however. The only person whose heart was on the
line was himself. He had handed his business over to his
younger brother Patrick, said farewell to his entire family,
and traveled hundreds of miles just to ask a little, green-
eyed girl if she would take him. All Ella had to do was say
yes or no.

Ella sighed and dismounted after Muffin plodded up to
the edge of the creek and began to have herself a long,
leisurely drink. If she had not been so lost in thoughts of
Harrigan every time she had gone riding, she would have
noticed how Muffin had so faithfully gone to the same
spot at the creek. She had been deluded enough to think
that she had found the cool, tree-shaded spot all on her
own.

"I seem to have become as great a creature of habit as
you, old girl," she murmured as she knelt by the creek,
wet her handkerchief in the water, and wiped the dust
from her hands, face, and neck.

Just as Ella proceeded to cup her hands together,
intending to scoop up some of the clear water and take a

drink, she tensed. She was sure she had just heard a horse
snort. Muffin had not made the noise, she mused, as she
looked at the horse who was placidly munching on some
of the sweet grass at the creek's edge. It took her a moment
to realize that it was silly to look to Muffin for some sign
of an intruder or danger. The horse probably would not
blink an eye if a rabid bear was thundering through the
brush.

As she turned her head to look around, beginning to
doubt that she had heard anything, for it had been quiet
since that one abrupt sound, a pair of boots entered her
line of vision. Her heart crept up into her throat even as
her gaze crept up the tall lean body standing in those
boots. She knew it was Harrigan even before she saw his
face. That strong body was painfully familiar. Shock
numbed her mind and the only word she could clearly
form in her confused thoughts was *why?*

"Speechless?" Harrigan asked, aching to yank her into
his arms, but knowing that he had to go very slowly. "I must
record this moment in my journal. Silence is something I
have never inspired in you before."

As he had hoped, his gentle sarcasm helped her recover
from her shock. She abruptly snapped her mouth shut
and the color returned to her cheeks. The look of mistrust
and anger that flared in her beautiful eyes was something
he had expected and was prepared to deal with. What
troubled him as he sat down beside her was the hint of
fear he could see in her expression. He was not sure what
she feared and could not fathom why she would fear anything he could say or do.

Ella's first thought as her mind cleared was that someone
had told Harrigan about the child. A small, calm voice
which kept saying firmly that no one at the ranch would
ever betray her was all that kept her from panicking, jump-
ing up, and running away. The fear that somehow he knew
her secret did not go away completely, however, for there
was still the big question as to why he was sitting there,

miles away from the family and the work in Philadelphia that he had been so determined to stay with.

"Did you come to attend George and Louise's wedding?" she finally asked, praying it was as simple as that, even though it could mean a lot of pain for her to endure. Harrigan would be close, renewing all the feelings she had for him, but would still be completely unattainable.

"That was part of it," he replied. "A small part. Actually, I came for you."

"For me?" She tensed, terrified that he was going make her repeat the agonizing parting of three months ago. "I cannot return to Philadelphia, Harrigan. I'm not sure I'll ever be able to, even though my family is buried there."

"I was thinking that I could find some way to earn a living here in Wyoming. It's a growing place. There must be a great deal of work a man can do out here."

Ella heartily wished she had some warning of his arrival. She was still reeling from the shock of his abrupt appearance. Her emotions were running rampant and she needed time to get them back under control, time Harrigan clearly had no intention of giving her. She ached to throw herself in his arms and taste again the passion that had been haunting her in her dreams. She wanted to be cold to him, to shield herself from any further hurt. She was also angry with him, infuriated by the way he could so confuse her.

"Harrigan, what are you talking about? Perhaps it's the surprise of seeing you, not only in Wyoming, but right here, that is making it so difficult to understand you."

Tentatively, Harrigan gave into the urge to touch her, smoothing his hand over her hair, stirred by the way it hung in a loosely tied, silken mass down her slim back. Ella tensed and eyed him warily, but did not pull away. Harrigan decided that a reluctant, tense acceptance was better than a complete rejection.

"I'm not sure how I can make myself any clearer," he said. "I came here for you." He gently grasped her by the shoulders and turned her until she faced him directly. "I beat the Templetons, brought them to their knees, and restored the livelihood they had stolen from my family. That's why I had to stay in Philadelphia. When it was all over I realized that it was the only reason to stay there."

"No, there was your family and your work." The intensity in his voice and in his expression made her heart beat so hard and fast she could hear the throbbing in her ears. Afraid to allow her reckless heart to lead her, however, she struggled to remain calm and listen closely to everything he had to say.

"I can find work anywhere or start a business here. I have a great many skills. My father always believed that the wider your knowledge, the better your chances of succeeding. I'll miss my family. It would be a lie and an easy one for you to see through if I tried to claim otherwise, but they're not completely out of my reach. I love them all dearly, but even they could not fill the emptiness I was afflicted with."

"The emptiness?"

"There's no other word for it." He sighed and touched his forehead to hers. "From the moment I saw you, Ella, I have fought you as hard as any man has ever fought a woman, but I couldn't kill what I was feeling. I need you, Ella, and I don't mean just in my bed, although I grow weary of waking in the middle of the night all asweat from a hunger no other woman can feed."

"No other woman?"

Ella cast aside the last of her wariness and doubt. He had not spoken of love, but a deep, rich feeling weighted his every word and she knew she would be a fool to demand it all right now. A sense of emptiness without her and a strong need for her had brought him to her. Both were feelings she easily recognized. If he did not love her now, there was every chance that he soon would. There was also a very good chance that he already did, that he had simply not put the word love to what he felt.

Harrigan smiled crookedly and began to smooth his hands up and down her arms. "No other woman, and it wasn't just because I was busy. Hell, I hadn't had any woman for months before I met you."

"Which probably provided a reasonable explanation for why you wanted me," she murmured, a teasing tone to her quiet voice.

"You know me too well. Ella, I have treated you poorly from the start. It was not only wrong of me, but unfair. I know that now. I knew it then, more or less, but could not seem to stop myself. You had me twisted in knots from the start and in my confusion it made perfect sense to *not* believe you simply because I wanted to so badly."

"You had good reasons for your suspicions. People of my class had deceived and betrayed you, people closely tied with my own family. Yes, I know it was unfair, but I also understand it." Ella relaxed in his hold when he enfolded her in his arms and savored the feel of his body next to hers.

"My prejudices nearly got you killed. It was cowardice too. You made me feel things I did not want to feel. I knew any betrayal by you would cost me far more than Eleanor's ever did or would. I still find it hard to believe that I allowed that fear to make me hand you over to your killer. If Harold had succeeded, I would have been guilty of your murder." When he felt her fingers against his mouth, he kissed them, then looked down at her.

"Only Harold is guilty of his crimes," she said. "I never thought of you as his cohort or sharing his guilt. Stupid and pigheaded, maybe." She smiled when he laughed. "I never liked or trusted the man, but I was slow to believe he would try to kill me, and I never suspected him of murdering my parents. Why should you have believed it when you don't know him or me very well?"

Ella was finding the conversation exciting as well as a heady revelation, but she decided it was going to be very hard to keep listening if Harrigan did not stop brushing soft, warm kisses over her face and neck. For far too many nights she had been tormented by the memory of his touch only to find her arms empty. She had decided that, sometimes, memory could be a hollow, cold thing. Now that he was there and she was in his arms again, could touch him and hear the steady beat of his heart, talking was no longer a priority for her. She slipped her hands beneath his coat and began to move them over his broad back, resenting the vest and crisp shirt that barred her fingers from reaching his warm skin.

She realized he was having the same difficulty when he gently pushed her down onto the soft grass. As he sprawled on top of her, she could feel the taut need in every inch of his lean form and her body responded to it with a dizzying greed. Although she did not yet know what plans he had for her, he had left everything that mattered to him to seek her out and he had both explained his actions and apologized for them. He had said enough for now.

"No more to say?" she asked in a husky voice, shifting her body so that he could more easily tug off her gown.

"Do you need to hear more?" Harrigan could not take his gaze off her slender form as he reluctantly left her arms just long enough to tug off his boots, coat, and vest.

"Can you talk and make love at the same time?" She shuddered as she undid his shirt and greedily stroked his smooth skin.

"Not this time." He laughed shakily at the awkward way he tugged off her linen drawers. "I am not sure I can even wait to get all these damned frilly clothes off you."

"Then just try not to rip them too badly," she whispered as she tugged his mouth down to hers, kissing him in a way that revealed her need, and, she suspected, her love.

His kisses and caresses were feverish, but Ella shared his greed and the need for haste. Her passion already possessed her so completely and so fiercely that his every touch was almost painful. When he finally cast aside all attempts at a sweet, leisurely lovemaking and almost roughly joined their bodies, he apologized. Ella laughed, giddy with the feel of their bodies united again after so long. She wrapped her body around his and held him as close and as tightly as she could, matching and equaling the desperation behind his every move. Her release swept over her with such force, her cry was almost a scream. Harrigan quickly joined her, calling her name in a way that only enhanced her ecstasy. He said something else, but, even as she heard those three little words and acknowledged the fact that they were vitally important to her, Ella lost all ability to think.

Harrigan inwardly grimaced as he tossed aside the cloth he had used to refresh them both, then sprawled at Ella's side and took her into his arms. He had been a coward again, telling her how he felt only when he knew there was a good chance she could not hear him. Neither had he intended to lose all control and make love to her before they had said all that needed to be said. His only consolation was that she had been in as great a fever as he had. That also told him that perhaps, he did not need to be so afraid of baring his heart and soul. Ella had to care about him in some manner to be as starved for the passion they could share as he was.

"That was undignified," he murmured as he nuzzled her thick, tousled hair. "Sorry."

"Stop apologizing," she said, idly trailing her fingers over his rib cage. "If I hadn't been completely willing, I'd be going after my shotgun by now and you'd be trying to run and tug your clothes back on at the same time." She smiled when he chuckled, then grew serious. "I think, however, that it'd be wise to finish our talk." Taking a deep breath to steady herself and shore up her flagging courage, she asked, "What do you mean when you say you came here for me? You haven't really explained that."

"Do you know how often those beautiful, big green eyes have haunted my dreams and my every waking moment?" He gently traced the fine bones of her face with his finger.

"That's very flattering," she said, feeling a blush heat her cheeks, "but it doesn't answer my question."

"I was trying to be romantic. I came here to ask you to marry me."

Ella tensed, pulling away from him a little. She had briefly thought she had heard the three little words she was so starved for just as she was swept away by passion, but she had discarded the idea as the result of some delusion. Now she began to wonder. Surely he must love her or why would he want to marry her?

"Are you sure?" she asked, her voice so soft it was little more than a whisper.

"Very sure. Ella, I gave up all I know and all I have worked for to come to you. I realize that I have been unkind and stupid in the past, but I'm not sure what more I can do to prove my sincerity."

"Tell me how you feel while I'm thinking straight and looking you in the eye."

Ella's heart was beating so fast and hard she was sure he could hear it. She could not believe her own daring, but decided that, if she was going to be waking up beside this man for the rest of her life, she needed to know what was in his heart. Her eyes widened slightly when he blushed faintly and looked a little embarrassed.

"I've already confessed that I'm a bit of a coward when it comes to you."

"Marriage is for life, Harrigan. I need to know how committed you are to it and to me."

He held her face between his hands and brushed a kiss over her mouth. "I'm here because I love you," he whispered. When she trembled and a sheen of tears brightened her eyes, Harrigan felt a lot braver. "I tried very hard not to and then I spent a lot of time trying to call it anything but love. When I finally beat the Templetons, the joy of that success was somewhat hollow, for you weren't there to share it with me. I think that was when I stopped trying to fight what I felt. And, although I ask this question with some trepidation, I think I need to know how you feel about me."

Not surprised to see that her hand was shaking, Ella

caressed his cheek, her emotions so strong that it was a little hard to speak. "I think I began to love you the moment I saw you." An unsteady laugh escaped her when he wrapped his arms around her and held her almost too tightly. "I fear I wasn't as strong a fighter as you and had to face the fact that you had stolen my heart fairly early in the game."

"Despite how I treated you?"

"I didn't say it was the wisest thing I have ever done." She laughed along with him.

Although she ached to savor the tenderness of the moment, Ella gently pulled away from him. There was one more thing she had to tell him. She thought it a little odd that, even though he had asked her to marry him and had told her that he loved her, she was still afraid of telling him about the child. The only way to tell a man such news, she decided, was as directly as possible.

"One last time—are you certain about your feelings and about wanting to marry me?"

"Of course. I've said so. While even I feel that words are inadequate, they're all I have. I'm not sure what else to do to make you believe me."

"I just wanted to hear you say it one more time before I tell you something."

Harrigan tensed and slowly sat up. "You're sounding ominously serious. All of a sudden all I can think of is that you haven't actually accepted my proposal."

"The answer is yes, although you may be so angry in a moment, you will consider taking it back." She held up her hand, gesturing him to be silent when he began to speak. "Please, let me say this. Trust me, it needs to be said. Remember the last night we were together in Philadelphia?"

"Those memories were both a torment and a comfort."

"I know what you mean, but I think that time of indulgence left me with a great deal more than a memory." She waited tensely as his expression slowly changed from one of confusion to one of wary understanding and shock.

"You think you're carrying my child?" he asked hoarsely.

"Oh, I don't think it. I know it. I just think it happened that night."

"You weren't going to tell me, were you?"

"No," she replied honestly. "I wanted a husband, but only a willing one. I wanted love and caring, not obligation and duty. Are you angry?" she asked, no longer able to accurately read the expression on his face.

After taking a deep breath, Harrigan admitted, "For a moment, I was furious." He looked at her, let the full realization that she carried his child sweep over him, and felt pure joy push away the last of his anger. "Are you sure you aren't accepting my proposal just because of the child?"

"Idiot," she replied gently. "If I didn't want you, I wouldn't have gotten pregnant to begin with." Ella sighed with relief and hugged him when he took her into his arms.

"Ah, Ella, my wild mountain rose, how I love you. I'm here, I have no idea what I'll do to earn a living, and I already have a family on the way. You have a true skill at turning my life upside down. What am I going to do with you?"

"Just love me as much and as madly as I love you."

"Oh, I do, and I will."

"Forever?"

"Even when my rose's thorns are at their sharpest." He grinned when she gave him a mock scowl, then grew serious again. "Yes, forever. Ten times forever," he added grandly.

Ella smiled as she touched her lips to his. "That will do for a start."

Please turn the page for an exciting sneak peek of
Hannah Howell's newest historical romance,
HIGHLAND SINNER,
now on sale!

Scotland, early summer 1478

What was that smell?

Tormand Murray struggled to wake up at least enough to move away from the odor assaulting his nose. He groaned as he started to turn on his side, and the ache in his head became a piercing agony. Flopping over, he cautiously ran his hand over his head and found the source of the pain. There was a very tender swelling at the back of his head. The damp matted hair around the swelling told him that it had bled but he could feel no continued blood flow. That indicated that he had been unconscious for more than a few minutes, possibly for even more than a few hours.

As he lay there trying to will away the pain in his head, Tormand tried to open his eyes. A sharp pinch halted his attempt and he cursed. He had definitely been unconscious for quite a while and something beside a knock on the head had been done to him for his eyes were crusted shut. He had a fleeting, hazy memory of something being thrown into his eyes before all went black, but it was not

enough to give him any firm idea of what had happened
to him. Although he ruefully admitted to himself that it
was as much vanity as a reluctance to inflict pain upon himself that caused him to fear he would tear out his eyelashes
if he just forced his eyes open, Tormand proceeded very
carefully. He gently brushed aside the crust on his eyes until
he could open them, even if only enough to see if there was
any water close at hand to wash his eyes with.

And, he hoped, enough water to wash himself if he
proved to be the source of the stench. To his shame there
had been a few times he had woken to find himself stinking, drunk, and a few stumbles into some foul muck upon
the street being the cause. He had never been this foul before, he mused, as the smell began to turn his stomach.

Then his whole body tensed as he suddenly recognized
the odor. It was death. Beneath the rank odor of an un-
clean garderobe was the scent of blood—a lot of blood.
Far too much to have come from his own head wound.

The very next thing Tormand became aware of was that
he was naked. For one brief moment panic seized him.
Had he been thrown into some open grave with other
bodies? He quickly shook aside that fear. It was not dirt or
cold flesh he felt beneath him but the cool linen of a soft
bed. Rousing from unconsciousness to that odor had obviously disordered his mind, he thought, disgusted with
himself.

Easing his eyes open at last, he grunted in pain as the
light stung his eyes and made his head throb even more.
Everything was a little blurry, but he could make out
enough to see that he was in a rather opulent bedchamber,
one that looked vaguely familiar. His blood ran cold and he
was suddenly even more reluctant to seek out the source
of that smell. It certainly could not be from some battle if
only because the part of the bedchamber he was looking
at showed no signs of one.

*If there is a dead body in this room, laddie, best ye learn about
it quick. Ye might be needing to run,* said a voice in his head

that sounded remarkably like his squire, Walter, and Tormand had to agree with it. He forced down all the reluctance he felt and, since he could see no sign of the dead in the part of the room he studied, turned over to look in the other direction. The sight that greeted his watering eyes had him making a sound that all too closely resembled the one his niece Anna made whenever she saw a spider. Death shared his bed.

He scrambled away from the corpse so quickly he nearly fell out of the bed. Struggling for calm, he eased his way off the bed and then sought out some water to cleanse his eyes so that he could see more clearly. It took several awkward bathings of his eyes before the sting in them eased and the blurring faded. One of the first things he saw after he dried his face was his clothing folded neatly on a chair, as if he had come to this bedchamber as a guest, willingly. Tormand wasted no time in putting on his clothes and searching the room for any other signs of his presence, collecting up his weapons and his cloak.

Knowing he could not avoid looking at the body in the bed any longer, he stiffened his spine and walked back to the bed. Tormand felt the sting of bile in the back of his throat as he looked upon what had once been a beautiful woman. So mutilated was the body that it took him several moments to realize that he was looking at what was left of Lady Clara Sinclair. The ragged clumps of golden blond hair left upon her head and the wide, staring blue eyes told him that, as did the heart-shaped birthmark above the open wound where her left breast had been. The rest of the woman's face was so badly cut up it would have been difficult for her own mother to recognize her without those few clues.

The cold calm he had sought now filling his body and mind, Tormand was able to look more closely. Despite the mutilation there was an expression visible upon poor Clara's face, one that hinted she had been alive during at least some of the horrors inflicted upon her. A quick

glance at her wrists and ankles revealed that she had once
been bound and had fought those bindings, adding
weight to Tormand's dark suspicion. Either poor Clara
had had some information someone had tried to torture
out of her or she had met up with someone who hated her
with a cold, murderous fury.

And someone who hated him as well, he suddenly
thought, and tensed. Tormand knew he would not have
come to Clara's bedchamber for a night of sweaty bed play.
Clara had once been his lover, but their affair had ended
and he never returned to a woman once he had parted
from her. He especially did not return to a woman who
was now married and to a man as powerful and jealous as
Sir Ranald Sinclair. That meant that someone had brought
him here, someone who wanted him to see what had been
done to a woman he had once bedded, and, mayhap, take
the blame for this butchery.

That thought shook him free of the shock and sorrow
he felt. "Poor, foolish Clara," he murmured. "I pray ye didnae suffer this because of me. Ye may have been vain, a
wee bit mean of spirit, witless, and lacking morals, but ye
still didnae deserve this."

He crossed himself and said a prayer over her. A glance
at the windows told him that dawn was fast approaching
and he knew he had to leave quickly. "I wish I could tend
to ye now, lass, but I believe I am meant to take the blame
for your death and I cannae; I willnae. But, I vow, I *will*
find out who did this to ye and they will pay dearly for it."

After one last careful check to be certain no sign of his
presence remained in the bedchamber, Tormand slipped
away. He had to be grateful that whoever had committed
this heinous crime had done so in this house for he knew
all the secretive ways in and out of it. His affair with Clara
might have been short but it had been lively and he had
slipped in and out of this house many, many times. Tormand
doubted even Sir Ranald, who had claimed the fine house

when he had married Clara, knew all of the stealthy approaches to his bride's bedchamber.

Once outside, Tormand swiftly moved into the lingering shadows of early dawn. He leaned against the outside of the rough stonewall surrounding Clara's house and wondered where he should go. A small part of him wanted to just go home and forget about it all, but he knew he would never heed it. Even if he had no real affection for Clara, one reason their lively affair had so quickly died, he could not simply forget that the woman had been brutally murdered. If he was right in suspecting that someone had wanted him to be found next to the body and be accused of Clara's murder, then he definitely could not simply forget the whole thing.

Despite that, Tormand decided the first place he would go was his house. He could still smell the stench of death on his clothing. It might be just his imagination, but he knew he needed a bath and clean clothes to help him forget that smell. As he began his stealthy way home Tormand thought it was a real shame that a bath could not also wash away the images of poor Clara's butchered body.

"Are ye certain ye ought to say anything to anybody?"

Tormand nibbled on a thick piece of cheese as he studied his aging companion. Walter Burns had been his squire for twelve years and had no inclination to be anything more than a squire. His utter lack of ambition was why he had been handed over to Tormand by the man who had knighted him at the tender age of eighteen. It had been a glorious battle and Walter had proven his worth. The man had simply refused to be knighted. Fed up with his squire's lack of interest in the glory, the honors, and the responsibility that went with knighthood Sir MacBain had sent the man to Tormand. Walter had continued to prove his worth, his courage, and his contentment in remaining a lowly squire. At the moment, however, the man was openly upset and his courage was a little weak-kneed.

"I need to find out who did this," Tormand said and then sipped at his ale, hungry and thirsty but partaking of both food and drink cautiously for his stomach was still unsteady.

"Why?" Walter sat down at Tormand's right and poured himself some ale. "Ye got away from it. 'Tis near the middle of the day and no one has come here crying for vengeance so I be thinking ye got away clean, aye? Why let anyone e'en ken ye were near the woman? Are ye trying to put a rope about your neck? And, if I recall rightly, ye didnae find much to like about the woman once your lust dimmed so why fret o'er justice for her?"

"'Tis sadly true that I didnae like her, but she didnae deserve to be butchered like that."

Walter grimaced and idly scratched the ragged scar on his pockmarked left cheek. "True, but I still say if ye let anyone ken ye were there ye are just asking for trouble."

"I would like to think that verra few people would e'er believe I could do that to a woman e'en if I was found lying in her blood, dagger in hand."

"Of course ye wouldnae do such as that, and most folk ken it, but that doesnae always save a mon, does it? Ye dinnae ken everyone who has the power to cry ye a murderer and hang ye and they dinnae ken ye. Then there are the ones who are jealous of ye or your kinsmen and would like naught better than to strike out at one of ye. Aye, look at your brother James. Any fool who kenned the mon would have kenned he couldnae have killed his wife, but he still had to suffer years marked as an outlaw and a woman-killer, aye?"

"I kenned I kept ye about for a reason. Aye, 'twas to raise my spirits when they are low and to embolden me with hope and courage just when I need it the most."

"Wheesht, nay need to slap me with the sharp edge of

your tongue. I but speak the truth and one ye would be wise to nay ignore."

Tormand nodded carefully, wary of moving his still-aching head too much. "I dinnae intend to ignore it. 'Tis why I have decided to speak only to Simon."

Walter cursed softly and took a deep drink of ale. "Aye, a king's mon nay less."

"Aye, and my friend. *And* a mon who worked hard to help James. He is a mon who has a true skill at solving such puzzles and hunting down the guilty. This isnae simply about justice for Clara. Someone wanted me to be blamed for her murder, Walter. I was put beside her body to be found and accused of the crime. And for such a crime I would be hanged so that means that someone wants me dead."

"Aye, true enough. Nay just dead, either, but your good name weel blackened."

"Exactly. So I have sent word to Simon asking him to come here, stressing an urgent need to speak with him."

Tormand was pleased that he sounded far more confident of his decision than he felt. It had taken him several hours to actually write and send the request for a meeting to Simon. The voice in his head that told him to just turn his back on the whole matter, the same opinion that Walter offered, had grown almost too loud to ignore. Only the certainty that this had far more to do with him than with Clara had given him the strength to silence that cowardly voice.

He had the feeling that part of his stomach's unsteadiness was due to a growing fear that he was about to suffer as James had. It had taken his foster brother three long years to prove his innocence and wash away the stain to his honor. Three long, lonely years of running and hiding. Tormand dreaded the thought that he might be pulled into the same ugly quagmire. If nothing else, he was deeply concerned about how it would affect his mother who had already suffered too much grief and worry over her children. First his sister Sorcha had been beaten and raped, then his sister Gillyanne had been kidnapped—twice—the second time leading to a forced marriage, and then there had been the trouble that had sent James running for the shelter of the hills. His mother did not need to suffer through yet another one of her children mired in danger.

"If ye could find something the killer touched we could solve this puzzle right quick," said Walter.

Pulling free of his dark thoughts about the possibility that his family was cursed, Tormand frowned at his squire. "What are ye talking about?"

"Weel, if ye had something the killer touched we could take it to the Ross witch."

Tormand had heard of the Ross witch. The woman lived in a tiny cottage several miles outside of town. Although the townspeople had driven the woman away ten years ago, many still journeyed to her cottage for help, mostly for the herbal concoctions the woman made. Some claimed the woman had visions that had aided them in solving some problem. Despite having grown up surrounded by people who had special gifts like that, he doubted the woman was the miracle worker some claimed her to be. Most of the time such *witches* were simply aging women skilled with herbs and an ability to convince people that they had some great mysterious power.

"And why do ye think she could help if I brought her something touched by the killer?" he asked.

"Because she gets a vision of the truth when she touches something." Walter absently crossed himself as if he feared he risked his soul by even speaking of the woman. "Old George, the steward for the Gillespie house, told me that Lady Gillespie had some of her jewelry stolen. He said her ladyship took the box the jewels had been taken from to the Ross witch and the moment the woman held the box she had a vision about what had happened."

When Walter said no more, Tormand asked, "What did the vision tell the woman?"

"That Lady Gillespie's eldest son had taken the jewels. Crept into her ladyship's bedchamber whilst she was at court and helped himself to all the best pieces."

"It doesnae take a witch to ken that. Lady Gillespie's eldest son is weel kenned to spend too much coin on fine clothes, women, and the toss of the dice. Near everyone— mon, woman, and bairn—in town kens that." Tormand took a drink of ale to help him resist the urge to grin at the look of annoyance on Walter's homely face. "Now I ken why the fool was banished to his grandfather's keep far from all the temptation here near the court."

"Weel, it wouldnae hurt to try. Seems a lad like ye ought to have more faith in such things."

"Oh, I have ample faith in such things, enough to wish that ye wouldnae call the woman a witch. That is a word that can give some woman blessed with a gift from God a lot of trouble, deadly trouble."

"Ah, aye, aye, true enough. A gift from God, is it?"

"Do ye really think the devil would give a woman the gift to heal or to see the truth or any other gift or skill that can be used to help people?"

"Nay, of course he wouldnae. So why do ye doubt the Ross woman?"

"Because there are too many women who are, at best, a wee bit skilled with herbs yet claim such things as visions or the healing touch in order to empty some fool's purse. They are frauds and ofttimes what they do makes life far more difficult for those women who have a true gift."

Walter frowned for a moment, obviously thinking that over, and then grunted his agreement. "So ye willnae be trying to get any help from Mistress Ross?"

"Nay, I am nay so desperate for such as that."

"Oh, I am nay sure I would refuse any help just now," came a cool, hard voice from the doorway of Tormand's hall.

Tormand looked toward the door and started to smile at Simon. The expression died a swift death. Sir Simon Innes looked every inch the king's man at the moment. His face was pale and cold fury tightened its predatory lines. Tormand got the sinking feeling that Simon already knew why he had sent for him. Worse, he feared his friend had some suspicions about his guilt. That stung, but Tormand decided to smother his sense of insult until he and Simon had at least talked. The man was his friend and a strong believer in justice. He would listen before he acted.

Nevertheless, Tormand tensed with a growing alarm when Simon strode up to him. Every line of the man's tall, lean body was tense with fury. Out of the corner of his eye, Tormand saw Walter tense and place his hand on his sword, revealing that Tormand was not the only one who sensed danger. It was as he looked back at Simon that Tormand realized the man clutched something in his hand.

A heartbeat later, Simon tossed what he held onto the table in front of Tormand. Tormand stared down at a heavy gold ring embellished with blood-red garnets. Unable to believe what he was seeing, he looked at his hands, his unadorned hands, and then looked back at the ring. His first thought was to wonder how he could have left that room of death and not realized that he was no longer wearing his ring. His second thought was that the point of Simon's sword was dangerously sharp as it rested against his jugular.